THE SERPENT AND
THE STAFF

The talents of Dr. Duncan Childers are those of the men of the Renaissance. He is as handsome as a god and as skilful at the piano as in the operating theatre. Many different people and experiences shape his tempestuous career, among them the New Orleans slums where he was born; gentle, dark-haired Jenny Greenway and Hester, his blonde, sensual wife; the terror of a malaria epidemic; the stately Viennese salons; and Dr. Jarvis Phelton, who cares more for publicity than for sound practice. In spite of some of them, and with the help of the others, Duncan begins to learn that the goal of medicine is the saving of lives, not of money.

FRANK YERBY

THE SERPENT AND THE STAFF

THE BOOK CLUB
121 CHARING CROSS ROAD
LONDON W.C.2

William Heineman Ltd
LONDON MELBOURNE TORONTO
CAPETOWN AUCKLAND
THE HAGUE

First published in Great Britain 1959

© 1958 by FRANK YERBY

Made and printed in Great Britain by
William Clowes and Sons, Limited, London and Beccles

FOR

BLANQUITA, MY BRIDE

WITH LOVE AND

GRATITUDE

Chapter 1

THE ALARM CLOCK shrilled hideously. Duncan put out his hand to shut it off. His groping fingers touched cold metal, strayed along it to the catch, then halted. No. Let it ring. If he shut the alarm off now, he would surely go back to sleep. And he couldn't go back to sleep. He couldn't.

He lay there, letting that ferocious jangle stab into his consciousness. He could feel his protesting nerves come alive, twanging like harpstrings in a slow, dissonant, off-tempo response to the clock's imperious cry. But his muscles were dormant still; laden with months-long accumulation of fatigue, they remained impervious to the commands of his mind. He stared at his legs, showing too long, too lean beneath the coverlet.

'Move!' he ordered them furiously: 'goddam you, move!'

A knee crawled upward, creaked dismally, made a tent of the coverlet. The other joined it, even more slowly. Then, in an explosive burst of pure will, Duncan Childers, M.D., threw back the bedclothes and swung his bony frame up into a sitting position on the edge of the bed. He sat there, running his long, powerful, surgeon's fingers through his thick red hair. It was going decidedly grey now, despite the fact that, in this Year of Our Lord 1903, Duncan Childers was only thirty-three years old.

"Duncan," Hester cried, "will you shut that damned thing off!"

He put out his hand, pushed down on the catch. The silence reverberated. He turned and looked at Hester, his dark brown eyes still heavy with sleep. 'My bride,' he thought mockingly; 'my beautiful, beautiful bride....'

"Duncan," she said, in that throaty, husky voice that once he had loved so well, that perhaps he loved a little still, "come back to bed. I'll call Jarvis and——"

"No," he said. "I've a patched-up œsophagus that wants looking after. Early cancer. I think I've got it all, but——"

"And there's nobody else down there to look after your patient? Neither Lester, nor Tom, nor Jarvis himself?"

"No. The man's a charity patient, Hes. Window-dressing. The august Doctor Jarvis Phelton always takes one or two. Gives him a reputation for heart. The heart he hasn't got. Eases public resentment towards our fine Cutting and Sewing Emporium for Ailing Millionaires. Tom would take care of my patient, only Jarvis won't let him. The rest? Hell! 'What difference does it make if a beggar dies? The bastard's better off, dead.'"

Hester stared at her husband. When he was angry, he was very fine. And he was angry now. He was tall, and a little stooped from bending over the operating-table for hours without end. His face, strangely, was losing some of that duality it had had when he had come back from Vienna. Then it had been an exciting face. You looked at it and saw the countenance of the Archangel Michael, the morning star, so wonderfully handsome, with that serene, almost unearthly beauty that was somehow frightening; until he turned. Then you saw that little half-moon scar high on his cheek—the scar he never would explain—and met his eyes that were not Michael's eyes, but those of Lucifer, screaming down through space; the eyes of a soul in hell.

Now? It was still an exciting face. Perhaps even more exciting. Only that soul was coming back from hell; only Lucifer was halting in mid-fall, spreading his wings to mount, to climb, to soar—he was getting to be all of a piece. She didn't like that. She had no patience with Archangels. She much preferred Lucifer. She wanted to see him lift those bushy brows in that characteristic expression of pained incredulity at the extent of human stupidity; watch those sardonic lip corners curl, hear him snarl out of the corner of his mouth:

"Money won't buy everything? The hell it won't! The salvation of my immortal soul? I'll wait, thank you. Talk to Peter at the Gate. Want to bet I can't make a deal even with him?"

"What's getting into you, darling?" she said now. "I've heard you say much the same thing. And it's true, when you come to think of it. Those poor devils from the Irish Channel would be better off dead. At least they wouldn't drink themselves to death then, or starve."

He stood there, looking at her. A little brush-fire started in his brown eyes, leaped, blazed. But, when he spoke, his voice was beautifully controlled.

"Yes," he said slowly. "It's true. They would be better off, as things stand now. But that isn't the only alternative, Hes. Those filthy, rat-infested tenements could be pulled down, and decent flats built. Something could be done to give those people hope. Jobs could be found for them. A basis for self-respect, so they wouldn't have to get their dreams out of the whisky bottle. Only, nobody

2

cares. So: let the beggar die! I want no part of that, Hes. I refuse to be an accessory after the fact to murder by neglect."

"Strange," Hester murmured. "This doesn't sound like you at all, darling."

"On the contrary, it does. I was born down there, remember. I spent the first fifteen years of my life in that roaring hell. I was a thief. I stole food. Or went hungry. I begged, to get the money to buy medicines for my mother. For my good and gentle mother who died in that pest-hole because a member of the class you came from didn't consider her good enough to marry after he'd gotten her with child. That was how my adoptive grandmother found me. I was robbing a grocery store and she was there when they caught me. It seems I was practically a duplicate of the grandson she'd lost. So she stopped them from beating me, brought me back to the Twin Towns, to Caneville-Sainte Marie. Scrubbed me, combed my hair, ridded my hide of vermin. Fed me till I looked human again. Hired tutors. Browbeat me into the realisation I had a mind. Lifted me into your world. Your pretty, leisurely, expensive world. Where I didn't belong. Where I don't belong still. Where I met you——"

"And I," she whispered, "spat into your face!"

"Into mine," he said softly, "and into the faces of all God's poor. Which ye have with you always. The mistake I made was to come back here. Me, with my hide of boiler-plate and my armoured heart. I, who knew the price of everything and the value of nothing. Doctor Duncan Childers, Physician and Surgeon. The fashionable young healer with the bedside manner. Who was going to make a mint out of practising medicine. Who is making a mint out of it. Only——"

"Only what, Duncan?" Hester said.

"The boiler-plate cracked. The armoured heart hadn't steel encasement enough. A dying child wrapped her fingers around it—her tiny, fleshless fingers—and smashed it all to hell."

"So that's what happened? I was afraid of that. I knew something——"

"Not something. A thousand things. That child was only one. She was dying, and she wanted me there—nothing I could do for her, except that. Malnutrition, rickets, a heart damaged by rheumatic fever ... So I sat with her, let her hold my hand. Gave her what comfort I could while she went about the lonely, pitiful business of dying. And, right in the middle of it, Jarvis summoned me to come and see after Mrs. Minton. Rich Mrs. Minton, who hasn't a damned thing wrong with her. Fat, useless pink flesh,

3

and a vacant mind turned hypochondriac to fill up the vacuum of her life. She always calls for me. She likes my pretty red hair and my bedside manner. To listen to her gush, to her illimitable whining, I was supposed to leave that baby to face the onrushing dark—alone. . . ."

"You didn't go?" Hester asked drily. "Then you were a fool, darling. You've said that there was no chance of saving the child."

"I didn't go. I sent Jarvis and Mrs. Minton both to hell. I got an immense satisfaction out of that."

"Oh, Duncan! You could be fired!"

"And spoil all Jarvis's hidden advertising about his Vienna-trained surgeon? Lose him his 'ace', who on three occasions has intervened directly into the heart itself? The only man in the state who knows the Mikulicz-Radecki technique for the plastic reconstruction of the oesophagus? Not on your life, Hes. He didn't even call me down. He was furious; but he kept his trap shut. His chief fear is that one day I'll quit."

"And mine," Hester said flatly.

"I know. Only you needn't worry. I haven't the guts."

He turned then, and went into the bathroom. A moment later Hester heard the rush of water in the shower.

'Oh, damn it!' she thought; 'damn it, damn it all!'

Duncan was on out-patient calls that morning, so he didn't have to go to the fashionable private hospital that Doctor Jarvis Phelton so charmingly called Rosebriar Clinic until afternoon. Instead, he had to drive his buggy through the shady streets of New Orleans' wealthy Garden District, stopping at imposingly hideous steamboat gothic houses, thrusting thermometers into querulous, complaining mouths to keep them shut a while, murmuring soothing platitudes into the ears of men and women whose chief illness lay in the fact that they had too much money, too little brains, and shrivelled, under-developed hearts.

'Not a damned one of them,' he thought bitterly, 'who needs more than an aspirin, or a dose of Epsom salts. No. That's wrong. They need far more than that. To be born again, I suppose. Tell them that and they answer like Nicodemus: "Can I enter into my mother's womb and——" To hell with it. That child, now. Ah, yes, that child. How gallantly she died. The poor get used to death. They see so much of it.'

There was one good thing about a well-trained horse. You could give him his head and he'd take you where you had to go. Leave you time for thinking. For remembering.

4

Strange. What he had told Hester that morning was true. He had been born in the Irish Channel section of New Orleans. But the implications of his words were a curious mixture of truth and falsity. He had never been completely an Irish Channel child. He had not run with the gangs. He had fought, but only in self-defence. He had stolen, but out of hunger, not out of that complicated entwining of real need and ferocious hatred for society that motivated them. He had lacked entirely their delight in destructive vandalism. He had owned, and on more than one occasion used, a switchblade knife; but only to keep bigger boys off his neck. And he had shared none of their precocious vices. Even now, at thirty-three, he drank but little, and did not smoke at all.

His mother had kept him from that. His beautiful, aristocratic Creole French mother, who had taught him her native tongue from the cradle, taught him French, not patois, so that he still spoke it as well as he did English. Perhaps better. Name of God, how had she come to that? How had Gabrielle Aubert, whose family had arrived with Sieur Bienville, ended her life in the Channel, coughing up the bloody shreds of her lungs?

He knew, all right. His father, James Childers of Caneville-Sainte Marie, who had gotten her with child, then refused to marry her, over the expressed doubt that, she being French and the morals of the French being what they were, he had no proof that this tiny, red-haired image of himself in sin was actually his own. That, and her parents' stern rejection of the daughter who had brought disgrace upon their patrician heads.

'Paternal love,' Duncan thought bitterly, 'is a form of Narcissism. I love thee because I made thee in mine own image, close coupled with thy mother in the dark. Out of my desire, out of my lust I made thee ... For which we must be eternally grateful. For being the accidental by-products of a thoroughly enjoyed coitus we must be grateful and never injure our fathers' pride. Because our sufferings don't matter. Only what people will say when they find out that the great man has such a child. *Merde!* That's only love of self, mental auto-eroticism....

'Poor Mama. God, how fiercely she tried to guard me from my world! She failed, of course. The attempt could not possibly have succeeded, given the circumstances of my life. But she did buy time; she did not fail entirely. At twelve, I was altar boy in the church— I, with my angelic, girlish face that infuriated the Channel brats into beating the living hell out of me every time I ventured from the house; I, with my precise speech, beautiful diction, collection

5

of holy images given for scholarship in the parochial school. Teacher's pet. Sœur Herminine used to swear I was a musical genius, predict great things for me...I wonder if I could have been a concert pianist, really? I wanted that. Until I found out that musicians usually starved. And I'd had enough of starvation.'

He pulled up the horse before the imposing house. Got down. Went in. Poked in the thermometer. Spoke the vaguely reassuring words. Wrote out a prescription for harmless placebo pills that would give imaginary help to an imaginary illness. Came out again. His bill would reach them in due time. And it would be steep.

Enough of starvation. He had known hunger all his life. His stepfather, Johann Bruder, had been a musician. A good musician. It had been he who had taught Duncan to play the piano and the violin. Oh yes, Johann Bruder had been first-rate. But that hadn't kept hunger from being a constant guest in that tiny flat down in the Channel where Herr Professor Bruder had lived with the wife, twenty-five years his junior, whom he had married out of love and pity—for her, and for her bastard child.

'I,' Duncan thought suddenly, 'can't bear the smell of potato soup even yet....Funny, how my life was twisted up with Caneville–Sainte Marie, even then. Strange town, Caneville. Well, here we go again....'

He went about his second call. It interested him more, because the patient was actually sick. John Templeton had what looked damnably like yellow fever. That was bad, because Duncan was going to have to report it to the health authorities. And the Templeton Manse—they actually called it that, by God!—would be quarantined. The Templetons would scream to high heaven to Jarvis Phelton over the phone. They were rich enough, important enough, aristocratic enough to be allowed to spread the fever as they pleased, rather than lose their precious liberty. To hell with them! He'd damn well report it. Let them scream. Them and Jarvis Phelton, too.

Hester was right. He had changed. 'If you practise medicine long enough, you finally get to be a doctor,' he thought wryly.

He was remembering now how carefully his mother had scrubbed him, combed his hair, adjusted his faded, patched, too tight clothing when his stepfather was going to take him to visit his uncle—by courtesy—Martin Bruder.

"*Sois sage,*" she always said; "*tu dois leur faire un bon effet.*"

"*Oui*, Mama," he said. He knew how important it was to make a good impression on the Bruders. They were very rich. If he were *sage*, that curious French expression which meant wise in the sense

6

of being wise enough to mind your manners and hold your tongue in the presence of your betters, they might give him one of Stanton Bruder's cast-off suits. It would be too big for him; but it would be warm, and it wouldn't have any holes. He hated Stanton Bruder, who was two years older than he and an outrageous bully and sneak. 'Funny,' he thought now, 'I still hate the bastard. But then, Cousin Stan's nobody to be loved.'

All the same, he had liked going to Martin Bruder's house. There he always had enough to eat. He usually made himself quite sick by stuffing his unaccustomed stomach with the heavy German dishes. Martin Bruder was always kind in his lofty, intellectual way. And Frau Hildegarde, Martin's wife and Stanton's mother, had been more than kind. Her sentimental Bavarian heart overflowed at the sight of Duncan's thinness—a thinness in part inherited, because James Childers had been like that, too. It was she who had stuffed him to the point of making him sick. Poor soul—even then she had had death in her. Invisible death, exploding among her cells. Cancer wasn't supposed to be contagious. Why then had Uncle Martin also died of it so many years later? 'Dear God, how pitifully little we know! What is the practice of medicine anyhow but legalised murder, approved mumbo jumbo, not two inches above the black arts of the jungle?'

On the way over to Martin Bruder's house Old Johann had made him practise his German phrases. His German had been very bad. It hadn't really got to be adequate until his second year at Vienna. And now he was forgetting it again....

He went about his calls mechanically. There was a thing inside him now, gnawing at his vitals like the fox of the Spartan boy. He was going to have it out one day. He was going to have to face it. He was afraid of facing it. It meant turning his back upon simplicity. Out of the materials of his life he had built a code. It was a very simple, pragmatic, demonstrably effective code. If he had put it into words, it would have gone like this: Money is power. The rich rule the world. The poor get kicked in the teeth, suffer hunger, misery, death. There is nothing worse than being poor; no price too high to pay for being rich. Dishonour, deceit, practising medicine à la mode, are only a means to an end, and of no importance once that end has been gained.

Well, he had achieved that end. He had his luxurious flat, his lovely, rich, lazy, sensual blonde wife; even the grudging respect, the flattering envy, of his peers. His bank account was in five figures now. His reputation as a surgeon was nation-wide since the sensational trial in the Jim Vance case. He was sitting on the top of

7

the world. "Doctor Duncan Childers, the brilliant young Vienna-trained surgeon who——"

Can't look in the mirror to shave in the mornings without wanting to puke. Who has everybody's respect, except his own. Who went into medicine instead of becoming the pianist he was perhaps born to be, because he looked upon medicine as a money-making game; not knowing it was going to get him, not realising that perhaps the twelve years that good, gentle Johann Bruder had been there to guide him, the fifteen that *les Sœurs Religieuses* and Gabrielle Aubert Bruder had had to shape him, had been enough, after all. And that when Minna von Stürck Bouvoir had got her forceful hands upon him the core of his being had been set, never really to be broken. The years afterwards—the wrenching of his being by the girl called Calico; by Marta Schlosser, that raven-haired, blue-eyed Viennese beauty; by Hester Vance—had twisted that iron inner core of rectitude, of idealism; but they hadn't broken it. There were words for what he felt now, for what he was going to have to face. Old, old words: "Man doth not live by bread alone . . . Render unto Cæsar the things that are Cæsar's . . . What is a man profited if he shall gain the whole world, and lose his immortal soul?"

He had the bread; Cæsar's coin; the whole teeming world. But the price he had given for them had been damnably high: his smart New School of Vienna medical training, bought by what was his recompense for helping Uncle Martin Bruder pay God his owed debt of death; his good clothes, flat, costly instruments, bought and paid for by his rich wife; his post in the most exclusive clinic in the South, got him by the Vances' influence, though held by his indisputable skill—all this at the cost of breaking Jenny Greenway's heart, at the price of giving up the one woman he could have loved truly, for legalised bedplay with the one he merely lusted after.

He should go back to the hospital now. But he didn't want to. He took an almost masochistic pleasure in remembering. All of it. Every fleeting, tiny detail.

To hell with the hospital! There came a point in time when a man needed to embark upon the search for himself. To sort things out and put them in order. To find what truly he was; and upon that basis erect the structure of his future.

He turned his magnificent grey's head—a gift from Hester, too, like so many, many things—towards the Irish Channel. Towards that filthy, roaring, drunken pest-hole in which he had been born. He would go back now. Back to what he was at his heart's core. Back to the child he had been.

8

Chapter 2

THE BOY, fifteen-year-old Duncan Childers, edged along the counter to where the tinned goods were. It didn't particularly matter what was in those tins. Hungry as he was, he could eat tinned fish-hooks, he reckoned. He looked back to where the grocer stood, waiting on a lady. The grocer wasn't looking at him. His hand shot out, grasped a tin, disappeared under his coat with it, came out again, empty.

Duncan guessed that the tin he'd swiped contained some kind of potted meat. Corned beef, likely. He had had only a brief glance at it; but the picture on the outside of the tin had looked like that. Corned beef would be all right for him; but his mama couldn't eat things like that. She was far too sick.

He looked at the grocer. The grocer was a big, hulking man with a handlebar moustache and a mean face. Not the kind to let catch you hooking things. But two more ladies had come into the store now. That made it easier. Duncan studied the pile of tins with some care. He swiped two more of potted meat, and put them in the pillow-case he had under his ragged coat. Then he saw what he was looking for: tins of all kinds of soups and broths. He was in luck. His mama could eat soup. Even sick as she was, she could.

But, looking again, he realised he wasn't in luck after all. The tins of soup were under the tins of peas and beans, under the corned beef, under everything! It was too risky to try to hook one or two. He stood there, the tears stinging his eyes. There were hot ashes and sand at the back of his throat. He remembered his mama's face the last time he'd seen it, four days ago. So white. And that coughing, that coughing that never stopped now.

There had been a few potatoes in the bin when he had left the flat four days ago. That was why he had left. He'd wanted his mama to eat them herself, instead of giving them to him. His mama was almost too weak to walk, these days. He reckoned those potatoes would be just about gone now. He had to get her some soup. He had to!

His hand crept out. His fingers closed around the tin. He tugged, easing it forward. It gave. Inch by inch he pulled it, putting his other hand against the tins above it to steady them. But it hung up at the last minute. He gave one more tug.

9

And the whole pile of tins crashed to the floor. They rolled.

"What th' divil be ye a-doin', boy?" the grocer roared.

Duncan's eyes darted from side to side, seeking some opening. There was none. The grocer's heavy bulk filled the gangway.

"I—— I wanted to buy—some soup," he got out, "and, seeing that you were busy——"

The grocer took in his rags at a glance.

"Ye damned little thief!" he bellowed. He lunged forward with a speed surprising in one of his bulk and grabbed Duncan by the arm. He pinned the boy's arm behind him, twisting it. The sack fell out from under the tattered coat. It clanked dully when it hit the floor.

"Ah ha, me foine lad!" the grocer rumbled. "So ye wanted to buy, did ye? I'll buy ye, ye ragamuffin! Take that!"

His big, beefy hand, striking, jetted the tears from the boy's eyes. He slapped Duncan's face right and left and right again, jerking the boy's head upon the thin column of his neck.

"Serves 'm right, th' dirty little thief!" the ladies screeched. "Hit 'm ag'in, Mike!"

Mike complied, with evident pleasure.

Then the old woman's voice cut through the heavy smash of the grocer's palm against the boy's thin face, like a knife.

"That is quite enough!" she snapped.

The grocer stopped; glared at her.

She was quietly, elegantly dressed. Her coat and hat alone had cost more than all the groceries in the store. Her hair was snowy. She had a velvet ribbon around her sagging throat. She leaned heavily upon a cane. The head of that cane was solid gold.

"Now see here, ma'am!" the grocer growled.

The old woman looked at the grocer. She didn't say anything. She didn't need to. Her eyes said enough. They were the eyes of an ancient she-eagle, icy with contempt. She took off her gloves, and Duncan could see the blue veins in her thin, old hands. She opened her handbag, brought out a twenty-dollar bill, laid it on the counter.

"This, I think," she said, "will compensate you for whatever the boy has stolen. Now will you please to turn him loose!"

Duncan had caught the noticeable accent in her rich, contralto voice. She said 'vill' for 'will'. Here 'this' sounded more like 'dis'. German. Like Papa Johann. But different, somehow. Proud, rich—even beautiful, for all her years. She looked like a dowager queen.

The grocer turned him loose.

"Well, for that much money, me foine lady——" the grocer began.

"It is more than you are worth," she said, "but I can afford to be generous—even with a cowardly *Schwein* who abuses *Kinder*. Come with me, *mein Sohn*."

Freed from the grocer's grasp, Duncan scurried to her side. They went out into the street together, the old woman leaning heavily upon her cane. She looked at him with those old, she-eagle's eyes. They melted very slowly into tenderness.

"Zo," she said, "I haf found you at last!"

"You—you were looking for me?" Duncan said.

"*Ja. Ach, Gott*, but you are zo like him!"

"I—I'm like whom, ma'am?" Duncan said.

"My grandson, who is dead. Your half-brother. You *are* Duncan Childers, are you not?"

"Yes'm. But how on earth——?"

"Run and fetch me a cab, Duncan," she said. "I will take you home with me now, to my city flat. After you haf eaten, *und* a bath had, so that you no longer offend my nostrils, we will talk."

He sat in the kitchen, wrapped in a heavy dressing-gown. It had belonged to Saint-Juste Bouvoir, the old lady's husband, who had been dead for many years. Hungry as he was, she hadn't let him eat until he had had a bath. It was the first time he'd ever had a bath in a full-length tub that a body could stretch out in, in hot, slightly perfumed water. No wonder rich folks smelled so good and were so clean! Hell, if he had all these fancy fixings for washing he'd take a bath every day!

She opened the ice-box and began to take out the food. His eyes opened, stretching wide at the sight. He started trembling. There was a whole chicken. Milk. Cheese. The half of a cherry pie. One by one she carried them to the table and placed them before him. She got out a plate, knives, forks, spoons, a heavy linen napkin with a monogram on it.

"I have" (she pronounced it, of course, 'haf') "not a maid here," she said, "since I only came down for a few days to look for you. You see, it was no accident I was passing that store. Your mother told me you would be in one or another of those terrible streets. So I walked them all. *Ach, Gott*, but I am tired!"

She sat opposite him, staring at him all the time.

"Eat, *mein Sohn*," she rumbled in her very musical voice. "I can see that you are hungry."

He began to eat very slowly, watching her all the time. This crazy old woman liked him. He could see that. The thought was strangely comforting. His hunger came back. He dropped his knife and fork, picked up the chicken, tore it apart with his hands. He began to wolf it down. He made more noise than a starving dog. He was perhaps hungrier than most dogs ever get to be. Hungrier, more neglected, more lost.

"Now," she said, "we will talk. You are puzzled that I know your name?"

"Yes'm," Duncan said.

"Your step-uncle, Martin Bruder, told me about you when he was up at Schwartzwald, his plantation, for the holidays. And he told me how you looked. He is right. You are *wunderschön*."

"But ma'am," Duncan said, "I don't see——"

"I know. You see, Duncan, I a grandson had. You know who your real *Vater* was?"

"Yes. A man named James Childers."

"*Jawohl. Und* he was a *Schwein*. After he deserted you and your mother he came back to Caneville-Sainte Marie. My daughter, Melisse Bouvoir, fell in love with him. Like you, he was wonderfully handsome. Only he had no heart. I tried every way I knew to keep her from marrying him——"

"But she did?"

"Yes. And had for him *einen Sohn. Dein Bruder*—your brother. You are his image. Only you are handsomer. He was twelve years old when he died. When they all died. *Ach, Gott*, but yellow fever is a terrible thing!"

"My—father is dead too, then?" Duncan said.

"Yes. *Und* my poor Melisse, who never a happy day had after she met him. *Und* my grandsohn. That is why, when Martin told me, I started to look for you."

"But Uncle Martin knows where I live!"

"I know. I went to your house. But you were never there. Your poor mama is so worried. She was afraid that this 'job' of yours that kept you all night oudt from the house was something bad. I see that she was right."

"I couldn't let her starve!" Duncan burst out. "Ever since Stepfather Johann died——"

"I know, *mein Sohn*. I do not blame you. Even Our Lord forgave the Good Thief. *Und* from your face I see you are not bad. I came back every day for the last four days; but you haf not come home in all that time. Nor did you go to Martin Bruder for help. He is a kindly man. He would have helped you gladly. But you did not ask him. It seems to me that these things badly want explaining. Why did you not come home? Why did you not go to Martin? Is it that you prefer to be a thief?"

"No," Duncan said. "I didn't come home because I had nothing to bring my mother. I couldn't stand seeing her so hungry, and so sick . I didn't go to Uncle Martin's because I didn't know he was in New Orleans. You see, ma'am, I never got to see them very much. They were awful nice to me—all except Stan——"

"That boy!" Minna snorted. "Go on, son."

"But I was still the poor relation. The poor relation who wasn't really kin at all. They made me feel it, all the time. Not meaning any harm, I reckon; but still they made me feel it. So I didn't go there, much. I would have gone this time; but when Aunt Hildegarde died, Uncle Martin went to Europe and took Stan with him. They must have just got back. I didn't know."

"Three months ago," Minna said. "Was then Johann Bruder so terribly poor?"

"Yes'm. He gave music lessons, but he didn't have many rich pupils. And they were the worst of all about paying their fees. I reckon I've been hungry all my life. But after Papa Johann died, we really starved. That's why I started stealing. I had to, ma'am! I only steal food from the grocers. All us kids do that. I'm not even good at it. That's why I got caught."

"Which," Minna said, "was just as well this time."

"What else was I to do, ma'am?" Duncan said earnestly. It had suddenly become important that this kind old lady should believe him. He wanted her approval more than anything else in the world except that God should give his mama back her health. "We had to eat, and Mama needed medicines. There just isn't any work. I didn't steal to get medicines, though. For that I begged the money, making like I was a cripple. You learn all kinds of tricks in the Channel. I hate stealing! I hated all those things I had to do."

"You will never have to steal or beg again, *mein Sohn*," Minna said. "I have put your mother in the hospital. You will stay here with me until she better is. Then we will go up to Caneville. Now you will go to bed. In the morning we will go see your mama."

"But why, ma'am? Why are you doing all this?"

"Because God took pity on my loneliness and gave me back my grandson. Or his image," Minna said.

But in the morning Gabrielle had been worse. Much worse. Duncan had seen at once that his mother was going to die. Three days later he was an orphan. But infinitely better off than he had been while both his parents lived. He did not cry. Fifteen years in the Irish Channel had taught him that death was often a blessing. And in the very young, as in the very old, there are some feelings that lie too deep for tears.

The first thing Minna did, the morning after their arrival in Caneville-Sainte Marie, was to take him for a drive. The weather had broken by then, and all the air was warm and slumberous with spring. It was even getting a trifle hot. They went first to the Bayou Flèche, the lake of the arrow, named, doubtless, after some ancient Indian tribal war. Lifting her buggy whip, Minna pointed out the mounds along its edge.

"Those," she said, "are the Chitimacha's burial mounds. One still finds arrowheads there, and shards of broken pottery. The little church beyond them is Our Lady of Sainte Marie. It contains a miraculous image. It was found by fishermen from here near Barataria. They call it *Notre Dame des Pêcheurs*. Our Lady of the Fishermen. They brought it up in their nets. So now they ask its blessing each time they go down the river to the sea."

"You believe that?" Duncan asked. "I mean, that a wooden image can——"

"Yes," Minna said serenely. "All things are possible with God, my son. I will have Father Gaulois come to see you. He is a good man. He is French, truly French, not Creole. He comes from Bordeaux."

She rambled on, her voice rising and falling through the clip-clopping of the horse's hooves.

"Here is the quarter of the Cajuns. See how their houses are built out over the bayou on poles? They live by trapping musk-rats. And that makes them the slaves of Nelson Vance."

"But who is Nelson Vance?"

"A swine," Minna said. "Perhaps the dirtiest swine who ever lived. Let us not speak of him."

They drove on. Minna pointed again.

"This is the quarter of the Creoles who are French. Descendants of the original settlers. The Cajuns came later. They were driven out of Nova Scotia by the British. They called their cold bleak land Acadia. That's why we call them Cajuns—a corruption of Acadians. They, too, are French, but a strangely different breed of French. I do not know why. Even their patois is different. The Creoles, now, are patrician and proud. Some of them, of course, are Spanish. A few. A very few. The Spaniards did not hold this section very long.

"And this quarter to which we come now is called Law's Coast, after John Law, that piratical swindler who brought the Germans here. Some of the Germans are Bavarians, and hence Catholic. The rest are Lutheran. See how neat and clean it is? We Germans have a passion for order and for neatness."

"Did your ancestors come over then, ma'am?"

"Do not call me ma'am. Call me grandmother. No. I was born in Berlin. I was *hochgeboren*, highborn. I was called Minna von Stürck, Countess Landsfeldt. Only your grandfather—I forget, he was not your grandfather—already I confuse you with little James— only Saint-Juste Bouvoir passed through Berlin on his grand tour. One look at those flashing black eyes, and I was lost. I eloped with him, thereby losing my title and my estates. It did not matter. I came here to Belle Bouvoir, his great plantation. And I was happy with him until he died. Even throughout the war, and the terrible reconstruction time, I was happy. I have never regretted it. No, Duncan, my son, the German folk who came here were peasants— and poor. But good people, fine people. Like the Bruders. They were among the families whom Law brought here. And they have grown with the years. See how great and gentle they have become now!"

"What is this part?" Duncan said.

"Caneville. The American town. They came last—like a plague of locusts. 'The Kaintocks' the Creoles called them, the Kentuckians. Thieves, brawlers, cut-throats. Men of immense bravery, but want-ing in honour, in delicacy. They have improved now—some, at least. Many have married among the Germans and turned Luth-erans, or among the French and become good Catholics. But some, like the Childerses and the Vances, ugh!"

"But who are the Childerses, ma'am—Grandmother? My father's family?"

"*Ach*, that is better. You will learn to say it easily enough. Yes, son, the Childerses are your family. They are Scotch Presby-terians. Tight-fisted, dour, unloving. Somehow they manage to make even virtue seem an evil. I do not know how they manage that, but they do. James, your father, was actually the better of the two brothers. At least his sins were the normal sins of the flesh. But Vardigan, your uncle, the Reverend Vardigan Childers, the pastor of their kirk, as they call their church, is beyond my comprehension. He makes a loathsomeness of such simple, pleasant things: like dancing; like boys and girls bathing together in the bayou. He has a sickness of the mind, I think. Unfortunately, we have to pay him a visit. That is where we are going now."

"Lord God, ma'am, why?"

"Because he telephoned me early this morning and asked me to bring you. It seems he feels some concern for your spiritual welfare. You must try to be patient, Duncan. For, although he is a most unpleasant man, he *is* your uncle."

"Yes, Grandmother, I'll try," Duncan said.

But it proved difficult. The Reverend Vardigan Childers would have tried the patience of Job himself. He was not a bad-looking man. None of the Childerses ever were. He was tall, and his hair was red like Duncan's except that it was going grey. His face was too long, and his teeth too big. They were yellowish.

'Why,' Duncan thought, 'he looks just like a horse!'

"This," Minna said, "is Duncan, Reverend Childers."

Vardigan Childers did not say 'Hello,' or 'How are you?' or any other word of greeting. Instead, he laid his big, bony hand on the boy's shoulder and rolled his eyes heavenwards.

"I pray Thee, O Lord," he intoned, "to visit Thy favour upon this poor orphan and sinner——"

'How,' Duncan thought, 'does he know whether I'm a sinner or not?'

"—who bears upon his youthful shoulders the burden of his father's sins! Verily, they were as scarlet! Cleanse him, O Lord; wash him white as snow. Root out of his heart any festering remainder of the brutish lust that brought him into the world. Remove from his heart his mother's people's tendency to levity. Wring from his soul his father's fondness for the strange woman and the cup that cheers. And, finally, save him, I pray Thee, from pagan influences, from image worship and idolatry. Thy blessings upon this orphan-sinner, Lord. Amen."

Duncan stood there staring at him with that expression which afterwards would become characteristic: a pained wonder at the bottomless depths of human stupidity. He shook his head. 'No,' he thought, 'not a horse. A jackass. A braying jackass.'

"Well, Duncan," Vardigan Childers said, in what was meant to be a genial tone, "I'm pleased to see what a fine-looking lad you are. I rather imagine, though, that your spiritual education has been somewhat neglected."

"No, sir," Duncan said firmly. "I was altar boy at the Cathedral until I got too big; and I was taught by the Sisters at the parochial school——"

"That is far worse!" Vardigan Childers snapped. "I'd rather it had been neglected than perverted! There is nothing worse than Popery——"

"Except," Minna said drily, "ignorance and bigotry, of which you, Herr Reverend Childers, have more than your share."

"I forgot you were of that persuasion," Reverend Childers said. "Your faith seems to me an abomination, but I will not enter into controversy now. Permit me to examine the boy. You, of course, Duncan, believe in God. And you must know the difference between good and bad, so let us start from there."

"No," Duncan said flatly. "Don't let's start from there, Uncle Vardigan. Don't reckon there's any place we can start. I don't understand all this, anyhow. Don't think I even want to. I've had to spend my whole life scrambling and scratching just to stay alive. Doesn't leave much room for holy thoughts. Don't know if I believe in anything very much, now. I cried and begged, and my mother, my poor little *belle* mama, who never harmed a living soul, died just the same, with the blood coming out of her mouth in clots. So now, to tell the truth about it, I don't give much of a damn——"

"Duncan, I cannot permit you such language!" Vardigan Childers thundered.

"I'm sorry, sir. On the Channel you don't learn to talk nice. I don't even know what all those highfalutin words mean. But I do know what good is. It's a full belly. And bad's going to bed with your guts asking your backbone if your throat's been cut. You talk a lot about God. All right. Maybe He's up there, some place. But He sure doesn't give a damn. Not for us. Not for the kids in the back streets of the Channel, stealing rotten fruit to stuff our gullets with. Not for the women who die of being too tired, too hungry and too cold. . . ."

"Duncan," Minna said, "you must not. What you say are half-truths and less. For instance, at the final extremity I found you. And, from now on, you will be safe, cared for, fed, loved. You talk like a cynical old man twice your years. But I am here. I was sent, surely sent, to give you back your youth."

"Just as I thought!" Reverend Childers snarled. "I must insist, Madame Bouvoir, that you send me this boy twice a week for lessons and for prayers!"

"Grandmother," Duncan said desperately, "you won't, will you? I won't come! I'll run away first!"

"No, Duncan," Minna said quietly. "Good day to you, Reverend Childers."

"Madame, I demand——" Reverend Childers began.

"You are scarcely in a position to demand anything, Herr Childers," Minna said. "You have ignored the boy's existence all his life. You let him almost starve to death and did not lift a hand. I am his legal guardian. I have adopted him. A very good day to you, sir. And keep your lessons and your prayers for yourself. You need them far more than Duncan does. Come, *mein Sohn*——"

She put her arm around Duncan's shoulder and led him out of there. Vardigan Childers didn't say another word. There was nothing he could say that would make any difference. And he knew it.

As they drove away from there, Duncan saw a buggy coming towards them. He looked at it. Then he heard the sharp intake of Minna Bouvoir's breath. "*Ach, Gott!*" she said. "That swine! Well, it's too late to turn off now."

Duncan stared at the oncoming buggy.

"Who is it, Grandmother?" he said.

"Nelson Vance. And his daughter, about whom, although she is a year younger than you, rumours have already begun to spread. Nelson Vance, Caneville's Lord and Master. The Twin Towns' richest man; owner of the Vance Sugar Mills, the Vance Fur Company; Chairman of the Board of Trade; Vestryman—since, in his efforts to claw his way upwards out of the dirt from whence he came, he gave a new and larger edifice to Saint Mark's—of the Episcopal Church. Which means he has arrived. Here, to be Episcopal is to be someone. Catholicism is the religion of the poor. People have asked me to my face why I have not changed."

Duncan sat there, staring at the huge mountain of sweating flesh perched upon the buggy seat. Nelson Vance was an unlovely sight. His little blue eyes were lost in creases of fat. Two or three buttons of his shirt had popped open, revealing the vast pink expanse of his belly. It was covered with coarse, reddish-blond hair, as was every visible inch of him, except his head, which, but for tufts of the same colour about his ears, was as bald as an egg. His mouth was flabby, sensual, cruel. A dark stain of tobacco juice dribbled from one corner of it, staining the reddish stubble of his beard. His black broadcloth suit was sweat-soaked and streaked with dirt; his broad-brimmed planter's hat, pushed back on his glistening bald dome, would have disgraced a vagabond. Yet, Grandmother Bouvoir had said, this was the town's richest man!

But what brought Duncan bolt upright, every fibre of his being locked into tingling rigidity, was the girl sitting beside the fat old monster on the buggy seat. At that time, 1885, Hester Vance was only fourteen years old; but she was already rounding and softening into womanhood. And she was as blonde and beautiful as the angels of the Nordic painters. She had her father's mouth, but

18

where Nelson's lips were flabby hers were full, generously full. Duncan had seen negroes with lips thinner than Hester's. He kept staring at that mouth. It disturbed him strangely. He didn't know why. For a Channel urchin, Duncan Childers was a singularly innocent boy. As a small child, he had been almostly completely protected from his environment. Johann and Gabrielle had kept him away from his fellows. While the average ten- or twelve-year-old in that jungle was already crawling under the stoop steps with some grimy, ill-smelling *gamine*, Duncan had been busy with his music and his books. Later, when their protection had been tragically removed, the normal sexual drives of a post-pubescent boy in him had been sharply diminished by hunger. The starving have little energy left for lust. And his own fragile beauty had made an outcast of him. The Channel brats resented furiously a boy who looked like that. They had done their damnedest to mar that beauty. It was Duncan's speed that had brought him through unscarred.

Nelson Vance pulled up his horse and bowed grandly to Minna.

"Why, howdy, Madame Bouvoir!" he boomed. "Heard tell you was back, and that you'd done brung a orphan boy to care for. Reckon this be him——"

"Yes, Mister Vance," she said.

Nelson stared at Duncan. So did Hester.

"Reckon I see why," Nelson said. "Spittin' image of that grandson o' yourn what died. And of James Childers. Sure Lord was a heller, that Jim. I'd say this here young'un was another one o' his yard-children. Right?"

"I fail to see what business it is of yours, Mr. Vance," Minna said icily. "But if you must know: yes, Duncan is also James Childers's son."

"I knowed it!" Nelson Vance crowed. "See that you keep a tight rein on him, ma'am. With that blood in him, he'll sure Lord have an eye for the likely fillies. Why, even ol' Pious-Bones Vard——"

"I am not prepared to discuss the morals of the Childers family with you, Mister Vance. Nor should you have the nerve to do so. It seems to me that you have enough to occupy you in that regard with your son, Jim. Not to mention that 'likely filly', if I may quote you, you have sitting at your side. Good day to you, sir!"

She whipped up the horse. Her buggy rolled past them. Duncan turned, looked back, and met Hester Vance's eyes. She made a face, stuck out her tongue at him. Then, tossing her ash-blond curls, she turned away.

That afternoon, Duncan went for a walk alone. He was hoping he would meet Hester by chance. He did meet her. But not by chance. At fifteen, he had everything yet to learn.

She was not alone. Jenny Greenway was with her. Duncan had no way of knowing that, under ordinary circumstances, Hester wouldn't have been found dead with Jenny Greenway. It was just that she had seen Jenny passing the Vance mansion, and seized the opportunity to take the promenade she would not have dared to take alone. Jenny was enormously flattered. She had never dreamed of being accepted on terms of equality by Hester Vance. The Greenways came from the wrong side of the railway tracks. So did the Vances; but Nelson Vance had crossed them twenty years before. Now the Vances were somebodies. People climbed fast in America. The trouble was that the Greenways had stayed where they were, and that made all the difference. Not that they were poor. Jenny's father, Iron Mike Greenway, was a section boss on the railway, and his salary amounted to more money than many a Caneville merchant ever saw.

As he walked towards them, Duncan studied Jenny. At fifteen, his own age, she was still built like a fence post. But her eyes, a warm and sunny brown, were nice, he decided. Her freckles were larger and darker than his own, and she had more of them. Her heavy, dark brown hair was lovely. And her little face, with its pert, upturned nose, was interesting and alive. She was pretty, decidedly pretty. But Hester Vance was beautiful. More than beautiful—exciting. Electric currents ran along his skin, just from looking at her.

"Howdy, Miss Vance," he said in his soft, grave voice. "Nice day, isn't it? Who's your friend?"

Hester stopped dead. She was, even then, a perverse little witch.

"Whatever gave you the idea, Duncan Childers," she spat, "that you could speak to me? I'm a Vance, remember. And we don't associate with nobody's yard-children! Your father wasn't married to your mother! Know what that makes you?"

Duncan stared at her.

"No," he said evenly. "What does that make me, Hester?"

"A bastard! And don't call me Hester, you bastard!"

Duncan hung there, white and speechless.

"Irish Channel brat!" Hester went on, her streak of feline cruelty dominating her. "You're half French. Your mother was a Creole. And you know what they're like—all whores!"

Jenny stared at her. She was older than Hester; but she had seldom heard language like Hester was using now. On the job,

'Iron' Mike had a tongue that could curl a pair of steel rails; but he didn't use profanity in his house, before his daughter. Nelson Vance did. Constantly. Even habitually. Which was precisely where the difference lay.

"Hes——" she began.

"Oh, come on, Jen!" Hester snapped, and turned away.

Duncan came alive. He had a temper to match his hair. His hand shot out, caught Hester's shoulder, whirled her about. He stood there, gripping her hard.

"Listen," he snarled. "I came from the Channel, all right. But I never met a girl there with a mouth as filthy as yours! You keep my mother's name out of it, you hear me? You aren't fit to talk about her! You ever do it again, I'll——"

That was as far as he got. For it was then that Hester spat full in his face.

He reeled back. Hester whirled, already running. Jenny stood there. Then, very slowly, she opened her handbag and took out a white handkerchief. Carefully, even tenderly, she wiped his face.

"Oh, Duncan," she whispered. "I'm so sorry!"

Duncan stared at her.

"Why should you be?" he said. "You didn't do anything."

"I know. But I was with her, so you must think——"

"Why do you care what I think?" he said angrily.

"I don't know," she got out; "but it seems I do—awfully."

"Why?" Duncan said. His tone was gentler now.

"I—I don't know, Duncan," Jenny faltered. "There's something about you. Your voice is—nice. Your face is, too—I think."

"You think?" Duncan said. "Can't you make up your mind?"

"It's not my mind," she said. "I had yellow fever as a child, and it affected my eyes. I can't see very well, Duncan."

"Then why don't you wear glasses?" Duncan said.

"I do. But they're so hideous! So I don't like to——"

"Put them on," Duncan said firmly. He did not realise it then, but the pattern between them had already been set.

Jenny brought out the glasses, with the heavy, tortoise-shell rims, and fitted them to her eyes. She was right. They were hideous. They spoiled her whole face. She stared at him.

"Oh, Duncan!" she breathed.

"Now what's got into you?" he growled.

"You—you're so handsome! Most too handsome! Almost pretty —like a girl."

"Well, I'm not like a girl," he said, a trifle nettled by this phrase

21

he had heard so often before. "Come on, let's take a walk, you and me."

Jenny smiled. Not even those glasses could destroy that smile. Her teeth were even and white, and her mouth was the colour of pale claret. It would be nice to kiss that mouth, he decided suddenly.

"Second choice, Duncan?" she said. "Oh well, I'm used to that. Nobody can quite compare with Hester, mean as she is."

Duncan didn't answer that.

"I still don't know your name," he said.

"It's Jenny. Jenny Greenway. Well, shall we go?"

They started up the street. They had not gone a hundred yards before they saw Stan Bruder and Douglass Henderson coming towards them. Doug was the most popular boy in Caneville. He deserved his popularity. He was darkly good-looking, a fine athlete, good-humoured, smooth with the girls and a very decent person. Stanton Bruder was the town's most unpopular boy. He deserved that reputation, too. Stan lived at Schwartzwald, the Bruder Plantation near Caneville-Sainte Marie, most of the time. Martin Bruder had long since decided that his son was much too wild to live in a town as wide open as New Orleans, except occasionally. Otto Bruder, the third and oldest of the Bruder brothers, ran the plantation. He was a good man; but he drank.

Stanton Bruder was sixteen and built like a young bull. Everything unlovely in the Teutonic race was concentrated in his heavy, scowling face. He was not much taller than Duncan, but he was far wider and thicker. He was heavily muscled, immensely strong.

"I was looking for you, Childers," he growled.

"Now take it easy, Stan," Doug said gently. "You know Hes's mouth is nobody's prayer-book."

"So now you've found me," Duncan said evenly; "both of you."

"I'm not in this, friend," Doug said. "Stan's big enough to fight his own battles. Besides, I don't even know you, so what can I have against you?"

"All right," Duncan said, "and thanks for keeping out of it."

"Don't mention it," Doug said.

"Hes says you insulted her," Stanton said, "and Hes is my girl."

"Now do tell!" Duncan mocked. "Reckon you're mighty proud, aren't you, Cousin Stan?"

"Don't claim kin with me, you snotty-nosed Channel brat! Even if my Uncle Johann was fool enough to take in a nameless little bastard and his whorish ma——"

22

Duncan hit him then, a hard right-hand smash to the mouth. Even after all his struggles in the Channel, he still didn't know that for a right-handed fighter to lead with his right was near suicide. Stanton took the blow on his left forearm, flicking it out and away from his face like a professional. Then he jabbed with his left, crossed with his right, and the sky fell in on Duncan Childers's head.

Duncan didn't know enough to stay down. He came up almost at once. And Stanton knocked him down again, closing his left eye, bringing blood from his nose.

Then Jenny stopped it. She flung herself upon Stanton, clawing, slapping, screeching like a small, dark-haired fiend.

"You bully!" she shrieked. "You coward! You're twice his size, and you've hurt him! Oh, I'll kill you! I'll scratch out both your eyes!"

Stan drew back his hand, open-palmed, ready to slap her. But Doug Henderson's hand closed over his wrist.

"That's enough, Stan," he growled. "Don't know what you fellers do down in New Orleans, but up here we sure Lord don't cotton to menfolks that hit girls!"

Stan jerked his hand away from Doug's grip. But he didn't raise it again.

"Well," he sneered, "since you have to let your girl fight your battles, Childers, reckon I'll bow out. Till the next time, you womanish little bastard, till the next time!"

Then he turned and left them there.

Jenny knelt beside Duncan in the dirt, dabbling at his bloody nose with her handkerchief. She was crying so hard she could not speak. Doug bent down too, to help Duncan up.

Duncan pushed his hands away furiously.

"Go away!" he snarled. "Leave me be, both of you! I don't need you! I don't need anybody!"

Doug straightened up, looking at him pityingly.

"All right, old man," he said, "if that's the way you want it."

"That's the way I want it! I can do without your help!"

Doug shrugged. Then he turned and started off up the street.

Duncan reeled to his feet.

"Duncan!" Jenny's voice was imploring.

"You heard me, Jenny, get!" Duncan howled.

She stood there, staring at him. Then, very slowly, she turned away from him, her thin shoulders shaking. And that was the first time that Duncan Childers broke her heart.

Duncan walked slowly down to the Bayou's edge. He sat there, staring out over the waters. His mother was dead. He had been brought to this strange town, where, apparently, nearly everybody hated him. He was alone. Utterly alone. Slowly, he put down his head, and let the tears run scaldingly down his cheeks. He was, after all, only fifteen years old.

"What for you cryin' for, whiteboy?" the dark, rich voice said gently.

Duncan's head jerked upright. He stared into the pleasant ginger-cake-coloured face of a boy his own age.

"What's it to you, nigger?" he spat.

"Nuthin'. Only I purely hates to see folks cry. Gone done a mighty heap o' it myself, so I reckon I know how it feels. What's yore name, whiteboy?"

"None of your goddamn business. Get away from me, you hear?"

"Nope," the negro boy said. "Not till you quits cryin' an' I'se shore you feels better. Folks do some mighty damn-fool things when they's upset. 'Specially whitefolks. Coloured's more patient. Plumb got to be."

There is a point beyond which it is impossible to resist pure, disinterested kindness. In Duncan Childers that point was easily reached. He had seen so little of it.

"I'm all right now, nig—boy," he said. "What's your name?"

"Mose. Mose Johnson. You th' orphan boy Madame Bouvoir done brung home?"

"Yes. How did you know that, Mose?"

"Hit's all over town. Now you git up from there 'n come home with me. Ma'll fix that shiner up so nobody can't hardly tell it. Who beat you up like that? Stan Bruder, or Jim Vance? Got to be one or t'other. They's plumb the meanest whitefolks in town."

"Stan," Duncan said. "The lousy bastard!"

"Ain't it the truth!" Mose sighed. "He kicks my tail eve' times he runs across me. So I keep out of his way. With me it's worse, 'cause I ain't 'lowed to fight back. Come on, now. What you be called, you?"

"Duncan Childers. You—you're a good boy, Mose."

"Tries to be; 'n Ma whales th' livin' tar outa me when I ain't. Tell you what. How you like to take some lessons?"

"Lessons?" Duncan said. "What kind of lessons?"

"Fightin'. Boy I knows down in Smoketown, done won th' Battle Royal in Nawleens three years runnin'. Whitefolks give 'im ten dollars every fight. He's plumb rich. What Tiger don't know 'bout fightin' ain't in th' books. He'd learn you, I was to ax him."

24

Duncan stood there, fierce hope surging through his heart.

"Done!" he said, and put out his hand.

Shyly, Moses Johnson took it. It was the first time in all their lives that either of them had shaken hands with a person not of his own race.

But there has to be a first time. For everything.

Chapter 3

'TIME,' DUNCAN THOUGHT, as he drove towards Rosebriar Clinic, 'is a curious thing. Seems to foreshorten itself as you look back in the direction you came from. It's been eighteen years since I shook hands with Mose that day. But it seems less than a week. Such a simple act; but, God, what it cost me! That was a thing I had to grow out of. And I have. At least I can say that, thank God.

'Such a simple act. And yet, look at its consequences. Because of it, our parish is going to have a coloured doctor any day now. What we've needed all along. Needed damned bad. What we'll get because a Channel urchin was big enough to call a negro "friend".'

He pulled up the horse before the Clinic. Then he saw young Tom Hendricks waiting for him at the top of the stairs, his boyish face shining with excitement. Tom was a fine young surgeon. But his accomplishment that impressed Duncan most was Tom's life of deep, sure, unwavering happiness with Millicent, his bride of two years. They already had a child. Apparently they'd never even disagreed, not to mention quarrelled. And that was quite a trick, Duncan thought.

'The real trick,' he mused bitterly, 'is to marry the Millicents, the Jennys, of this world, instead of—the Hesters. That's not fair. Hes is all right. Only——'

He went on up the stairs to where Tom Hendricks waited. Tom was all right. Very much all right. A native of New Orleans, he had taken his degree in New York. But he knew quite a lot about the Twin Towns, because his uncle, Matthew Hendricks, ran the drug store there.

"Dunc!" he said. "It seems you're a hero again. Tell me: what have you done now? The Press is waiting for you in the ante-room. You're to meet them, old boy. But first I'm to bring you to Old Arctic Regions' office. He wants to brief you."

"Damn!" Duncan said feelingly.

"Play the game, old boy. Do or die for deah Old Rosebriar. The publicity will do us good. Every damned millionaire with a belly-ache in the whole South will read it and——"

"*Merde!*" Duncan said. "Let me out of here. I don't want——"

26

"Now, now, old boy. Is that the team spirit? We're on the five-yard line. Last down and five seconds to play——"

"Don't!" Duncan groaned. "Damn you, Tom, shut up!"

"Why be a sorehead, Dunc? Instead, be a good fellow and tell me all about it."

"All right," Duncan said, "though it was nothing much. They brought in a charity case. Nine o'clock at night, day before yesterday. Choking to death with a blocked œsophagus. Literally choking to death. Phelton went in and found—cancer. Apparently localised. Hadn't started to spread yet. At least, I hope so...."

"And?" Tom said.

"You know how he hates hopeless cases," Duncan said. "I suppose all directors of private hospitals feel that way about them—from pure economic necessity. One really bad case, and the talk starts. Two, and somebody who doesn't know a bloody, damned thing about surgery shouts 'Butcher Shop!' That does it. You're done, Tom. Finished. I don't agree with him, but I understand his point of view. Anyhow, he stood there peering into that beggar's slit throat for a hell of a time. Then he turned to me and ordered me to sew the poor devil up. And walked out of there."

Tom Hendricks stared at him. When he spoke, the words came out very slowly.

"You mean he walked out of surgery," he said, "in full possession of his faculties, nothing wrong with him, neither sick, faint, nor dizzy; and left an operative case in——"

"The hands of his assistant. Yes. He didn't want to see it, couldn't face it, believing as he did that it was maybe a matter of an hour or two, say, even if we cleared the passage so the man could breathe. Post-operative shock, alone, should have been enough to finish the beggar. You should have seen Jarvis's case. He was more than half hating that poor dying bastard for threatening his security, hurting his reputation for success. But not a drop of pity, Tom. No pity at all. Still, I was glad he left. Gave me a chance to——"

"Extirpate it, resection the tube, and——"

"Not exactly. It wasn't that easy. I had to make a plastic reconstruction of the œsophagus, using the technique that von Mikulicz-Radecki showed us in Vienna, the one he invented himself. I think I described it to you once. Regis was absolutely flabbergasted. You know she knows damned near as much surgery as any doctor in the place."

"More than a lot of them I could name," Tom said. "Best head operating-room nurse I ever ran into. Go on, boy."

27

"I could see she was just itching to get out of there and call Doctor Phelton. So I kept her busier than old hell. Not that I had to; there was enough to do, anyhow. When it was over, she flew. Like a bat out of hell. Flapping her skirts and squeaking. You should have seen her. But it was too late by then. He'd gone. Yesterday morning, before anybody got a chance to warn him, he walked into our minute charity ward and found the ward nurse holding a glass of iced water for my boy with the rebuilt œsophagus to sip with a straw. As you know, I don't dare give the patient anything even warm for several days because of the danger of his hæmorrhaging. So far, he's living on ice-cream and loving it."

"What did old Frozen Phiz do, faint?"

"Damned near. He rushed out of there to look for me; but, as luck would have it, he ran into Regis in the corridor."

" 'Doctor, I never!' " Tom mimicked in a high falsetto. " 'Absolutely marvellous! Just thrilling to watch him, Doctor, just thrilling!' "

"Her exact words." Duncan grinned. "Well, let's go get it over with."

They walked down the corridor together. They had almost reached Doctor Phelton's office, when the mention of Duncan's name coming through the slightly open door stopped them.

"Childers?" Dr. Phelton was saying. "What about him?"

"Is he as good as folks say, Doctor?"

The speaker's voice was not entirely familiar. It took Duncan some seconds to identify it.

Dr. Lester Ryan, he realised at last. 'Hearty, jovial type. Always pretty decent towards me. Brings an occasional patient in here for major surgery.'

"Absolutely," Jarvis Phelton said. "Perhaps better than most people realise. We don't get graduates from the New Vienna School of Medicine every day, Lester. They're far ahead of us. I never realised how far until I saw Childers operate. You've heard about his heart surgery, of course?"

"Yes," Dr. Ryan said. His tone was extremely dubious.

"Well, I've seen him do it. It's fantastic, Lester! He handles the heart as if it were an ordinary piece of muscle, say. Mortality under thirty per cent."

"Knowing you," Lester Ryan said drily, "the most fantastic thing of all to me was your getting up enough nerve to let him try it."

Dr. Phelton laughed. He didn't sound very amused, Duncan thought.

"I didn't at first," he said. "I waited until after I'd seen what he can do. But the first week he came here, by a pure fluke, Lester, they brought in a gunshot case while I was out begging money from old Harvey; and Ramson and Hendricks were up to their elbows in a hysterectomy—you know how damned short-handed we always are down here. Well, Childers went in there, removed a forty-five-calibre bullet from—of all places—the pylorus, the opening of the stomach into the small intestine, you know——"

"Damn it, Jarvis, I'm aware of what the pylorus is! I did go to medical school, Doctor," Lester Ryan snorted.

"Sorry. I've done so much lecturing to laymen here, of late, that I've formed the habit of explaining everything. No reflection upon your professional knowledge, Doctor. Anyhow, as I was saying, after taking that slug out of the patient's pylorus, Childers resectioned it; and six weeks later the patient walked out of here on his own two feet. Saw him no later than yesterday, back on his old job, working at hard manual labour in a boilerplate factory."

"Well," Ryan said, "I, for one, am damned glad your ace lives up to his advance billing. You're going to need him, Jarvis—bad. Maybe they taught him something over there we don't know. Anyhow, it's your problem. Decidedly your problem, since it concerns our sterling local philanthropist, Ernest Harvey, who's been keeping your private butcher shop going so many years. Last year, if I remember rightly, he gave you all of fifty thousand——"

"More. Closer to a hundred. Good God, Lester! Don't tell me he's got something serious!"

"No. He's as sound as a dollar. It's his daughter, Grace. She has a clear-cut case of Myxœdema, Jarvis. She's young and pretty. Or she was. You know what Myxœdema does to a girl's looks."

"I also know there's no known cure for it. For God's sake, don't dump that on us, Lester!"

"I won't. But old Harvey's going to. You don't think it hasn't occurred to him, after all the money he's given you? He's bringing the girl down here tomorrow."

Inside Duncan Childers's mind the pages of the heavy German tome flipped over. Came to a certain page. Stopped. One paragraph leaped into focus: "Myxœdema, failure of the thyroid function. Insufficiency of secretion, resulting in dryness and swelling of the skin." Pop-eyes, too. Legs and arms like—God, the girl would be a horror! Then coldly, the cure. In French, this time: "Description of thyroid transplant from a sheep to a human patient. Technique of the illustrious Doctor Odilon Marc Lannelongue. Successfully performed at the University of Paris in 1890." All of thirteen years ago, and these jingo types hadn't heard about it yet!

He touched Tom's arm, cleared his throat loudly. Inside the office the talk came to an abrupt halt. Duncan rapped upon the door.

"Come in!" Jarvis Phelton said; then: "Ah, Childers, Hendricks. You both know Dr. Ryan, I presume?"

"Yes, sir," Tom said. Duncan merely nodded.

"There're some gentlemen here, Dr. Childers," Jarvis said, "to meet you. Members of the Fourth Estate. The Press. It seems word has got about of your feat in rebuilding that cancerous œsophagus——"

"You mean," Duncan said drily, "that word was let slip. Damned unethical, Jarvis. The medical profession doesn't advertise. We're not—hucksters."

"Now see here, Childers!"

"Oh, skip it," Duncan said wearily. "My ethics aren't that robust yet. Maybe they'll get to be, but, so far, I'm still the mercenary type. Money in large, folding batches is what I practise medicine for. Now, about Grace Harvey—yes, I eavesdropped. That rule about eavesdroppers never hearing good of themselves didn't hold. You were being very sweet, Doctor. I'm grateful. So I'm going to tell you how to save your hemstitching factory. Myxœdema, eh? Well, you take a sheep——"

"A sheep!" Ryan and Phelton chorused.

"A sheep. Four-footed beast. Gives wool. Out of which your smartly-tailored, well-cut suits are made. A live sheep. You trot him up to the operating-room——"

"Childers, have you lost your mind?"

"Perhaps. I sometimes think so. Influence of my surroundings, what? Are you going to listen? I'm merely trying to help you keep Ernest Harvey happily shelling out the coin of the realm."

"Go on," Jarvis Phelton said grimly. "But if this is your idea of a joke, Childers——"

"No joke. Didn't it ever occur to you, Doctor, that a sheep's thyroid and the human article are remarkably similar?"

"Jarvis, I think he's got it! Seems to me I read somewhere——"

"You probably did, Doctor," Duncan said. "It's been all of thirteen years since Dr. Lannelongue performed the first successful thyroid transplant in Paris. *He* used a sheep as donor. So I don't see why all this prejudice against our four-footed pastoral friends..."

Dr. Phelton stopped him with a wave of his hand.

"Will you do it, Doctor?" he asked. "I'm afraid we're hopelessly outmoded over here. I haven't the faintest idea where to begin."

"Begin by getting me a sheep. I'll do it, of course. For dear little Grace. When she's pretty again, she might even give me a donation. Not money. I'll take my fee out in trade. Now, where is your crew of hired scribblers, Jarvis?"

"Childers, I beg you, I implore you, not to be flippant."

"Don't worry. I'll be as serious as Robert Koch. Lead on, good physician."

The Press was an ordeal. Dr. Duncan Childers was disarmingly modest.

"Nothing to it," he said; "merely a technique I was taught in Vienna. They're quite advanced over there."

"Will the patient live?"

"I don't know. I hope so. But with cancer you can never tell. That he will recover from this operation is certain. Also that he will live a number of years. But no honest doctor can guarantee more than that. If so much as one cancerous cell got into his bloodstream he will die of cancer, later. It will show up somewhere else in his body. I devoutly hope that there was no cancerous tissue left. I took every known precaution. But Sean Murphy's life is in the hands of the Almighty. None of us, gentlemen, have the skill of the Gentle Physician of Galilee."

He could see Dr. Phelton nodding approvingly. That was good copy. Damned good copy. But his words almost choked him. What was he—a paid publicity agent, or a doctor?

"What about the Vance case, Doctor? Would you care to give us an opinion?"

Duncan recognised the reporter who had asked that question. He was Fred Baynes of *The Picayune*. A good reporter, who specialised in chasing ambulances in gory accident and murder cases. Which was why Duncan knew him. Their paths had crossed often enough. Still, he had to admit that, as reporters go, Baynes was not a bad type.

"As a matter of fact, Fred," he said quietly, "I'd rather not. James Vance was my wife's brother. Naturally, that whole matter is still a painful subject to her. After all, it was only three years ago."

"Sorry, Doctor," Fred Baynes said.

"Say, Doc—how about some background? You're a local boy, aren't you?" another reporter asked.

"I was born in the Irish Channel," Duncan said. "I'm rather

31

proud of that fact. I'm also proud to say that my parents were dirt-poor. Seems to prove that opportunity is not dead in this country. Later on I was taken to the town of Caneville-Sainte Marie by my late and eternally blessed benefactress, Minna von Stürck Bouvoir. It was there that I met the girl who afterwards paid me the supreme honour of becoming my wife...."

The pencils scribbled busily. He talked on, prettying it up, falsifying it into a penny romance. In his mind, the reporters faded out; and he was there again, in the sultry back bayou country, seeing it again, living it....

The boy, seventeen-year-old Duncan Childers, walked down Miller's Lane towards the swimming-hole. It had been a crowded two years since he came to Caneville-Sainte Marie. He had been swamped with tutors brought from Boston, New York, New Orleans by Minna Bouvoir. And he had caught up with his class, even passed it in some subjects. His German was becoming better than fair. He'd be ready for the Berlin Conservatorium when the time came. Only he wasn't sure he wanted to be a pianist any more. The memory of his mother's death held him. To cure disease was a wonderful thing. A nobler thing than playing a piano. And the way that people looked at Dr. Hans Volker—they surely didn't look at Prof. Augustus Bergdorf with anything like that much respect. Still, it was a hard choice. When he had said to Professor Bergdorf that he might change over to medicine, the old music teacher had almost cried.

"Any *Esel, mein* Duncan, can saw bones!" he roared. "But few —very few—can play everything from Beethoven's 'Diabelli Variations' to a Chopin mazurka the way you can!"

'A musician's a kind of a freak,' he reasoned painfully, 'and I'm damned tired of being a freak. They don't call me bastard to my face any more, not since I learned to fight; but they still think it. Funny that I haven't tangled with Stan any more. Maybe he's heard what I can do with my fists now. That Tiger sure knows his business. Pivot off the ball of your foot. Lean your weight behind the punch. Left jab first, always. Then cross with your right....'

Miller's Lane was not the shortest way to reach the pool. By cutting across the Vance place he could have saved half a mile of trudging through the July heat. But, for several reasons, he didn't dare. He knew well that if he were seen, even by one of the negroes, inside of five minutes Toby Williams, the overseer, or even old Nelson Vance himself, would be there, shouting and damning him off the place. Worst of all would be Jim Vance, Nelson's twenty-six-year-old son by his first marriage. Jim wouldn't shout. He would simply plant his size-eleven hobnail boots in Duncan's seat with all his force.

These were the reasons he gave himself, and they were all true. What was not true was the belief that any of them, singly or in combination, actually kept him from crossing the Vance place. He had in him a good bit of the natural ferocity of the slum-bred. He took a savage delight in combat, because it allowed some of the dark poisons festering inside his heart an outlet. He had been beaten, kicked, abused, throughout a goodly portion of his younger life. He had learned to take it, and give back in equal measure as he received. But now his hurts were subtler ones, against which he had no defences. One word encompassed them all; and the name of that word was: outcast. He was—apparently—rich, pampered, cared for. But the invisible stigma of his illegitimacy was upon him like a brand. He had no friends, except Mose Johnson. There was no girl he could go walking with of an evening, buy sodas for at Matt Hendricks's pharmacy. Except Jenny Greenway, whom he, in turn would not accept, out of a subconscious feeling that there must be something wrong with her or she wouldn't like him, since nobody else did.

Youth is a terrible time; a suffering, hurtful time. Groping towards manhood, youth needs to be morally reinforced by friendship. Conformity is its hallmark. But Duncan Childers could not conform with the customs of his contemporaries because he was not allowed to. Cut dead, avoided, sneered at covertly, he was beginning to accept the idea of his own worthlessness. His natural reaction, to explode into anger little short of murderous, didn't help matters much, if at all.

And if all his problems could be summed up in the word outcast, no one cast him further out, banished him more cruelly beyond the pale, hurled taunts distilled of purer venom at his head, than sixteen-year-old Hester Vance. He had aching, unformed dreams in which that shell-pink, sensual mouth floated on the darkness inches from his own. Lately he had begun to dream of seeing her naked— and those were the vaguest dreams of all. He had very little idea of how she would look, naked. He had never seen an unclothed female form. Again, his outcast state contributed to his emotional retardation; boys like Stan Bruder and Doug Henderson drove over to Mertontown, ten miles away, and picked up the lint-heads, mill-fluff, white-trash girls who worked in the textile mills, and early and easily achieved carnal knowledge. But to Duncan Childers were left only his agonising, formless dreams.

The route he was taking now led him near the section where Jenny Greenway lived with her widowed father. Duncan hoped he wouldn't see her; but he was sure he would. Jenny always managed to be underfoot, somehow. Like him, she had few defences; none at all as far as he was concerned. He thought cruelly of using her to explore the aching business of sex; but her candid eyes shamed him out of the notion. He was strangely afraid of her great innocence, her serene and untroubled innocence, which, seemingly, did not suffer dreams.

He saw her almost at once, running down from the ridge on which her father's shotgun cabin was perched, her dark brown pigtails flying out behind her. He slowed his steps. Perversely, he wanted to see her, to talk to her; and did not want to, at one and the same time.

She jumped down from the high bank beside the road.

"Hi, Dunc!" she got out. That was all she had breath for.

Duncan studied her. She was still built like a fence post. But now the post was gradually losing its angularity. Small breasts, the size of oranges, broke the straight fall of her calico frock. Slim as she was, her hips were not quite boyish any more. She was one of those girls who develop late. Hester had been more provocatively female at fourteen than Jenny was now at seventeen.

"Hi," he said gruffly.

"Where're you going?" Jenny said.

"Swimming."

"Can I come?" Jenny pleaded. She had no subtle, feminine wiles. "I'm a good swimmer, Dunc."

"No," Duncan said.

"Why not?" Jenny whispered.

"There're going to be just boys. And we're going to be—well—naked."

"Oh!" Jenny said.

He studied her, his brown eyes crinkling with pure deviltry.

"Maybe you could come, at that," he said. "I could send Mose away."

"Oh, Duncan!" she breathed ecstatically. "Just you wait two minutes till I put on my bathing-dress."

His mouth curled into sardonic mockery.

"If you're going to need a bathing-dress," he said, "I don't want you to come. What the hell fun would that be?"

She stood there staring at him, her brown eyes wide behind the ugly glasses. Horror crept into them.

34

"Oh, Duncan!" she said. "What do you think I am?"

"A girl," he said. "At least I reckon so. You look something like a girl, though not much. Maybe I could turn you into a real live one, given the chance."

She didn't answer him. She stood there, staring at him, her eyes big with hurt.

He took two quick steps towards her, caught her by the shoulders, dragged her to him. He tightened his arms about her ferociously. Ground his mouth into hers. Her glasses fell off, and were trampled underfoot. She struggled with him in fear, in disgust. Then the fear became terror, the disgust, shame, because of what was happening inside her. The sudden explosion of warmth along her veins. The slackening, the incurving ache, the breath-strangle, heart-hammer, the loosening of loins, the thrust irresistibly forward so that their bodies arched and curved and fitted into one another, the calico mingling with the white of shirt, its red flaming against the blue of his denims——

Horror gave her strength. She tore free. Whirled. Fled, driven headlong by the whiplash of his laughter.

"I take it back!" he called. "Reckon you're a girl after all, Jen!"

"Why, Duncan Childers!" the throaty voice behind him said. "Whatever did you do to poor Jen?"

He turned. Hester sat there in her smart little buckboard, drawn by one of the Vances' matchless greys. Despite the heat, she was crisp, starched, fragrant, her ash-blond hair piled high, her full lips smiling.

Smiling. At him. At him! Then he remembered.

"What's it to you?" he snarled.

"Nothing. She's a tacky little old thing. Get in. I'll take you wherever you're goin'."

"I was going swimming. In the altogether. So I reckon I'd better go alone."

She smiled.

"It is hot, isn't it?" she said. "Wish I could come. Only I reckon it wouldn't be—'zactly nice."

"You fishing for an invitation, Hes? All right, you've got it. Go get your bathing-dress."

Her smile never wavered.

"What—what about you, Duncan?" she said.

"I'll keep on my under-drawers," Duncan said recklessly, "if that won't shock you too much."

35

"Of course not, silly! I do have a brother, remember. You wait right here. I'll go get my bathing-dress. Be back in a jiffy!"

He stood there waiting, his whole body a quivering jangle. But when he saw the buckboard coming down the lane, Hester was dressed exactly as before. 'Damn!' he thought. 'I knew this was too good to be true.'

He waited. When Hester was close enough, he frowned at her sternly.

"Where's your bathing-dress?" he demanded.

"I've got it on," Hester giggled. "Under my clothes, Duncan. Only way I could have got out of the house with it. Aunt Sarah would have seen it and told Pa. Then there really would have been trouble. Come on, hop it. It's too hot for walking."

"All right," he said, "as long as you promise not to spit in my face this time."

Hester turned her enormous blue eyes on Duncan's face. They were petal-soft, suddenly. She laid a hand on his arm.

"I'm sorry about that, Duncan," she whispered. "D'you know I cried myself to sleep that same night? I was so ashamed over what I'd done. I don't know why I acted like that. It's not your fault who your parents were, or what they did. Besides—you're handsome. Very, very handsome. Reckon you're the handsomest boy I ever did see."

Duncan's heart leaped, soared. But he contained his joy. He had had too many bitter lessons by then, over how quickly joy can turn to grief.

"You've had a hell of a long time to say you were sorry in," he said flatly, "and you never did. Why now, Hester?"

"Couldn't get up the nerve. I've grown up now. And I know what people say doesn't make much sense. Besides, I know what I want——"

He stared at her.

"Am I what you want?" he said quietly.

"Yes, Duncan," Hester said, "and—for keeps!"

Duncan turned away, and sat there staring straight ahead. This had to be absorbed, slowly. He had no capacity for joy. They rode along until they came to the pine wood. Hester turned the horse into the little path. They could hear the water falling over the rocks. It made a noise like laughter.

Mose Johnson was there, waiting for Duncan. He had grown tall and strong in those two years. But his eyes were sorrowing.

"Howdy, Dunc," he said, then more timidly: "Howdy, Miss Hester."

Hester didn't answer him. She sat there staring at him in pure astonishment. When she did speak, her voice was ice.

"What," she said, "are you doing here, Mose?"

"I come—came to swim with Duncan," Mose said. He was trying to mend his grammar, under Duncan's teaching.

"Well, I never!" Hester said. "I must say you have some mighty peculiar friends, Mister Duncan Childers!"

"Why?" Duncan said blandly. "What's so peculiar about Mose?"

"Nothing," Hester spat. "He's just a nigger. What's peculiar is your running around with him!"

Duncan stared at her, his brows making thunderclouds above his eyes.

Hester ignored the storm warnings, plunged on.

"You are queer. When I came down the road, I do believe you'd been kissing that tacky little Jenny Greenway."

"Jen's all right," Duncan said. "I like her."

"Well, let me tell you one thing, Duncan Childers! If you want to be friends with me, if you want to be my beau, you'd better give up all your peculiar friends! I won't have—why! Where are you going, Duncan?"

"Home," Duncan said evenly. "I've changed my mind. Guess I don't want to go swimming after all."

"Oh!" Hester gasped. "You come back here, Duncan! You think I'm going to let you run off and leave me like this?"

"I," Duncan said, "am not running off. You sent me away, Hester."

"I did not! I only said——"

"That I would have to give up the best friends I have in the world, if I wanted to be your beau. Well, I want to be your beau, Hes, but not that bad!"

"Look, Dunc," Mose said gently, "I'm going. I shore Lawd didn't mean to cause no trouble 'twixt you'n Miss Hester."

"No," Hester said gaily. "Don't go, Mose! You stay here and have a nice swim. I'm sorry I called you a nigger. I was just mad at Duncan."

"Reckon I'm used to it, Miss Hester," Mose said. "Sho don't like being called that. None of us coloured folks do. But we don't take on over it. Only, Miss Hester, I can't strip off 'n go swimming whilst you's here."

"I know. Dunc and I are going to take a walk. We've got something to talk about."

Duncan stared at her. He hadn't even begun to learn the ways of women.

37

"Fine," Mose grinned. "Reckon three's a crowd, eh, Miss Hester?"

"Right." Hester laughed. "Shy like Duncan is, I don't want anybody around to scare him." She locked her slender arm through Duncan's. "Come on, now," she said.

Duncan walked beside her, frowning.

"Damned if I can understand you, Hes," he said.

"Of course not. You're a boy, and I'm a girl. Boys never understand girls."

"While girls——?" Duncan said.

"Understand boys perfectly. But then, we're smarter," Hester said.

They moved through the woods, following the meanderings of the little stream. Neither of them said anything. It didn't seem to be a time for talking.

"Let's sit down here—under this tree," Hester said. "We can put our feet in the water."

"Well——" Duncan said, "we can still swim. Water's deep enough for that."

"Don't want to," Hester said. "It would get my hair all mussed, and Aunt Sarah would be sure to notice. I will take off my frock and petticoat, though. I'll be cooler in my bathing-dress. Besides, what I really want to do is to talk to you."

They sat down under the tree. Duncan bent forward, tugging at his shoe-laces. He watched Hester undressing out of the corner of his eye. It was disappointing. The feminine bathing-dress of the 1880s was an exceedingly modest garment.

"What'll we talk about?" he said.

"Oh, I don't know. F'instance, you're still aiming to be a doctor when you grow up?"

"How'd you know about that?" Duncan said.

"Reckon everybody knows. You didn't think you could ride around with Doctor Volker on his house calls without anybody noticing, did you? 'n besides, he and Prof. Bergdorf had a terrible fuss over you."

"They did?" Duncan said in pure astonishment. "Lord, Hes, why?"

"Because Prof. Bergdorf thinks you've got the makings of a concert pianist; and Doc Volker thinks you'll make a great doctor. I was there, having my piano lesson, when it happened. You should have heard them shouting at each other! Prof. Bergdorf was really mad. Says anybody can treat a belly-ache, but to play the piano the way you do—— And you know what, Duncan? I think he's right!"

"I'll do both," Duncan said. "A surgeon and a pianist need the same kind of hands. The two careers aren't mutually exclusive."

"Mutually ex-clusive," Hester repeated. "How fine you do talk, Duncan! You know what?"

"No," Duncan said. "What?"

"I like you. I like you—heaps!"

Duncan stared at her. The moment stretched itself wire-fine, to the point of breaking.

"Hes," Duncan whispered huskily, "would you—would you mind if I—if I kissed you?"

"'Course not," Hester said. "I was wondering how long it was going to take you to think of—that."

He kissed her then, clumsily. She drew away her small face after a moment, and loosed a peal of silvery laughter.

"Why," she said, "why, Duncan Childers! You don't even know how to kiss!"

Duncan looked at her, his brown eyes filled with puzzled hurt. She sprang up suddenly and began to run, deeper into the woods. He pounded after her. She was doe-swift, agile. It took him a long time to catch her.

He jerked her to him, roughly. He ground his mouth into hers. She pushed him away with surprising strength.

"Not like that—either," she said.

"How?" he growled.

"Like this," she whispered; "like this——"

She knew how. Already, at sixteen years old, she knew.

They lay there, under the trees, locked in each other's arms. Duncan kissed her endlessly. There were dark woodwinds in his blood, trumpets, drums. But he didn't know what to do about it. He had a clinically exact knowledge of pregnancy, drawn from his reading of medical books. He knew all the precise scientific words for the act of love. But these words are not descriptive. They are nomenclature; nothing more.

Instinct instructed him. Tentatively he touched her knee, just below the full skirt of the bathing-dress. She made no effort to push away his hand. Slowly, trembling as much from fear as from anything else, he let it stray upward.

Hester twisted her face away from his.

"No, Duncan——" she said.

"Hes——" His voice was imploring.

"No, darling. I—I'm human, too, Duncan. If I—let you go—too

39

far, with me—I might not be able to stop you—later on. You—or me. So don't, please!"

He took away his hand.

"Lord, Hes——" he began, but her fingers bit into his arms.

"There—there's somebody in there!" she hissed, "watching us!"

Duncan rose to a sitting position. He sat there a long moment, staring at the trees. Then he got up and walked towards the place where Hester had pointed. It was a thicket, denser than the rest of the woods. Just before he reached it, he thought he heard a twig crackle under someone's step; a rustle of branches, brushed aside in passing. He thought he heard those things. But he was not sure. They were as slight as that.

He plunged into the thicket. Vines caught at him. Thorn-bushes hung in his clothing. There was nothing there. Absolutely nothing at all.

Girls, he thought morosely, have the damnedest ideas—then he saw the blue streamer of smoke, spiralling up from the cigarette butt on the ground.

He stood there, staring at it, the word 'Who?' printing itself inside his mind. He was not a woodsman. He knew he had not the slightest chance of following the trail of a man who could come and go with the ghostly stealth with which this one had come and gone. He was miserably sure that whoever it had been was already on his way to tell Nelson Vance. Then he shrugged. It was too late now. That particular music would have to be faced.

When he came back to where he had left Hester she was already up, nervously brushing the twigs and leaves off the back of her bathing-dress.

"Oh, come on!" she wailed. "We'd better get out of here! I'm scared! Oh, Duncan, did you see?"

"No," he lied calmly. "There wasn't anyone. Just your imagination, Hes."

"No it wasn't! There was somebody, I tell you! Oh Lord, Dunc, if Pa finds out——"

"He won't," Duncan said. "Besides, I haven't finished kissing you yet."

"Oh yes, you have! Enough of a thing is enough. You were already trying to get me to go the limit and——"

Duncan's face was ludicrous with shock. Not from the fact that she had so accurately defined what had been his intentions; she had acknowledged them before, and her own ready response to them; it was, instead, the way she pronounced that phrase, as though the words were—old, familiar things.

40

He caught her by the shoulders, roughly.

"Tell me, Hes," he grated, "have you—ever?"

"Have I ever what?"

"Gone the limit with somebody?"

Hester's face flamed scarlet.

"Why, Duncan Childers," she said, "I think you're perfectly horrid!"

He stood there, looking at her; the shame inside him bone-deep.

"Lord, Hes, I'm sorry," he mumbled. "I didn't mean——"

"Oh yes, you did! And what right have you, Duncan, to think a thing like that—about me?"

He was years away from the correct answer. His inexperience prevented him from even conceiving of it. He didn't even know that at this time the vast majority of young women in their twenties could not have displayed the practised familiarity with the ways of love of this precocious child. But his ready temper saved him.

"I said I'm sorry," he snapped. "What do you want me to do, Hes—get down on my knees? Anyhow, you put the words in my mouth. I never heard another girl talk like you. Besides, if I knew of a fellow who'd been fooling around with you, I'd——"

"What would you do, Duncan?" she said, a little breathlessly.

"Kill him," Duncan said evenly. "Come on."

But she stood there and loosed the silvery lift and soar of her laughter.

"Why, Duncan Childers," she said. "I do believe you're jealous!"

"I am," he said grimly. "Come on!"

Mose had gone by the time they reached the swimming-hole. Duncan guessed sadly that he and Hester had spoiled Mose's day. It was his first experience of the conflicting loyalties that mark adulthood. He didn't like the feeling.

They got into the buckboard and started back towards the Vance place. The nearer they came to it, the more visible Hester's nervousness became.

"Dunc——" she quavered.

"Yes, Hes?"

"Would you mind awf'ly getting down here? Pa's so—so strict. If he saw me riding with a boy, he'd——"

"All right," Duncan said, "if you'll kiss me good-bye, Hes."

She wound her slim arms about his neck. She kissed him until the sky spun dizzily above his head. Then she hung back against the circle of his arms.

"I—I love you, Hes," Duncan groaned. "It's awful how I do love you!"

She smiled at him then, gently, tenderly.

"And I love you," she said. "But it's not awful. Oh no, Duncan, it's not awful at all!"

'I'll go home,' Duncan thought, as he watched the buckboard rounding a curve until it was out of sight. 'I'll tell Grandmother I kissed Hester. That way, if old Vance phones her, she'll be prepared. Lord, what a girl Hester is! Makes me feel like a fool. I should know more than she does; but—I don't. How the devil can she know so much? If I thought——"

"Here he is, boys!" Stan Bruder said.

Duncan had been so lost in his thoughts that he hadn't even seen Stan Bruder and his crowd. He stopped short, the waves of anger already beginning to beat about his ears. He was a prey to many conflicting emotions; but his feelings about Stanton Bruder weren't among them. His hatred of his cousin-by-courtesy was both un-mixed and pure.

The boys fanned out, encircling him.

"Today," Stan said, "this snotty little bastard took advantage of my girl. My ex-girl. Naturally I wouldn't touch her—lil' whore that she is—with a ten-foot pole after this! Long as I was the only one she did it for, it was all right. But I don't share my wimmen. 'Specially not with no Irish Channel punk. There I was, walking through the woods all peaceful-like——"

"So," Duncan whispered. "It was you!"

A roar of laughter went up at his words. He stared from one of them to the other like a trapped animal. He was far too angry to read the admiration and envy in their eyes.

"And there he was," Stan snarled furiously, "stretched out on the sweet-smelling grass with——"

"Don't you say it!" Duncan spat. "Don't you put her name in your filthy mouth!"

"Why not?" Stanton sneered, "since I've had her sweet lil' body in my filthy ol' hammock out in back o' my Uncle Otto's filthy ol' hunting-lodge, I don't see why——"

Duncan hit him then, a hard right-hand smash to the mouth. He was so enraged that he forgot Tiger's first instruction: "Never lead with yore right, Dunc!"

Stanton stepped back, shaking his head. A thin trickle of blood trailed down from the corner of his mouth.

"Well, you bastard!" he snarled, "you asked for it!" Then he pivoted on the ball of his left foot, and caught Duncan full in the middle with a left jab. It travelled less than six inches; but it doubled Duncan in half. Then Stan crossed with his right, and

Duncan went down. He lay on his back, staring at the tree-tops.

He didn't get up at once. He knew better now. He lay there until the damage those mule-kick powerful punches had done him ebbed.

"Get up, you yellow bastard!" Stan Bruder roared.

Duncan got to his feet. Fell into a crouch. Tucked his chin down behind his left shoulder the way the negro fighter had taught him to do.

Stanton Bruder knew the rudiments of boxing, and these had served him well against Duncan's total lack of skill. But now Duncan had been taught by an expert. It was an almost classical combat: the slugger against the boxer, the fancy dan. Stanton came in like a bull. Duncan wasn't there. He bobbed, weaved, ducked, sidestepped. Stan's blows whistled past him, venting their explosive force upon the naked air.

"Stand still and fight, you bastard!" he howled.

That was the last thing on earth Duncan had any intention of doing. Stanton Bruder was far stronger than he was. To stand still was to get murdered. Instead, he closed Stan's big mouth with a left that had all his wiry strength behind it. Stan's knees buckled. He straightened up, shook his head, and bored in. To be met by a left that worked like a riveting hammer. Always there, jabbing into his face, moving piston-like, jab following jab so fast that their speed blurred sight. When he pulled back, his gang saw, in mute astonishment, the blood flowing from a cut over his eye.

Duncan saw it too. It awoke something primitive in him, a pure and ancient blood-lust. His lips curled away from his teeth in a smile crueller than a snarl. 'Concentrate on that eye,' he thought. 'Close it. Then the other. But first I better bring his guard down.'

He came forward in a half crouch. His fists beat a tattoo on Stan's blubbery middle. Stan was going soft, running to fat. His mouth jerked open, gasping for air. His punches slid harmlessly off Duncan's shoulder, forearms; grazed the top of that red head. Mercilessly, Duncan worked on his belly, waiting for his guard to drop. Stan's hands came down, and Duncan snapped a left to the uninjured right eye. It closed at once; puffed, ballooned, turned purple. The left was already half blinded from the blood that flowed from the cut.

Then, without pity, Duncan cut him down. He wasn't strong enough to bring Stan to earth with one blow. It took him twenty. And it wasn't pretty. It wasn't pretty at all. Stan Bruder's face was a bloody hash by the time he fell. Duncan stood over him, panting. He glared at the others. Uneasily they moved back, back....

"Get going, you yellow rats!" Duncan roared. They broke, scurried. Triumph beat through his veins in waves. He moved off. Looking back, he saw Stan get to his hands and knees and crouch there, his head hanging. Inside Duncan's veins joy distilled itself into crystalline purity. He'd done it! He really had.

Then it ended. All at once, with no interval of transition, the joy drained out of him, leaving him trembling, cold, and sick. And thick black misery rose to fill his heart. Stan's sneering phrases swarmed into his mind: "Long as I was the only one she did it for ... her sweet lil' body in my filthy ol' hammock out in back of my Uncle Otto's filthy ol' hunting-lodge ... I don't see why——"

Inside Duncan Childers something died, screaming. He clamped his jaw down tight lest the agony in him tear bloodily upward through the tight-locked cords of his throat.

'Damn her!' he thought. 'Oh damn her, damn her, damn her! Filthy little whore! Does it for anybody! Anybody but me!'

He whirled, raced back to where Stan crouched, trying to rise. He drew back his foot and kicked. His foot made a dull thud against Stan's shredded face. The red drops made a bright shower against the bone-dry, thirsty earth. Duncan kicked him again, again, again, until Stan loosened all over like a punctured air-sack. He lay there without moving. Then Duncan Childers walked his fallen foe up and down, grinding in his heels. He had seen the Channel gangs do that, and it had sickened him. But now he gloried in pure, feral savagery.

Then his rage left him. He broke into a slow jog-trot, headed for the Bayou. He gained it, sat down on the bank, at the place where the old landslide had cut it off, forming the marshes from which the musk-rat trappers added to Nelson Vance's wealth. He sat there a very long time, perhaps two full hours. He did not cry. He had, by then, moved far beyond mere tears.

Then he heard her calling his name.

"Duncan!" she wailed. "Oh, Duncan, where are you! Duncan, please!"

He lifted his head. "Over here!" he called out.

Hester flew to him.

"Oh, Duncan!" she sobbed, "I've looked and looked for you! Mose told me you'd probably be here! We're in trouble! In terrible trouble! It's all over town that we—that we—— Oh, why did you have to fight Stan Bruder? They say that you beat him nearly to death! Everybody's saying that your grandmother shouldn't have brought you here! That you've got killer instincts because you came from the Channel! And that's not the worst of it! Father

44

and my brother Jim are both out looking for you! They're going to kill you, Duncan!"

Duncan looked at her.

"Let them. What have I to live for now?"

"Duncan!" she shrilled, "don't talk like that! I'm in trouble, too! Father's going to have me examined by Dr. Volker to see whether I——"

"Made love with me. And you can't prove you didn't. Because you've done it with Stan Bruder. Maybe with a half a dozen others!"

She stared at him. What was in her eyes was—horror.

Slowly, wordlessly, she sank down beside him. Took his hand. He jerked it away.

"Get away from me, you little whore!" he snarled.

She sat there, looking at him. Then she started crying worse than ever. He had never seen or heard anybody cry like that. Her sobs came grating up from her throat. They made a noise like tearing.

Clumsily he put up his hand and stroked her bright hair. He was not yet impervious to a woman's tears.

"Don't, Hes," he croaked. "Please don't—please!"

"You believe that about me!" she stormed in an agony of grief. "You! Oh, Duncan, I could be examined by a million doctors! I'm still the way I was the day my mother bore me! Stan's lying! He's tried dozens of times, and I never let him! Oh, darling, darling, if I wouldn't let you—loving you like I do, you think I'd——"

Joy leaped, flamed, towered. He put his hand under her chin and lifted her tear-streaked face, bent and kissed her mouth. A long, slow, heart-stopping time.

She jerked away from him.

"Duncan!" she whispered, "take me into the woods! Do what you want—what I want too! Since they think so, why not? If we're going to be punished, why shouldn't we be guilty?"

Duncan looked at her, his brown eyes tender.

"No, Hes," he said. "I'll wait until we're wed."

They were still sitting there, when Mose Johnson found them.

"Dunc!" he got out. "Miss Hester! Y'all better git outa here! Mister Jim's on his way down here, 'n he's mighty mad! Miss Hester, please! You go home round about. I'll take Dunc home with me. My ma'll hide him until——"

Duncan shook his head.

"No, Mose," he said. "I'm not hiding. Come on, Hes——"

"No, Duncan! If Jim sees you with me, he'll kill you sure! Maybe even kill me! I know a short cut——"

Duncan considered that. It was better that way. For Hester's own sake, it was better.

"All right," he said. "C'mon, Mose."

"Not that way, Dunc! We'll meet him, sure!"

"I want to meet him," Duncan said. "Get going, Hes!"

She hung there, her face white. She came to him, and kissed him, hard. Then she turned and ran along the Bayou's edge.

"Come on, Mose!" Duncan snapped.

"Dunc, I'm scairt! I'm purely scairt o' that mean ol' Jim Vance! He done caused 'nough trouble in my family. He—he's been picking at my sister, Ruby. Pa's fit to be tied. Ma done took his shotgun and throwed it in the river. Says she ain't going to see a good man hanging from no tree, or burnt alive over no nocount whiteman, nor no fool gal, either."

"All right," Duncan said. "You take the short cut. I'm going home straight."

"Dunc——" Mose pleaded.

"No. You get going, Mose," Duncan said.

He met Jim Vance in the middle of Miller's Lane. Jim was mounted on his big chestnut. He pulled the horse up, his face turning purple. He was, as usual, a little drunk.

"Fool around with my lil' sister, will you!" he roared. "Why, you gawddamned Channel brat, I'll——"

"You get down off that horse," Duncan flared, "and see if you can talk so big on the ground!"

Jim lifted his crop, brought it whistling down. It cut through Duncan's shirt like a knife. Brought blood. Duncan leaped backwards. Jim spurred the horse forward, striking. Half his blows missed; but the ones that didn't did fearful damage to Duncan's chest and back.

Duncan groped desperately in his pocket; his fingers closed over the knife. It was a relic of his Irish Channel days—a murderous switchblade, seven inches long. He touched the button. The blade flicked out like blue lightning. He waited.

Jim reined-in the dancing chestnut and tightened his grip on the crop. But he did not strike again. With a neigh that was curiously like a woman's scream, the big chestnut went back almost on his haunches, pawing the air with his forefeet. Jim had all he could do to keep in the saddle. He fought the horse down again; and the chestnut dug his hooves into the earth, soaring forward into a gigantic leap. Jim sawed at the bit, forcing the animal to a halt; but before he could stop the beast's frantic prancing, the curious neighing scream came again; and the gelding was off, the bit between his teeth now, running, going on.

"Come on, Dunc!" Doug Henderson called out tensely. "I'm here—right here in the woods! Be two miles before that big nag's winded enough for Jim to rein him in. By that time we can be a hell of a long way from here!"

"But how——" Duncan said—"how'd you do it, Doug?"

For answer, Doug held up a catapult and a handful of those ball-bearings that the boys had stolen from the round-house of the Trans-Mississippi and Louisiana to use for marbles.

"Started to let Jim have one of these steelies," he chuckled, "but then he would have known. This way, he'll swear you put a grisgris on him. Lord, boy, are you ever in a mess!"

"I know," Duncan said gloomily. He folded the blade of the knife back into the handle, and put it in his pocket. He stared at Doug. "Mind telling me why you did that—for me?" he said.

"Because you're one hell of a man! My personal vote of thanks for peeling off Stan's hide. He sure Lord had it coming."

"Thanks," Duncan said.

"Don't mention it. And the next time you aim to get into Hester's frilly pants, you let me know. I got the sweetest lil' hideout——"

"Doug!" Duncan got out. "I never!"

"That's the ticket! Never admit it out loud, not even in church. Reckon you better get going, boy, before that big bastard comes back."

"Doug, I swear!"

"All right, you swear," Doug grinned. "Just you make tracks—right now!"

There was no point in staying, Duncan saw. Convincing Doug would take all evening. If he ever could. He made a beeline for his home.

That evening, Nelson Vance paid a call on Minna Bouvoir. He had, by then, achieved a state of rage capable of inspiring fear in a stone image. Which was a mistake. Even to go there at all was an error. For he wasn't assailing a stone image. He was confronting Minna von Stürck Bouvoir, who was a good bit more formidable than any image.

For Minna, after all her years in America, was still uncontaminated with democratic ideas. She knew who she was. She knew also who, or rather what, Nelson Vance was. In her appraisal of him she was unmoved by his wealth, his power, or the respect that the citizens of the Twin Towns accorded him.

On the other hand, Nelson Vance believed certain things about himself, and certain different things about other people, including Minna von Stürck Bouvoir. But Minna knew. The difference was immense. Nelson Vance hadn't a chance from the beginning.

"You will sit down, Mr. Vance?" she said coolly. "Perhaps a glass of beer would be pleasant in this heat?"

"Hell and damnation, woman!" Nelson Vance roared. "I come here to have it out with that adopted brat of yourn, and you gab about the heat! Can't you even understand talk?"

"Talk, yes. Shouting, no. And exceedingly bad manners, least of all. You are in *mein Haus*, Mister Vance. First of all, you will please to remove your hat."

Wonderingly, Nelson Vance took it off.

"*Ach*, that is better. And now, you will please to talk quietly. My grandson is badly hurt. Your loutish son did that. He has fever, and noise disturbs him. It disturbs me also, though I am not hurt. You were saying?"

"That I come over here to lay a buggy whip on that whelp of yourn's hide! Why, th' mannish little puppy, he——"

"Of whom are you speaking, Mr. Vance? We have not dogs on the place. We have here only human beings, loved and cared for. I am afraid I do not understand this mode of talking."

"You understand it, all right!" Nelson grated. "But I'll put it to you, straight. Your grandson was seen fooling around with my daughter! And when I git my hands on him——"

"*Ach, so?* But you will not get your hands on him, Mister Vance. I shall not permit it. If you should so much as touch him, I shall have you arrested."

"Arrest me? Hell, woman, you don't know who I am! Ain't a soul in town who'd dast lay a finger on me!"

"But I do know who you are, Mr. Vance. I sometimes think that I alone truly know. Perhaps you are right about their not arresting you. But it would not be necessary. Even though you are, by your own admission, *Schwein* enough to use force against a child, this will not happen because you are already aware that you would have afterwards to deal with me. And of that you are not capable. Noise and bluster and the kind of cowardice that abuses the weak are one thing. But what is necessary to face me is quite another. *Und* this you do not have. A blooded boar from barnyard pigs never comes, Herr Vance."

"Pigs! You're calling me a pig, Missus Bouvoir?"

"No. That would be to insult the real ones, I think. Listen, Mr. Vance, *und* quietly. I have spoken to my grandson about your little daughter. Duncan tells me that nothing happened between them. This story was invented to plague him by those ruffians who follow the Bruder boy. And Duncan does not lie. Now what does your little girl have to say about the matter?"

"Naturally, she says the whole thing ain't so, but——"

"But you, doubtless, have good reason to doubt the word of your daughter. She is, after all, of your blood. But Duncan has never lied to me since I have had him. He knows that he has no need to. If you are so concerned about your daughter I should suggest you await the results of the medical examination that Duncan tells me you have already asked Doctor Volker to perform. Though it will prove nothing. There are many more boys in this town besides my Duncan; and she is, after all, a Vance."

"So," Nelson rumbled in baffled rage, "that's all the satisfaction I'm going to get out of you?"

"You have already had too much. I have permitted you to enter *mein Haus* by the front door. Your *Vater* always came to the back, for in those days the Vances had not yet forgotten their place. You have, I am told, much money now; but money cannot, Herr Vance, buy birth, breeding, or gentility. With those things one has to be born. Now I must ask you to leave *mein Haus*, and not to come back. Also, you are not to even look at *meinen* grandsohn. Is this clear, Mister Vance?"

"Why, you old Dutch witch, I'll——"

"You will do nothing, but to leave quietly, Herr Vance," Minna said.

"No," Nelson growled. "I'm expecting a message from Dr. Volker. I told him I'd be here. And if he says what I think he's a-going to, I'm swearing out a warrant for your boy's arrest. Assault 'n battery on young Bruder. Assault with a deadly weapon ag'in my boy. Carnal knowledge of a girl below the age o' consent——"

"I see you know the law," Minna said.

Duncan, who had been listening to all this from the landing of the curving stairs, did not wait for more. He went back to his room, got into his clothes, climbed down the drainpipe, and headed for the railway tracks. A freight would be along any minute now. He knew very well how to ride the rods; he had done it several times before, once as far as Baton Rouge, when he was looking for a job after Johann Bruder died. He'd go to New Orleans and ask Uncle Martin Bruder for work. Uncle Martin would give him a job. He was sure of that. He could tell his step-uncle frankly

49

about the fight with Stan, holding back only how badly he'd beaten him. Uncle Martin knew Stan only too well. That was why he kept him out of New Orleans most of the time. . . . Maybe, one day, after things cooled down, he could come back.

He should have waited. He had scarcely swung aboard the freight when the telephone rang in Minna Bouvoir's home. She picked it up, spoke into the receiver, turned.

"It's for you, Herr Vance," she said.

Nelson Vance took the receiver from her hand.

"Well?" he barked into the mouthpiece.

"Your daughter, sir," Doctor Volker's voice came over grim and slow, "is perfectly intact. Still—virgin. And you, sir, are a filthy swine!"

Chapter 4

DUNCAN LAID *The Picayune* back down upon his desk. The three-column story it carried under a banner lead about his feat of saving the cancer patient was perhaps symbolic of something. Of, it might well be, the distance he had journeyed in those sixteen years since he had rolled out of the Twin Towns on a fast freight, riding the rods, the whiplashes that Jim Vance had inflicted upon him aching with every jolt, fleeing—from what?

From a Nelson Vance bent on jailing him for his damnably in-complete enjoyment of Hester's favours? That had provided him with motivation enough that summer of 1887; but now, in 1903, the man realised what the boy had not been able to: that old Nelson's threats had been only a minute part of what he had been fleeing; that what he had run away from then had been a world that was too much with him, and which he never made.

'As I am fleeing it now,' he thought quietly; 'but it's time to call a halt; high time to turn and face the pack. To face—myself. Especially that. For the whole problem of man boils down to a question of identity: who am I? Or rather—what? A skilful surgeon with a surgeon's hands. But with a surgeon's heart? Ah, that is the question!'

That story helped. It was under Fred Baynes's name. It praised him for his humanitarian behaviour. For the humanitarianism he had spent half a lifetime denying. Yes, the story helped. It made the choice clear. He was grateful to Fred Baynes.

All the same, he hoped there wouldn't be any more stories. There was a certain antithesis between good medicine and fame. And he was getting closer to what practising medicine really meant. He was gaining the strength to truly begin. Yes; he'd be just as happy if they didn't print anything more about him.

As it turned out, his luck in that regard proved dismal. New Orleans was very quiet at the moment. There hadn't been a decent murder in the last six months. Reading copy, the city editor of *The Picayune* got one of those ideas that had made him city editor in the first place. He called his star reporter in.

"Fred," he said, "you hop over to Rosebriar Clinic and talk to Dr. Phelton. We're going to do a series on the romance of modern medicine, as personified by young Dr. Childers. See if you can't get Phelton to let you ride herd on this boy. He's hotter than a two-dollar pistol. All the angles: local boy makes good; New Orleans' own surgical whiz abroad showing the greasy furriners how it ought to be done; Childers talks with Koch; Childers studies under von Whatchamaycallit; his courtship of, and marriage to—who the hell was that fluff he married?"

"Vance," Fred Baynes rasped, "Hester Vance. Sister of the guy who made Childers famous. You remember that stabbing case in Caneville-Sainte Marie three years back? Not just another cutting. Prominent people. Jealous husband. Juicy scandal."

"Great! Play that up. How does the babe look?"

"Like she could start a forest fire just strolling past the woods. Blonde. Built like a million dollars. Got the look. You know: the kind friend hubby's got to renew his claim to every night or—or I don't know wimmen."

"A natural. You ride with him on his calls. Watch him operate——"

"Chief, doctors are plumb tetchy. Most of 'em don't cotton to publicity none a'tall."

"Phelton does. I know him from way back. He's in th' pill-pushing business for the long green, not for love of humanity. And he's Childers's boss."

"All right," Fred Baynes said. "I'll get over there right now."

Duncan listened very quietly while Jarvis Phelton explained it to him. The publicity would do Rosebriar no end of good. Bring in other philanthropists like Ernest Harvey; enable them to improve the equipment, extend their services...

Duncan yawned.

"What's in it for me?" he said.

"I'll put you on a commission basis," Dr. Phelton said. "It'll double your take, Childers! Fifty thousand a year ought to appeal to you."

"It does. I even know what I'm going to do with it—the surplus, I mean. You own that old building next door, don't you, Jarvis?"

"Yes, but I don't see——"

"With your permission, I'm going to put beds in it. Make Tom resident. Hire eight or ten new nurses. I'll plough my extra twenty-five back into that. A real charity ward, Jarvis, where all the physicians practising in the Channel and other neighbourhoods like that can keep their hands in; one set-up in this lousy town where neither the medicine nor the care given the poor will be less than first-rate."

"But why, Duncan? Name of God, why?"

"Salve for my conscience. I've recently discovered that I still have one, Jarvis. Did you get me my sheep?"

"Yes, but——"

"No 'buts' about it, Doctor. I'll let the beggar pry into my life on that basis, and no other. I've been an unmitigated bastard for a long time. My stomach's no longer up to it. Getting tired of tossing my cookies at the sight of my own beamish, boyish countenance. Come on now, Good Physician, Gentle Healer, let's go scrub. Dear Grace must be made pretty again. I only hope she doesn't go 'B-a-a-a-a!' from now on when she tries to talk."

It was a tricky operation. They let Fred Baynes watch it. He was clad in a white gown and a cap like the rest. It didn't sicken him. As an old accident and crime reporter, he had seen far messier sights.

He went to lunch with Duncan.

"Tell me, Doc," he said, "after you left N'Awleans at fifteen, you didn't come back till you finished Harvard, did you?"

"Once," Duncan said. "I spent my seventeenth summer here."

"Doing what, Doc?"

"Working for Bruder, LaVallois and Company. Export, Import. Martin Bruder was my stepfather's brother, so he gave me a job; not because I knew a damned thing, but because he was fond of me and knew I needed the money."

"But weren't you living at Madame Bouvoir's by then? She was quite rich, for all I ever heard tell."

"She wasn't. She was keeping up appearances, that was all. She spent her last dime on my education. Of course, I didn't know that until too late. Or I wouldn't have let her do it. But that wasn't the problem that summer, Fred. It so happens I'd run away."

"Mind telling me why, Doc?"

"Not at all. I was a Channel brat, remember. A trifle rough for Caneville. I beat up the wrong guy. So badly that he had to be hospitalised. So things got rather thick."

"Why'd you do that, Doc? A girl? What was her name?"

"Yes—a girl. But let's say I don't remember her name, Fred," Duncan drawled. "Anything else?"

"What did you do at that Export Company, Doc?"

"Shipping clerk. Then Mr. Bruder got sick—and, as my German was pretty fair by then, I more or less took his place...."

53

'Yes. Had the incredible good luck to have Uncle Martin drop out before he discovered the fight I'd had with Stan was something more than a boyish exchange of fisticuffs. Before he learned that I'd all but flayed that oaf alive. And he had to keep me on after he did find out, because he was too sick to come back, and there was nobody in the office who knew German. Not even, if the truth were told, me. But I did know enough to get by. Made a go of it. Took care of the German language correspondence. Learned to make invoices, keep ledgers, even—give orders. Heady business for a snotty little seventeen-year-old. Of course old Jacques really made the decisions. But he let me think I was making 'em. Good of him. Gave me confidence. I needed that then; damned fine antidote to what the Channel and Caneville had done to me.

'Taught me an awful lot, too. But I must have been worth at least a little; because, even after Uncle Martin came back, they kept me on in the office instead of sending me back to the shipping room. My seventeenth summer. The summer of my discontent. The summer I met—Calico. Nothing was ever the same after that. God, but she was lovely! How could I have believed that she——'

At the end of three weeks Duncan had learned all the commercial terms he needed to know in both languages. What's more, he had learned the quirks and peculiarities of both partners. They quarrelled incessantly; but at bottom they were very fond of each other. And both of them took a strong paternal interest in Duncan. This, of course, was natural enough in Martin Bruder, who considered the boy an actual nephew; but in Jacques LaVallois it was strange. In fact, Duncan provided them with a new theme for argument, LaVallois holding that a young man should get all the amatory experience possible, while Uncle Martin Bruder insisted upon a stern Lutheran code of morals. Duncan ignored the arguments, and did his work very well indeed. So well that LaVallois, who was cursed, or blessed, with that typical French frugality that no mere Scotchman ever even approached, raised the boy's pay to twenty-five dollars a week without either Duncan or Uncle Martin suggesting it.

One thing, however, Duncan refused to do: he would not live at the Bruder residence, though his Uncle Martin very strongly insisted upon it. Instead, he took a little flat on Conti Street. Duncan put his refusal on the basis that he didn't want to be a burden to a family who, after all, were not really his relatives. The truth was he wanted to be free.

The business was enormously profitable despite the dingy appearance of the offices. The modern improvements that LaVallois wanted to institute—buying a typewriter and hiring a typist (preferably, that cynical old sinner declared, a young, good-looking girl)—were fast becoming absolutely necessary. Nearly all the firm's correspondence was still entrusted to the beautiful copper-plate script of the ancient clerk, who possessed the astonishing talent of being able to copy letters without error even when they were written in a language he knew not a syllable of; but matters were progressing to such an extent that even a dozen hand-copyists could not have kept the correspondence up to date. Besides, the system made dictation impossible. Jacques and Martin had to scrawl out their own letters and hand them over to the clerk to make fair copies of. In this, too, Duncan proved very useful. He could take dictation in French at a fairly rapid pace—rapid, that is, when due consideration was given to the fact that he knew no shorthand. He could even take them in German, but so slowly that it was hardly worth the trouble. Uncle Martin could scrawl them out faster himself.

Finally, reluctantly, Martin Bruder gave in to progress, and put a sign in the window: "Wanted, Secretary Typist. Preferably Female. Must know shorthand and be able to take dictation. Those failing to meet these qualifications please do not apply."

A week passed, and no young female came. Wedded as they were to their ancient habits, it never even occurred to the partners to place an advertisement in the newspapers. Duncan thought of suggesting the idea to them; but he decided to keep his own counsel. He had already noticed that Uncle Martin did not take very kindly to new ideas.

In the meantime Duncan had written his grandmother; and had received her reply. Her consent to his remaining in New Orleans was less reluctant than he had expected. For one thing, she was glad he was working for Martin Bruder, who, she knew, would keep an eye on him. For another, she was happy to keep him out of the clutches of the Vances and Stan Bruder, at least for a while. She warned him against New Orleans' obvious perils: loose women and strong drink. Duncan didn't drink at all, beyond a little wine with his meals; and purchased favours disgusted his curiously fastidious soul. He wrote her a reassuring letter, promising to write her every week and tell her how he fared.

As it turned out, he did not keep his promise, not even for the first week. For the very next day after writing to her, as he was leaving work, a girl stopped him on the pavement.

"Excuse me, sir," she said. "You—you work there, don't you?"

He stared at her. Her voice was low, husky, warm. His precise musical ear caught the fact that her careful pronunciation was not natural; that it had been learned with some effort. Then, seeing her clearly, he forgot all about the way she talked.

She was very young; no older than he was, he guessed. She was dressed in a severe shirtwaist and skirt, and wore a boating straw hat on top of high-piled blond hair that was a glory. Her eyes were the pale, milky blue of star sapphires; and her mouth, her mouth——

He fought for words to describe it, even to himself. What came were clichés, drenched in purple, but he did not know then, as he would later, that they were. A passion flower. A great exotic blossom, blooming in the midst of her small, pale face. Full-lipped, moist. He stood there, staring at her.

"Yes," he got out. "Why?"

"I—I'd like to apply for that job. This is the third day I've come; but I just can't get up the nerve. Maybe you could help me."

"I," he said gravely, "would be delighted. If I can be of any service to you, Miss——?"

"Landis. Elizabeth Landis. Only my friends call me Calico, because I'm so fond of wearing it. Besides, people always call you Liz or Lizzie when you're named Elizabeth. And that's awful, isn't it?"

"No. Nothing about you could be awful, Miss Landis. Now, if you'll tell me how I could be of help——"

"Tell them—that—that you've known me a long time. That I'm a friend of yours...."

"The second part won't be a lie," he said gaily. "I am a friend of yours—that is, if you'll let me be."

"Oh," she said huskily, "you're so sweet! But then I knew you would be, the first time I saw you."

"And when was that?" Duncan said.

"The day they put the sign in the window," she said.

"Why, that was a week ago!"

"I know. I wanted to ask you before, only I was scairt—afraid. But now I'm glad I finally did. You needn't be worried about recommending me, Mr. Childers. I really can type, and I know the Pitman system backwards. I'm a business school graduate. I've got my diploma right here—see...."

But he did not look at the elaborate, gilt-edged scroll she proffered him. He was staring at her in pure astonishment.

"How did you know my name?" he said.

"I—I asked the janitor. You don't mind, do you, Mr. Childers?"

56

"Heck no! I'm glad you did. Only I'd like it better if you called me Duncan."

"All right, Duncan," she said shyly; "and you can call me Calico."

"Good. Now, Calico, since we're friends, how about having supper with me?"

"You're quite a man of the world," she said slowly. "I'd put you down as being more timid, sort of——"

"Well, I'm not. Come on, Calico, what do you say?"

"I'd be delighted, Mr. Chil—Duncan. To tell the truth, I'm as hungry as a bear."

He took her by the arm and started walking. He liked the way she walked, swaying a little like a willow sapling in a light spring breeze. He cast a covert, sidelong glance at her figure. Her breasts under her shirtwaist were high and firm, up- and out-thrusting. Her waist was a handspan; her hips wide and sweet-curving. Her feet were tiny.

" 'How beautiful are thy feet with shoes, O prince's daughter!' " he quoted under his breath.

She turned those pale, milky blue eyes upon him. Ice and fire coursed simultaneously through his veins.

"What did you say?" she whispered.

He repeated the verse from the *Song of Songs* aloud.

"That's pretty," she said. "Reckon you're a mighty smart boy, Duncan."

"No. Only I've got eyes," he said boldly. "For which, God be praised!"

He sat across the table from her in Antoine's, watching her eat. He ate very little himself, partially from the natural frugality of his temperament, but mostly because the thunderous swelling of his youthful heart didn't leave him room. It was astonishing the amount of food she managed to tuck inside that tiny form. The meal was going to cost him a young fortune, but he didn't care. He was preoccupied and troubled by something else.

"How long has it been since you've eaten last?" he said, accusingly.

"Day before yesterday," she said sadly. "My rent's paid up to tomorrow. And the typewriter I hired for practice, till the day after. Oh, Duncan, I've just got to get that job! If you'll help me, I'll— I'll do anything for you!"

There was a quality in her voice that reminded him of Hester,

57

suddenly. He stared at her bleakly. He wanted her with all the pent-up anguish of his youthful loins. He had, almost from the first moment he had seen her. But she was spoiling things, talking like that. Gratitude was too close to outright purchase to suit him. In the wildly erotic dreams that tormented his sleep he had pictured his nymph goddess swooning nakedly into his manly arms for pure love of him. None of his dream maidens had ever said to him: "I will kiss thee with the kisses of my mouth, because thou gavest me the right to type Uncle Martin Bruder's letters!"

"Tell you what," he said. "Let's go to your place. I'll dictate a letter, and you read it back to me, then type it. That way, I'll know what I'm talking about when I recommend you."

The sapphire eyes narrowed, then widened again under the youthful candour of his gaze.

"All right," she said slowly. "Shall we go now?"

"Yes," he said, "but don't think what you were thinking just now—not ever again. I'm not like that. I don't play dirty tricks."

"I know," she said huskily. "It's just that——"

"It's just what?" he demanded.

"That so few men don't," she said bitterly. "I'm sorry. Reckon I knew you were different from the rest. Come on, let's go."

. . . . .

"Ready?" Duncan said, manfully not looking at the pitiful poverty of that furnished room.

"Yes," Calico said quietly.

"Messrs. Thomas Swaithe and Sons, Limited, Fleet Street, London, England," Duncan began. "In regard to yours of the 15th instant, we are pleased to reply——" he went on dictating the imaginary letter with brutal speed. When he had finished, with, "I beg to remain, your obedient servant, etc.——" she was there waiting, pencil poised.

"Is that all?" she said.

"Yes," Duncan said. "Now type it, please, Calico."

Her fingers on the keys of the machine matched his own speed on the piano. In minutes she handed him the typescript. It was letter-perfect.

"Great!" he exulted. "If you don't mind, I'll keep this, Calico."

"Why?" she said.

"To show to Mr. Bruder in the morning. Mr. LaVallois you don't have to convince. One look at those eyes, that figure——"

"Oh dear!" Calico wailed.

"Don't worry," Duncan said. "I'll tell him we're engaged, sort of."

She sat there staring at him, her eyes luminous in the dusky room.

"I—I wish we were!" she said in an intense whisper.

But there was something wrong with that, too; something in her tone, her expression, that killed his joy half born.

"Why?" he demanded.

She looked him straight in the face and said it. She spoke clearly, softly, truly.

"Because I'm tired of being alone. Of being scared. I'm even tired of my hair, my eyes, my figure. They—they're a curse, Duncan. I wish I were ugly, sometimes. Or that a man, just one man, some-place, some day, could be—kind. . . ."

"You think I'm not?" Duncan said darkly.

"I think you are," she whispered; "only——"

"Only what?"

"Only so many started out pretending to be, and later——"

He stood up, looking at her, his dark eyes filled with hurt.

"Goodnight, Calico," he said.

"Don't go!" she said. "I didn't mean to hurt your feelings! I shouldn't have said——"

"You were perfectly right," Duncan said gravely; then, a smile breaking through his wry look, he said: "Have breakfast with me tomorrow morning, little Calico, and I'll present you when I go to work."

"Oh, Duncan, would you?" she said. "You get me that job, and I'll——"

"Let me get it for you first, Calico," Duncan Childers said.

It proved to be ludicrously easy. Calico knew the work, which pleased Uncle Martin; and she was a pretty young woman, which pleased Monsieur LaVallois. Nor did Duncan's broad hints that an understanding existed between the girl and himself dampen the old Frenchman's spirits. He seemed to get a sort of vicarious satis-faction out of his unshakeable belief that young Childers was at last indulging in a piquant little affair.

Calico, under Uncle Martin's severe gaze, took off her boating straw, sat down at the desk before the bright new machine that Duncan was sent out to buy, and in one day caught up with three weeks' arrears in the correspondence. Duncan, from his own desk, clasped his two hands together and gave the pugilist's sign of victory. She smiled at him sunnily.

After Herr Bruder had grudgingly confirmed her employment,

59

she and Duncan snatched a lunch of 'Poorboy' sandwiches at a nearby cafeteria.

"We'll have to celebrate," he crowed. "I'll take you to Antoine's tonight, and——"

"Not Antoine's," she said gravely. "It's much too dear, Duncan. You'd better start saving your wages."

"Why?" Duncan said.

"You just should, that's all. Besides, I don't want you spending your hard-earned money on me. You've done enough for me now."

"I," Duncan said, "haven't done anything at all!"

"Oh yes, you have. I never could have got the job without your help. And you'll find I know how to show my gratitude, Duncan."

Again there was something in her tone that made him feel cold. But he didn't know exactly what it was.

They had supper in a little French Quarter restaurant, where the food was good, plentiful, and cheap. So was the wine.

It bubbled through Duncan's veins and loosened his tongue. He poured out his dreams to her, laying them in tribute at her feet. He told her of his plans for becoming a doctor, and how they had been frustrated—at least temporarily. But he told her nothing at all about Hester Vance.

"You'll do it, yet," she said. "I just know you will, Duncan!"

He reached across the table and took her hand in his.

"Thanks for believing in me, Callie," he said. "Not many people have."

She gave his hand a gentle squeeze.

"Then they were blind, and fools," she said.

Duncan ordered another bottle of wine. Then another. The celebration was becoming increasingly gay.

"Here's to us!" he cried out, lifting his glass.

"To us!" she echoed, and drank the wine down. Then slowly, unsteadily, she stood up.

"Pay the bill, Duncan!" she said tipsily; "and leave the man a nice tip."

Duncan stood up. The ceiling reeled about his head. Her face had become a whitish blur to his eyes. Only the great exotic blossom of her mouth bloomed pink-petalled and clear in her indefinable face.

"Well," she said, when the waiter had come and gone, chuckling happily over the size of his tip, "shall we go to your place—or to mine?"

Duncan stared at her. His tongue was a hot thickness, blocking his speech.

"My place," he croaked, and took her arm.

He unlocked the door and let her in. She stood in the middle of the room, staring around her.

"Oh, Duncan, it's so nice!" she said.

He realised suddenly, despite the wine he had drunk, that he had never heard such real warmth and longing in her voice before. Her tone sobered him. He was beginning to understand her now. 'Poor little thing,' he thought; 'her folks must have been dreadfully poor—as poor as mine. But she went to business school, and that costs money. I wonder how the deuce she managed it?'

Calico put up her hands and drew the hatpins that held the straw boater to her head out of her golden hair. Then she loosened her hair. It fell over her shoulders in a shimmering cloud, reaching half-way to her waist. Her fingers worked at the buttons of her shirtwaist. When she had them all undone, she slipped it off and turned to him.

"Aren't you going to undress?" she said.

Duncan remembered the day he had kissed Hester in the woods. It was like that now. Only worse. He wanted Calico. There was a knotting in his middle, a heaviness in his loins, an ache, an agony —but the thing was wrong. Wrong in a curious way that had nothing to do with morals or standards of behaviour. Time was oddly out of joint, and he not born to set it right; the scene false, permeated with a slow and deadly coldness that broke through the agony and the ache, that wrote a momentary *finis* to his need.

"Calico——" he said.

The sound of her name, spoken like that, thrust out on the moving tide of his anguish, stopped her in the curious motion of pushing her skirt down over her wide, sweet-curving hips. She stared at him.

"What ails you, Duncan?" she said. "Don't you want me?"

"I do," he said, his voice breaking over the words, splintering into the planes and angles of purest grief. "I—dear God! But not like this. I don't want you to be grateful to me. I don't want to be paid with your body because I helped you get a job. I don't want——"

'This feeling of coldness. This arranged, untender meeting of two strangers in this alien room. This unceremonious getting into bed. This hired body to ease the hell inside me. This love purchased even with the gentler coin of gratitude. These things cannot ease or comfort me; for what I suffer is no simple thing like lust, but very love. My loins are undivided from my heart; the white-hot jetting of my seed must have a purpose more profound than the mere relieving of desire. I—oh God—I——'

But he could not find the words for these things he felt, so he stood there, staring at her.

"Then what do you want, Duncan?" she said.

"I want you to love me," he said humbly.

"Love you? That was just what I was getting ready to do," she said.

"No. You don't understand. I mean love *me*—a person, living, breathing, hoping, Calico. Love me with your mind, your heart; because I'm dear to you, because I mean something to you—not——"

She came towards him then, her white arms bare, the bodice of her chemise caressing her proud and pointing breasts. She stopped a little space away from him.

"Am I," she said huskily, "am I dear to you, Duncan? Do I mean something to you?"

"You," he croaked, "are more than dear, Callie. And what you mean to me is just—my life."

She stood there, staring at him, until the tremor of her mouth was an uncontrollable thing; until her eyes were blinded by the slow welling up of her grief, her joy. Then suddenly, startlingly, she dropped to her knees before him, and seizing both his hands in hers, covered them with incoherent kisses, bathed them with her tears.

He bent and lifted her to her feet.

"No, Callie!" he wept. "Please, Callie, no!"

They stood there like that; two children in a lonely room, clinging mouth to mouth and crying.

"Duncan!" she sobbed.

"Yes, Callie?" he whispered. He was much calmer now.

"I want you to love me. I want you to love my body. Because I don't know the words you do and that's the only way I can let you know——"

"Callie——"

"—how I love you. For I do love you, Duncan, so much, so very much. I always did, I reckon, before——"

"Callie, Angel, Love——"

"—I even knew you. I dreamed you before you were there. I knew there had to be one man somewhere who was kind and good and beautiful."

"Beautiful?" he said.

"Yes, yes! How else could I describe you? All the way through, inside and out. I want you to touch me. I want to feel your hands——"

"Callie!"

"—on my body—because it's yours; it belongs to you. I belong to you; my body, my soul, my life! To do what you want to with; to——"

"Callie, Callie, Callie——"

"Help me off with my things, Duncan," she said.

He had not known a woman could be so beautiful. He searched her with his eyes, etching the image of that form upon the tissues of his brain. He knew that, until death should blind his sight for ever, that glory would blaze unending there.

She was willow-slender, perfect. Upthrusting, sweet-curving, deep-hollowed, perfect. Shellpink-crested, gold-tufted, lithe-limbed, waiting, unashamed.

"Now I'll help you," she said.

The loosening, the freeing, the coolness. Her small hands, lighter than a breath, moving over him as though, in her, memory were a tactile sense. The long, long clinging of the sweet underflesh of lip and tongue-tip. The wonderful trembling warmth of her.

It was right, perfect, glorious. More than mere limb-entangled writhing on a narrow bed. More than the gasp and strangle of tortured breath. It was searching, finding—the place where the soul lies hidden, wedding of seeking seed with waiting cell; union true and right and perfect beyond all belief and past all bearing, so that he was thinking, while he still had power to think, 'I am not alone. There is no longer I, nor she, but us. And we are one.'

"Duncan——"

"Callie?"

"Oh, Duncan, I——"

"Yes?"

"I can't tell you——"

"What Callie, Love?"

"How I love you!"

'But you are telling me,' he thought exultantly; 'your thighs are saying it like music; your breasts are sounding it like trumpets; your mouth——'

He heard then her high, wild, far-off, despairing cry.

And then he, too, died the good, momentary dying, the explosion out of life, the jetting of the very stuff of his being out on a tide of anguished ecstasy, more exquisite than mere pain.

63

They lay still in a soft nothingness, no place, no time, nothingness, until life ebbed back again. He could hear her crying very softly against the hollow of his throat.

"Callie," he murmured tenderly.

"Y-yes, Duncan?" she sobbed.

"This is for always," he said.

"No, Duncan."

"Why not?" he said.

"It—it can't be!" she wept, in a torrent, an inundation of pure grief. "I'm not fit——"

"You're an angel, Callie. My Angel——"

"You mustn't say that, Duncan! You mustn't believe——"

"What mustn't I believe, Callie?"

"That I'm an angel. You mustn't treat me like anything more than—than just a girl. A girl who loves you. Because, if you do—I won't——"

"You won't what, Callie?"

"I won't be able to bear it, when you leave me."

"I'll never leave you, Callie."

"Yes, you will. But not now, Duncan. I must have you, keep you, love you until—— Oh, Duncan, couldn't I just stay here with you until——"

Until—until——

"Until the day I die," he said solemnly.

"No. But as long as you let me," she whispered brokenly. "Like man and wife. I want to cook for you, mend your things, wash——"

"We'll get the licence in the morning," he said.

"We can't. You're not old enough. And it shows. They'd ask for your birth certificate or your baptismal papers. I'm old enough —two years older than you. But it isn't that. I—I couldn't marry you. You're too good, too fine——"

"I'm not. For you no man on earth could ever be," he said.

But he could not change her mind. They settled down to their quaint, unhallowed, precocious domesticity. They were very nearly perfectly happy. At least Duncan was. But time and time again he surprised Calico looking at him with deep and brooding sorrow, her eyes filled with a kind of fear that chilled him to the bone.

Yet, except for that, they were very nearly perfectly happy all that summer; until, one September day, their private doomsday came——

Walking into the offices of Bruder and LaVallois in the form of a drummer. Tall, well-fleshed, small-eyed, sensual. Tight-fitting drummer's suit. Tilted drummer's bowler. Turned-up drummer's shoes. Little drummer's soul.

He stopped in the doorway and stared.

"Well, bless my horny hide," he roared, "if it ain't little Calico!"

He moved over to her desk and lifted her horrified face with his beefy hand.

Duncan got up and started towards him.

"Howdy, baby!" the man chuckled. "You mean to tell me the bustle-hustling trade's so bad you're doing honest work?"

"Jim—please!" Calico whispered.

Duncan's hand came down on his shoulder, hard.

"Take your filthy paws off her!" he spat.

The drummer turned, still grinning.

"Look, son," he drawled, "you ain't got no call to take on so. There's been many a filthy paw on this here milk-white hide. Jealousy don't make no sense, when we're talking about this particular piece o' commercial goods. Anybody can have this who's got the price——"

There was a rustle of a skirt, the swift clicking hammer of high heels, and Calico scampered past them, running for the street.

"Callie!" Duncan cried, and started after her. But the drummer caught him by the arm, holding him back.

"Let her go, son," he said kindly; "that kind o' cheap goods is a dime a dozen." Then, seeing the boy's face: "You didn't know! You actually didn't know! Gawd damn it, son, I'm plumb sorry I opened my big mouth."

"You're lying!" Duncan got out; but he knew it was true. He had seen the damnation in her eyes.

"Wish to hell I was, son. But I ain't. You just go down to Big Mame's on Basin Street and ask anybody——"

But Duncan was no longer there. He was running towards that door, that street——

That empty street that bore no trace of her.

He came home that night to a room that echoed with vacancy. Whose very air was scarred with memory of her presence. The faint aroma of her perfume. The dresses he had bought her, hanging with anguished muteness in the cupboard. The little stove on which she had cooked their simple meals. The bed.

It was impossible, unendurable. He walked out into the thronging streets, moving without aim or direction. He saw a bar, and entered it. He left it reeling, going straight to Basin Street. To Big Mame's.

She was there. Parading half-naked with the rest. Flaunting before the eyes of lecherous swine that nakedness that had been his alone, and a glory. She faced him with dead eyes, and did not flee.

"Which one do you want, son?" the Madam said.

He did not answer her.

He stood there. He did not move or speak. He could not. There was no motion appropriate to that hour, nor anything to be said.

"I said, which one——" the Madam grated; but the sound of her voice released him. He turned. He took a step towards the door. Another. His feet weighed tons. The smoke-filled, perfumed air was fluid, was quagmire-thick. It dragged about his ankles, his knees.

The lights were dancing blobs. Faces, bosoms, naked legs shaded off into distortions, blurred away into the smoke.

The sounds rose, tinkling of glasses ringing like maniac bells, laughter lifting, edging into shrieks, male voices sinking, rounding, booming into reverberations, the echoes of far thunder.

He pushed the door open.

He went out into the street. It was raining. The night wept for his anguish and his loss.

He walked the streets all night. In the morning he sent his grandmother a wire, saying he was coming home. He could now. His troubles in Caneville-Saint Marie had blown over. Stan Bruder had gone to Nashville. Dr. Volker's pronouncement had taken the Vances off his back. He could go home. It was the only thing to do.

He entered a restaurant, ordered the Number Two Special. It turned out to be pancakes and coffee. He tasted the pancakes. Put his fork down after the first bite. Drank the coffee. Paid. Walked out. Went back to Conti Street.

He smelled, as he rounded the last landing of the stair, the elusive fragrance of her perfume. He had a moment of panic; the desire to turn and run back down those stairs seized him, but he mastered it. He walked up the last steps slowly, and stood there, facing her. They stayed there, looking at each other, for a long, long time.

"I came to get my things," Calico said. "That is, if you want me to have them, Duncan."

"Of course," he said evenly, and opened the door for her.

She walked in ahead of him, and sat down on the bed.

"Duncan——" she said.

"Take your things and get out, Callie," he said flatly.

She got up very slowly.

"All right," she said. "I reckon they could be considered payments for—my services. Though I generally do get more."

He put his hand in his pocket.

"How much," he said, "how much more do I owe you?"

"Nothing," she whispered. "You've already paid me, Duncan. By being kind to me. By saying—I was your life."

He stood there, staring at her.

"But that's finished, isn't it?" she went on. "You helped me up a rung or two of the ladder before you kicked me in the face. All right. I was a fool for ever trying to climb. The world is what it is. And I——"

"Callie," he burst out, "how did you ever do it? What made you ever start it? And why, for the love of God, did you ever go back?"

She threw back her head and laughed aloud. The sound of it was like someone ripping a coarse cloth in two with his hands.

"That's what they always ask—all of them. When they're through, Duncan. When they're lying there all spent, and stinking of sweat. 'Tell me, Baby—how'd a sweet lil' gal like you ever get to be a floozy? Whatever made you start hustling in the first place?' They can be sentimental then, when the heat is out of 'em; when I've worn 'em down from slobbering beasts to something that even looks sort of like a man. Some of them even get real soft and start talking about taking me out of that life. As if I'd have them! As if I'd spit on the kind of poor, half-male devils who have to buy it——"

"Forget it," Duncan whispered. "Forget I ever asked you."

"No," she said. "I won't forget it. In fact I'm going to tell you. And because, in a way, I have given you a raw deal, I'll even tell you the truth. Sit down, kind sir, and listen to the story of my life. I was born in a wagon, in Jones's Alley, because, at the time, my mother didn't have a roof over her head. She didn't know who my father was, because there were too many gentle friends and old acquaintances who could have been guilty. Later on, we lived in a flat on a back street; I and Ma and all my half-brothers and sisters whose fathers she couldn't pick out either.

"The flat didn't have any lights or running water. It was so rotten stinking dirty that we got used to the cockroaches, the bedbugs, and the lice. My little brother didn't have any tip to his nose. The rats bit it off while Ma was asleep. And drunk."

"God!" Duncan whispered.

"Don't bring Him into it," Calico said. "Fat lot of good He ever did me. I, Duncan dearest, was different from the others. I taught myself to read and write as a little girl. I even kept myself clean. Do you know how hard it is to be clean in the kind of a district I lived in? Have you ever had to go down to a street pump with a leaky tin-pail for water to wash yourself with? To beg, borrow, or even steal soap? A neighbour gave me a comb. I kept it hid like it was made out of gold, when I wasn't using it. I grew and I was pretty. So my mother sold me to a man who ran a cat-house——"

"Callie!"

"——when I was fifteen years old. I know. You can't believe it. I couldn't either; but it was so. They kept me locked up for almost a year. They sold me every night to the highest bidder. You see, I was the House 'Virgin'. Can you understand that? Can you explain to yourself or me what goes on in the mind of a man who will pay money to torment a child?"

"No, Callie," Duncan croaked, "I can't explain it. I only know——"

"You don't know anything. Not a damned thing. You're just a sweet kid, not even dry behind the ears, who I was going to use to get out, to get away. Because I'd got myself ready by then. I'd used the money they gave me, to buy books. When they saw they didn't have to worry about my running away any more, they let me out in the daytime. I went to school. I learned to talk like a lady; I learned to dress myself properly—neat, but not gaudy. After it came to me I'd have to have some way to make an honest living, I went to that business school——"

"Callie, forgive me, I didn't know. I——"

"You still don't. And there's nothing to forgive you. As I said, I planned to use you. I picked you out for that. You looked like such a lamb. Only it didn't work. I forgot I was still a woman. I was fool enough to think I didn't have a heart any more. I was wrong—on both counts, Duncan. You got to me. You hit me down deep where I lived. I got so I was even dreaming of fixing it so I could really spend the rest of my life with you. Me, little Calico Landis, turning into a soft slob!"

"You can," Duncan said. "Oh, Callie, you still can if you want——"

"Shut up!" she said. "Don't be a fool, Duncan. I'm surprised that you came back here. I thought by now you'd be half-way home—you and your busted heart!"

68

"I was going home," Duncan said. "I only came to get my clothes."

"Then take them and go, sonny-boy. Run home to Grandma. Your feelings have been hurt, haven't they? Come on, let me help you pack. I'll keep the flat. Nice place to rest on my nights off."

"Callie," Duncan said.

"Get down the valises, Duncan. I can't reach them. There. You sit down. You're useless. You'll only get everything all wrinkled."

He sat there, watching her. He was old enough now to know he wasn't going to die from the way he felt. And that was the worst of all.

"There," she said. "Take them and go. That's it. Bye-bye, baby boy."

"Callie," he whispered, "I'll never forget——"

"You'll never forget what, Duncan?"

"How sweet you were—how tender——"

She stood there looking at him, her pale blue eyes strangely opaque. She came to him and took the valises from his hand.

"Then," she said flatly, "I reckon I'd better give you a sample of my professional style."

Her hands came up, locking behind his head. She dragged his face down to hers, ground her mouth into his.

"Callie," he muttered, "I don't want——"

"Oh yes, you do!" she mocked. "Men always want—this. And you *are* a man, aren't you, Duncan?"

His brown eyes darkened into near blackness.

"Yes," he growled, "I'm a man, all right. Come on."

It was like nothing he had ever dreamed of. It was actually beyond even his great powers of dreaming.

Not Callie, his mind made an idiotic refrain of the thought; not Callie not Callie not Callie—— This is not——

Callie. Not ever my down-soft undulant Callie drawing the fear out of me, the hurt, the hot sickness of being young, the long fever of living. No——

Not this whipcord-sinewed savage with no softness in her anywhere. No——

Not Callie; not this wild-thrashing, loin-scalding, furious she thing. This stranger.

This molten, incandescent Ishtar with cruel, flagellate limbs. No.

She spread her ten fingers wide against the smooth flesh of his back. She curved them until her nails were touching him lightly. Then she dug them in.

69

She saw his face go ludicrous with shock. Like a child's. Like a hurt child's, slapped while offering a kiss.

She was motionless as stone, searching his face with eyes no longer opaque milk-blue sapphires set in a heathen idol's face. But warm suddenly; moist, warm, tender. Then crystalline with grief.

"Oh, Duncan, I——" she whispered; and, surging up, sought and found his mouth, clinging her own to it for that age-long moment of metamorphosis while brazen Ishtar fled out of time and mind, and in her place——

Was Callie. The Callie that he knew.

Softer than swansdown; warmer than spring; enveloping him in a tenderness that trembled on the edge of anguish. Slow, sweet-moving. Clinging to him: mouth, and cushioning soft fire-pointed breasts, and undulant loins, and lithe comforting thighs, in one long, total kiss——

Of farewell.

For it was that. He knew it by the pure, calmly contemplated, acceptable pain inside his heart.

He stumbled from the bed, gathered his scattered clothes, got painfully into them. She lay there, propped up on one elbow, watching him, her mouth a little bruised and swollen from his kisses, her body sweat-glossed, glistening.

"Duncan," she said suddenly, oddly, "want to bet I won't get what I'm going after now?"

"And what are you going after?" he said.

"The whole damned world—on its own terms, Duncan. Want to bet I won't get it?"

Wordlessly, he shook his head.

"No," he said. "I wouldn't bet against you, Callie. I'm not that big a fool."

He turned then, hobbled out of that room, stumbled down those stairs. He had no wish, hope, or need to drive him back again. Which was a pity. For he might have completed his education in the ways of women, then and there. Had he even so much as turned just after he passed through that open door, he would have seen Calico, stretched out upon that bed, her face crushed into the pillow—and crying.

Chapter 5

CRYING. Because in those days she could still cry. In 1891, when he had seen her again, she had moved beyond tears. Got to the place where bitterness had burnt her eyes into hard dryness. What had she reached by now after twelve more years? Dear God, what?

He climbed into his buggy before the Clinic, turned his horse towards home. But he didn't even notice his actions; his memories held him still.

'When I walked out of that flat (sixteen—years? ages? æons? ago) I knew I'd lost her. I had. Eighteen ninety-one didn't change matters. And that on top of already having lost Hester—was too much.

'Only, I hadn't lost Hes. Not then. Not even yet—entirely. But I am losing her. Because the way I have to go, she wasn't made to follow. Not yet. But I'm sure to, if I ever do what one day I'm going to have to: go back to Caneville; start practising medicine instead of being a fancy sawbones. The risk must be faced. Even accepted. Oh God, I——'

He was remembering with bitter clarity that brilliant day of sun. The day he thought he had lost Hester Vance for good. Remembering how it felt. 'I snapped back easily enough then,' he thought; 'but then I had youth's elasticity. And Hes hadn't become the habit' (habit—or vice? the mocking, questioning part of his mind jeered) 'that she is now. The day I got back to the Twin Towns. The day after—Calico. . . .'

That day, Duncan had walked with Mose Johnson towards the swimming-hole. It was only a week before school began again, but it was still hot enough for swimming.

"Five more days—not countin' Sa'day 'n Sunday," Mose said.

"I'm glad," Duncan said.

"You is?"

"Not is, are," Duncan corrected him patiently. "Yes. I'm glad."

"Why?" Mose said.

"Because it will give me something to do. Study French again. Learn to talk German well enough to study over there."

"Gonna study doctoring, ain't you, Dunc?"

71

"Medicine," Duncan corrected him again. "Yes—why?"

"Wish I could. Got me a powerful hankering to be a doctor. We sure Lord need one in Smoketown. Most coloured folks ain't got money enough to pay what white doctors charges."

"Then how could they pay you?" Duncan said.

"I kin live cheaper. Charge 'em two bits—to half a dollar a call. Give 'em credit. Take it out in grub. Chickens, eggs, collard greens."

"Got it all figured out, haven't you boy?"

"Yep. All but how to go to doctor school. My folks is gonna send me to Tuskegee. They's saving up for that. But doctor school —Lord God!"

"Maybe if I asked my grandmother——" Duncan said.

"No, don't. Ma wouldn't let me take no help. You know how proud she is. What was that kind o' talk you's gonna learn?"

"German," Duncan said.

"Folks got too many different ways o' talking," Mose said. "Maybe they's got too many different colours, too——"

Duncan grinned at him.

"Which would you choose, Mose—black or white?"

"Neither one," Mose said easily. He had long since learned he could speak freely to Duncan. "Black is too strong a colour, kind of. And white ain't really pretty. All faded and washed out. Give me highbrown, ever' time!"

"Like Renée?" Duncan teased. "How are you making out, Mose?"

"Just fine. She lemme kiss her the other day. Only she don't talk American so good yet; and when she switches off into that Gumbo talk, she leaves me a fair mile. Glad I ain't black, though."

"Why not, Mose? One colour's as good as another."

"I know that. Only Renée's Pa'n Ma don't. You think white folks is death on niggers, Dunc, but you don't know them light Creole coloured folks! Reckon they'd pizen a chile of theirs 'fore they'd let her marry a black boy."

"Then they're stupid," Duncan said. "I don't see what difference it makes."

"Reckon they thinks like whitefolks, being so near. Anyhow they don't seem to mind me."

They were passing the Vance place now. Duncan slowed his pace, staring at the house through the trees.

"She ain't there," Mose said kindly.

"Who isn't there?" Duncan snapped, though he already knew whom that 'she' meant.

"Miss Hester. Old man Vance done sent her up to St. Louis to his sister's place—'cause o' you."

Duncan stopped there in the middle of the lane, under the blazing sun.

"How'd you know that?" he demanded. "Nobody else does!"

"No whitefolks," Mose said complacently. "Coloured people got ways of knowing."

"Is she—is she," Duncan struggled to get it out, "coming back?"

"Don't know. But if she ain't here for school opening, she ain't a-comin'. You can bet your bottom dollar on that."

The first day of school was, as always, a dead loss. Boys and girls alike were almost painfully aware of each other. Notes were passed. From behind the books rose a cloud of half-smothered tittering. Duncan had expected to be horribly bored, but he wasn't. He sat there in rigid misery, staring at Hester Vance's empty seat. 'Maybe she'll come tomorrow,' he thought. But he knew she wouldn't. It would be years before he saw Hester again—that is, if he ever did.

He was so unhappy that he failed to notice that the girls were looking at him with new interest in their eyes. Last summer's scandal had done him a world of good. When they saw him looking at Hester's seat, the titters grew. But Duncan didn't notice that either.

He did look at Jenny Greenway, finally; but she turned away from him with an angry toss of her head.

'Now what the hell is wrong with her?' he thought. It was characteristic of him that he didn't know.

Leaving the school at closing time, he saw Jen a little ahead of him. He quickened his steps until he caught up with her.

"Hi, Jen——" he began, tentatively.

She whirled upon him.

"You go away from me, Mister Duncan Childers!" she said.

He opened his brown eyes very wide, looking at her.

"I don't remember having done anything to offend you, Jen," he said softly, "but if I have, I'm sorry."

"You haven't," Jenny said. "It's just that—oh, foot! Leave me be, Duncan Childers!"

"You," Duncan said, "have been listening to tales out of school, Jenny."

"And if I have? The tales don't interest me. If that fast little Hester Vance let you take advantage of her, that's her business!"

73

Duncan grinned at her suddenly. He hadn't had his summer of discontent for nothing.

"I'd much rather take advantage of you, Jen," he said.

She stared at him, speechless.

"Now," he said, "while you're getting your breath back, maybe I can get in a word edgewise. Don't you think it would be a lot fairer if you listened to my side of that story, Jen?"

"And what is your side?" she snapped.

"The truth, Jen. Want to hear it?"

"Well—I reckon so. I don't want to be unfair to you, Duncan."

They walked home together, while Duncan told her. Everybody saw them. Several of the girls were moved to remark: "Don't see what he sees in that tacky ol' Jen Greenway!"

At her gate, he stopped.

"You kissed her," Jenny whispered, her voice humid with choked-back tears. "You kissed Hes! You said so yourself!"

'If the idea of my kissing Hes bothers you like that,' he thought, 'what the devil would you think or say if you knew about—Callie?'

"Lord, Jen, what difference does that make? A kiss isn't anything. The reason I told you all that is I want you to do me a favour. I want you to be my girl——"

Jenny's heart stood still, compressed by too much joy.

"—sort of," Duncan went on, recklessly. "That way, the next time Stan or anybody else makes up tales about me that just aren't so, I can say I'm all tied up with you."

"Tied up," Jenny whispered, "with—with me!" The tears were there now, flooding her freckled cheeks. "Oh, I hate you, Duncan Childers! I hate you I hate you I hate you! You're the meanest, most inconsiderate, most thoughtless boy I ever——"

She whirled then, and marched with funereal slowness towards the gate. Duncan kept pace with her.

"You mean you won't go out with me?" he said.

"No! If I ever even speak to you again, I hope I drop down dead!"

She was inside the gate now; but Duncan reached across it and caught her arm.

"You're pretty when you're mad, Jen," he said. "To heck with the silly gossip. Be my girl for true."

"No," Jenny choked, "I hate——"

But he leaned across the gate and kissed her mouth, the way Hester had taught him to. With practised variations supplied by Calico. Three girls, homeward bound, saw it. They hugged themselves with pure delight, thinking about what a sensation they'd cause when they told this tomorrow to the whole school.

Jenny didn't even see them. She hung there, wordlessly, staring at him, twin constellations of limpid tenderness glowing in her dark eyes.

She turned, already running. He stood there, watching her go. Then, with a very Gallic shrug, he turned away.

"Girls!" he muttered.

But the next morning, when he came out of the gate of the Bouvoir house, his books slung over his shoulder on a strap, she was there, waiting for him, in the shade of the big oak tree.

On 5th June the Class of 1888 was graduated from Caneville High. Among its members were Douglass Henderson, Duncan Childers, Stanton Bruder, and Jenny Greenway.

Hester Vance should have been, had she been there. But she wasn't. It was popularly believed that she was graduating from a fashionable girls' school in Saint Louis some time that same week. The belief was incorrect. She wasn't. Where Hester was at that moment wouldn't be found out in Caneville until several weeks later, when the scandal finally filtered back, as scandal always did.

For, even as the young scholars of Caneville High were receiving their diplomas, Nelson Vance sat in his study, his heavy jowls quivering as he read his sister's letter:

We found them in a hotel room just across the state line, two weeks before graduation. The boy, thank God, had actually married her, so it's not an out and out scandal. He's a nice kid, for a Wop. I waited to write you this long, because I wanted to make sure whether I should have the marriage dissolved— whether Hester mightn't be—oh, you know. Well, she isn't. So yesterday, I went to see the judge. Since you sent me her birth certificate so I could enter her in school here, I had no trouble convincing him she was under legal age; and he handed down an annulment decree at once. The boy's father, Enrico Rossini, St. Louis' richest contractor—these people are coming up, Nels; they should, pushy as they are—came and took him home. Swears he's going to send him off to military school. But, as for Hester, she's impossible. Never would have believed a seventeen-year-old girl could have such a vile tongue in her head. Reckon you'd better come and get her, Nels; she's far too much for me!

On the afternoon of graduation day there were many parties, given by the good citizens of Caneville-Sainte Marie to celebrate the fact that their children were now cultured, responsible members of society. Naturally, with everybody giving parties, there were conflicting invitations. Even Jenny Greenway had three. She went to all three parties, hoping to find Duncan at one of them. He wasn't at any. Jenny went home and cried, her day completely spoiled.

Duncan was, in fact, at home. Minna was entertaining a group of friends on his behalf. Characteristically, Minna had planned, not a party, but a musical soirée. The guests were to bring their instruments and contribute to the solo and ensemble performances. Or to sing, if their voices were up to Minna's high standards.

By Caneville's standards, they were an odd assortment: Father Gaulois sat in one corner, quietly fingering the flute which lay across his knees. Jan Muller, who ran the general store, with his cello leaning against his chair, beamed at his son, Fritz, who was carefully tuning his violin to the A that Duncan was sounding on the Steinway Grand. Hilda Muller, with no instrument at all, except the invisible one of her magnificent coloratura soprano voice, beamed at them both. Only Professor Augustus Bergdorf, who was out of town, was missing. Hans Volker, who had been invited as a baritone, not as a physician, was late. Minna had expected that; one could never depend upon a doctor's being on time.

Fritz nodded briefly to Duncan.

"That does it, Dunc," he said. "I'm all set."

Minna studied the darkly handsome Bavarian boy. He was really very fine, she decided. She had no personal prejudices at all, only the stiff-necked pride of class. And though the Mullers were humble people by her lights, their obvious brilliance opened her doors to them. There was in this, of course, a certain amount of condescension. She was motivated by the aristocratic idea of upholding her natural position as patroness of the arts. But Minna's manners were so good, her graciousness so nearly inborn, that not even the talented Mullers, sensitive to a fault, as they were, ever realised that she was patronising them.

There was but one uninvited visitor: young Moses Johnson, who had come seeking Hans Volker. At the doctor's office he had been told that Dr. Volker would come to the Bouvoir house at the completion of his calls. He waited in the passage, trembling a little. And Minna had been too preoccupied to notice that his brown eyes were scars of grief in his gingercake-coloured face.

"Well, folks," Duncan said cheerfully, "which will it be first: Schubert or Beethoven?"

"Schubert! Schubert!" the Mullers chorused; then, looking

apologetically at Father Gaulois, "if that's all right with you, Father?"

"Just fine, Jan," the priest said, "as long as you include a flute piece later on."

"For you, Vater," the storekeeper said, "we got a special treat. I put the 'Beethoven 25' third on the programme."

Father Gaulois smiled contentedly. The Opus 25 was the Serenade for Flute and Strings.

"Ready, everyone?" Duncan said.

"Ja!" Jan said happily.

Duncan swung into the irresistibly melodic opening of the Schubert Opus 99, for violin, piano, and cello. Minna leaned back and closed her eyes, listening to the lovely, lovely music of the trio. How many times in Berlin had her father paid good reichsmarks to hear playing less expert than this!

She drifted along to the haunting beauty of the melody. Seeing her eyes closed, Duncan wondered if she were asleep. When they had finished the Schubert, he began at once, almost without a break, the powerful, dramatic, poetic Beethoven Opus 97, 'The Archduke', Minna's eyes flew open at once.

"Ach, Liebchen!" she cried, "why did you not give me the chance to applaud? Did you think I was sleeping?"

Duncan nodded, and went on playing. The music held him entirely. His fingers were blurs, fingering the keys. Behind him the violin cried whitely against the air, and the cello, muted and deep, answered it.

Outside in the passage, Mose felt the tears sting his eyes. This was music! Not like that hot-licks stuff he got fifty cents a night for hammering out on the battered piano in Midge's barrel-house. Lord God, if he could only play like that! If he only could....

Hans Volker came very late. He walked along the passage with his face darkened by a frown. That Meremée case, now; was it, or was it not, yellow fever? The symptoms were obscure; but yellow fever symptoms were very often obscure. There was no jaundice, but that didn't mean anything. He had known a great many people to die of the fever without that yellowish tinge putting in its appearance at all.

'It's that damned swamp,' he thought angrily. 'If we drained it, Nelson Vance couldn't profit from the musk-rat skins those poor devils of Cajun trappers bring him. Drain it—and no more musk-rats. But, perhaps, no more fever either. Get rid of those miasmic vapours and——'

The music caught him, penetrating even the heavy armour of his

77

thoughts. Fritz was playing the last of the six Bach violin sonatas that are called 'Partitas'. Hans stood in the passage, listening to it. He was vaguely aware of Mose's presence; but only vaguely. He did not look at those grief-scarred eyes, pleading for his attention.

Then Duncan began to play again, the Opus 57, Number One, that almost never-played companion piece to the Number Two, the famous Number Two that people insist upon calling the 'Moonlight' Sonata, though Beethoven himself never called it that.

'I'm wrong, wrong,' he thought, 'Bergdorf is right. It would be a crime to make a mere doctor of a boy who can play like that!'

The white cry of the music entered into him, like a stab of something beyond pain. He put out his hand, letting it rest on Mose's shoulder. He could feel the negro boy trembling; but he stayed there without moving until Duncan finished the sonata, then he started towards the door.

"Please," Mose whispered, "please, Doc—will you come see my Pa ag'in tonight?"

Hans looked then and saw the boy's eyes.

"Still not eating?" he growled.

"No, sir," Mose said, "an', Doctor, sir, he—he can't even sit up no more. Ma had to put him to bed——"

"I see," Dr. Volker said gruffly. "All right, boy; you go tell your mother I'll be there in about an hour."

"Ruther wait on you, Doctor, if you don't mind. Ain't no fun being at home, these days."

"Buck up, Mose," Dr. Volker said. "Your Pa's going to be all right."

But he wasn't going to be all right, Hans Volker knew. Big Mack Johnson would never be all right again. There was no medicine for what he had. The surprising thing was that he had survived it so long, for he had had it all his life. Big Mack had been born both black and proud—a combination one hundred per cent fatal in the South.

Still thinking about it, this case beyond medicine, requiring perhaps the services of the priest, or even the intervention of God Himself, Hans Volker walked into the salon under the cover of the bravos and handclaps which greeted Duncan's performance. He sat down very quietly, nodding to the others. Duncan smiled at him, and flexed his fingers.

"Duncan," Jan Muller announced, "will now play the Liszt Sonata, 'Années de Pèlerinage'—the last number on our programme."

'No, no, I cannot,' Hans thought, hearing even from the open-

78

ing bars Duncan's complete mastery of his instrument. 'I've got to talk him out of it; I've got to. The town needs doctors; but what this boy can give the world far outweighs whatever claim this place may have upon him.' He settled back, listening to the flamboyant, prophetic fantasy. 'A true *Paradestück*,' he thought, 'a showpiece for a virtuoso. The boy's technique is miraculous; but——'

He stiffened, listening now to Duncan's absolutely flawless playing with a keenly critical ear. 'But his heart isn't in it!' The realisation entered Hans Volker's mind like a shout of joy. 'It isn't in it at all!'

He stared at Duncan, reasoning very slowly: 'The boy is perhaps something like your man of the Renaissance: multi-talented. He will do absolutely everything he sets out to do, so well that people will be deluded into thinking it a true vocation. Yet there always must be one thing, in a boy like this extraordinary one, that he must do not merely very well, but superbly. And it must be a thing he loves; a thing that consumes him. I know he loves medicine; but how much of that love is not merely the product of his adolescent imagination? And how much of my reasoning now is not mere rationalisation, born of my own desire?'

He applauded with the rest when Duncan brought the piece to a masterly conclusion; but his mind was far away. He answered Minna's "*Ach*, Hans, how goes it with you, today?" almost absently; then he saw Father Gaulois looking at him.

"Well, Doctor," the priest said, "which are you going to prescribe for our boy: medicine—or music?"

"I don't know," Hans said humbly. "I thought I knew before, but now——"

Father Gaulois turned to Duncan.

"Which do you want it to be, my son?" he said.

"Medicine!" Duncan said at once.

"Why? Playing like you do——"

"I can go on playing," Duncan said, his voice dark, intense; "but it will always be just that—playing. To me that doesn't compare with saving lives."

"I see," the priest said. He turned to Doctor Volker. "Well, Doctor," he said, "are you reassured?"

"Not quite," Hans Volker said. "Frau Bouvoir, may I borrow your grandson for one entire day? Say—tomorrow?"

"Of course," Minna said.

"Good," Hans Volker said. Then he turned to Father Gaulois. "Father," he said, "how would you like to come with me on a call tonight?"

"I'd be delighted. One of my people?"

"No. Not even of your faith. But I need your help. And he, poor devil, needs it worse. Actually, it's your department. There's not a blessed thing wrong with his body. It's his soul that's sick, Father."

"I see. You interest me profoundly, Doctor. Will you call for me at the rectory?"

"No. We'd better go now, if you can. It's terribly serious, Father."

"Very well. As soon as we have thanked our hostess for this truly delightful evening I am at your service, Doctor."

"Doctor," Duncan said, "couldn't I——"

Hans Volker shook his head.

"We'll have all day tomorrow," he said, "and this particular call is not of a nature I'd care to have you see. Thank you, Madame Bouvoir, for your hospitality. I enjoyed the little of the music I managed to hear."

"Don't mention it, Hans," Minna Bouvoir said.

They stood there in the neatly whitewashed cabin, staring at the big negro in the bed. Big Mack Johnson was a giant of a man. Or he had been. But after fourteen days during which not a particle of food had passed his lips he was down to skin and bones. He wasn't black any more, but grey. Hans Volker had attended too many negroes not to know what that meant. When the blackness started fading out, they were as good as dead.

"Mack," he said angrily, "for God's sake, man! Don't you realise what you're doing? Ruby's not the first gal in history, black or white, to get herself knocked up. You'll get used to it. But this—this is a crime! Same thing as using a gun."

Mack Johnson stared at the two white men stonily.

"Luvinia," he croaked, "throwed my shotgun in the river——"

"Or else you would have used it?" Father Gaulois said quickly. "That is a mortal sin, my son."

Mack Johnson didn't answer him. He lay there, looking at the priest.

"You have much to live for," Father Gaulois went on. "You've a fine wife. Your daughter needs you more than ever now. And your son——"

Mack Johnson turned over very slowly. The bed creaked under his weight. He lay there with his back turned towards them, facing the wall. In the corner, Ruby cried very quietly.

"Ain't no use, gentlemens," Luvinia Johnson said. She was a

tall woman with a heavy mixture of Indian blood. A true red-bone woman, Hans Volker thought. Her dignity was monumental. "Come on out on the porch, where we kin talk, us," she said.

They sat in the rocking-chairs, Luvinia between them. The chairs were new. The contrast between Big Mack's neat, well-kept cabin and the ramshackle shanties of the rest of the negroes was, in itself, a measure of the man. Luvinia rocked back and forth. The motion was the only indication of the pain inside her. Mose sat on the porch steps, motionless as stone.

"You-all don't understand him," she said. "He's a man, him."

"We're all men, Luvinia," Hans said shortly. "I don't see what that's got to do with it."

"Hit's got a mighty heap to do with it," Luvinia said patiently. "All right, you's a man, Doctor. You kin afford to be. Don't cost you nothing. Ain't nobody gonna cut off your fingers and your toes for souvenirs whilst you's still alive, like they done——"

"Luvinia!" Hans said.

"—to that poor nigger over in Mertontown. Then they burnt him. And he was defending his home, too, him. No sir. Man gits your chile in trouble, you takes a shotgun to him, makes him marry her, or you kills him. But my Mack cain't do that. Not neither one."

"I don't approve of either force or murder," Father Gaulois broke in, "but it does seem to me that the man should have been persuaded to marry the child."

Luvinia threw back her head and laughed aloud. The sound of it made Hans Volker shiver. He leaned quickly towards the priest.

"The man is—white, Father," he said.

"I see. And I'm sorry. I'm terribly sorry. This sort of thing is shameful!"

"You ain't a-telling me nothing I don't know, Father," Luvinia said. "But there hit is, yes. And my Mack, being a man, and loving that fool chile like he do, wanted to kill him. So I throwed his shotgun away, me. Then I talked to him, telling him what would happen: how they'd drag him behind a wagon through the streets, tie him to a green log, so the burning wouldn't be quick, so they could hear him a-crying and a-screeching a long time. Talked to him, me. Talked the heart right out o' him. Oughta knowed better. Ought to of remembered hit was Big Mack Johnson I was a-talking to. Six foot four, a railroading man, with a backbone holding him up. Us being married all these years, and I didn't have sense enough inside my thick head to realise that to sit back'n watch hit'n not do nothing was the one thing my Mack couldn't stand. So now he's gonna die."

81

"Ma!" Mose cried.

"Hush, chile. Your Pa's gonna die. He's gonna cause he'd druther be dead than live with shame. An' he's right. 'Member that, son. All your livelong days remember that your Pa was Big Mack Johnson, and he was a man."

"Luvinia," Hans said drily, "you're giving that boy some awful bad advice. He's got to live in the South and——"

"No, he ain't. Not in the South, not nowheres he cain't be a man, him. Living's just fine, Doctor. But it ain't the only thing. Hit ain't even the most important."

"And what is, Luvinia?" Father Gaulois said.

"That he don't never bow his head to nobody, 'cepting to his God. My Mack never did. Now, if you gentlemens'll 'scuse me, I got to go look after my man."

"Goodnight, Luvinia," Hans Volker said. "See if you can't get him to——"

"He won't," she said flatly. "I'm mighty thankful to you-all for coming. Wants my boy to know they is some good whitefolks. Not very many, but some."

"You must try to rid your heart of bitterness, Luvinia," Father Gaulois said. "I will pray for you that——"

"You do that, Father," Luvinia said. "Maybe he'll listen to you. 'Cause hit 'pears to me your whitefolks' God just don't hear no niggers' prayers. Goodnight, gentlemens; thanks ag'in for coming."

The two of them walked down the path and got into the buggy. They didn't say anything, neither then, nor the rest of the way home. There was, perhaps, nothing to be said.

The testing that Hans Volker planned for Duncan Childers, that of having him witness the very worst cases, to see whether his determination to become a doctor could be shaken, proved an unqualified success. In one way, it exceeded Hans's expectations. For Duncan had insisted upon bringing Mose Johnson along. Seeing the coloured boy's interest in medicine, as keen as Duncan's own, Doctor Volker came to a decision. He would back Mose's studies for the medical profession. For two reasons: it would take the heavy burden of his practice among the negroes off his shoulders; and it would rid him of the curious emotion of shared guilt he felt.

'But nothing,' Duncan thought, looking back across the gulf of fifteen years, 'can rid me of this subtler guilt I feel. We were so clean of heart then, Mose and I. I reckon Mose is still. He wanted the right things even then; even back in 1888 he asked only to be

82

allowed to serve. Had it all planned: how he could live off the chickens and eggs and garden truck the coloured folks could bring him. How he wouldn't need money. While I, while I——

'While I,' he thought savagely, 'needed my blonde filly, my fancy flat, my flossy practice. How the hell did I get this way? Name of God, how?

'Maybe,' he thought, 'Grandmother's death had something to do with it. More than something. Perhaps—everything.'

He was crossing the north end of the yard, just in front of Stoughton Hall, when the Western Union boy came pedalling up to him on the bicycle. He had been at Harvard two years by then; and he loved it as much as it was possible for a man to love his school. Which, in Duncan, was a great deal. He had found a certain measure of acceptance there—even a kind of peace.

"You're Mister Childers, sir?" the messenger boy said.

"Yes," Duncan said; "why?"

"Telegram for you, sir," the boy said.

Duncan took it, signed the receipt, gave the boy a coin. Opened the telegram, read it. His world collapsed.

Minna von Stürck Bouvoir was dead. Unexpectedly, of a heart attack. He hadn't even known she was ill.

The pain that entered his heart was very nearly mortal. All the love he had felt for his martyred mother had been transferred intact to Minna Bouvoir. And it had grown with the years, fired by her tenderness, guarded by the great respect he felt for her.

'Not many fellows,' he thought woodenly now, 'have had the luck to be brought up by—a Queen!'

He crossed the yard towards Holden Chapel, his eyes so blinded by the scalding rush of his grief that he could not even make out that tremendous coat of arms above the door. He went in, knelt down and said a prayer for her, a prayer that poured up from the depths of his anguished soul—he, Duncan Childers, who proudly proclaimed himself an atheist.

When he came out, he was calmer. He crossed to his Hall. Packed his things. Went to Boston, caught a train headed south to Louisiana.

To bury her who had been the very bulwark of his life.

Then, afterwards, the second blow. Minna had got into debt to pay for his education. The last of her money had been gone even before he left Caneville High. The plantation had to be sold to meet those debts. And Duncan Childers was left with the Bouvoir house, and not one red copper to his name.

83

He could, of course, have sold the house. It would have brought him in enough money to finish Harvard. He could have, in the sense that the possibility existed. Being himself, remembering her, he could not. The very thought was sacrilege.

Work, then. But where? North. In some factory, some mill where the wages would be high enough to make the time lost from his studies as brief as possible. Work at some task so hard, so dirty, so dangerous, that they had to pay high wages to get men. Like a boiler factory. A rolling mill. A steel foundry.

He went north. To Pittsburgh. Starved for two months, until he found a job. Working as a puddler's assistant in a foundry. Enduring the closest approximation to classic hell ever designed by the mind of man.

It was murderous. You knocked out the fireclay plug of the furnace's pouring-gate with a long steel rod; and the molten metal exploded out, white, pure white, sun-bright; no, brighter than that, so that he never afterwards could find a word that would say that brightness, that awful, awe-inspiring brightness that seared your eyes even through the deep purple lenses of the goggles. And with that whiteness, the noise: the belly-deep rumble from the bowels of a Titan; that sound somhow deeper than sound, so low-booming that you felt the impact of it as much as heard it.

Then the heat. The heat leaped out upon you, smote you hip and brow and thigh; dried your mouth into cracked blisters, dried the blood from those blisters into black crusts, evaporated your sweat instantly so that you burnt, drily, the skin on your face peeling off, lashes and brows gone, any wisp of hair that escaped your cap crisped into powder within minutes. And you, dragging it into your lungs, dragged in fire, dragged in death. The average furnace tender lasted just five years before his lungs went, in those days.

The metal storming into the ladles, held there like liquid sunlight. The heat rising, simmering, the poured arc dividing the dark. The spilled droplets making dancing stars upon the floor. The smoke, the smells, the heat, the hell.

Killing a 'wild heat' of steel with aluminium powder poured into the ladle, you made a pillar of fire as tall as the one God sent the Hebrew children. Stirring the open-hearth heats with a puddling rod, throwing in fluorspar, manganese, cobalt, nickel, vanadium, tungsten; the heat in and around you was like a presence, your hands burning raw through your armoured gloves.

It was terrible, back-breaking, man-killing work. But he gloried in it. It was a job for men.

Coming out of that heat, dirt, blast-furnace roar, the cold of a

84

Pennsylvania winter penetrated your lungs like a knife. Yet he held on, endured, suffered it, for a year. At the end of that year he got pneumonia. Nearly died.

"Look, son," the doctor said, "you just aren't built for steel work. You're too lean and rangy. Steelworker ought to be made like a bulldog, low, heavy, close to the ground. You go back into that foundry, and you'll be a T.B. case in six months. You talk like an educated man. Why don't you find yourself something lighter? Like clerical work say. In a warm climate."

"All right," Duncan said weakly.

He would have to do something. The money he had nearly killed himself to get was all but gone, eaten up in hospital bills, medicines, doctor's fees. His chances for getting back to Harvard, for beginning to study the art of healing, were gone with it. He had played it straight, and life had kicked him in the teeth—again. He had worked like hell, and all he'd got out of it were a pair of damned sick lungs.

Well, he wouldn't again. He'd take it easy for a while, then look for the main chance, for the facile, dirty, crooked way. The world was like that. He had known that as a child, but the interval of salvation with Minna had illusioned him. The world was like that; and now he was prepared to join the world. He had been too long away.

A warm climate. Clerical work. Light tasks. He added it up. It spelled New Orleans, and Bruder & LaVallois again. He didn't want that. It would remind him too much of—Callie. Perhaps he would even run into her again.

Which was both a fear—and a hope. And the hope was greater than the fear.

He took a train.

Chapter 6

"MADAME BOUVOIR'S DEATH must have been quite a blow," Fred Baynes said.

Duncan got the drift now. A good reporter always strove for the emotional impact. Make 'em laugh. Make 'em cry. That was the ticket.

"Yes," he said quietly. "You see, Fred, she was almost the only human being who had been kind to me since my mother's death. I remember feeling at the time that all the people whom I loved, and more especially those who loved me, seemed fated not to live. Damned egotistical reaction. But the young always imagine themselves at the centre of the stage, playing the leading rôle in the tragedy of the universe. Takes quite some time to learn that the fate of any one individual is of no more importance than that of a —cockroach."

Calico had said that. The second time. The time he had found her again.

Fred Baynes scribbled busily.

Duncan looked at his watch.

"I'm sorry," he said, "but I really can't spare any more time today. Calls, you know."

"Let me ride with you while you make them," Fred said. "That way I can get more down, and you'll be rid of me that much faster."

"On the contrary, I've been enjoying your company," Duncan said. "In fact, you're helping me immensely."

His tone was completely sincere. The reporter stared at him.

"Mind telling me how, Doc?" he said.

"There's a thing I have to do. A decision to make. You're helping me to get to the place where I can make it. It's a rather serious decision that wants thinking about. And it can only be made on the basis of experience, that is, out of the materials of my life. You're forcing me to recall a great many things I'd all but forgotten. Because of that, I believe I'm going to be able to decide quite soon now."

"Decide what, Doc?"

"I'd rather not say, at the moment. But I promise to let you know at the proper time. Well, Fred, shall we go?"

"Right. Thanks, Doc. When you came back to New Orleans in 1891, after you'd worked in that steel-mill, what did you do?"

"I got my old job back—at Bruder & LaVallois again," Duncan said.

The first person he saw, when he walked into the offices that morning in the spring of 1891, was the typist. She had her back turned to him, but she was small and well formed and blonde, so that for a long moment his heart stood still.

"Please, miss," he said.

She turned and his heart started beating again. It wasn't Calico, after all.

He tried to analyse his feeling of disappointment. What good would it do to see Callie again? What earthly good at all?"

"Yes, sir?" the new typist said.

"I'd like to see Mr. Bruder, if you don't mind," he said.

"I'm afraid that's impossible," the girl said.

"Why?" Duncan said bluntly.

"Mr. Bruder is very ill. He only comes to the office because there's no one to take his place. And the doctor says he shouldn't receive anyone. You can talk to Mr. LaVallois, if you like."

"Later," Duncan said. "But first, if you'll just trot in there like a sweet girl and tell Mr. Bruder that Duncan is here, I'm sure he'll see me. Tell him that's what I came for—to take some of the load off his shoulders. Go on, baby-doll, scoot!"

She didn't know whether to display indignation or pleasure. So she compromised.

"Fresh!" she said, with a toss of her head. But she said it with a smile.

While she was gone, Duncan reasoned the matter out: 'Uncle Martin's sick. Again. The same thing, probably. His stomach. LaVallois said that Dr. Terrebonne suspected—cancer, before. Then it cleared up. Now, again. Uncle Martin's a fine man. It's a pity—but, damn it all, it's an ill wind that blows nobody any good. Sick people are dependent. A little extra kindness and——

'You bastard!' the icily honest part of his mind said.

'Yes,' he mocked himself: both literally and figuratively. 'Why not? What has sweetness and light ever got me? I want to be a doctor. Not from any overwhelming love for humanity, but because I happen to like the profession, and it—commands respect. Not to mention the crisp, green, sweet-folding cash it brings in. So I need money for my medical education. How to get that money? Why, be nice to Uncle Martin, of course!

'You dirty bastard!' his mind said.

The girl came back.

"Mr. Bruder will see you now," she said.

"Thanks, baby-doll," Duncan said. "Supper tonight?"

"Of course not," she sniffed. "I'm engaged."

"Lucky, lucky man," Duncan said. He thought: 'Poor devil! She's got a face like a horse. And those buck teeth, ugh!'

He went into the office. Stopped still. Stared at Martin Bruder.

Uncle Martin had lost forty pounds. Before, even when he had been sick that time, he had always been plump. Now he was skeletal. His face was grey. His cheeks were dark hollows. His eyes were lost in their cavernous sockets.

"Uncle Martin!" Duncan gasped. "Good Lord!"

"I know," Martin Bruder said with a gentle smile. "I'm a dreadful sight. Cancer of the stomach is not a pretty way to die, Duncan. Nor," he added with a grimace of repressed pain, "a pleasant one. Sit down, my boy. I do hope you've come back to work for us."

"There could be some mistake," Duncan said furiously; "doctors aren't infallible, Uncle Martin! Have you seen more than one?"

"Dozens. They all give the same advice: 'Make your will, Martin Bruder.' This is the end of it, Duncan. And because it is, I have never been so happy to see anyone in my life."

Duncan sank into a chair. He was thinking: 'Oh, no; this is too much! This is too bloody rotten goddamned much! All the swine there are on earth, and this had to happen to him. To one of the kindest, best——

'Forgetting something, boy?' his mind mocked. 'This was what you were going to take advantage of. This. Pretty, isn't it? All right, get going! Butter up to this poor, dying hulk of rotting flesh. . . .

'Shut up!' Duncan screamed at his mind.

"You see, my boy," Uncle Martin went on, "I need you. I'm trying to leave this business in such a state that it will run itself, or that it can be liquidated profitably. That gibbering idiot I have for a son is of no use to me. I'll leave him well fixed, of course. Even rich. But inside of five years he'll have thrown every penny of it away, even if I were to leave him twice the sum I'm able to now. That's why——"

"Uncle Martin," Duncan said, "should you talk so much? You look dreadfully tired."

"I shouldn't, but I have to. Listen to me, Duncan. I've got eight

88

months to a year. I've taught you a lot already. Your German is better than fair. Your commercial German, which is almost another language, was coming along nicely when you left. I now investigate the characters of my typists before I hire them."

"*Touché*," Duncan said wryly. "You—you never heard what became of her, did you, Uncle Martin?"

"Yes," Martin Bruder said. "In fact, I know precisely where she is. But before I tell you that, one question: are you entirely over her, Duncan?"

"Yes," Duncan said.

'Are you?' his mind mocked. 'Are you, boy?'

"Good. She has a flat down on Conti Street. And," Martin Bruder smiled mockingly, "before you follow the impulse I see in your eyes, Duncan, I'd better add a postscript: my good-for-nothing son, Stanton, is keeping her as his mistress."

Duncan sat there. He did not move.

"The blow was intentional," Martin Bruder said, "with malice aforethought. Though it happens to be true. Now, if you've sufficiently recovered——"

"Go on, Uncle Martin," Duncan said quietly.

"In that year I want to train you enough so that you can take over for me. During it you can lift a considerable load from my back. I'm prepared to be generous: how would two hundred dollars a month, to start, suit you?"

Duncan didn't answer. In 1891 two hundred dollars a month was a princely fortune.

"You don't have to pay me anything," he said. To his own surprise, he found he meant it. "Anything I can do to help you, Uncle Martin, shouldn't have a price tag put on it. As long as I have enough to pay for a room, my food, a book or two——"

"You won't need a room, Duncan," Uncle Martin said. "I'm taking you home with me."

"But—Stan?" Duncan said.

"Can take it and like it. He's never there. Too busy with his dalliance. And I need someone there. Not to take care of me; I have a trained nurse for that; but just there—someone of my blood——"

"I'm not of your blood, Uncle Martin," Duncan said.

"Then of my spirit, by means of the love that poor Johann bore you. What you can do, no nurse can. I need someone to put my hand out to, when the pains get really bad. A substitute son—I know; I have a son. Flesh of my flesh, blood of my blood—and yet —no son at all!"

"Uncle Martin, you shouldn't——"

"I know. There are so many things that I shouldn't, Duncan. This way of dying is tiresome. The worst of it all is the loneliness. I thought I'd got used to loneliness, after Hildegarde died. But I hadn't. This thing in me saps not only my strength, but my courage, my will. So I need you, Duncan. For the business—and to help me die—well."

"Uncle Martin!"

"The last act, Duncan. One should ring down the curtain with dignity and with grace. I know, I'm asking a dreadful lot. You're young, you have your life, your friends——"

The tears stung Duncan's eyelids suddenly. He fought to push them back. Succeeded; but not quickly enough. One at least traced light down his cheek.

"Thanks, son," Martin Bruder said. "It's hell when an old man has to be grateful for a boy's tears! But I am. Profoundly grateful. You'll come?"

"Of course, Uncle Martin," Duncan said.

There was no question after that day of using his Uncle Martin for his own selfish ends. His very entrails were wrung with pity as he sat night-long by the old man's bed, holding his hand until the morphine did its work. Dying is a lonely thing; but this awful, ugly, tortured dying that left a man neither courage, nor peace, nor dignity—God! To find something that would stop this! To find a way, a way——

In the office he gradually came to do all Martin Bruder's work; to sit there hour after hour making invoices, writing letters, keeping ledgers that caught up in columns of neat figures a commerce sprawled around the globe. He seldom had time to even talk to old Jacques LaVallois. Nor, for that matter, to think of Calico.

He saw Stan Bruder only once, when that worthy came to the office to beg of his father the fifty dollars he had lost at poker the night before. With him was young Forsythe Bevers, heir to the Bevers' Knitting Mills in Mertontown. Forsythe, too, was a student at Tulane. Duncan thought he was a better sort than Stan. Not much better, but some.

Stan knew his father would give him the money. With icy, studied contempt, of course; but give it to him he would. Why was the old fool taking so long to die? All that money! When he got it, he'd——

Then he pushed open the door and stared into Duncan Childers's face. Forsythe Bevers was behind him, but, at the last moment,

Bevers stepped back and remained in the outer office. 'Doesn't want to get mixed up in it,' Duncan thought.

Martin Bruder was sitting at his desk, with his eyes closed. It was Stan's outraged roar that wakened him.

"What," Stan bellowed, "is this miserable bastard doing here?"

Martin Bruder stared at his son. What was in his face was less contempt than pity.

"My executive secretary has every right to be in my office, Stanton," he said quietly; "the most excellent one being that of work superbly done. And, if you are capable of understanding me, bastardy of the flesh is entirely pardonable. I don't believe in a God who visits a father's sins upon the head of the son—the quite innocent son."

"Innocent!" Stan sneered.

"Yes, innocent. What is not pardonable, Stanton, is bastardy of the soul. Nor the life of a parasite; nor any of a number of things it would be bootless to name. Now tell me—what do you want? You're interrupting our work."

"Fifty dollars," Stan mumbled automatically. "But I still don't like——"

"What you like is of less than no importance. Here's the money. Take it and get out. No—wait. Will you deliver a message to Miss Landis?"

Stan's eyes bugged out.

"To—to Beth?" he said.

"Yes. You might tell her that my will is made. And that it contains a certain clause—a very interesting clause, to wit: 'That if ever in the future said Stanton Bruder should contract matrimony with the woman known as Elizabeth "Calico" Landis, the money held in trust for said Stanton Bruder and from whose interest his income is derived shall automatically cease to be held in his behalf, and shall be turned over to certain worthy charities, a list of which is hereinunder affixed.' Is that clear? Will you be so kind as to tell her that?"

"Think I'm a fool?" Stanton grated. "Why, she'd leave me flat!"

"I rather imagine she would," Martin said imperturbably. "So you're going to keep her living upon vain hopes?"

"And on your money, after you're dead! What the hell do you think we'll need a pretty piece of paper and some long-faced ugly jackass mumbling out of a Bible for? Contract matrimony, ha! The mixture as before, old man; but this time on your cash!"

"Uncle Martin," Duncan said quietly, "would it bother you too much if I hit him?"

"No, don't. He'll receive his lumps soon enough. Sooner than he thinks—the first week he tries to keep that wench on the sums I've arranged to have doled out to him. But enough of this. Stanton, will you please go?"

The next morning, Duncan went to the flat on Conti Street. His old flat, the one she had shared with him. The one she was sharing now with Stanton Bruder. He went very early, on his way to work, knowing that Stan wouldn't be there. Stan was a Junior at Tulane University, studying—if what Stan did could be called study—agriculture, with a view to taking over his Uncle Otto's plantation near Caneville.

Calico opened the door herself. Her blond hair was tousled, her eyes heavy with sleep. She had made love the night before. He could see the blue circles of fatigue below her eyes, the drawn mouth, the faintly trembling hands. He could well read the signs. He had put them there too often himself.

She did not move, nor speak, nor even breathe.

"Supper tonight, Callie?" he said, gently. "At Broussard's, say?"

She looked at him a long time, a very long time.

"All right," she whispered huskily. "Stan isn't going to like it, but——"

"I don't think you need be concerned about what Stan likes or doesn't like, Callie," Duncan said.

At Broussard's he sat across the table from her, looking at her face illumined by candle-light. The weather was fine, so they were eating outside in the long, narrow courtyard. Dark shrubbery lined the walls. Rambler roses climbed them. Between the tables, in pots, were long-stemmed roses, calla lilies, violets, chrysanthemums, and hibiscus. Duncan turned to the waiter and ordered for them both: *huîtres à la Broussard, poulet en papillote, salade verte mixte, vin rouge*; and, for sweet, *la Surprise Broussard*, which turned out to be nothing more than extra-fancy *crêpes suzettes*.

He sat there, studying her, trying to decide how she had changed. He had the feeling she had grown more embittered. Much more. But he didn't say anything.

"All right," she said harshly, "go on, Duncan, ask me."

"What am I supposed to ask you, Callie?"

"How I managed to get mixed up with—a thing like Stan Bruder."

"Doesn't interest me. I know. Part of getting the world on its own terms. Revenge, perhaps, because Uncle Martin refused to take you back after you left Big Mame's the second time."

"How'd you know that? Did Mr. Bruder tell you?"

"No. He has never discussed you with me. I guessed you'd left. I didn't think you could stay. I'll even bet you left very shortly, within a week, say, after I saw you there."

"Less than that," she whispered. "That same night, with my guts in knots, remembering your eyes. Without having entertained a client. Determined to be straight, to make you proud of me—fat chance!"

"Then—no job," Duncan said softly, "hunger, after a while— and only one commodity the world, the male half of the world, wants to buy. So—Stan. Better than Big Mame's, at least."

"Not much," she said bitterly. "He's a brute, a lout, and a coward. And," she smiled maliciously, "no damned good in bed."

"Then," Duncan said, "my conscience is clear. If you don't love him, I have no reason to allow you to suffer him in the hopes of one day being rich. You won't, Callie; here's why."

Then he told her.

What was in her eyes was almost relief.

"I'm glad," she said; "I'm really glad, Duncan. I was getting to the place where even the hope of all that money wasn't enough." She smiled at him mockingly. "You didn't by any chance tell me this to get me back yourself, did you, Duncan?" she said.

"No," he said; "we've no future, neither of us, Callie."

"And too much past," she said bitterly. "Pay the waiter, Duncan; then go call me a cab."

"Why?" he said; "what's your hurry?"

"I have packing to do," Calico said.

"But where will you go?" Duncan said. "What will you do? Callie, I pray God——"

She looked at him.

"He doesn't care," she said quietly. "We're like cockroaches to Him. That is, if He even remembers we're here. Call me that cab, Duncan."

He called it, helped her into it, watched her ride away out of his life. Out of Stanton Bruder's, too; which was small consolation to him.

Duncan sat at the grand piano in the parlour of the Bruder residence. He had been playing all evening: Chopin, chiefly; the Mazurkas; the Fantasies Impromptu; that old warhorse of a show piece, the Polonaise Number 6. Some Liszt: the Second Concerto; the *Totentanz*, not because he wanted to play a piece with so grim a name, but because Martin Bruder asked him to. He was playing now, smoothly, softly, the Beethoven Opus 57, Number 2, the so-called 'Moonlight' Sonata.

Uncle Martin lay on the sofa listening to him. His eyes were closed. And death was upon him visibly.

The door crashed open; Stan Bruder stormed into the room. Forsythe Bevers was with him. Duncan knew why Stan had brought Forsythe along: for reinforcement. He hadn't the guts to tackle Duncan alone.

"She's gone!" he howled; "she's gone! You took her away! You lousy rat-bastard Channel scum, where've you got her? Where?"

"I don't have her, Stan," Duncan said quietly; and went on playing. "If you must know, I told her you'd never get your money if you married her. I'm not ashamed of that. Why make the poor thing live on empty hopes?"

Stanton caught him by the shoulder, jerked him round.

"You know where she is!" he grated. "Tell me, you bastard! Tell me!"

"I'm getting a little tired of that word, Stan," Duncan said, "and I don't know where Calico is. She didn't tell me where she was going."

"You lie!" Stan spat, and smashed his fist with all his force into Duncan's face.

The piano stool crashed over. Duncan got to his feet very slowly, blood trailing from his mouth.

"I won't fight you, Stan," he said. "Not now. Not here."

"Quite a hero, aren't you, Childers?" Forsythe Bevers sneered.

"You were brave enough to drive Beth away!" Stan bellowed. "Come on, you yellow bastard, fight!"

"Stan," Martin Bruder said, "must you drag your whore even into my dying bed?"

Stan whirled.

"You're not that sick!" he jeered. "You'll be around here for years to plague me!"

Martin Bruder smiled.

"I only wish I had more time in which to plague you, Stan," he whispered. "It is one of the few pleasures I have left. Duncan, if you'll be so kind as to help me up to bed—I do not believe you'll have to play for me another night."

"Uncle Martin!" Duncan whispered.

"Don't let it trouble you, my boy. I think I shall manage it well.

94

Goodnight Stan. And your friend, whatever his name is. Or perhaps I should say—good-bye."

"Father," Stan got out, "I didn't mean what I said! I hope you don't think——"

"What I think is no longer of any importance, son. Come, Duncan. You'll stay with me for a while?"

But Martin Bruder did not die that night. Not for many more nights. Death was not so kind. Death required more of him: that he reach the place where the morphine had no effect; the time when his screams tore the night, when Duncan had to hold him in the bed to prevent his hurling himself from the third-storey window to end the agony that devoured him.

Death was not kind. He died, weeks later, screaming, in his foster-nephew's arms. At the last instant, he locked his teeth and muttered through them:

"I will do it well!"

But his mouth tore open again, his neck arched back, back, and his tortured lungs dragged air. Then, before he could let that final anguished shriek out, Duncan clamped his strong, tender hand over his mouth.

"Well, Uncle Martin!" he wept. "Die well! Oh God, let him, please!"

He drew his hand away. There was a faint rustle. It went on for ten full minutes longer. Then silence.

He left Duncan Childers ten thousand dollars in his will. So it was, and at such a price, that Duncan embarked upon his studies in Vienna.

Chapter 7

"But, Doc," Fred Baynes said, "since Mr. Bruder was so set on having you run the business after he died, appears to me he would have tied a few strings to that money he left you."

"No," Duncan said softly, "he didn't. I was with him constantly, both day and night. We talked quite a lot to each other during that period, about art, music, philosophy. I told him what I wanted out of life, Fred. I guess the word 'doctor' must have cropped up with considerable frequency. At any rate, when his will was read, I found he had left me the money for the specific purpose of studying in Vienna—I must have mentioned that city a thousand times to him—either medicine or music or any other appropriate career."

"And the business?"

"Was sold to new owners. Jacques LaVallois retired. The money from the sale was divided between him and Martin Bruder's estate. That is, it was added to the trust that Mr. Bruder had set up for his son."

Fred's face showed disappointment. No drama in that. He fished about for a new lead.

"Tell me something about your life abroad, Doc," he said.

"All right," Duncan said. He was going to have to leave an awful lot out of that part, too. But, thank heavens, that was one section of his life that Fred Baynes had no way of checking upon. He said: "I went to Vienna in the fall of 1892. I finished my studies, pre-medical and medical, by the spring of 1898. Then I had two years of internship in Berlin. So I didn't get home until 1900, three years ago."

"How about a few details, Doc?" Fred said.

Duncan walked very slowly down Dresdner Strasse until he came to the Praterstern. Then he turned and walked to the Kai behind Saint Stephen's Cathedral. He moved into the Ring. Then he saw Wolfgang Heimer waiting for him on a stone bench in front of the Cathedral.

Wolfgang was his best friend in Vienna. They lodged together, because Wolfgang came from Berlin, not Vienna. Therefore the Austrian medical students considered him as much of an *Ausländer*, a foreigner, as they did Duncan. He had a wonderfully sunny disposition, which was sometimes hard to take.

"Why the overwhelming gloom, old boy?" Wolfgang said. He had been educated in England, and was proud of his accent. He frequently overdid his Anglicisms; and they never rang quite true. But his accent was very good indeed. "I'll wager you a fiver that it's a girl," he said.

Duncan smiled.

"The lack of a girl," he said wryly. "No letter from Jen again this week. I'm beginning to think she's thrown me over."

"Then I prescribe more of the same. A hair of the dog that bit you, what? In short, another girl. I've already arranged it. Gret's bringing her along tonight—for you. Ravishing dark-haired creature, named Marta Schlosser. Damned aristocratic. The Emperor's going to make it 'von' Schlosser soon. Services to the Imperial Throne and all that sort of ruddy rot."

"You mean she serves the Throne?"

"Oh no. Her father. Insufferable old prig. Blast him! I'd rather talk about Marta: that hair, those eyes, that figure—absolutely ripping. You'll see. Never could hit it off with her, though I tried...."

"So you settled for Gret Pfeifer?"

"Quite. Glad I did; Gretchen's jolly well fun. At least in bed. Tell me: what are your plans for the summer, Duncan?"

"I was thinking of going up to Berlin to hear Virchow lecture. That cellular theory of his——"

"*Die Cellular-Pathologie in ihrer Begründung auf die physiologische und pathologische Gewebelehre*, Berlin, 1858," Wolfgang pronounced sententiously. "I've read it. Great man, old Rudolf Ludwig Karl."

"I don't know," Duncan said. "His modification of cellular structure under the influence of disease is indisputably correct; and would be of great help in diagnosis, if you didn't have to get the tissue for microscopic examination out of cadavers. By then it's too late. But he stubbornly fights Koch, and he sneered at Pasteur."

"The germ theory of disease, eh? Jolly well proved by now. But Pasteur had too many weaknesses."

"He did stop hydrophobia and anthrax."

"And silkworm disease, and bad wine and all other kinds of ruddy nonsense. But his anthrax vaccine killed as many sheep as would have died of the disease without it. Rum type, that Pasteur. Look what Koch did to him! The vaccine that Pasteur said wouldn't even kill mice, really wouldn't, but it would kill rabbits; and the

97

vaccine weak enough to be effective on bunnies, killed sheep! He simply wasn't scientific. Too French, I guess. Lacked the beautiful precision of the Teutonic mind."

"Don't be so bloody chauvinistic," Duncan said. "Wolf—about this girl——"

"Marta? Stunning creature. Positively ripping. You'll see."

"To tell the truth, I'd rather not," Duncan said. "I'm in no mood to——"

"Which is exactly why you must come. What do you say, old boy?"

"Oh—all right," Duncan said tiredly.

When Wolfgang and Duncan got there, the beer-garden was already filled with lights and laughter and music. From the bandstand the uniformed, and uniformly fat, musicians pumped away at Viennese waltzes. Equally fat waiters rushed among the tables bearing huge and foaming steins of beer. In the centre, well upholstered burghers danced with their plump and pretty Fraus. An enormous Brunhilda, out of the ancient legends, drenched the night with her matchless coloratura soprano. It was all very warm, moving, *gemütlich*, Viennese. Duncan was already feeling a good bit better.

He sat there thinking about Calico and all the time and space between them. He had treated her badly. But what else could he have done? It was all beginning to subside into a dull ache now. Callie would make it. Wherever she was, she would make it. She was smart enough. Even tough enough.

He thought about his first year at the University. It had been brutal. In the 1890s the difference between a German Gymnasium—which meant a school, not a place to play games and take exercise—and any American high school whatsoever was so great as to be frightening. German students had completed trigonometry and calculus before their American counterparts had even begun algebra. A Gymnasium graduate could speak Latin and Greek, was fluent in three or four modern languages. And between the training of the students—whom the fame which Karl Rokitansky had solidly established for the New Vienna Medical School, before his death in 1878, attracted to the five-hundred-year-old University—and the pitiful dabbling in the arts and sciences to which Duncan had been exposed at Caneville High, the distance could only be measured in light-years.

What saved Duncan from failing his courses was the fact that he was truly brilliant. And his two years at Harvard had cut that distance somewhat. But his true salvation lay in the fact that his work-toughened body could support an incredibly great amount of study, while sustained by an equally incredibly small amount of sleep. He made up his deficiencies with private tutors at night. Professor Zauber taught him the Latin and Greek which he was supposed to have already learned at Caneville High, but which, of course, he hadn't, since the instructors who had taught him hadn't known the first principles of the ancient tongues they were supposed to teach. Wilhelm Zerenczi ground mathematics into him. Stephenov caught him up in physics and chemistry. In the daytime he studied the pre-medical and later the medical courses, began to learn the ten thousand and fifty words which would finally make a doctor of him.

He was not the only foreigner. There were students from every European country and from the British Isles. Small, smiling Japanese bobbed about, their tiny, deft fingers making apparent child's play of the most delicate experiments; Scots from Edinburgh; Frenchmen from the famed Pasteur Institute; Americans from Harvard and Yale; all the world making freely or grudgingly the admission that, in those days, German medicine was king.

He found, in the midst of all these herculean mental labours, free time to follow his natural bent. He took lessons in piano technique from Livinsky on the one night he could have stolen a little sleep. At intervals, when the work slackened, he cut himself a wide swath among the *Mädchen* of the *Weinestuben* and *Bierhallen*.

But it was nearly summer now; and Duncan knew what he wanted to do. He had decided to go to Berlin, hear Virchow, find some way of begging, fighting, or stealing his way into the presence of Robert Koch, that prince of germ fighters, the man who really proved that microbes cause disease. His good friend and fellow medical student, Wolfgang, preferred to remain in Vienna and amuse himself mightily. Vienna was certainly the place for that.

Duncan looked at his watch and growled:

"They're damned late!"

"Oh ho!" Wolfgang laughed. "Thought you weren't in the mood?"

"I'm not," Duncan said. "But this business of sitting here, drowning my insides with beer and waiting. . . ."

"You can relax, old boy," Wolfgang said gaily. "Here they come now!"

They stood up and waited as the two girls came towards them, weaving their way among the tables, under the dancing lights that were suspended from the trees. They took off their hard straw hats and stood there, the light and shadow flickering over their striped blazers. The girls came up to them.

"*Grüss Gott*," they said in their soft, Viennese fashion; "Greet God."

Duncan and Wolfgang stood there. They didn't say anything. Duncan drew in a deep breath. Let it out. Said, "Good Lord!"

Gretchen Pfeifer might as well have not been there as far as he was concerned. He was staring at Marta Schlosser. Gretchen was plump, rosy, clean-scrubbed, blonde. But Marta——

She was tall, slender, graceful. Her hair was black, which, of course, was no rarity among the Austrians, with their heavy mixture of both Italian and Slavic blood. But her eyes, instead of the brown that Duncan had expected them to be, were blue. The contrast was startling, especially under brows heavier than any woman's he had ever seen before, half veiled by lashes as inky as her hair, and longer than he had thought it possible for lashes to be.

Her mouth matched her brunette shade. It was wine-red without the slightest help from paint. Her throat was of that Victorian slenderness so greatly admired in that day.

And her figure, under the white bell-flare of her summer dress, was a pure miracle.

He recovered at last.

"Yes," he said. "Greet God—and thank Him, too!"

"Marta," Gretchen said, "may I present Herr Childers? You already know Wolfgang. *Mein Herr, die Fräulein Schlosser*."

"I am honoured, Fräulein Schlosser," Duncan said, and shook hands with her.

"Which do you prefer, ladies?" Wolfgang said. "Beer? Wine?"

"Wine," Gretchen sighed. "I have to watch my figure."

"What's wrong with your figure?" Duncan said gallantly.

"A lot. At least I always think so when Marta comes with me. The boys look at her and fairly swoon."

"Gret, please!" Marta said. Her voice, Duncan noted, was like woodwind: rich and dark-toned.

"I'm still swooning," Wolfgang groaned. "Pour some beer over me, Dunc!"

Duncan picked up the huge stein.

"No you don't!" Wolfgang cried.

"*Was gibt's bei Dir*, Wolfgang?" Marta said. "Are you always so mad?"

"No, sometimes he's crazier," Duncan laughed. "This is one of his sane nights."

"I do not mind," Marta said. "He is amusing. I like that."

"Amusing," Wolfgang wailed. "*Gnädiges Fräulein*, you see before you a man smitten unto death, and you find his death throes —amusing! You are crueller than the Lorelei, Marta dear!"

"I can be kind," she said gravely, "when it pleases me, Wolfgang, and to—people who please me."

"Then may I have the honour of this waltz, Fräulein?" Duncan said. "That is, if I am among the people who please you."

"I should be delighted, Herr Childers," Marta said.

By that time he had learned to waltz very well. That was one of the things you learned in Vienna. To waltz and to hold your beer. He knew the words to all the hits of 1895. He sang them softly, in his deep, rich baritone, not into her ear, but looking upward, as though she were not there. His voice was not extraordinarily bad; and he could carry a tune.

"I must say you sing beautifully, Herr Childers," Marta murmured. "What else do you do?"

"Piano—fairly. No, better than fairly. I play very well. False modesty is stupid. You probably know that you're lovely. But I'm sorry that you are.

She looked at him with startled eyes.

"What a strange thing to say! Why, Herr Childers——"

"Duncan, to you. And I'm going to call you Marta, whether you like it or not. I'm sorry you're so beautiful, because I'm just getting over one unfortunate love affair. I don't want to start another. And I could fall in love with you. Very easily. Too damned easily."

She opened her blue eyes very wide.

"You mean a girl jilted—you?" she said.

"Jilted? Yes, you could call it that. Does this seem strange to you, Marta?"

"It seems incredible. She was a fool, this girl. Was she Amerikanner?"

"Yes."

"Ah, that explains it. They are not very bright, your girls."

"But you would be smarter. You would not jilt me?"

"No. Because I should not permit myself to fall in love with you. I am already engaged, Duncan."

"Oh, damn!" Duncan said succinctly. "Who is he?"

"The Oberleutnant Count Franz von und zu Landsgrave-Hesse. My parents are very pleased. Franz *ist sehr hochgeboren*."

That word again. He had heard it all his life. Or its American equivalent. Very highborn. Was there nothing he could ever do that would make up for his lack—of that?

"But you," he said evenly, "don't love him. Not the slightest bit. I can tell."

The blue eyes darkened.

"No," she said candidly, "I don't suppose I do. But in our position in life, marriages for love don't occur very often. Besides, I like Franz well enough."

"Then hang your position in life, Marta! I'm going to take you away from him!"

She looked out over the swirl of the dancers, her night-smoke lashes veiling her day-blue eyes. She didn't speak for a long time. Then she said: "I shall ask *meinen Vater* to take me with him to Salzburg when he goes next week."

"Lord God, Marta, why?"

"You. You are far too handsome, and forceful, and impetuous. I like you. I like you too much. That could be troublesome. Oh, why did you have to be *ein Ausländer*!"

"Why," Duncan snapped, "do you have to be Austrian? Neither of us were allowed to choose our parents."

She hung back against the circle of his arms, staring at him.

"*Da haben sie recht*, Duncan," she whispered. "You are very right."

The music died with a flourish.

Duncan did not bring Marta to the table. He danced twelve waltzes with her in a row.

"Duncan——" she said, "your family is—rich and distinguished?"

"I have no family. I am an orphan. And I was born in a slum where the rats climbed into bed with me and bit my toes."

"Oh! That is bad. *Mein Vater* would never accept——"

"Hang your Father! Have you also this disease of snobbery, Marta?"

"Yes," she said sadly. "But now I wish I hadn't. Perhaps, if you tried, you could cure me of it. Will you undertake the case, Herr Doctor?"

"Gladly," Duncan said, "if you will promise not to go to Salzburg."

"I shall not go to Salzburg," Marta said. "I don't think I could —now."

Nor did Duncan go to Berlin, as he had planned. He remained in Vienna, using as an excuse his need to catch up in the many basic studies in which Caneville High had left him so sadly deficient. His real reason, of course, was Marta Schlosser. He would have got exactly nowhere without the help of Wolfgang Heimer and

Gretchen Pfeifer. They not only watched from without the curiously difficult effort to breach the very nearly impenetrable walls of the aristocratic Austrian mentality, but, being both of them from families who from 1848 onwards had shed their life's blood in the cause of liberalism and democracy, and hating the nobility with great cordiality, they also took an active hand in furthering matters. Wolfgang, himself highborn, got permission to take Marta out of an evening along with his own fiancée, Gretchen. That was permissible. Since Marta was engaged, even Wolfgang would not have been allowed to take her out alone.

Sometimes, on these occasions, Wolfgang was able to enjoy her company for as long as five whole minutes before Duncan appeared, seized Marta by the arm with a brisk, "Come on, Süskins, let's make tracks!" tossing backwards over his shoulder, as they fled, a laughing "Thanks, Wolf, old boy!"

Later those same nights, Duncan would pour into Wolfgang's ears the painfully detailed story of his progress and his setbacks. The setbacks were many. Marta fought with all her stubborn, aristocratic will the inclination of her heart towards him. She quarrelled with him, insulted him; then begged his pardon very prettily with tears in her great blue eyes. The night, two months after they met, she permitted him to kiss her for the first time, he came home and turned handsprings all over the sitting-room of the flat he shared with Wolfgang.

After Calico, he should have behaved less childishly. The trouble was that he was basically a romantic, and hence unable to achieve a simple transfer of training between these two quite dissimilar events in his life. Later he would achieve it. Later he would learn that women are simply women, with coronets or without them.

Duncan was walking alone before Schönebrunn Castle, a week before the autumn term opened, when he saw Marta coming towards him. She was dressed all in white and balanced a saucy little white lace parasol over her head. Her way of walking was indescribably graceful. But her face was troubled and sad.

"So," Duncan said mockingly, "here we are, three long months later, and you still haven't fled to Salzburg, Marta darling."

"No," she said seriously. "I saw I couldn't. I simply wasn't strong enough to give up seeing you. That was wrong of me."

"Why was it?"

"Because, oh, Duncan, it's terribly wrong! I shouldn't encourage you, give you hopes——"

"Or give yourself hopes, either," Duncan said flatly.

"Or give myself hopes, either," she repeated wistfully. "Father will never, never consent——"

"That bad, eh, Marta?"

"Yes, Duncan," she said, "that bad."

"Then what are we going to do?"

"I don't know. I'd always thought that love would be such a happy thing. Last night—I cried, Duncan. I was dreaming about our wedding—the wedding we'll never have; and I woke up, crying."

"We could run away," Duncan growled.

"No, Duncan. My parents have been wonderfully kind to me. I don't see how I could hurt them the way I would if I ran away with you. Besides, you'd have to give up your career. I'm under age. My father is very close to the Emperor, and he could get the marriage annulled at once. And have you expelled from the country. So we couldn't even live in Vienna while you finished your studies."

"I could finish them in Berlin, Strasbourg, Munich, Leipzig——"

"No, Duncan, I couldn't. There must be some other way."

But there wasn't.

In some ways, Duncan was very practical. During the three full years that *l'affaire Marta* lasted, he did not give up his beer-hall *Mädchen*, his little waitresses of the *Weinstuben*. Since any sort of physical intimacy with Marta was all but impossible, in part because of her scruples, in part because of the lack of any real opportunity, and in very large part because of Duncan's own reluctance to spoil their idyll, he cheerfully made use of his little safety-valves, as he cynically called them. He had, he told himself, completely got rid of the last vestige of bourgeois morality. He was deluding himself. The stern Lutheran code of ethics that his stepfather, Johann Bruder, had instilled in him from his earliest childhood may have been, in Freudian terms—already all the rage in Vienna since it was in that very city that the great psychologist had published his first epochal work only a year or two before—buried deep in his subconscious; but it was, none the less, there. All Wolfgang had to do was to see the melting tenderness in Marta's eyes each time she looked at Duncan to realise that she was very probably incapable of denying him anything whatsoever. But Duncan himself held back. Somewhere deep in the racial memory that goes far beyond the consciousness of any individual there remained for him, unrecognised, unacknowledged, the concept of the pure and spotless virgin bride come to her lord before the altar of the Most High. He loved his Marta with a love that was boundless and deep; which he knew in his heart of hearts was for always.

He was, without knowing it, influenced in his behaviour towards Marta by the disastrous affair with Calico. He had a deep, unexpressed need to differentiate between them. Therefore he treated her as though she were made of delicate Venetian crystal. Marta admitted to herself that she found his consideration excessive. The one way he could have won her did not occur to him until too late: to sweep her off her feet, drag her off to his lair, reduce her (or exalt her?) from pale nymph of the fogs and fens of myth to panting, passionate woman. But, for slum-born Duncan Childers, this princess out of the legends was to be treated with awe. He didn't even remember that he had won her attention in the first place by being his hard, male self.

So Duncan and Wolfgang came to the fifth year of their studies. They both sported full beards, and weary, worldly-wise looks. They had all but forgotten the terror of the first days, as they bent desperately over their first cadaver, their faces green, their entrails revolting within them, counselling each other in hoarse whispers: "Don't faint! Whatever you do, don't faint! You pass out, and by tomorrow you'll be packing to go home!"

They hadn't fainted. They got to the stage where they placed a plate of sandwiches on Otto's forehead—Otto being the name they had christened their cadaver—and ate while they slashed, probed and poked into his noisome insides. They learned to prepare beautifully thin sections of tissue for microscopic examination and to stain them with a variety of dyes. They duplicated Robert Koch's hanging drop cultures of microbes; they learned thousands of words for nerves, bones, blood-vessels, tissue. They played learned games in which one of them would start a single sentence on any one of the pages of the anatomy book, and the other would pick it up in midphrase, completing the entire page verbatim. Once, for a bet, alternating with one another, they recited an entire chapter of Virchow, to the astonished delight of their friends. They waded through pathology, bacteriology—so new then, so excitingly new—hygiene, gynæcology, obstetrics, surgery—all the old and new disciplines with which the world of medicine was so crowded. And, in that flowering of the art of healing during the last days of the nineteenth century, they could never quite catch up. They journeyed to Berlin with a select group of students to watch Wilhelm Conrad Röntgen demonstrate his magic rays that saw through human flesh as though it were not there. They followed the vulgar argument between Ross and Grassi over to which of them was due the honour for the discovery that malaria was mosquito-borne. In the last forty years, because of men like Pasteur and Koch and Metchnikoff and Virchow and Conheim, to name only a few, the sum total of what was known had more than doubled in the field of medicine. And every day the horizons were widening. They would learn a series of facts, undisputed since the time of Galen, and some keen-eyed searcher, peering into his microscope, would throw those same facts into the dust-heap of mythology, or primitive superstition, replacing them with other facts, beautifully simple, clear, and demonstrable. By their fifth year, much of what they had learned in their first year had to be revised. There was no end to it.

And they themselves changed during those years; changed and grew. They found it possible now to get away from medicine during the summers. They spent one entire vacation in Paris, supposedly studying art—a vacation that Duncan was pleased to finance, and Wolfgang brash enough to accept. They painted hundreds of exceedingly bad pictures; and made love to dozens of plump, complaisant little models. They smoked huge black pipes, and discussed life, love, literature and art at the top of their lungs from the heights on Montmartre, till the sun came up over the rooftops of Paris. Duncan wrote daily letters to Marta, sometimes with his latest Marcelle, Yvonne, or Suzette on his arm as he penned his burning lines. Wolfgang also wrote carefully non-committal letters to Gretchen, whom, he now realised, he would never bring himself to marry, having grown far beyond her.

Back in Vienna, at the beginning of their fifth year, Duncan was finding it increasingly difficult to see Marta at all. Someone had seen them together; someone had talked; and now Marta was forbidden to leave the house in the evening at all. They had to snatch minutes together in public places: the Artistic History Museum; the gardens of the Hofburg; the Albertina Museum of Graphic Arts; the Museum of Natural History; the Imperial Museum in the Capuchin Church . . . .

"I," Duncan swore fervently, "will never enter another museum as long as I live—after things straighten themselves out, of course."

But things didn't straighten themselves out. They got worse. Weeks passed without his being able to see Marta at all. He managed to send her notes by Gretchen; but notes were no substitute for having her near him. And Marta missed him as sadly as he missed her. Finally, in desperation, she arranged a rendezvous in the garden of her home. Duncan duplicated the athletic feats of a Renaissance gallant in scaling those high walls. They walked in the garden, hand in hand, and made impossible plans for escape, for an elopement. So preoccupied were they with each other that they had wandered down by the kennels, where Marta had wisely taken the precaution of chaining up her father's fierce Dobermann Pinschers; and the dogs, scenting Duncan's alien presence, made all the night hideous with their barking. Before Duncan could reach the walls again, the gatekeeper was there, his long fowling-piece levelled.

Herr Schlosser came down in nightshirt, monocle and cap. He didn't even shout. He simply said, with icy quiet:

"Heraus mit Ihnen, Ausländer," and took his daughter by the arm.

"Out with you, foreigner," Duncan muttered bitterly, as he walked the dark streets back to the flat. "The one phrase that sums up my life. Where haven't I been an alien and a stranger? Where and with whom?"

And the very next day, bag and baggage, the Schlossers left Vienna. They went to Innsbruck in the Austrian Tyrol, which is about as far as it is possible to go from Vienna and still remain within the borders of the country. Herr Schlosser had an estate there.

Duncan, of course, obtained the address from the Heimers; but in six months not one of his letters was answered. He guessed, correctly, that Herr Schlosser was intercepting them. He tried the expedient of enclosing a note in one of Gretchen's letters; where-upon Professor Pfeifer received the curt command from Herr Schlosser kindly to forbid his daughter to meddle in affairs that were no concern of hers.

Duncan did get, finally, a tear-spotted note from Marta, in which she begged him to forget her. She could not, she declared, for the sake of her own happiness, cause her parents so much pain. She would always remember him; she would for ever be grateful for the joy of having known him; but there was too much between them; too many insurmountable difficulties, which she, for one, had not the strength to overcome.

So Duncan threw himself into his work as an antidote, immersed himself in a round of pleasure as an opiate. Spurred by his example, Wolfgang found himself working even harder than he had that brutal first year. And at the end of the term, Wolfgang stood first in the class, and Duncan second. That summer they went on a bicycle tour of Italy, making sketches of Renaissance buildings, Gothic churches, and Roman ruins. They came back to Vienna as brown as Indians and bursting with life and health.

They needed both, for, that final year, there was no time for

107

anything but work. They subsisted upon two hours' sleep a night, upon sandwiches gulped furiously down while their eyes remained glued to the heavy German tomes propped up against the beer steins. Duncan hadn't even time to grieve over Marta. The work, which had been merely brutal before, became ferocious. They were down to skin and bones, red-eyed, bad-tempered. But they got through it.

On the last day of the examinations they reeled out into the sunlight, delirious with the conviction that they had passed. They had already made their applications to do their internship at the famous Burgholtz Hospital in Berlin. Wolfgang's family's influence would help them there.

As they came out into the street, they found Gretchen Pfeifer waiting for them.

Wolfgang slapped Duncan on the back.

"Well," he said cheerily, in English, "how did it go?"

"Great!" Duncan roared. "God be thanked! I passed. There's not the slightest doubt of that! And you?"

"Rippingly!" Wolfgang crowed.

Then they saw Gretchen's face.

"She's back," Gretchen whispered. "She's to be married in a week to Oberleutnant Count Franz von und zu Landsgrave-Hesse. Oh, Duncan, I——"

"Doesn't matter," Duncan muttered.

"But it does matter! She doesn't love him! She's fairly dying to see you."

"Foul type," Wolfgang said. "Twenty-seven monocles to match his changes of uniform. Sabre scar. Callouses on his heels from clicking them. I tell you, old boy, the creature prob'bly goosesteps in his sleep."

"She—she wants to see me?" Duncan said.

"She sent me here to find you," Gretchen said. "She said that if there were any way at all——"

"I," Wolfgang said, "have a plan that's quite jolly! She and his nibs will prob'bly be at the Biergarten tonight. All the engaged couples go there. We'll all get there early, and take a table on the far side, near the gate. Then I'll ask her for a dance. I'll waltz her over to where you'll be sitting, old boy, where we'll all be sitting, ready to watch the fun. I'll have a *fiacre* waiting at the gate. Ripping, isn't it?"

"I don't know——" Duncan said.

"Oh, for God's sake, take a chance, Duncan," Wolfgang said.

The fires of hope were there now, leaping and blazing in Duncan's dark eyes.

"Damned right!" he said. "It's jolly ripping for fair!"

It went off like clockwork. The Oberleutnant, who looked like something carved out of ice and granite, bowed stiffly at Marta's flustered introduction. When Wolfgang requested the favour of a waltz, he grew stiffer still.

"Oh, just this once, Franz!" Marta begged. "Herr Heimer and I are old, old friends."

Like clockwork. Waltzing through the swirl of dancers at a beat far quicker than the music, Duncan standing up, wordless, drawn, trembling; the dash through the gate.

But there was one small detail that Wolfgang hadn't anticipated: when he came home to the flat at two o'clock in the morning and turned the key in the lock, he found he could not open the door. He pushed against it, hard. It gave a little, and he heard the scrape of the sofa and the two heavy chairs that Duncan had piled against it. He stood there a long moment, staring at that door. Then, very quietly, he turned and went back out into the night.

Two days later the lists were posted. They had both passed with honours. But, seeing Duncan's face, Wolfgang couldn't find it in his heart to rejoice. It wasn't until the day after graduation that he got the story out of him.

"She wouldn't elope with me," Duncan said grimly. "She didn't have what it takes to defy the conventions of her world that far. So I took her to the flat. Piled those things before the door. She sat there watching me do that. She didn't say a word. But when I turned round, she was crying. I'm a fool. I can't stand seeing a woman cry."

Wolfgang stood there, staring at him pityingly.

"So you took her right back down again?" he said.

"No. We talked for hours. She asked me not to dishonour her. Said that she loved me; that she would not, could not resist; but wouldn't I please spare her sacred honour! Name of God, Wolf, in this day and age, she used those exact words! I was out of my ground. I don't know how to manœuvre in my grandfather's times."

"Perhaps," Wolfgang said drily, "those words still have meaning."

"For her, it seems, they do. Then you came. Tried the door. I'd had enough. I took her home—untouched. She kissed me very

109

prettily. Said good-bye with tears in her eyes. And that, my friend, was that!"

"Brace up, old bean, there are other dainty creatures in this world," Wolfgang said.

But that was not quite that. There remained one other thing. That same evening the Oberleutnant's seconds waited upon Duncan Childers. The Count had taken so long to present his challenge because for several days he didn't know exactly whom to fight. After that, more time was spent in investigating whether his proposed opponent's lineage was sufficiently exalted for him to be able to meet him on the field of honour without degrading himself. His investigations turned up exactly nothing, so he decided to chance it. Afterwards he could invent patents of nobility for this *Ausländer*, who would soon be leaving Austria, anyhow, well decorated with the scars the Count meant to inflict upon him.

Duncan was delighted. He chose sabres, fully intending to cut Count von und zu et cetera down to size.

Which was a mistake. Duncan had never had a sabre in his hands in his life, while Oberleutnant Count Franz von und zu Landsgrave-Hesse had had fencing lessons since he was nine years old.

And that, of course, was how Duncan got his romantic, half-moon-shaped scar high on his cheek. The one he never would explain to Hester. Or, for that matter, to anyone else.

A week later, Duncan and Wolfgang entrained for Berlin. There, under the man-killing labour of a big city interneship, Duncan's pain grew dim. The sabre-cut on his face healed within a fortnight. But he was sure the wound within his heart would bleed for ever.

He was wrong. Within two days after his return to Caneville-Sainte Marie, in the spring of 1900, he had almost forgotten that Marta Schlosser existed.

Which was, in some ways, sadder still.

Chapter 8

"You mean to tell me," Hester said, "that this reporter, Baynes, is going to follow you around for weeks, watching everything you do, and asking questions?"

"Yes," Duncan said. "Publicity for Jarvis's Hemstitching Factory, Hes. But Baynes has been damned decent. So far, he hasn't printed a thing I asked him not to."

"Glad of that!" Hester laughed. "You've had one spotted past, haven't you, love! Guess that's what makes such an interesting man. What's he working on now?"

"We're up to my return from Berlin," Duncan said.

"Then he should interview me! That's where I came in, darling. Just in time, too. Dear little Jen in her nurse's cap was all set to grab you. Why, I could tell him——"

"Enough to get me lynched. Only you won't. Because I won't let you, Hes," Duncan said.

The day Duncan Childers, M.D., came home from Germany, Hans Volker gave a party for him. He invited the musical Mullers, all but Fritz, who was off on a concert tour. Father Gaulois. And Jenny Greenway. Jenny wouldn't come. She was afraid that Duncan might think she was throwing herself at his head. Which is precisely what she should have done. It would have saved everyone an awful lot of trouble.

So Duncan went after her. All Hans Volker's guests had arrived before he got back.

"Where is Duncan?" Father Gaulois said.

"He's gone to look for Jenny," Hans Volker said. "I tried to reach her by phone; but it was impossible. There's an awful lot of sickness among the Cajuns this year."

"I know," said Father Gaulois. "And now that Dr. Walter Reed and the Army Medical Board have just about proved it's the mosquito that carries yellow fever, we're going to have a fight on our hands."

"Why so, *Vater?*" Jan Muller said.

"The Bayou Flèche and the swamplands around it will have to be drained, Jan. It's as plain as the nose on your face. There always has been more yellow fever among the trappers than among anyone else. Why? Because they live right on top of the mosquitoes' breeding-places."

"But, *Vater*," Hilda said, "if we drain the swamps, what will those people do for a living? Without the swamps, there will be no musk-rats."

"*Und* no profit for Nelson Vance," Jan said bitterly.

"That is the major problem," Father Gaulois said gravely. "I'm sure that the Cajuns could be absorbed into other industries if people really tried. Mr. Henderson tells me that he could use half the men in his lumber business alone; but they don't apply. They're creatures of habit. And Nelson Vance sees that they have no opportunity to change those habits, by keeping them hopelessly in debt. Actually that's not the way to tackle the problem anyway."

"What do you suggest, Father?" Hans Volker said.

"Much as I am opposed to the idea of using base motives for good," the priest said, "that appears to be our only chance for success. Yellow fever doesn't confine itself to Cajuns. There are three cases of it in town now. If we can convince the citizens of Caneville-Sainte Marie that their own lives and those of their loved ones are endangered by the continued existence of the Bayou and the swamps——"

"*Und* that it won't cost too much," Jan Muller said drily.

"We can get past that," the priest said, "if the threat becomes serious."

"You mean if enough people die, eh, *Vater*," Jan said, "to show them that yellow fever is not really the stranger's disease, as they call it."

"Which heaven forbid," Father Gaulois said, "I'd rather try to get them to see that even strangers have a right to live; that to neglect the most elementary precautions because they believe only chance visitors will die of that neglect is nothing short of criminal, and——"

They heard, at that moment, Duncan's tread upon the veranda. With it, punctuating it, came the staccato click of high heels. Everyone stood up, turned towards the door.

Duncan came in with Jenny Greenway.

"Welcome home, Duncan!" they chorused.

"We're proud of you, my son," Father Gaulois said.

Hilda Muller kissed him. All the men shook his hand.

Duncan looked at them. He was very moved. He did have friends here, after all. Good friends.

"Surprise!" he laughed, to hide the impulse toward tears he felt. "Just look what I found!"

Jenny blushed. She was clad in the spotless white uniform of a nurse. She had the badge R.N. pinned to her shoulder.

"But we knew, Duncan," Hilda Muller said. "It is no surprise that a girl as sweet and smardt as our Jen shouldt became a nurse. What surprises me is——"

"Hilda, you shut up!" Jan Muller said.

"She's been working for Dr. Volker a year and a half—and a half," Duncan said reproachfully, "and none of you ever wrote and told me! That wasn't fair. Little Jen—a graduate, registered nurse. Just what this old burg needed. Doesn't she look grand?"

"I—I wanted to change," Jenny said breathlessly, "but he wouldn't let me. I don't see what's so wonderful about it. If you could become a doctor, Duncan, I reckoned I could put my two cents worth in and——"

"But it *is* wonderful, Jen!" Duncan exulted. "Doc Volker's going to take me into partnership with him, and with you to help us—boy!"

"That is good!" Jan Muller laughed. "A new young doctor to help the old quack! Maybe they taught you in Germany, Duncan, something better than snake-oil for rheumatiz, and roots——"

He stopped short, staring at the door.

Duncan followed his gaze, his brown eyes widening in his thin, freckled face as he stared at the tall, willowy blonde girl who lounged with effortless grace against the door-frame.

He had seen that face before, a thousand times. He had never in life beheld that face. She was not too young, about twenty-seven, he guessed; yet she looked far younger. But her blue eyes were the oldest things in all the world. They had that ancient candour of one who has lived past the need for concealment or deceit; who has gazed upon men as they are, evaluated the importance of pride, pomp, and circumstance and found them hollow; in whom, in fact, the necessity of lying about anything whatsoever has long since gone.

She was lovely. Her loveliness was frightening. *La belle dame sans merci*, he thought; without respect or pity for the world, and especially not for herself. She was smiling at him, her wide, sensual mouth caught up in an expression that had gone beyond even the bitterness of mockery. He had the feeling that she thought he was funny, that she was funny, that all the world was sadly comical. And that she accepted the wry, antic humour of life completely;

that she was free from either the immature vice of hope or the senile futility of regret.

She was utterly unlike any other woman he had ever known. The impact of her presence was almost tactile in the silence—in the abrupt cessation of sound that greeted her coming. He saw Jenny standing behind her, and he was conscious that no comparison could be made between them, that they were opposites in everything. He realised that she was less lovely than Marta had been; that her beauty had a certain tired fragility that set her apart even from Calico, to whom her resemblance was marked, perhaps from the fact that in Callie there had been no surrender of hope.

"I'm sorry," she said, in that slightly husky voice which was the only thing about her that hadn't changed. "I guess I'm intruding. But when I heard that you'd come back, Duncan—I just had to come. I hope you'll forgive me, Doctor Hans."

"Hes!" Duncan got out. "Lord God, Hes, I never would have known you!"

"I'd have known you anywhere, Duncan. You've still got the face of an angelic choirboy, except for that interesting little scar where some girl probably tried to find out if you really were good enough to eat. But then, you've had a good life, I suppose." She came up close to him, ignoring the others as though they were not there. She put up her hands and took his face very quietly between them, so that her long, tapering fingers lay along the slant of his jaw.

"For old time's sake, Duncan," she said easily; and kissed his mouth.

"Well, I never!" Jenny gasped.

"Then you should have, Jenny, darling," Hester drawled. "You don't know what you've been missing."

Sitting in the buggy with Hester, three or four nights later, Duncan was conscious of how long he had journeyed—and how far. He had come back to a world whose apparent sameness was an illusion; in which everything had changed in subtle, almost indefinable ways.

'We die piecemeal,' he thought; 'we perish by inches. Where is that boy—lost, forgotten, no longer I—who kissed the golden-haired child this lovely stranger was then, by the stream's edge in the forest shade? Where is that girl so full of light and love and laughter? Dead, both of them, fled out of time, departed, unmourned, forgotten; while we sit here like dense and solid ghosts, talking of them and of all the lost and lovely days that maybe never were; that I dreamed, perhaps, as I am surely dreaming now. . . .'

But Hester's voice, speaking, broke into his reverie.

"So you see, Duncan," she said, "I'm more or less the town's fallen woman—or I would be if I were not Nelson Vance's daughter. They don't know the true story. In fact, they don't want to know it. Not interesting enough, I guess."

Duncan stretched his arm across the buggy seat and put it around her shoulders.

"I like that," Hester said lazily, "but you shouldn't, you know. Playing with fire, and all that sort of thing. Don't mean to lead you on, old dear."

"Why not?" Duncan said. "Time I lost my boyish laughter, don't you think?"

"As if you hadn't already," Hester laughed. Then her mood changed. "No, Dunc. Let's control the romantic impulses, shall we? At least until we get to know one another better."

"But I've known you all my life!" Duncan said.

"You don't know me at all," Hester drawled. She straightened up, and sat there, staring moodily into the darkness. "I don't even know me," she added drily.

"What do you mean by that, Hes?" Duncan said.

"Simple. I told you my father kept me practically a prisoner for years. He was afraid I might give way to my animal nature. Though, as a matter of fact, all I was guilty of was getting married to a boy I was in love with. It was only about five years ago that Dad started letting me go out again. By then all the good available material was taken. Except Doug Henderson, and he and I have never hit it off; I don't know why. About a year ago I started going out with Stan Bruder, who isn't bad-looking in a sort of ox-like, hangdog way. But Stan fixed that up very nicely. You know the Fontaines?"

"No," Duncan said.

"You'll meet them. Jeff Fontaine is one of Doctor Hans's patients. Poor dear, he's the sweetest, nicest man. Paralysed from the waist down. He caught infantile paralysis while fishing, about three years back. So dear Abigail, his not too blushing bride, started getting restless. It seems the paralysis extends to Jeff's manly functions—do I shock you, darling? I remember I always used to."

"I'm shockproof," Duncan grinned. "Go on."

"So it settled down to a race between the town's two champion stallions—or so they fancy themselves, at least: my somewhat less than angelic brother Jim, and my beloved Stan."

"And Stan came home first?" Duncan said.

"Right. But then Jim was handicapped by a wife and a child; while Stan had only me. Not much of a handicap. Then he started flaunting her about town and lost even that poor handicap. I threw in the towel. Quit."

"In a wild and jealous rage?" Duncan mocked.

"My pride was hurt," Hester said gravely. "I've never considered Abbie Fontaine anything very much. But I really didn't care about Stan's playing footsie, or, more accurately, bedsie, with her. I would have married Stan long ago—I was lonesome enough to marry Bluebeard—but for a certain squeamish reluctance to undertake my wifely duties with such a lout. The case actually did my reputation no end of good. Furnished proof to all and sundry that I wasn't letting Stan into——"

"Hester, for God's sake!" Duncan said.

"Sorry. Musn't shock you, must I?" Hester drawled. "Let's see, what's a nice homey synonym for unlawful carnal knowledge? That I wasn't letting Stan have his boyish sport of me. All right?"

"It'll have to do," Duncan groaned.

She turned to him, her eyes glowing.

"I'm glad you came back, Duncan," she said. "I was beginning to despair...."

"Of what?" Duncan said.

"Of ever seeing you again. So many years, darling."

"Too many," Duncan said. "I'd given up. I was sure you'd be married. I never did hear anything about you. Jenny used to write me every week, but——"

Hester threw back her head and laughed aloud.

"Dear Jen," she said. "Dear, dear Jen! You don't really think she merely forgot to tell you about me, do you?"

"Why not?"

"Because Jen's no fool. Why should she remind you of me? You might have got to thinking of me and that wouldn't have helped her hopes . . . Tell me the truth, darling: how did you get that scar?"

"You told it the other day, Hes. A girl bit me. About Jen——"

"Let's drop the subject of Jen, shall we, darling? What were we talking about before I got so far afield?"

"You were saying that I didn't know you. And that you didn't know yourself."

"Yes. That's so. You, Dunc, the other day when I came barging into Hans Volker's house, and kissed you like a shameless hussy right in front of everybody—you seemed to me absolutely the most terrifically attractive male creature on the face of creation. But after I'd gone home again and got a chance to think——"

"You changed your mind?"

"No. You've always been terribly attractive. And I've been more or less in love with you all my life—with time out, of course, for Gino. I just wondered how much of that gone-in-the-middle, weak-as-water feeling I got seeing you, was due to the way I've had to live."

"Your father started letting you go out again quite a while ago," Duncan said drily.

"I know. After he became convinced that I hadn't the slightest interest in the local yokels—and that I was unlikely to make a fool of myself with some man socially unfit to be my husband. Perhaps even after he began to get afraid that he was going to be stuck with an old maid daughter on his hands."

"You're not old," Duncan said.

"I'm twenty-nine. That, you know, is positively ancient for a girl not to have caught herself a meal-ticket in this benighted part of the world. Of the class of eighty-eight, only Jen Greenway and I aren't married—and possibly for the same reason——"

"And what was that?" Duncan demanded.

"We were waiting for you," Hester said.

Duncan tightened his arm about her shoulder.

"No, Duncan," she said quietly.

"Why not?" he growled.

"I don't want to start playing post-office with you, right off. Neither childishly, nor grown-up style. I don't want to drag you into anything you'd regret. I'm awf'ly fond of you. I may even be in love with you all over again, for all I know. But I'm not sure I'm suited for you. I don't know if I'd make you a good wife, the kind you deserve—Lord God, but I'm being brazen, aren't I?"

"Brazen, how?"

"All this talk about wives and husbands as if I were sure you wanted to marry me. Perhaps you've other ideas. Maybe you're all set to reward dear Jenny for her years of patient waiting, even for her being smart enough to train herself to be your partner."

"Jen's nice," Duncan said, "but somehow I can't see her——"

"Occupying the other pillow? A pity. You should. She is suited for you. She's good as gold, sweet, kind, intelligent—everything that I'm not."

"What are you doing, Hes? That feminine trick of damning with faint praise is pretty ancient."

"You, love, are much too smart to be a man. But I wasn't being

117

snide about Jen. I called myself being honest. I don't suppose that after bursting into your party and hurling myself into your arms I have any right to ask you what you really have on your mind as far as I'm concerned. Still, I'd like to know. Were you planning a week-end trip to New Orleans, where we'd register in a side-street hotel under assumed names?"

"And if I were?" Duncan said.

"I'd go with you, of course. Even knowing it would be a fool trick because you'd despise me afterwards. Men always do. Is that all you want of me, Duncan?"

"No," he said. "I think you've grown up to be something pretty fine, Hes, and I——"

She put her fingers across his mouth.

"Don't say it!" she said sharply, "or I'll always think I dragged it out of you. No, darling. You've got your practice to build up. Or, better still, Dad could get you a job in New Orleans at Rose-briar Clinic. You know, Dad and Ernest Harvey and a few other wealthy men actually built it. So Jarvis—Dr. Jarvis Phelton—couldn't very well refuse you, if Dad asked him. Besides, knowing Jarvis, I'd say he'd be delighted to have a Vienna-trained surgeon on his staff. Would you like that, darling?"

Duncan stared out into the darkness.

"I don't know, Hester," he said slowly. "A few years ago, before Uncle Martin died, I'd have jumped at the chance. Medicine seemed to me a rather respectable way of making money. But seeing him die like that—so horribly, it came to me that maybe what doctors are for is to cure the sick. Still——"

"Still, it would speed things up enormously. There your practice would be ready-made—and rich. Not that I care, darling; but we are going to have to get over father's objections—if we do decide to put on double harness. And if you can show him that you can support me in the style to which I am accustomed. . . ."

"I see. Tell him to write Doctor Phelton, then, Hes, if you please. Because speeding things up is damned well what I'm after!"

"Wait, Duncan," she said quietly. "I want to make one thing abundantly clear. All you'll be speeding up will be the practical side, making our marriage possible—even probable. But I'm not saying I'll marry you, even so."

He stared at her.

"Lord God, Hes," he said, "why not?"

"Not because I don't want you. My mouth hurts now from the strain of not kissing you all evening. And having been, temporarily, a bride once before, I know a few other things, too. If you got started in—that way, I'd probably resist five minutes. No, three. Which is why I don't want you to start. I want to know it's something else beside the fact that I was born so damned female. So off with you to New Orleans, my love! Come back to see me whenever you can. I'll come down there properly chaperoned, of course, to visit you. In a year, say, we'll get to know each other again, learn each other's ways well enough to know whether we should part with regret or make the outrageously indecent impulses just being near you gives me both legal and proper. I've made one bad mistake in my life. I don't want to make another. And I don't want you to, either."

He sat there, looking at her, seeing her slim, golden, achingly lovely in the moonlight. He saw the poise she had acquired, the very real dignity, the almost painful honesty. He was very sure, suddenly.

"No, Hes, it won't be a mistake," he said.

. . . . .

"Like old times, eh, boy?" Hans Volker said.

"Well, not quite," Duncan smiled. "In the old days I wouldn't have understood one half of what you were doing. Now I do, practically all of it."

"And even wonder why I continue to follow such outmoded and obsolescent practices, eh, son?"

"Frankly, yes—some of them, at least. Those pills you gave old Miss Pritchard for her sick headaches—they weren't aspirins, and, as far as I know, there isn't anything——"

"Perfectly right. They're dried bread-crumbs with a sugar coating. Damned most effective pills I have, for some cases."

"You mean?"

"That Milly Pritchard's a hypochondriac. There's nothing wrong with her. Or rather, everything's wrong with her. What she's got, it's far too late to cure."

"And what has she, Doctor?"

"Loneliness. Disillusionment. An empty life. The effective cure for that she should have arranged for herself thirty years ago: a good, lusty husband and six kids. So now it's my placebo pills. Milly believes in them implicitly—so they work, as long as I don't make a mistake and give her the wrong colour."

"Well, I'll be damned!" Duncan said helplessly.

"You'll learn," Doctor Volker chuckled. "Nine-tenths of local medicine consists in treating the patient, not the disease. Most of their illnesses are imaginary, anyhow. You get so you welcome a clear-cut sickness—as long as it's a thing you can cure. But, damn it all, when they do get sick it's things like yellow fever, cancer and late syphilis—awful lot of paresis hereabouts, some families have been congenital syphilitics for generations. Sometimes I feel like giving up. There are so many things we can't cure."

"We can prevent a heck of a lot of things," Duncan said.

"Sure we can: malaria, yellow fever, syphilis, rabies, smallpox, cholera. But we haven't learned to prevent human nature yet; and, until we do, all our bright new scientific knowledge is danged nigh useless."

"What do you mean?" Duncan said.

"You tell a Cajun trapper you're going to drain the marshes to get rid of the mosquitoes that carry malaria and yellow fever, and what does he answer? '*Mon dieu*, Docteur! How'm I gonna feed my kids, me, if you dry up the musk-rat's breeding grounds?' You tell an old sport like Jim Vance or Stan Bruder that if he keeps on frequenting whores he'll sure as hell get syph, and he laughs. The soft chancre goes away, and he feels fine for five or six years. By the time locomotor ataxia or paresis or an aortic aneurysm sets in, it's too late. Tell him to come in for a prompt treatment of gonorrhoea, and he snorts: 'Hell, Doc, clap ain't no worse than a bad cold!' So the babies keep right on being born blind, and wives keep right on going sterile. We know a hell of a lot, all right, Duncan; but what's beyond us is to get people to follow what we know. That's why I'd like to find out how to cure those things. It would be out of their hands then. Look, boy, ever since Semmelweis we've known that the way to prevent puerperal fever consists of one of the simplest methods in the world: asepsis in obstetrics, nothing more than absolute cleanliness; but the same old childbed fever is still the number-one killer of young mothers in this parish—because the Cajuns prefer their filthy *sages-femmes*, and the farmers their country midwives, to a doctor. Can't blame 'em. Day before yesterday, Thompson argued like blazes that all this germ theory business is nonsense. Three hundred years after Leeuwenhoek, forty years after Pasteur's first discoveries, thirty-odd after Koch's, and there are doctors—doctors, mind you!—who still don't believe that microbes cause disease!"

"I didn't realise that people were so stupid," Duncan said.

"You'll learn, boy," Hans Volker growled, "that the two absolutely invincible forces in this world are ignorance and stupidity. We never win more than a partial victory over them. What we need in this parish is a good psychiatrist to cure them of what's eating them inside, and a medical commissioner with completely dictatorial powers to damn well make them do what they ought to do. A five-dollar fine for each unscreened window in a house would cut the incidence of yellow fever seventy per cent in two years. Or a murder trial for Nelson Vance every time a trapper's kid died of it. That might get some action."

"Or maybe a couple of sticks of dynamite at the place where the landslide blocked the Bayou Flèche from running off into Merry Creek, eh, Doctor?" Duncan said.

"So you've thought of that, too?" Hans Volker said. "We ought to do it one dark night, you and I. I've even suggested it to the City Fathers. But they're too scared of Nelson Vance. Got the colossal gall to argue that we still aren't sure it's mosquitoes that carry it—and this with Havana without one case of yellow fever for the first time in one hundred years! No, that way we can't win. We have to make slashing raids around the perimeter, instead of a frontal assault. And for that, thank God, I'll have you—and Mose."

"Good Lord, yes! How's he doing, Doctor?"

"Just fine. Graduated near the top of his class. He's learned to talk almost like a white man; and he eats and sleeps medicine. He's interning now, down in Tuskegee, Alabama. He would have finished before, but he didn't want to take money from me if he could avoid it. Played in a coloured dance band in the summers to help out. His last two years, I didn't have to send him a cent."

"Mose," Duncan said, "is one of nature's noblemen. That's a platitude; but platitudes are sometimes true. I'll be glad to see him."

"And I," Hans Volker said.

"Where do we go now, Doctor?"

"The Hendersons. I've got to look in on the old man. Not long for this world, poor old fellow. He's had one stroke already."

He paused, looking at Duncan.

"Tell me, boy," he said bluntly, "what are you going to do about —Jen?"

"Nothing," Duncan said. "I'm going to marry Hester Vance."

Dr. Volker stared at him. The old man's face was slack with—shock. Then it tightened. Became hard.

"You'll be making a damnfool mistake if you do," he said.

Duncan met his eyes. The silence played itself out, fathoms deep.

"What do you mean by that, Doctor Hans?" Duncan said.

"Well——" Hans Volker hesitated, "wasn't there some talk, ten or twelve years ago?"

"Twelve. Hester eloped with the son of a rich Italian contractor in Saint Louis. Her aunt had the marriage annulled because she was too young. A fool kid's trick. There hasn't been any talk since, and that's what matters."

Hans Volker was still looking at him. What was in his eyes was a mixture of anger and—pity.

"But," Duncan went on evenly, "that's not what was on your mind, Doctor Hans. So—there was something else?"

"I didn't say that, boy," Hans Volker growled.

"You implied it. Aren't you going to tell me why you think I'd be making a mistake?"

"No," Hans Volker said.

"Why not?"

"Because I can't," the old doctor said; then he lifted his white-maned head like a tired old lion, and roared: "Marry her, damn it! But don't say I didn't warn you!"

"'Or else hereafter for ever hold his peace,'" Duncan quoted, smiling. "Come off it, Doc. I'm perfectly capable of beating her when she needs it. Don't be cross with me on our first calls together."

"Oh, all right," Dr. Volker rumbled, then he laid his hand on Duncan's arm. "Forgive an interfering old fool, won't you, boy? It might work out all right. I doubt it; but it might."

They rode towards the Henderson place. Dr. Volker went on talking. He seemed to find relief in having someone to talk to, someone who now, at last, really spoke his language, understood fully the problems confronting a man of science in the backward, culturally starved area of the Twin Towns.

"Too many children," he grumbled. "One every blasted year until a fallen uterus, senility, or death stops 'em. Try to teach them a little birth control, and Father Gaulois is down on your head like a ton of bricks. I asked him: 'Look, Father, which is the greater sin: stopping a child from being conceived'—I don't hold with abortion; I agree with him that it's murder, as well as highly dangerous to the woman involved, herself, 'just preventing conception from taking place, since there's no life until it does—or letting him be born to hunger, poverty, disease, and the inevitable incentives to crime and vice such a life offers?' But he's got all the answers, right out of the book: 'No man has any right to interfere with the will of God.'"

"No man," Duncan said drily, "has any right to assume he knows the will of God, or that his particular book is the right one."

Hans Volker stared at him.

"Damned if I ever thought of that line of attack," he said. "I'll spring it on him the next time."

"Don't," Duncan said. "It won't do any good. To my mind, the religious man is not so much irrational as anti-rational. He hates logic. Tackle him with that weapon, and you don't even dent his armour. He serenely assumes you're a fool. He may be right. What's so bloody rational about the world we live in? Lord God! Who—or what—is that?"

"Abbie Fontaine," Hans Volker said drily; "one of our two potential sources of some damned bad trouble. Or she would be, if Jeff weren't paralysed."

"She looks like she invented sex," Duncan said, "and still holds the original patent."

"She damned near did," Hans chuckled. "Well, here she comes. You got your chastity belt fastened down tight?"

She came towards them, smiling. She was dressed in a summer frock; but she looked naked. Naked and proud of it. Duncan had the feeling that the frock was an optical illusion. Any moment now, he thought, it's going to disappear!

Her hair was auburn. Her eyes were the lambent yellow of the great cats. She walked like them, too, sinuously, the motion flowing. Her mouth was the raw wound of passion. But the pain of it wasn't in her face. It was in the tangled guts of the man looking at her.

"Hi, Doc!" she said in a clear, moronic soprano. "How's tricks?"

There was a long, long pause while the air between her and Duncan Childers went smoky, seethed; then she murmured: "Just who is this beautiful, beautiful man?"

"I told you!" Hans Volker laughed. Then he said: "This, Abbie, is Dr. Duncan Childers, my new assistant. Who knows damned well you're married. I told him. Who is safely engaged. And who, unlike a couple of other retrogressions to apehood I could mention, is not a goatish swine."

Duncan threw back his head and roared.

"I've heard some mixed metaphors in my time," he said, "but that one ties it! Got in damned near the whole animal kingdom, didn't you, Doc?"

"Except Abbie," Hans said. "She's a new species. A fire-bird, say. Touch her, and you get burnt. Well, Abbie, are you going to be a good girl, and go home?"

"No," she said brightly. "I want him. Give him to me."

"No, thank you, Abbie," Duncan said. "At the risk of seeming ungallant, I must decline. I want to live a long time."

"You're mean!" Abbie said. " 'Bye, now!"

Then she went on down the road.

123

"Is she a mental case?" Duncan said. "She sounded like one."

"Hell, no! Abbie's as smart as a whip. That's an act. She calls herself being girlish and cute. And she's thirty-two. But it must work—at least with idiots. She's kept Stan Bruder on her string for over a year now."

The Henderson place was about two miles out of town, but on the other side. They had to go back through Caneville to get to it. The streets were crowded. People passed, greeted them, staring at Duncan with the frank curiosity of the small-town dweller.

"There'll be many a filly setting her cap at you, now that you're a doctor," Hans said. "Whatever their background, doctors are always respectable. And Abbie's right: you're damned good-looking——"

"Thanks, Doc!" Duncan gibed. "You're pretty, too!"

"Don't be flippant, damn it! I'm serious. I'd like to see you wed as soon as possible. Provides protection. But not, I must confess, to Hester Vance. I'd hoped that you and Jen——"

"No soap, Doc," Duncan said. "Jenny's—well—too sisterly to suit me."

Hans Volker turned and looked at him. A long time.

"Sisterly!" he exploded. "How big a fool can a body be!"

"Fair to middling big," Duncan grinned. "Now I've seen everything! There are witches; there really are!"

The ancient crone coming towards them was, truly, a sight to see. She was black—not that rich nightshade, velvety blackness having its own sable beauty, often found in people of her race—but grey-like, shading off into a cadaver-like purplish tinge about the lips. Her face was a mass of wrinkles; she seemed immensely old. Yet she did not shuffle, or hunch her back; but strode up-right like a woman half her age. And somehow, unaccountably, Duncan had the feeling that evil moved with her, emanated from her, just barely invisible, not quite tactile, but there, surely there.

Doctor Volker looked at the old negress, and his face purpled with fury. His hands on the reins shook visibly.

"I don't believe in lynching," he grated, "but if they ever string that old black bitch up, I'll pull the rope!"

Duncan stared at him. This wasn't like Doctor Hans. Not the Doctor Hans all the negroes in the parish brought their illnesses to—even their troubles. Not like the man who had sent gingercake-coloured Moses Johnson to college at his own expense.

"Howdy, Doc!" the old woman cackled with serene insolence. "Been snatching any babies lately?"

Hans Volker sat there. He didn't say anything. But the veins at his temple swelled and beat visibly with his blood.

Duncan stared at him. He had never seen Hans Volker like this before.

"I'll see you hanged yet, Charity!" the old Doctor snapped, and brought the whip down across the horse's back. The buggy moved off with a jerk.

"Why do you want her hanged, Dr. Hans?" Duncan said. "Didn't think you had anything against black folks."

"It's not Charity Mance's hide I object to," Hans Volker said; "it's the colour of her evil heart!"

"Same question, Doctor," Duncan said. "Why?"

"Something I suspect her of. Suspect, hell! Something I know damned well she's doing, but can't prove. Don't ask me what it is. I won't tell you. Especially not you—now."

Duncan opened his mouth to protest. Then he saw Hans Volker's eyes. He closed his mouth again. Kept it shut.

They moved on out of town. The crowds of Saturday shoppers thinned out, disappeared. It was very peaceful. But there was a brooding tension underneath that peace that ran along Duncan's nerves like a galvanic current. For the life of him he could not tell why. But the feeling was there. Very definitely there. He tried to shake it off. He couldn't. Time seemed to be waiting. For what?

Dr. Volker touched Duncan's arm.

"Remember I said *two* potential sources of trouble?" he growled. "Well, here comes the second one. The Willis boy. Dick!" he called out. "Oh, Dick, wait a minute, will you?"

But Dick Willis plunged past them without answering, his head down, walking very fast, grim purpose in his every stride.

"I say, what's eating him?" Duncan said.

"Got wife trouble. Married that flighty Meg Clouter; and, of course, God's gift to womankind, Jim Vance, is rallying round in his absence. Everybody in town knows it except Dick—and, from the way he looks right now, I'd give you odds that somebody's finally told him."

"You mean Jim's still carrying on? Lord God, he must be damned near forty!"

"Which isn't old, son. Besides, age doesn't cure that particular itch; at least not as quickly as most folks think. Thought for a while Jim was going to settle down. He married that sweet little Rosemary McCullen, about three years back. They've got a baby daughter, who's a pure treasure. But not even that stopped Jim Vance."

"What," Duncan said, "do you think is going to happen now?"

"Blessed if I know. But you can bet your bottom dollar it won't be good," Hans Volker said.

They came upon the porch of the Hendersons' home. Doug, who had been sitting in a rocking-chair, his sock-clad feet propped up on the banisters, jumped up at once.

"Dunc!" he roared. "Dunc! Good God, boy, it's great to see you! Lord, you look fine! Got sawbones written all over you! Put her there!"

Duncan took his outstretched hand. Afterwards he looked at his fingers to see if the bones had been crushed.

"Been a baldheaded coon's age, ain't it, boy?" Doug said. "Tell me, did them foreign fillies treat you good?"

"Just great, Doug," Duncan laughed. Doug hadn't changed. He was still his old, warm, cheerful self.

"Jen's with your father, I suppose?" Hans Volker said.

"Yep," Doug said happily. "Great lil' girl, Jen. Been trying to get her to take my case on a permanent basis. So far, no soap."

"Keep after her, boy," Duncan said. "She's worth it."

He wondered why the thought of Doug's marrying Jen was painful to him. But it was. It very definitely was.

"And while we're on the subject of balls and chains," he added slowly, "you can offer me your sympathies, Doug. Hester said 'Yes' last night."

"Great!" Doug cried. "Shake on it!"

Again Duncan suffered that bone-crushing grip.

"Jen!" Doug bellowed. "Come out here, honey! I got news for you! Great news!"

"Do you have to make so damned much noise, boy?" Hans Volker growled. "Scaring your old man out of his wits won't help his condition at all."

"Gosh, Doc, I forgot," Douglass said contritely.

The screen door opened. Jenny stood in it. She didn't have her glasses on, and the way she looked then, at that moment, brought Duncan's heart to his throat; then it dropped to the pit of his stomach.

'Hell of a reaction for a newly engaged man,' his mind said.

" 'Lo—Jen," Duncan said.

"Hello, Duncan," Jenny whispered. She already knew about those buggy rides. In Caneville everybody knew everything.

"Congratulate him, honey!" Doug said with malicious glee. "Dunc 'n Hester are going to jump over the broomstick!"

'Not like this!' Duncan thought miserably. 'I didn't mean to have it flung in your face like this with no preliminaries, nothing to soften it.'

She looked at him a long, heart-stopping time.

'Sure you know what you're doing, buddy boy?' his mind said.

"Aren't you going to say anything, honey?" Doug said plaintively.

"Yes." Jen's voice was clear now, beautifully controlled. "My congratulations, Duncan. And, believe me, my heart goes with them, too."

She turned to Doctor Volker.

"Your patient is ready, Doctor," she said calmly. "Will you come in now, please?"

"Coming, Duncan?" Hans Volker said.

"If you don't mind, Doctor, no," Duncan said. "I'll just sit here and chew the fat with Doug a while."

"That was an awful funny thing to say," Doug growled, after Jenny and Dr. Volker had gone into the house. "'My heart goes with them too . . .' Now what the devil did she mean by that?"

"Just a way of putting it," Duncan said. "Like: 'With all my heart,' but fancier. Women just love to twist words around."

They sat on the veranda and talked. Duncan answered all Doug's questions about life in Europe with a casualness that gave no hint of the raw nerve ends that jangled inside him.

Then Jenny came out of the house with Hans Volker. She stood there looking at Duncan in perfect silence.

Duncan hoped that Doctor Volker would leave at once and take him away from there. But the old man sank with tired contentment into a chair.

"He's no better—nor worse," he rumbled. "I give him four to six months. If you kids are really thinking about getting hitched, you'd better do it now, or you'll have a funeral and a period of mourning to stop you. Sorry, but that's the way it is."

"Reckon we'd better, at that," Doug said, looking at Jenny with hopeful eyes. "What do you say, Jen-baby?"

"No, Doug," Jenny whispered. "I'm sorry, but—no. Nothing has happened to make me change my mind. Nothing could. Except, maybe, one thing——"

"Damned if you aren't in the queerest mood!" Doug exploded. "What could change your mind, then?"

"Nothing," Jenny said, "nothing in this life."

"Lord God! What's going on down there?" Dr. Volker said.

Duncan moved to the edge of the porch. He was profoundly

grateful for this interruption of a conversation that was twisting into dangerous ways. Doug came over and stood beside him. All four of them looked down the road to where a dust-cloud boiled furiously towards them, punctuated by whipcracks and shouting.

"That," Doug declared, "is old Nelson Vance. Nobody else could bellow so much like a bull, but him."

"Doc," Duncan said, "you remember—Dick Willis?"

"Lord, yes! Come on, Duncan! Bet you my bottom dollar that——"

Jenny came erect, crisp, starched, all nurse.

"I'll be at the office if you need me, Doctor," she said.

The three of them started for Hans Volker's buggy; but Jenny picked up her bag and went to her own little rig, behind the house. Napoleon, the doctor's ancient horse, was not distinguished for his speed. An ambling trot was all they were able to whip out of him.

Nelson Vance's sleek greys were fast enough. They came pounding up the road at a hard gallop, manes and tails flying, foam-covered, their eyes rolling red.

The shouting came clear:

"Doc! Lord God, Doc! Anybody seen Doc Volker?"

Nelson Vance stood up in the light wagon, his thick legs braced, his whip whining and cracking against the team's flanks, his gross body bouncing like some Plutonian charioteer out of Hades itself.

He nearly crashed into the buggy with his team. Old as he was, he jerked the big greys almost back on their haunches so that they thrashed against the wagon shaft, pawing the air wildly.

"Doc!" he roared. "Get down from behind that bag o' bones and come with me! My boy's dying! That rat-bastid Willis——"

Duncan and Douglass were already down, reaching up their arms for Doctor Volker. All three of them piled into Nelson Vance's wagon. The old man yanked his team round, sawing cruelly at the bits, and they were off, thundering back down the road towards town.

"Stabbed him!" Nelson Vance bellowed. "Came into the house without saying a word—just afore dinner. Everybody was there: Rosemary, Hester, lil' Ruth——"

"Where's the wound?" Doctor Volker shouted.

"Chest—left side. Can't be the heart, though, 'cause Jim was still mighty strong when I left! Jesus, Doc——"

"What happened to Dick?" Doug cried.

"Don't know! Run out o' there, 'fore anybody could—Goddamn you nags! Get the lead out o' your tails, and move!"

There was a crowd in front of the Vance mansion. Nelson Vance scattered them by the simple expedient of driving his team through them at a gallop. The four of them rushed into the house. Everything looked strange to Duncan. Unfamiliar. Then he remembered that this was the first time he had ever entered it.

Jim Vance was stretched out on the sofa, his face white, his breathing laboured. Hester bent over him, trying to stanch the flow of blood with an endless series of towels. Rosemary Vance lay in the corner of the room in a dead faint. Beside her, little Ruth shrieked, unnoticed.

Hester stood up, moved away. Doctor Volker bent over Jim, placing his stethoscope as close as he could to the gaping wound. Hester stared at Duncan, her face white, working. Doctor Volker straightened up with a sigh.

"Sorry, Mr. Vance," he said tiredly.

"Lord, Doc!" Nelson bellowed. "You don't mean he's gonna——"

"Yes. Heart. Right ventricle. There's absolutely no hope."

"Doctor," Duncan said crisply, "may I have a word with you, please?"

"Look, son," Doctor Volker said angrily, "there's nothing——"

But Duncan bent and took a roll of cottonwool out of Dr. Volker's bag. He handed it to Hester.

"Here," he said, "take this cottonwool, Hes, and pack the wound. We'll only be a minute."

Firmly he took the old doctor by the arm.

"Come on out on the porch, Doctor," he said.

"All right, Duncan," Doctor Volker said, once they were outside; "don't give me a lecture about some new-fangled technique! Jim's a goner. A stab wound to the heart——"

"No new technique, Doctor," Duncan said quietly. "What would you do if that stab was in the thigh, say?"

"Suture it, of course! Of all the fool——"

"Wait. The heart's the toughest organ in the body, Doc. You know that. It's the only thing that never rests. So let's go in there and sew it up. The right ventricle can be sutured. Doctor Gido Farina did it first in '96, just four years ago."

"What happened to the patient?" Hans Volker snapped.

"He died—but of pneumonia, four days later. Wait! Don't interrupt me, Doctor! Dr. Louis Rehn, of Frankfort, did it again the same year, and the man lived. Since then Dr. Rehn has performed the same operation three more times—always successfully. He was invited to lecture on his technique at Vienna. While he was there, they brought in a train-wreck victim—piece of wood through all three layers, endocardium, pericardium, and myocardium. He removed it, stitched up the wound, and that man was still alive when I left Vienna. I assisted at the operation, Doctor. It wasn't even spectacular. Just an ordinary purse-string suture that any jack-leg can do."

Doctor Volker was staring at him.

"Lord God, boy," he whispered, "I can't do it. I'm just not that good a surgeon. And if you try it, and fail, even though you have passed the State board, you know what'll happen?"

"Yes. I'll be charged with criminal malpractice. But if I don't I'll be guilty of homicide by neglect, in my own eyes. Will you back me, Doctor?"

Doctor Volker straightened up proudly.

"Goddamn it, you're a doctor, son!" he said. "I'm with you, all the way!"

"Good. Now call Doug for me. We'll have to give Jim a transfusion. Phone Jen to hop over here prepared to work. Tell her to bring a few cans of ether, and every damned instrument you've got in the place."

"And all we can borrow from every sawbones in town," Hans Volker growled. "We'll need rib-shears, retractors, spreaders—thank God Harris does chest surgery, so he'll have all those things——"

"Maybe we'd better get him to do it," Duncan said.

"Wouldn't touch it. Never take the risk. He'll lend us his instruments, though. Want him to assist? He'll do that."

"No," Duncan said firmly. "I want you, Doctor Volker."

"Harris is younger," Hans protested; "and he's done chest surgery, while I——"

"Have never cut into the chest cavity, placed hæmostats, mopped blood and so forth in your life, eh, Doc? Pure bull. How about the time you cleaned those rib splinters out of Paul Bleaker's lungs? You can do the job and I won't let you get out of it. Come on, Doc!"

"All right, then," Hans Volker whispered; then, his voice strengthening, filling with pride: "Let's get moving, boy!"

In the bathroom, scrubbing up for the operation, Duncan went over the steps in his mind. He was particularly worried about the transfusion. He knew that many a patient had unaccountably died after receiving the blood of a perfectly healthy donor. The thing was a mystery. Blood was blood, and yet——

It would be two years later before that particular mystery would be cleared up by Karl Landsteiner's discovery of the four blood groups and their combinations; and forty more years before the same physician and his assistant, Weiner, would demonstrate the elusive Rh factor which caused so many fatal transfusion accidents in supposedly compatible blood types, as well as the tragic abortion- and still-birth-producing *erythroblastosis foetalis*. But in 1900 these things were not known. A transfusion was a gamble with the patient's life. Yet, in this case, the gamble would have to be taken. Jim Vance would die without the transfusion. With it, he might live.

'I must not hurry,' he told himself. 'Rehn's first case underwent surgery a full thirty-six hours after being stabbed. The bleeding's already slowing down and——'

"Duncan——" Hester whispered.

He turned.

"Yes, Hes?" he said.

"You can do it! I just know you can! Jim's no good at all; but he's my brother, Duncan. You save his life and I'll——"

"No," he said angrily, "no promises, Hester! I'm a doctor. I swore my most solemn oath to always do what I can to save lives —and not for any rewards, nor anybody's gratitude. Not even yours."

He backed away from the sink, his hands and arms red from the scrubbing, dripping the hot water on to the floor. Hester handed him a towel.

"No!" he roared. "It's not sterile, Hes! I can't touch anything, not anything at all! You go see whether Jen's got the instruments sterilised yet."

"I can see," Hester said with a wry smile, "that as a doctor's wife I'll be a number-one dud. All right, love, I'll do just what you say."

He and Hans Volker stood in silence while Jenny buttoned them into their white gowns and adjusted their caps. They wore no masks. It would be several more years before that refinement would be introduced. Doug was stretched out on a cot beside the sofa, waiting. He was almost as pale as Jim Vance.

The transfusion went off without a hitch. Dr. Volker performed it with the sureness of long practice. Duncan could see the colour stealing back into Jim's face. All his life he had hated this man. Jim Vance was a blackguard, an adulterous scoundrel. But that wasn't important any more. He was just a human being now— and at death's door. That was all that mattered.

Rosemary and the child had been removed to another room.

Hester and her father sat in the hall, listening through the closed door.

"That does it," Duncan said. "Thanks, Doug. You go lie down somewhere. If you're going to faint, have the goodness to do it after you get out of here!"

"You ol' bastard!" Doug chuckled. "Can't I stay and watch? I've seen an awful lot of hog-butchering in my day."

"Get out of here, Doug!" Hans Volker growled.

Jenny was very pale as she poured the ether over the gauze cone covering Jim Vance's mouth and nose. She had witnessed and assisted in her share of major operations during her training at Massachusetts General. But Duncan was going to do this one. Her professional impersonality all but deserted her. She watched as Hans Volker mopped the area around the wound.

"Scalpel!" Duncan barked. She jumped, so that she almost dropped the knife. She placed the handle timidly into Duncan's rubbed-gloved hand.

"Harder, next time, Nurse!" Duncan snapped. "Slap it into my palm. I like to feel it's there."

"Yes, Doctor," Jenny whispered.

The thin red stripe, vertically crossing the wound. Hans Volker mopped it feverishly.

"Forceps!"

The crisp slap of the metal against the rubber glove.

Deeper. The red, striated muscular coat showed. He cut into it. A small artery spurted.

"Clamps!" Hans Volker's voice now, speaking with authority.

Jenny passed him the hæmostats. He clamped the blood-vessels one by one as soon as Duncan had cut through them. The old doctor had forgotten his fear, his hesitation. He worked with Duncan now, in beautiful unison. Cut. Spurt of blood. Clamp. And on, deeper.

Duncan worked without haste, yet with lightning-like speed. There was the horrid crunch of the great rib-shears biting through bone.

"Spreaders!" Hans Volker growled. Jenny passed him the bridge-like instrument. Hans turned the set screw, forcing the ribs six inches apart.

"Retractors!" Hans barked. Jenny passed them over. Hans pushed the painfully heaving lungs aside. The heart could be seen now, a great, reddish purple mass, beating fitfully, unevenly, under its semi-transparent sac.

"All yours, Doctor," Hans said with satisfaction.

Duncan's hand moved, slitting the sac, starting well above the rent Dick Willis's vengeful knife had made, passing lightly through it, continuing on below it.

"Sutures!"

She passed them over.

Duncan's hands were deft, moving with beautiful, effortless grace, sewing up the gash in the ventricle wall. It was enormously difficult, something like taking aim at a moving target each time he passed the ligatures through. But he did it. He knotted the suture, put out his right hand.

"Scissors!" he barked.

He worked on, sweat beading his forehead. Jenny wiped it off with a sterile pad. His hands danced, joining the ends of the severed blood-vessels with absorbable ligatures . . . The clank of the clamps into the tray as Hans took them out one by one. The fitting of the ribs back in place. The final suture of the great curving incision he had made, leaving only a space for the drainage tubes. He stepped back, trembling a little. Hans Volker stepped in with the sterile bandage, the disinfectants, the tape.

It was done now, all done. Jenny Greenway stopped being a nurse, became a woman. She turned away, her shoulders shaking, crying from pure excess of pride in him. Duncan draped an arm around those shaking shoulders. They stood there, staring at the patient. Jim Vance breathed normally. His colour was good.

Duncan looked at the grandfather clock across the room.

"Three hours," he exulted, "from skin to skin."

"Goddamn it, son," Hans Volker said, "I've seen surgeons and surgeons; but damned if you aren't——"

"A lucky bastard," Duncan said solemnly. "Looks like he's going to make it, eh, Doctor?"

"You're damned right he will—Doctor," Hans Volker said.

Chapter 9

"YOU MADE THE FRONT PAGE of every rag in the state," Fred Baynes said, "with that job you did on Jim Vance. Reckon that's what made you, eh, Doc?"

Duncan looked at him. He didn't want to talk about that. But it was all a matter of public record. All Fred Baynes had to do was to go and look in the back files of *The Picayune*. Better to tell him—a little. That way, maybe he wouldn't look it up. That way he might print a version of the Dick Willis–Jim Vance case that would be at least a little—fair.

"It helped," he said, "but not as much as you'd think, Fred."

"Why not?" Fred Baynes said.

"Well, it did get me an assistant residency here. My prospective father-in-law, Nelson Vance, wrote Dr. Phelton a day or two after the operation, asking him to appoint me. Quite understandably, Mr. Vance didn't want his daughter to have to undergo the three to five years of semi-starvation that are the usual lot of a young doctor's wife. Dr. Phelton was considering the matter. The rather too glowing newspaper reports of the operation decided him."

"Proves my point. All that free publicity——"

"Which was knocked on the head by Dick Willis's trial," Duncan said drily.

"Heck, Doc, after the three finest heart specialists in the state went to bat for you, there wasn't any question——"

"There was. It seems that there are other qualifications for a surgeon beside skill. He must also say his prayers, and never kiss the wrong girls in his youth, Fred."

"That was rotten. Didn't cover the Willis trial myself. But Bill Phelps told me about it. What did that Bruder character have against you, anyhow, Doc?"

"Many things, most of them imaginary. The point was, I was the defence's key witness, so I had to be discredited in the eyes of the jury. I was in a peculiar position, anyhow; my father-in-law-to-be was thirsting for revenge. My fiancée, bless her, stuck by me through it all. It was rough. First the prosecution attacked my professional qualifications, in order to cast doubt upon the medical and surgical opinions I'd expressed. That didn't work. I had the whole medical profession behind me. Then they tried to prove that I was an unsavoury character who had spent most of his younger days consorting with loose women. They rang in Stanton Bruder, who has known me all my life, to do that. He was delighted to oblige. They knew from the beginning that that line of questioning was irrelevant and immaterial; and that it would be objected to by Willis's counsel, the objection sustained, and Bruder's testimony ordered to be struck from the record. They didn't care. It wasn't the record they were interested in. It was the impression that testimony would make on the minds of the jurors. They probably succeeded there. Finally, at the suggestion of my uncle, the Reverend Vardigan Childers, who loves me with somewhat less than the usual avuncular love, they did get my testimony removed from the record on the basis that the oath of an atheist, sworn on a Bible he doesn't believe in, is worthless; and the court, therefore, has no right to accept his testimony as true."

"Golly, Doc," Fred said, "and are you?"

"Am I what?"

"An atheist?"

"Let's say I have some slight reservations about generally accepted beliefs," Duncan said drily. "Anything else?"

"Do you think your testimony did any good at all? All right they struck it from the record; but, like you said yourself, no matter how hard a judge tries, he can't make a juror forget it all. Do you think it did?"

"Yes," Duncan said slowly. "It reduced Dick's sentence from life to seven years. Which wasn't enough. They should have freed him, damn them!"

"That's so," Fred said, "but you shouldn't be so bitter over it, Doc. At least you have to admit all the newspapers were on your side. Bill Phelps wrote a piece praising you to the skies."

"All?" Duncan said. "Including Tim Evans, Fred?"

"Oh, him? Now really, Doc, you didn't expect the editor of *The Mertontown Courier* to say something nice about a Caneville boy."

"What did we ever do to those Mertontowners to make them hate us so?" Duncan said. "I know there's bad blood between the two towns, but I never did hear why. What did we ever do to them?"

"Enough," Fred grinned. "First off, Caneville's a plantation town. French people were planting cane there as far back as 1720. So you folks are real aristocratic, and you don't mind showing it. Every time a Caneville-Sainte Marie citizen runs into a Mertontowner, somehow or another such kind of lovin' remarks like 'lint-head', 'mill-fluff', and "bobbin-doffing trash' just seem to pop out of his mouth. But that ain't all. 'Bout twenty-five, thirty years ago, you uppity Caneville folks, finding out that Mertontown had got big enough to outvote you in the local elections, started in to engineer the prettiest bit o' gerrymandering a body ever did see. Wanted to put Mertontown clear out of the parish. Only you-all didn't put it down to the natural fact that the interests of the two towns, one manufacturing and the other agricultural, just plumb rides counter to one another, but on the real sweet, diplomatic basis that manufacturing was degrading to your traditions. Naturally, you lost. But Mertontown ain't forgot that cunning little compliment yet!"

"Lord God!" Duncan said. "So that's it!"

"That and a few other things I could name. Like the fact that your high 'n mighty planters' sons just plain look upon the Mertontown female millhands as their private stock o' fun fillies. Which don't help matters none at all. So Tim, being a Mertontowner born'n bred, and a millhand's son to boot, naturally ain't got much love lost for you all. He ever gets a chance, he'll make you all pay."

"Then we mustn't give him a chance. Anything else you want to know, Fred?"

"Doc, let's go back a bit. Just a word or two about Jim Vance. What kind of fellow was he, anyhow?"

Duncan paused. He was remembering the first day that Jim was well enough to talk. He was seeing it again, hearing the words. If Fred had been there he wouldn't have needed to ask that question. That quite unanswerable question, in any event.

He remembered it all. How he moved through the door, bent over the bed——

"Well, Jim, how do you feel?" he had said.

Jim Vance lay back against the pillows. The degree of his recovery in the one week since the operation was gratifying. They had taken the drains out after the fourth day. Barring an unforeseen accident, Jim would live to reach a ripe old age. But the expression on his face was—strange.

"Great," he croaked weakly. "Pa told me that you went right in and stitched up my heart. Jesus, boy! I don't know how to thank——"

"Easy on the talking, Jim," Duncan said. "You're not out of danger yet. You move around and burst the prettiest suture I ever made, and I'll never forgive you."

"Reckon I wouldn't be around for you to forgive, eh, Doc?" Jim whispered.

"Damned right, you wouldn't. You'd go out like a light. So just save all the talk for four or five weeks more. By then you'll be strong enough."

"Thanks, Doc," Jim muttered. "Say—anything wrong with me having a lil' drink?"

"Depends upon what you call a drink. Your body needs liquids. You can have all the water, milk, lemonade, or fruit juices you want. But no tea, and especially not any coffee. Caffeine is murder on a weak heart."

"Heck, Doc, I wasn't talking about kid stuff! It's a wee snort of bourbon 'n branchwater I'm purely pining for."

Duncan stared at him.

"Tell me something, Jim," he said slowly. "You want to live— or don't you?"

Jim lay there staring at the ceiling. He was motionless except for his eyes. They swept back and forth without ceasing. They looked like the eyes of a trapped beast.

"I asked you a question, Jim," Duncan said sharply.

"Now I reckon that kind of depends," Jim said. His voice was still very weak. Duncan had to lean forward to hear him. "You tell me something, Doc: when I get up from here, am I going to be all right? I mean will I be able to put down half a pint o' bust-head at a sitting, an' pinch every pretty behind in the parish, just like I used to?"

Duncan looked at him with icy contempt. 'This is what I put in three of the damnedest hours of my life to save,' he thought; 'this!'

"No," he said coldly. "You're going to have to take it easy, boy. No liquor. No wenching. That way, you'll see eighty."

"That way, I'll see hell," Jim Vance said.

"Look, man," Duncan snapped. "You've got a fine wife. Marital relations every fifteen days or so—maybe even once a week, if your condition warrants it later on, won't kill you. But whorehopping all over the parish, like you used to, will. That is, if the next husband you cross isn't smart enough to use a gun *before* that bum ticker you're going to have gives out on you. And if you pickle your insides with rotgut, I wouldn't give two cents for your chances —not even in Chinese money. You hear me, boy?"

"I hear you all right, Doc," Jim whispered, "but 'twixt that kind o' life, and sleeping real peaceful in my grave, don't 'pear to me to be no hell of a lot of difference."

"That choice," Duncan said evenly, "is up to you, Jim. I've done what I could. Now you just rest quietly, while I go have a little talk with your folks."

"All right," Jim said. "And thanks, Doc—even if you did leave me a spavined old gelding."

Duncan found Rosemary in the sitting-room with Hester. Nelson Vance stood by the sideboard in the adjacent dining-room, mixing himself a mint julep. The glass doors between the two rooms were open, so that he could hear every word. But Duncan didn't care.

"Rose," he said, "before Jim's up and about again, you have a lock put on the liquor cabinet. And you keep the key."

"What's that, Doc?" Nelson Vance rumbled.

"That damnfool son of yours," Duncan said flatly, "is already craving a snort of bourbon. Like he is now, even one jigger glass would do him more harm than Dick Willis's knife did. Later on, it won't kill him quite so fast; but it'll still finish him. Maybe with a ballooning aneurysm around the edges of the scar tissue from that cut. Maybe with a thrombosis. I don't know. I did the best I knew how in order to pull him through. Keeping him away from hard liquor is your job, not mine. He's your son. You can do as you like, of course. But remember that I warned you."

"Hell, son," Nelson growled, "you can count on me. I'll pour the damn stuff down the drain afore I'll let him even smell it. I can always have myself a snort at Mike's."

"And you think, Father Nels," Rosemary said grimly, "that Jim can't—or won't?"

"I'll keep him locked up!" Nelson roared. "I'll go down there and tell Mike that if he sells that fool boy o' mine a drink, I'll have his licence revoked, *after* I've had his hide!"

"Let him drink it," Rosemary said. "Let him go on chasing after every man's wife in town, except his own. It'll kill him, you say, Doctor Childers? Good. He's better off dead. He's——"

"Why, Rosemary!" Hester said.

"You don't mean that, do you, Rose?" Duncan said kindly. "All right, you're bitter. You've a right to be. But what you're saying doesn't jibe. What you do, the old saying goes, speaks so loud I can't hear what you say. So let's skip the hard words, shall we? Doesn't do you any good to feel that way. Because I, for one, will go right on remembering the girl who fainted dead away when she thought her man was dying. You're just overwrought. Wait a second, and I'll give you a little something to make you sleep."

He searched in the bag Doctor Volker had loaned him for the visit.

"Here," he said, "you take these two pills, and go lie down. You'll feel different about things tomorrow."

"It was the blood," Rosemary said sullenly. "I fainted because of the blood."

She got up awkwardly from where she was sitting. She was not a pretty girl, and life with Jim Vance had killed whatever attractiveness she had once had. She stood there facing them.

"You saved his life, Doctor," she said. "That was your job, and you did it. Oh, I don't blame you. They're saying all over town that your operation was a surgical miracle."

"It wasn't," Duncan said. "As a matter of fact, it was relatively simple. Except for not having to go through the ribs, an appendectomy can be worse at times. People have an exaggerated idea of how delicate the heart is. It's not. Actually, it's the toughest organ in the body."

"Thanks for the medical lecture, Doctor," Rosemary said drily; "and for your brilliant performance last week. But not for saving my husband's life. If he had died, I'd have been the merriest widow in the whole blamed state. All right, Doctor Childers, I'll take your pills and go to sleep now like a good girl. Sure you can't spare me a barrel of them? Enough to fix it so I can stay asleep all the rest of my life, and not have to ever——"

"Now look, daughter," Nelson Vance rumbled.

"—even have to look at that miserable rat-bastard in there again," Rosemary Vance finished calmly. Then she turned and walked out of the room without another word.

Hester jumped up and took Duncan's arm.

"Oh, Duncan, love," she said, "I'm so sorry you had to listen to that!"

"Doesn't matter, Hes," Duncan said easily. "I've already forgotten it. Pill-pushers like me have to forget two dozen unsolicited confidences every day."

"You're sweet," Hester smiled, "but then you always were. There!" she said, and kissed him full on the mouth. "There's your reward for today."

"Hester!" Nelson Vance thundered.

"It's all right, Father," Hester said. "Duncan and I are practically engaged."

"I hope you don't mind, sir," Duncan said. "I've been meaning to discuss the question with you; but Jim's getting hurt sort of side-tracked me."

Nelson Vance considered the matter.

"Mind?" he said, putting his thoughts into words as slowly as his brain formed. "Nope, don't reckon I do. Surgeon good as you are is damn sure going to build hisself up one hell of a fine practice, so there ain't much danger of my baby's sufferin' from want. And, with Jim an invalid, be a handy thing to have a doctor in the family. 'Sides, you saved my boy's life. I'm grateful for that. You always was a clean-living youngster, for all I ever heard tell. And you come from one of the finest Creole families in the state, on your ma's side, that is. Your pa warn't to be despised, neither. Reckon that's where you really got your brains from. You being a bas—a natural child don't make no difference to me."

"Dad!" Hester said.

"Nor the fact that Abbie Fontaine's done let slip to the wrong ears that she's aiming to add you to her string. Feller wimmen don't chase after ain't man enough to make no proper husband nohow, to my way o' thinkin'."

"Just as long as women in general, and Abbie in particular, don't come chasing after him now," Hester observed coolly.

"Ho!" Nelson guffawed. "Jealous lil' female, ain't you, baby? Well, son, you got my consent. Here's my hand on it, 'specially since you ought to be gittin' some inkling of what you're tanglin' yourself into."

Duncan took the proffered hand. He thought wryly of what a strange thing it was to be shaking hands with Nelson Vance. Almost as strange as being engaged to his daughter. There was, he was beginning to realise, no end to the tricks life played upon a man.

"Now that it's official," Hester said, "you may kiss me again!"

Duncan glanced uneasily at Nelson Vance.

"Go on, son," Nelson laughed. "Buss her a good 'un!"

Duncan kissed her. But it wasn't a good one. He was far too nervous.

"That reminds me," Hester said mischievously, "of the day we didn't go swimming."

"I know," Duncan said. "But I improved matters then, and I'll improve them still more in the future."

"I don't doubt it, darling—considering all the practice you must have gotten in with those ratty foreign females."

"Lord, baby," Nelson chuckled, "you better git the bridle on him proper afore you starts driving him so hard. You'll have the pore critter all windbroke an' useless ahead o' the wedding day. Smarter to go slow, I say."

"Thanks, Mr. Vance," Duncan laughed, "but you'll find I can manage her, for all her talk."

"That's what you think, Duncan, darling," Hester said.

Almost as soon as he left the Vance mansion, Duncan saw the posse coming towards him.

He stepped out in the street and waited. As they passed along, men dropped out, entered their houses. The remnants of the posse came up to him.

"Haven't caught him yet, Sheriff?" he said.

"Nope, Doc. Winged the beggar, though. Stan Bruder did it. Lord, that boy can shoot! Anyhow, Dick was losing a sight o' blood when we closed in on him last night. But he was smart enough to go wading in Merry Creek, and that throwed the dogs off the scent. We'll git him tomorrow, sure."

"Why didn't you split the posse, and send some men upstream and some down?" Duncan said.

"He's armed. And like that brush is back there, we need the whole bunch to flush him out of cover. Laying low behind some logs or rocks, he could pick off four, five men afore we could git him. Didn't want to take the risk."

"I see. You say he's hurt. Well, if you happen to need me later on, Sheriff—I'll be at Doc Volker's office."

"Gonna need you all right, Doc. He was bleeding like a stuck pig."

"I'm available," Duncan said.

Duncan went straight to the office. Until he got a reply from Doctor Jarvis Phelton about that job at Rosebriar Clinic in New Orleans, he was helping Doctor Volker with his office patients. Many of them were asking for him, now, saying haltingly: "Look, Doctor Hans—you don't mind if the young Doc has a look at me, too?"

His fame had already spread. The local newspapers had written a glowing editorial about his feat. The New Orleans papers had carried the story, emphasising the point that Dr. Duncan Childers had been born in that city. Papers from as far away as Alexandria and Baton Rouge had sent reporters to interview him.

Duncan was more than a little embarrassed about it all. Except for the deeply ingrained fear that most people, even doctors, have for diseases and injuries of the heart, they might have seen that, technically, the operation he had performed was nothing remarkable. Still, it was good to be launched.

He went into the office through the side door, thus avoiding the waiting-room and the patients who would have detained him with their symptoms and their pains as he passed through. He hung up his hat and took off his jacket. Doctor Volker was busy with an examination behind a screen in the corner. Duncan started towards the lavatory to scrub his hands and arms, but Jenny stopped him.

She had on her cape. Her bag was already in her hands.

"You'd better come with me, Duncan," she said quietly.

"Why all the mystery, Jen?" he growled. "What is it?"

"It's Dick," she whispered. "He's hiding out in the barn at Doug's place. He's been shot, and he's delirious. He's got a gun, and he won't let Doug come near him, good friends as they always were. Doug phoned me. He thinks you might be able to persuade him——"

Duncan stared at her.

"All right," he said. "Let's get going, Jen!"

Chapter 10

HE WONDERED WHY FRED BAYNES hadn't asked him about—that. The newspapers had printed that story, too, so Fred must know about it. He hoped the reporter wouldn't. That was one of the bad, painful memories. Of course, Fred wouldn't print it again if he asked him not to. The newspaperman had been blessedly scrupulous, so far. But he didn't even want to talk about it. That still hurt. It hurt damned badly.

Then it came to him that Fred wasn't going to ask about those particular happenings because they didn't fit. Fred had a wonderful flair for a neat, tight story with a dramatic, moving ending. But the ending of this one was wrong. It broke the established pattern of the series, 'The Romance of Modern Medicine: Interviews with Doctor Duncan Childers.' It spoiled the readers' anticipation of the usual happy ending. It hadn't the force of keenly awaited joyous inevitability implicit in the beginning.

For, from the readers' point of view, from Fred's, and perhaps even from his own, he had married the wrong girl.

No, Fred wouldn't ask him about it. He was sure of that now.

They came around the house together. Doug was waiting on the back steps, staring at the barn.

"Lord, you took your own sweet time!" he said. "Thought you'd never get here! God, boy, I don't know what to do! You know me'n Dick have been friends all our lives; but 'bout half a hour ago I tried to get close enough to talk to him—and he shot at me! Damn near parted my hair! Lord God, Dunc——"

"I'll get him out of there," Duncan said.

He was aware that Jenny's gaze was resting coolly on his face. His insides tautened. 'I'm scared,' he thought; 'I'm scared spitless, and my guts are in knots. But I'm going to walk in there and drag that poor devil out—or get killed trying. Why? Because I'm both male and a fool. Callie once said a body oughtn't to care what people think. But I care what Jen thinks. I care terribly. Come on, little boy, walk that high fence in front of your girl! Stand on your head. Swing upside down by your knees from the tallest tree limb you can reach. Risk your fool life to gain your lady's favour, which you don't want, can't accept, must reject—Come on, you atavistic bastard, move!'

He started walking straight towards the door of the barn, moving very slowly, his slim body a perfect target. Doug and Jenny watched him in frozen horror, walking there like that, already in easy pistol range, going on.

"Don't come no closer!" Dick Willis howled, from the barn. Duncan stopped.

"Look, Dick," he said, "I'm a doctor. I've come to help you; I——"

"No closer," Dick grated. "Done killed one lousy bastard! Can't hang me but one time. Might as well be for two as for one!"

"You haven't killed anybody, Dick," Duncan said. "Jim Vance is alive. You aren't going to hang, boy. We're going to get you off."

"Don't lie to me, Dunc! I put that knife through his filthy heart! Ain't nobody gonna take me back so's that no-good bitch I married can stand there a'grinning while I kick'n choke! Not nobody. I know you, Dunc. You're a good boy. Hate to kill you. So don't come no closer, please!"

"I'm coming closer, Dick," Duncan said. "I'm not lying. Jim's not dead. I opened him up, and sewed up his heart myself. You aimed too low, and too far right."

"I'll kill you, Dunc! Much as I hate to, I'll——"

"All right," Duncan said. "Give them something to hang you for. Because they haven't anything now. Kill the man who saved you from that by keeping Jim alive. Because I'm coming on in, Dick. I'm not going to run or dodge. I'm coming in straight. Aim well, boy, if you've got to shoot. See if you can't do a better job than you did on Jim, because I'm coming in."

He moved then. One step. Two. His mouth was dry as sand. His tongue stuck to the roof of it. Sweat beaded on his forehead, dripped from his chin. The fear that twisted inside him, clawing at his guts, wasn't good. It wasn't good at all.

He heard, at the last possible instant, the swish of stiffly starched skirts, the earth-muffled staccato of her running feet; and above it, through it, Doug's choking roar: "No, Jen! Goddamn it, no!"

He turned, dropped his bag, put out his hands in warning. Too late. She crashed into him with sickening force, caught his arms, wrestled him about with maniacal strength so that she was facing him, her back to that door; and he, seeing only her face, blurred out of focus by too much nearness, only the eyes clear, soft brown and clear, filled with desperate tenderness, until they flared suddenly with that white-hot stab of pain she must have felt, dimmed, glazed slowly, went opaque; and he, holding her erect by main force, raised his eyes towards the barn door, seeing the smoke rising from that shot he had not even heard, feeling only the reverberations of it in his deafened ears, saw Doug crash into that door, smash it open, screaming now, his normally bass voice as high as a woman's:

"Going to kill him! Gonna kill th' bastard!"

And he, letting her down gently, tenderly, straightening up again, shouting: "No, Doug! No!" and running through that door, saw Doug standing there, aiming with great care the revolver he had wrested from his fallen foe at Dick's head; and he, Duncan, not having time to think what afterwards he thought: *Love should be prohibited by law!*, leaped that intervening yard of space, clawed Doug's hand upward so that the shot crashed through the barn roof, wrestled with him furiously until he thought to say, through set teeth, forcing out the words:

"She's not dead! You're letting her die, you damnfool—keeping me here fighting with you!"

And Doug going limp at once, and he, Duncan, saying:

"Give me that pistol, Doug."

He pocketed it, already running. The two of them bent over her. Doug cradled her dark head on one knee, his hot tears splashing into her face.

Her eyes came open. She smiled up at Doug, gallantly.

"Quit crying, you big sissy!" she said. "I'm all right."

Then she fainted again.

Doug's eyes were shapeless blobs of terror, searching Duncan's face.

Duncan didn't say anything. He took the scissors out of the bag; he looked at Doug.

"Prop her up higher," he grated.

He cut into the stuff of her uniform, behind, near the waist, slipping one blade in, and, silently, thanking God she had no need for corsets or stays, ripped upward through uniform and chemise to the neckline, slashed through her long sleeves, and yanked the mutilated uniform down to her waist, baring her proud and pointing breasts to Doug's eyes. She was lovely. Duncan could tell that from Doug's face. But his own coldly professional gaze had no time for emotion now.

"Doc——" Doug quavered.

"High," Duncan said. "Smashed the clavicle, ranging upwards. Missed the lung, thank God!"

"Dunc——" Doug's voice was blade-sharp, urgent.

"Don't know," Duncan said. "It hasn't come out, Doug. I'm going to have to go in and find it."

"Here?" Doug said.

"No. We'll have to take her into town. You go tie up that crazy bastard in there. We'll bring them both in."

They laid them both down gently, blanket-wrapped, in the spring-bed of the wagon. Duncan had given them each a shot of morphine, slapped on temporary bandages.

They climbed up into the driver's seat.

"Go sit with her, Doug," Duncan said. "I'll drive."

"No, Doc—be better if you——"

"All she needs is comfort, son," Duncan said, "and that you can give her better than I."

"You think so?" Doug burst out. "It was you she went flying to save! You she cared enough for to put that pretty flesh 'twixt you and that ball!"

"You weren't in danger," Duncan said flatly. "She would have done the same thing for you."

"I don't know," Doug wavered, searching for comfort, his eyes sick with unbearable hurt; and it was then that Duncan thought it first: Love should be prohibited by law!

"You get on back there, boy!" he growled. "We're wasting time!"

They rode down the main street, towards Hans Volker's office, surrounded by a crowd that grew and grew. Eager hands lifted Jenny and Dick down, carried them through the waiting-room. Duncan stared with bleak eyes at the crowd of patients sitting there.

"You'll have to go home," he said. "Neither Doctor Volker nor I will have time for you today."

He stood there, watching them as they filed out. Before the last one had gone, Sheriff Martin was at the door, pushing his way through the last of them to leave.

"Hear you 'n Doug got him, Doc! Where is he? I'll——"

"You'll wait outside, Sheriff," Duncan said icily. "Post a guard, if you like. He isn't going to do any more running. Dr. Volker and I have two operations to perform. So, if you please——"

"Right, Doc," the Sheriff said. "You're the boss here!"

Hans Volker was just finishing his scrubbing. He stepped aside to let Duncan take his place.

"Duncan," he rumbled, his voice thick with emotion, "what happened? Why did Dick shoot—Jen?"

"He was shooting at me," Duncan said harshly. "She threw herself between us and took the ball."

"I see," Hans Volker growled, "but you still don't, do you, you damned young fool!"

"I'm ready, Doctor," Duncan said. "Doug, you get the hell out of here!"

"Thought maybe she'd need a transfusion," Doug muttered.

"You can wait outside," Duncan said in a kinder tone. "Go in the patients' lavatory, and scrub yourself just like you've seen us do. Then, if we do need you, you'll be ready. But I don't think we will —her colour's quite good. Right, Doctor?"

"Excellent," Doctor Volker said.

"All right," Doug said. "Goddamn it, I——"

"Go on out, Doug," Hans Volker said gently. "She'll be all right. She's in capable hands."

Duncan waited in silence as Hans dripped the ether over the gauze cone.

"That does it," Duncan said. "Now we'll turn her over and——"

Hans Volker shook his head, and grinned at Duncan.

"No, Doctor," he chuckled. "This isn't major surgery, which I'll admit you're a whiz at. Use your eyes, boy. Tell me, what do you see?"

Duncan stared at Jenny's inert form.

"Not a damned thing, Doctor," he said at last.

"Just for that, you assist, son. I'm going to show you a thing or two. Wonderful thing about medicine. Always manages to pull smart young whippersnappers down a peg. Ready, Doctor?"

"Yes, sir," Duncan said.

"Scalpel!" Hans Volker barked.

Duncan passed, slapping it into his palm.

Hans made a tiny incision, scarcely an inch long, just below the right collarbone. He didn't merely mark it. He cut in, deep.

"Forceps!"

Duncan passed them over.

Hans pushed them into the incision, turned them so that their jaws were under the bone. He opened them, closed them, drew them out. The bullet clanged into the tray. The whole thing had taken him less than one minute.

"Well, I'll be damned!" Duncan said helplessly.

"Didn't notice that slight bulge in the collarbone, did you, son?" Hans Volker said. "Almost missed it myself. Now you get busy. Cauterise that wound, slap on dressings, while I get to work on Dick."

147

"I'm sorry, Doctor," Duncan whispered. "I apologise for having missed that."

"Nothing to apologise for. Missed my share of diagnosis in my day. Probably will miss a few more before I pass on. In a way that job you did on Jim Vance was bad for you. A young surgeon ought to fail a few times first, for the good of his immortal soul. A little decent humility never hurt any doctor—and, damn it all, boy, it safeguards patients' lives, by keeping us from killing 'em by treating things they haven't got. Get busy now. I'll start on Dick."

Duncan worked furiously, cauterising and dressing Jenny's wound. Then he went to the sink, scrubbed again. He joined Hans over Dick's inert form.

Hans had made a tremendous incision in Dick's thigh. Duncan peered into the hæmostat-ringed gash. Slowly, painfully, Doctor Volker was picking out splinters of bone. The flesh was purplish, angry, already beginning to suppurate. The femur wasn't broken—not entirely. The ball had merely clipped a six-inch-long splinter off one side of it, smashing the splinter itself into tiny slivers which had penetrated everywhere.

"Name of God!" Duncan said. "What did that—a cannon?"

"Look in the tray, boy," Hans Volker growled, "and learn!"

Duncan stared into the tray. The slug that lay in it had flattened to a size larger than a five-cent piece.

Hans Volker straightened up.

"Forty-four-calibre, from a Winchester carbine. Hit a rock, flattened, ricocheted, and entered edgewise. He was lucky. Gone in whole, we'd have to take off that leg."

"Might have to yet, if it doesn't drain properly. Three tubes, eh, Doc?"

"Four," Hans Volker growled. "I've made that incision unnecessarily large."

"You didn't know where it had gone, Doctor," Duncan said quietly. "And if we miss one of these unmentionable splinters—just one——"

"I know, boy," Hans Volker said. "That's why we aren't going to miss one."

It took them four hours. Long before they were done, Jenny had come out from under the ether.

Duncan wheeled her out into one of the two rooms Hans Volker had for emergency patients who couldn't be moved. Lifted her from the stretcher, turned towards the bed.

"You know, Doctor," she mocked him gently, "it's nice feeling your arms around me again."

Duncan stood there, holding her.

"Jen," he choked, "Lord God, Jen——"

"Put me down now, Doctor," she said.

He put her down on the bed, drew the bedclothes up over her, arranged the pillows.

"There," he said. "How do you feel, Jen?"

"It hurts," she said frankly.

"You're going to be all right," he said. "But no thanks for saving my life! I didn't want it that way. The risk was mine. I'd accepted it. You had no right——"

She looked at him steadily. His voice trailed off into silence.

"I don't know about rights," she said weakly. "I only knew it was far better to die quickly than to see you killed, and die slowly afterwards. But then, being a woman, I don't reason with my head."

"Jen," he said, "you aren't going to——"

"Accept Doug? No, Duncan. It wouldn't be fair to him. A man like Doug deserves to be loved. And I haven't any to give—him."

He stared at her.

"Look, Jen," he said, "you want me to——"

"Break your engagement to Hester? No, Duncan. That wouldn't be fair to her, either. Or to me. I don't want—gratitude."

"Jen, it wouldn't be——"

"Oh yes, it would. Get back to your work, Doctor. I'm just fine."

Duncan went back into the operating-room. Hans Volker was taking out clamps. Then he was sewing, beautifully, perfectly. Duncan turned. He walked out of there. He got out of his white gown, his cap. He put on his tie, his coat, his hat. He went out into the street, seeing in astonishment half the town there, just beyond the cordon of deputies the Sheriff had placed before the door.

Norton of the *Clarion* called out to him:

"A statement, Doc! A statement! Anything at all. . . ."

"They're both out of danger," Duncan said. "Miss Greenway's wound is less serious than we believed at first. She'll be up and about in two or three weeks. Dick's wound is bad. He may lose his leg, though it's too early to tell yet. But there's one thing I want carefully noted, Norton: I performed neither operation. Dr. Volker removed the ball from Miss Greenway's upper pectoral region in less than one minute. Then he performed a surgical masterpiece on Dick Willis's leg. I only assisted. Guess that's all, now."

"No, it ain't," Bob Norton grinned. "Just one thing more, Doc.

149

Is it true that Nurse Greenway threw herself between you 'n Dick Willis, and took the bullet Dick was aiming at you?"

Duncan looked at him.

"Who told you that, Bob?" he said.

"Doug. Leasewise he told one o' the deputies."

"Yes," Duncan said. "It's true, Bob. Miss Greenway is a very gallant woman. I'm grateful to her for saving my life. But, before you start printing romantic nonsense, Bob, reckon I'd better make a public announcement that I wasn't meaning to for some time yet. Day before yesterday, Miss Hester Vance did me the supreme honour of consenting to become my wife. Is that clear, Bob?"

"You bet your sweet life it is!" Bob Norton cried. "Thanks, Doc! All right, folks, lemme out of here! I got to go set this up for tomorrow's paper!"

Duncan came down the steps. He was surrounded by the crowd. People reached out to shake his hand, voiced their congratulations, begged for additional details.

Duncan fended them off as best he could. He felt, suddenly, a hand thrust through the crook of his elbow. He turned, furiously, and stared into Hester's face—as white as death itself, and streaked with unashamed tears.

"Please, folks," Duncan said, "let us out of here, will you?"

Then, officiously, Sheriff Martin took command.

"All right," he barked. "Stand back now. Lou, you 'n Hank clear the way. Stand back, folks! Can't you see the little lady's plumb upset?"

Duncan helped her up into the offside of her buggy, then went round and climbed into the driver's side. She clung to his arm, her face crushed against his shoulder, crying helplessly.

He flapped the reins. The horse moved off.

"Lord God, Hes!" he said.

"I—I thought I'd lost you!" she sobbed. "I—I wanted to die, Duncan! Lou Travis talked to Doug in there—then he came out and told everybody. How you t-t-t-took your b-b-bag and walked straight into to D-D-Dick's gun! You mustn't be that b-b-brave any more! Oh, darling, you mustn't! If anything happened to you, I'd——"

"Hush, baby," Duncan said tenderly.

"That wasn't the worst of it! When he told how she—how she——"

"It's all right, baby," Duncan said.

"It's not all right! It'll never be all right again! Now you'll never know, never believe, that nobody on earth could possibly love you more than I do! You'll go on thinking, remembering, 'There was a woman once who was willing to die for me!' Oh, Duncan, that's a hell of a thing for me to have to live with! Oh, I hate her! I hate——"

Duncan lifted her chin with his free hand.

"Do you, Hes, baby," he said gently, "considering the fact that, without her, you'd have been a widow before you were a bride?"

She stared at him with wide and frightened eyes.

"No!" she breathed. "Oh no, I don't hate Jen, Duncan! I—I love her! I'll be a sister to her. I'll——"

"Hush, baby," Duncan said. "I'm going to take you home now —and give you a sedative. And, considering how those thunderheads are piling up over the river, reckon we'd better skip our little spooning for tonight. Good night's sleep will do you good, Hes."

"No you don't, Duncan Childers! You're taking me out tonight even if there's a cyclone! Lord God, you don't know how I need comforting, love!"

"All right, Hes," Duncan said fondly. "I'll be there at nine, come hell or high water."

Driving away from the Vance mansion that night, Duncan Childers was sad and still.

Hester was silent, too, her eyes, under the street lights, big with pain. The rising wind stirred her lovely hair. It was going to storm, as sure as hell, Duncan knew. So he turned the horse down the half deserted road leading toward the McPherson place. The stout home that Angus McPherson had built with his own brawny hands would provide shelter enough if the storm came. The McPherson farm was deserted, since yellow fever had swept the entire family away in a night, four years before. Nobody would buy the place now, even for the pittance of unpaid taxes for which it could be had. The beds were still stained with black vomit that no one dared to wash. Even though Walter Reed's most terrible experiment— that of locking his volunteers in fever-ridden huts for days on end, where they had slept in bedclothes and nightshirts befouled with black vomit, with the sweat and excreta of men who had died horribly; but keeping these men of unparalleled, unmatched heroism carefully screened against the winged marauders of the night— had conclusively proved that you got yellow fever from the mosquito's bite, and from no other source, nobody would go near the McPherson place, let alone buy it.

'Even I,' Duncan thought, 'don't want to go there. But it's better than getting soaked to the skin and coming down with pneumonia."

"Duncan," Hester said suddenly, "I—I've decided to release you from your promise. You don't have to marry me. I don't even think it's a good idea. I'd make an awful doctor's wife. I'm too jealous, and I can't stand being lonely! I can't, Duncan! I've been lonely so much that I—have a horror of it. I might even—even betray you with somebody else, if I got too lonely. I haven't got much courage or willpower, or anything else, like—like your Jen."

Duncan fished in his pocket and found the ring.

"Give me your left hand, Hester," he growled.

"Duncan, no! I——"

He took it, dragged it forward, slipped the ring on her finger.

"It was my mother's," he said gravely.

He knew she was crying, though it was too dark in that starless, wind-whipped night to see her eyes.

'Don't I even get a kiss?" he said.

She surged forward, flung her arms around his neck, and kissed his mouth in a blaze of passion that threatened to illuminate the night.

He drew away his face.

"Take it easy, baby!" he said.

"No,' she whispered. "We mustn't, must we? Not before. That's always a mistake. We women are such fools. When we love a man, we can't deny him anything—and afterwards, he despises us."

"Look, Hes," Duncan said drily, "I'm a doctor. If there's anything that's pure hogwash in this world, it's our tendency to deny that women have passions just like men."

"More than men," Hester said soberly. "Only we have them less frequently. Thank God for that—or life would be one unholy mess! I think that if I ever turned loose, really turned loose, darling, I'd kill you from pure exhaustion. You're right; it isn't merely a matter of refusing our lovers; it's also a matter of refusing —ourselves."

"I like your honesty, Hes," Duncan said.

"Thank you, kind sir!" she laughed. She was in much better humour now. "Oh, Duncan!" she wailed. "You were right! It's already starting to rain!"

"And we, damn it all," Duncan said, "are still three miles from the McPherson place!"

He whipped up the horse. There was nothing to do but to run for it now. The rain came down in solid sheets. The wind got into driving it under the buggy's high top. In minutes they were soaked to the skin. The wind rose, howling now. A tree crashed to earth seconds after they had passed. Lightning ripped jagged white wounds in the sky. Thunder crashed sickeningly, shaking all the night.

They raced on. The wheels of the buggy sent up yellow wings of muddy water. They lurched wildly, righted, sped on. The rain beat against them like solid blows.

'We'll never make it,' Duncan thought: then, in the blinding blaze of the lightning, he saw the house. They raced into the yard, leaped from the buggy, ran up on the porch. The way the wind was driving that rain, the roof of the porch was no protection at all. Duncan tried the door. It was locked. So he drew back his foot and kicked it in.

Inside, it was dry, except for a leak in one corner of the roof. When Duncan drew out his matches, he found that they were as soaked as the rest of him. But he realised that not even thieves had dared enter that house. There must be dry matches in the kitchen.

"You wait here, Hes," he said. "I'll go find a light."

"Oh, no, love!" she cried. "I'm scared! Let me come with you."

"All right, then," Duncan said. "Come on."

They groped their way to the kitchen. The matches were there, in a gaily painted box above that enormous range. There were oil lamps on a shelf. Duncan took one down, turned up the wick, lit it. The soft glow stole through the kitchen. He looked at Hester. She was shivering violently. Her lips were blue.

"You get out of those wet clothes," he growled. "I'll take another lamp and rummage around upstairs until I find one of Sally McPherson's dresses."

"Oh, no, Duncan—I couldn't! I'd die before I'd put on anything she'd worn!"

"Then I'll get you a blanket to wrap yourself in—a clean blanket out of the chest. Will that suit you?"

"Perfectly, darling; but first make a fire in the living-room grate. I'm so cold!"

He did so, shivering himself now. Outside, the rain thundered down with no sign of let-up. He went upstairs, found two blankets, found, what was even better, a bottle of Angus's good home-made whisky.

"I'll go undress in the kitchen," he said. "But I'll have to come back in here to hang my clothes in front of the fire. So wrap up good, baby!"

He came back into the living-room with his clothes dripping

from his arm. They stared at each other, dissolved into gales of helpless laughter. Then Duncan stopped laughing.

"Hes," he said soberly, "the way I feel right now, you'd better run!"

"I," she whispered, "don't think I have to run. I think my very gentlemanly fiancé can be trusted. Can he, darling?"

"Of course," Duncan said unhappily. He could see one snowy shoulder, one softly curving arm. His blood made dark thunder inside his veins.

She was still cold. Her teeth chattered.

"Can I have a drink of that, Duncan?" she said.

Silently he passed it over. She took a long pull at the bottle, another. It didn't seem to bother her at all. She gave it back to him. He took a long, long swallow. Good Lord, old Angus had known his whisky!

"Give it back, greedy man!" she said gaily. She tilted it skyward. When she took it down again, her cheeks were rosy once more, her eyes sparkling.

"Oh, hell, let's kill it," Duncan said.

He saw, as he turned to hurl the empty bottle into the fireplace, her filmy underthings spread out on the chair. He realised that under that blanket was only—Hester. There was a thickness in his breath. His tongue glued itself to the roof of his mouth.

"Oh dear!" Hester wailed. "It's going to rain all night!"

"Let it!" Duncan said.

"Father," Hester said merrily, "will be waiting for us with his best shotgun in the morning!"

"Then," Duncan said, "we might as well profit from the occasion."

"No, Duncan," Hester said.

"Why not, Hes?"

"Because I don't want to. No; that's not true. I do want to. Very much. Only I'm not going to."

"Same question, baby."

"It's—it's hard to explain. If this rain keeps up all night, Father really is going to be waiting, shotgun in hand. I want to be able to tell him truthfully that nothing happened. He won't believe me, but that doesn't matter. *I'll* know I'm not lying. That way, even though, physically, you may seem to have been forced to marry me, morally, you will not have been. Is that clear?"

"As mud. Mississippi mud."

"Which is the best mud there is," Hester said gaily.

"Hes——"

"No, Duncan."

"All right. Then as soon as our clothes are dry, we'd better pluck up courage, as the dime novelists say, and brave the storm."

"No. Not that, either. Duncan—did anybody die on that sofa?"

"Of course not. They died upstairs—in bed."

"Good," she said. "I'm going to lie down on it, all cosy-like. You come sit beside me, on the floor. Rest your head on my knees. You can take one of the cushions out of that chair to sit on, so you'll be nice and comfy."

She crossed to the sofa. Lay down on it. Her hands worked at the blanket she had wrapped so tightly around her, until it was loose. Then she whipped it off and up in the motion a woman uses to make a bed. In that half heartbeat before it settled down again, covering her, he caught a flash, one blinding flash, of a singing perfection of form that equalled Calico's. Exceeded it, maybe. He hadn't seen her long enough to tell.

"Come here, Duncan," she said.

"Lord God, Hes——" he breathed.

"Come here, love," she said tenderly. "Sit here beside me. Put your head on my knees, so I can run my fingers through your hair. Just like we were already married—except for—that. . . ."

"Good Lord!" Duncan said, "I'm a man, Hes! I've got blood——"

"I know that," she murmured drowsily, "but I also know you're a gentleman—who can be trusted."

Groaning, he moved over to the chair, picked up the cushion, put it on the floor beside her, sat down upon it, leaned back so that his head was resting against her knees. He felt her fingers moving through his heavy, deeply waving red hair.

"You've such pretty hair," she said, " 'specially with the firelight shining through it."

He didn't answer her. He sat there glumly, staring into the fire. Her fingers, moving in his hair, slowed, became still. Turning, he saw that she was asleep.

He got up, put more wood on the fire, pulled up a chair, sat down in it, stretched out his long legs.

Wolfgang, he thought, would never believe this!

He sat there without moving, except the times he got up to replenish the fire, until three o'clock in the morning, when the rain finally stopped.

He glanced at her. She was sleeping peacefully. Hastily he got into his now dry clothes. He crossed to where she lay, bent down, kissed her mouth. Her eyes came open, sleepily. She smiled at him.

"What do you think of me now?" she said.

"I think," he said flatly, "that you're the most heartless, the cruellest witch in all the world!"

"You'll find out differently, once we're married," she said. "Hand me my things, darling."

He passed them over. She stood up, wrapping the blanket around her carefully. But still an awful lot of Hester showed.

'Bait me, will you!' he snarled inside his mind; 'tempt me! By God, I'll——"

She saw his eyes, smiled at him tenderly.

"Am I—that pretty, darling?" she murmured. "Am I?"

"Pretty! Baby, you're the goddamnest most beautiful thing in this mortal world of sin!"

"Except for the profanity, I like that," she laughed. "I'll kiss you for it, darling—*after* we're dressed."

"Father Nels," Duncan groaned, "get that shotgun ready! In fact, you won't even need it. Look, baby, if you think I'm going to wait until after I work a year, you'd better think again!"

She was clad in the filmy underthings, now, the mist-like chemise. Which was just like being naked, only worse. She ran to him, put her arms about his neck, dragged his face down to hers, kissed his mouth endlessly.

"No," she said. "You won't have to wait, darling! I—I can't either—not any more, now. I'll marry you any time you say."

He pushed her away gently.

"But no sampling of forbidden fruit until then, eh, Hes?"

"Please, darling, let's not spoil things now," Hester said.

It was growing light when he drew the buggy up before the house. He got down, put up his arms to her. He felt her stiffen.

"Duncan!" she breathed; then her voice rose, edging into a shriek: "Oh, my God, Duncan, it's—it's Jim!"

Duncan whirled. Then he was running towards the nightshirt-clad figure lying in the muddy yard. He knelt in the mud, lifted Jim Vance's head. The face was blue. The breath came fitfully. The flesh burned to the touch. The rustling sound was there, audible to the naked ear—the râles.

Duncan stood up, put his arms under Jim, lifted powerfully. Jim was a big man, over six feet tall. Even after a week in bed, he weighed more than a hundred and eighty pounds. Duncan staggered up on the porch with him. Pushed against the door. It was locked.

156

Hester put her finger on the bell. It rang and rang and rang, awaking echoes. They heard at last the shuffle of slippered feet. The door flew open. Nelson Vance stood there in his nightshirt. He saw Hester first.

"Goddamnit, girl!" he roared, "I'm a-gonna——"

"Father," Hester whispered, and stood aside.

Nelson Vance whitened to the ears. He put out his massive arms.

"Here, give him to me, son," he said.

They put Jim Vance into his cold bed. Duncan piled the blankets around him.

"Get me more blankets!" he snapped. "Every damned blanket in the house! A hot-water bottle—you hear me, Hes!"

But Hester was holding the brown bottle up to the light. It had held a quart, but it was empty now.

"Look, Father," she said.

"Rose!" Nelson bellowed. "Goddamnit, Rose!"

Rosemary came into the room. She was yawning. Carefully, Duncan thought.

"Who the goddamned, bastardised, bluebottled Hell gave Jim that whisky, Rose?" Nelson roared.

"I'm sure I don't know," she said. "I had a little nigger boy raking the yard, right outside this window. Maybe Jim—sent him——"

"What nigger? Tell me his name! I'll have his——"

"How would I know, Father Nels? Just a little nigger. Can you tell strange niggers apart? I can't."

'She's lying,' Duncan raged. 'She's lying! She gave him that whisky herself! She's—she's murdered him!'

"Is he dead?" Rosemary asked brightly. Her voice held nothing more than casual interest.

"No," Duncan said flatly. "He's got maybe one chance in ten thousand—if that much."

They piled the blankets on Jim Vance. Put the hot-water bottle at his feet. Duncan bared one leg, began to massage it, forcing the blood upward.

"You take the other one," he said to Nelson Vance.

He leaned forward, put his ear against Jim's chest. Thumped with his fingers. It sounded like an oaken barrel, full of—mud.

"Meg, baby!" Jim Vance cried.

"Ain't forgot her yet," Nelson groaned. "If that murderin' fool Willis had of had sense enough to 'tend to his homework—his wife wouldn't of——"

"Meg!" Jim said again. His voice had an odd sound, a curiously

157

pectoral tone. Duncan felt his pulse. It was terribly weak. You could compress it. It felt—thready.

"What is it, son?" Nelson Vance's voice was anguished. "What the hell——"

"Galloping pneumonia," Duncan said.

He could hear Hester in the hall phoning Dr. Volker as he had told her to. No need of that now. What we need is a miracle worker. Jesus Himself, maybe, to raise the dead.

Jim was still alive when Hans Volker got there. But his face was indigo. He coughed. A line of sputum dribbled down his chin. It was not red, nor black. It was—Duncan's mind sought for the exact image—the colour of prune juice.

"Hæmoptysis," Duncan whispered.

"What's that, son?" Nelson Vance said.

"Lung hæmorrhage," Hans Volker said flatly.

"Isn't there anything——?" Hester sobbed.

"Well," Duncan said tiredly, "we could sponge him off with warm alcohol."

"Tried Digitalis, son?" Hans Volker barked. "Caffeine? Adrenalin? Strychnine? Any damned thing?"

"No. I didn't have my bag," Duncan said.

"Well, I've got mine! Let's see, about two grains of Digitalis ought to——"

"He'd be dead before you got the needle out," Duncan said. "Not only Digitalis—any of the things you named. You don't, Doctor," he added in that bone-deep weariness that came from pure loss of hope, "give any of the most powerful stimulants known to a man with a fresh suture in his heart."

Hans Volker stared at him.

"I'm sorry, boy," he said. "I'd plain forgot."

"Then what in God's name are you going to do?" Nelson Vance roared.

"Nothing," Duncan said grimly. "Sit here and watch him die. My punishment, I reckon; my penance for excess of pride."

"Duncan!" Hester cried. "Oh, Duncan, no!"

"There isn't anything known," Hans Volker said, "that's good for advanced pneumonia, child. The greatest physician on earth doesn't know any more than we do. I'd suggest that you send for your minister, Reverend Father Rayn."

There was a rustling in Jim Vance's throat. A sound like dry leaves blowing down a paved street on an autumn day. A rattle. Louder now, again. Then, abruptly, no sound at all.

Duncan stood up. He pushed aside Hester's groping hand. He

walked down the hall, out of the door, into the street. He kept walking aimlessly, until the sun came up, and even after that, until his feet were too numb for him to even feel them there.

He turned back into the main street at last, going towards the office. He went into the room where Jenny lay. Her dark hair was loose. It clouded her pillow. Her brown eyes, bright with tears, then, at that moment, were the loveliest things in all the world.

"Duncan!" she choked. "Oh, Duncan, Doctor Hans just told me! They—they——"

"What is it, Jen?" he said tiredly.

"They've changed the charge against poor Dick—to murder," Jenny said.

Chapter 11

MURDER. 'A charge they couldn't make stick,' Duncan thought, as he walked up the stairs into Rosebriar Clinic that bright September day of 1903; 'but homicide was enough. Especially with Uncle Vard and Stan Bruder putting their two cents' worth in. Seven years. Lord God! Let's see—Dick was sent up in the fall of 1900—three years ago. That means he's still got four more years to go. Not too bad. Sometimes I envy him. I'd rather be in jail right now than do what I have to do.'

He frowned. What he had to do that morning was a thing that he almost literally would have preferred going to jail to doing. He had to pay an extended call on Grace Harvey. There was no way to get out of it. He couldn't turn the case over to Avery Ramsom or even Lester Ryan or Tom Hendricks. Grace was asking for him specifically and by name. And you just don't give offence to that many millions. Especially not since, out of gratitude to Duncan for saving his daughter's looks, Ernest Harvey had made the new charity wing one of the best equipped hospitals in the state.

'The trouble is,' Duncan thought, 'that I'm quite fond of Grace. She's awfully pretty and damned sweet. Her greatest handicap has always been all that bloody money. Old Harvey seems to have convinced her that that's all her beaux are after. Jesus, how can a girl as fine as Grace have such a thumping, thundering inferiority complex? Old Harvey's fault, I guess. He's as canny in one way as he's generous in another. Over-protected her, and damned near ruined her life.'

He stopped at the entrance. This thing needed working out. He'd been at Vienna during the very years that Sigmund Freud had created the intellectual explosion of psycho-analysis. He hadn't believed in it very much, but some parts of it made sense. Grace's growing attachment to him was almost surely 'transference'. That business of falling in love with your doctor or psychologist. Well, he'd have to be both now. And he knew so damned little of psychology.

She wasn't sick any more. She could go home. The dryness, roughness, swelling, of her skin had disappeared. Her eyes were normal again. They were lovely eyes—the soft blue of cornflowers.

She could go home; only she was refusing to. She pretended illness, so that she could have Doctor Duncan Childers sit by her bed and hold her hand. Death and hell! Weren't there any end to the complications of life?

He pushed open the door.

"Good morning, Doctor," the receptionist, Nurse Tinkler, said. "There's a man waiting to see you. A Mr. Henderson. Awfully good-looking. He's waiting in your office."

Duncan stood there. Light broke behind his eyes. Doug. Just perfect. A godsend. Doug, whose father had left him more money than even the Vances had now. Doug, who was suffering from Jenny Greenway's continued rejection of him. Three years of that. Which was sure as hell why he was here now. Ready to be caught on the rebound. And Grace, whose defences were down—all the way down. Besides, they would suit each other to a T. Both good kids and——

He smiled. 'All right, Dr. Dan Cupid,' he thought; 'got your chance now. Go in there and get busy!'

He went into his office.

Doug stood up, his face mournful.

"Howdy, Dunc," he said. "Sorry to bother you this way, but——"

"Bother?" Duncan laughed. "I've never been so glad to see a body in my whole life!"

"You know what I came for?" Doug said.

"Yep. I'm to play John Alden to your Captain Miles Standish. It won't work. Jen's a stubborn little wench."

"She seems to be hoping that you'n Hes'll—break up——"

'And she may be right,' Duncan thought bitterly. Aloud he said: "Fat chance! We're very happy. Doug, look. I'm not very good at arranging other people's lives. Made enough of a mess of my own, it seems to me. And butting your head against that particular brick wall will get you exactly nowhere."

"Then what do you suggest, Duncan?" Doug said.

"That you come with me on a call. Right now. Here in the hospital."

"Dunc, I don't see——"

"Ah, but you will, Doug," Duncan said. "You will!"

An hour later, Douglass Henderson was sitting there, gazing into those cornflower-blue eyes with an expression on his face like that of a stunned ox. He had, Duncan decided, simply reached the stage where having someone to love had become an emotional necessity. Or a biological one. Or both. Romanticists to the contrary, the object of his affections wasn't really very important. There were any number of pretty young women who would do just as well. That "one and only" business was a product of adolescent imagination. Or a sign of arrested development. Needing to love, Doug had settled upon Jen because she was pretty, sweet, and—available. Only Jen herself, being a true romantic, had removed the availability. Well, Grace was also pretty, sweet and available. And she wasn't removing her availability. Far from it. With ludicrous ease, Doug would now settle upon her, perform the miracle of healing a hopelessly broken heart in a matter of hours. In fact, he was already performing it.

Duncan wanted to laugh. But the taste of repressed laughter on his tongue was strangely bitter-sweet. There was an element of sadness in the comedy. The tragi-comic difference between people's pretensions and their performances, he supposed.

And Grace, in equal measure. She was softly, prettily glowing.

"Oh, Doctor, you have such nice friends!" she said.

Duncan grinned, choking back the accurate observation that since Doug was the first and only friend of his she'd ever met, how the hell did she know?

"Look, kids," he said, "I have to go. Appointment with Fred Baynes of *The Picayune*. But I want to tell you both that I introduced you on purpose, with malice aforethought. Got damned tired of seeing two of the nicest people I know going around with hangdog looks. Part of my treatment, Grace. Doug, you got any good reason to go back to Caneville in a hurry?"

"Lord, no! And if I had, I'd sure as heck make some arrangements now."

"Good. So now I'm going to give Grace a prescription—verbally. You, young lady, are to go dancing with Douglass Henderson every night you can get out of the house. Buggy rides under the moon. The works. I'm discharging you right now. Doug will take you home. And, Grace——"

"Yes, Doctor?"

"You tell that horny-fisted old pirate of a Pa of yours just one thing for me: the Hendersons of Caneville-Sainte Marie haven't as much money as he has. But then who the hell has, except John D. Rockefeller and Jay Gould? Just tell him that Doug Henderson has enough long green to keep any girl in disgusting luxury for the rest of his life. So he can look into your bonny blue eyes without the dollar signs getting in the way. Forgive me if I sound crude. Hell, I am crude. What else can you expect of a Channel brat?"

"I think you're just perfectly wonderful, Doctor Duncan," Grace Harvey said.

"Dunc——" Doug croaked.

"Yes, boy?"

"Thanks. Thanks, loads!"

"After that," Fred Baynes said, "was when you married Miss Vance? That must have been romantic. You'd saved her brother's life. It was brought out at the trial that his death wasn't your fault."

"I wouldn't have married her, Fred," Duncan said, "if I had thought it was mere gratitude. We were engaged several weeks before Dick Willis stabbed her brother."

"Even better. More romantic that way. The readers like romance, Doc."

"Yes," Duncan said drily. "I guess they do."

He was thinking now how little romantic it had been. How close Nelson Vance had come to making a shotgun wedding out of it. Not that that made much difference. Not that anything did.

"Look, son," Nelson Vance said tiredly, "I ain't saying that I blame you two much. You're both young, and young folks is just plain nacherly full o' hell."

Duncan looked at the old man pityingly. In the two days since Jim's death and the funeral that afternoon at the Presbyterian Church—for Jim had refused to follow his father's lead and switch his religious affiliations as the Vances clawed their way upward, on the explicit grounds that "them Episcopalians is just too damn highfalutin for me!"—Nelson Vance had aged twenty years. Before, it had been impossible to tell he was actually sixty years old. Now he looked every day of it, and more.

"But, Father," Hester said tearfully, "what will people say? For us to go and get married the day after my brother was buried would cause an awful lot of talk."

"Heck of a lot less," Nelson rumbled, "than having a brat show up a damn sight too soon!"

"I've told you and told you!" Hester wept. "I am not in the family way, as you call it! I couldn't be, for the simple reason that we——"

"Didn't do nothing. You two jest sat there a-listening to the rain. Now who the hell do you expect to believe that, daughter?"

"Not you, in any event," Duncan said evenly. "You haven't the kind of mind that could, sir. Nevertheless, that's exactly what happened: absolutely nothing at all."

"I wish we had!" Hester burst out. "I wanted to! But I didn't because I didn't want to ruin the finest day in my life—the day I was going to marry Duncan because he loves me enough to take me proudly and publicly to wife, letting the whole world know what I mean to him! I won't let you shame that, Father! I won't let you dirty it!"

"It ain't me who's shaming it, daughter," Nelson Vance said stubbornly. " 'Twas you who stayed out all night with your young man."

"And how did I stay out, Father? Lying on a sofa, with Duncan sitting on the floor beside me, talking to me about the future, about our plans—until I fell asleep! Then he sat by the fire, keeping it going, watching over me, guarding me, protecting me, like a gentleman should! But you don't understand that. You don't even know what it means to be a gentleman."

"Reckon I don't," Nelson said wearily. "I'm just a plain, practical man, who don't believing in taking no chances. The facts is as plain as the nose on your face."

"All right," Duncan said. "But there are some other facts that you aren't taking into consideration, Mr. Vance. I'll skip all of them but one: you can't force me to marry your daughter. There just isn't any way you can do that."

"Great balls o' fire!" Nelson roared. "You want me to git up from here and git my ol' double-barrelled twelve-gauge, boy?"

"If you like," Duncan said coolly. "What good would it do you?"

"What good?" Nelson Vance bellowed. "You ask me what good?"

"Yes, sir. Precisely that. Even if, out of respect for your age, and love for your daughter, I refrained from taking it away from you, and bending it double around a stump, as I could—what could you do with a shotgun, sir? Frighten me into sneaking off and marrying Hes, like a yellow-bellied rat? I don't scare, Mr. Vance, not even a little bit. In fact, I don't scare at all."

"You, Father," Hester said—her voice vibrant with that ancient, even atavistic, pride of the warrior's woman, the champion's mate —"are talking to the man who walked barehanded right up to the muzzle of a known killer's gun! New experience, eh, Father? What do you do now? How are you going to handle a man? You've never had to before. All you've had to deal with were poor shivering starvelings dependent upon your bounty. Tell me, Father, what are you going to do?"

Nelson Vance surged to his feet, his face purple:

"Do? Why, I'll blow his gawddamned head off! I'll——"

"Sit down!" Duncan snapped. His voice was very quiet, but it had the quality, the ring, of suddenly unsheathed steel.

Nelson Vance stood there staring at him.

"Sit down, Mr. Vance," Duncan said.

Slowly, Nelson Vance sank back in his chair.

"Suppose you got that gun," Duncan went on, his voice easy, pleasant, conversational. "You then ordered me to marry Hester for a thing I didn't do. And I refused. You must then kill me, because you would have no other way out, no further recourse. What then, Mr. Vance? Your daughter remains—you insist—dishonoured, possibly pregnant. And the only man capable of righting matters is dead. Very intelligent. What's more, you're in jail. And if the case went on long enough, as it might, the simple fact that Hester is not going to have a child for the even simpler reason that we just didn't do what you accuse us of having done, inconceivable as that may seem to your type of mind, would become apparent. The court then, despite your position in the community, would be forced to hang you—or, at best, sentence you to life imprisonment. What then would you have solved? That's what you're faced with, sir. Because I do refuse to marry Hester under those circumstances. Much as I love her, I refuse."

"You mean—not never?" Nelson Vance said. His bull-like voice had a noticeable quaver in it.

"No, sir. I'll marry your daughter, sir—at Christmas time, in the church, before the usual group of relatives and friends. But I will not insult her by giving in to your suspicions. I will, however, make one concession to your concern as a father for your daughter's welfare."

"And that is?" Nelson Vance growled.

"I give you my word, as an Aubert, even as a Childers, for my father's word meant something, too, that nothing happened between Hester and me. Does that satisfy you?"

"Well," Nelson grumbled, "just your plain word——"

"Not my plain word. The word of an Aubert. The next time you're in New Orleans, sir, pay a visit to the Saint Louis cemetery. You'll find there, side by side, the tombs of three men who dared, on the same day, to question Jean Jacques Aubert's word. He was my grandfather, Mr. Vance. I don't think that blood has run thin yet."

"Well, all right," Nelson said slowly. "But if you're lying to me . . ."

"I never lie. The only excuse for lying is that you're afraid."

165

"Or," Hester said, "that you don't want to hurt—someone you love."

He was going to recall those words to mind, one day. But he did not know that then.

"In which case you can keep your mouth shut," Duncan said. "Well, sir?"

"Oh, all right!" Nelson Vance said.

It rained all Christmas Day. But that didn't stop matters at all. Outside the Episcopal Church there was a sea of umbrellas, sheltering the uninvited curious. The guests arrived early, despite the foul weather. Douglass Henderson, the best man, arrived first. After him, Stanton Bruder came. He, curiously, had rung up Duncan and asked for an invitation.

"Hell, Duncan," he said over the phone, "let's bury the hatchet. After all, you and I are sort of kin, and you won't be having any family there. Shouldn't hold my testimony in the Willis case against me. I was called to testify, and I was under oath. Now you tell me one thing. Did I tell one single lie?"

"No," Duncan said. Stan hadn't lied. All he had done was to twist the truth by inflections of his voice, sentences left uncompleted, until the implications had become far worse than any lie could ever have been. But it didn't matter now. "All right, Stan," Duncan said. "Come on. Glad to have you."

The only thing he couldn't figure was Stanton's motive. During the ceremony, it seemed to have been that he had come to catch Hester's eye and grin at her with mocking insolence. Afterwards it turned out that that was precisely what he had come for. But that was another thing that Duncan Childers didn't know then.

Next came Jenny Greenway, who, for the first time in her life, excited the admiring whistles and loud comments of the corner hangers, lounge lizards and drugstore cowboys, as she descended from a hired carriage in her white old lace dress, matching Hester's wedding gown, with her dark hair softly clubbed under her wide picture hat, and, best of all, not wearing her glasses, thus giving her extraordinarily large and beautiful eyes their full play. Even Duncan shaped his lips into a silent whistle, looking at her. She looked back, but she didn't recognise him. Without her hideous spectacles, she just couldn't see that far away. Jenny was maid of honour, a fact whose true basis she was unable to decide. It was difficult to say whether Hester's motive in asking her had been kindness—or cruelty.

The musical Mullers, all four of them, came next. Their presence excited little comment, for the crowd had been expecting it.

Then Doctor Hans Volker came with Professor Augustus Berg-dorf, and Doctors Harris and Thompson and their wives paid honour to their young colleague.

Last of all, the Vances came. The crowd did not know which to admire more: Hester, incredibly lovely in her gown of creamy white old lace, or Nelson, for the first time in his life groomed, scrubbed, polished and correct, from his top hat, morning coat, hickory-striped trousers, down to the patent-leather pumps that hurt his feet.

As they came in, Stanton Bruder succeeded in his intention to catch Hester's eye. Having done so, he grinned mockingly.

Hester's face flamed scarlet.

'Dear God!' she thought; 'I hope Duncan didn't see!'

Father Rayn, who had long since given up the attempt to con-vince even his own flock that his name was not Ryan, waited by the flower-smothered altar. Before it, Douglass, Duncan and Jenny also waited. The organ began the wedding march from *Lohengrin*. Nobody noticed Rosemary Vance, as she crept like a sombre, black-clad shadow into the church.

Doug was so nervous, he almost dropped the ring. Duncan, to his own surprise, was very calm—that is, until, turning at some half-heard sound, he met Jenny Greenway's eyes. They were twin dark stars, eclipsed by grief. Looking into them, at that moment, took more courage than he knew he had. He turned back again, hearing Father Rayn intone: "If there be one among you, who knows any reason or impediment for which this sacrament of mar-riage should not be performed, let him speak now, or henceforth forever after hold his peace. . . ."

"Wait!" Rosemary Vance shrilled. "I know the reason! Don't you hold me! I've got something to say about that!"

"Let her come forward," Father Rayn said.

Rosemary strode towards the altar, confident and smiling, un-moved by, even unaware of, that silence that rang like vibrating crystal through the church.

"Will you state your objections, Mrs. Vance?" Father Rayn said.

Rosemary Vance stood there, smiling, facing them.

Her hands moved. She dug feverishly into her handbag and came out with the paper. She began to read, brightly, her voice high and clear, like a child's:

"It is forbidden of God and also of my brothers the green-eyed

Irish Kings who on that day of rest the Sabbath did profane and more——"

She paused, peering at them, her face twisted into an expression of cunning.

"Besides, it is murder. Even with whisky it is murder and hate itself doth not suffice nor all my shame or my burning revenge. He drowned in the rain with a knife in his heart for this reason they must not wed. There is blood on this marriage and its consummation will be a sickness and a grief so sayeth my brothers the green-eyed Irish Kings who befouled the Sabbath Day by lying in filth and foulness with Meg Clouter and others of that ilk——"

"Mrs. Vance!" Father Rayn thundered.

Hans Volker stepped forward, his eyes full of pity.

"Let me take her outside, Father," he said quietly. "I'm sure I can handle her."

"Please, Father," Duncan said, "let him take her away."

Hester was crying helplessly now. Jenny was trying to calm her. Father Rayn spoke out clearly, calmly, as Hans led Rosemary away:

"My friends, may God have pity upon this poor broken mind! Let us say a silent prayer that her sanity be restored, and then proceed."

It was over very quickly, after that. Everything went off smoothly, beautifully. But it had been spoiled just the same. For on his bride's mouth, in that first nuptial kiss, Duncan Childers tasted neither warmth nor tenderness, but only cold and trembling and the salt of tears.

Chapter 12

DUNCAN CLUNG TO THE STRAPS of the wildly careering 'Meat Wagon' as they pounded at a hard gallop through the narrow streets of New Orleans. Up on the driver's seat, Fred Baynes sat with the driver. This was the last night. After this experience of emergency calls, Fred would have all he needed to finish his series of stories.

'And I,' Duncan thought, 'have all I need to make up my mind —or very nearly. To stop being a surgical pimp, and become a doctor. But can I? Have I got it in me?'

The ambulance gave a tremendous lurch, almost overturning.

"Tell that damned fool to slow down!" Duncan growled. "It's only an O.B."

"I've told him a thousand times," Tom Hendricks groaned, "but ever since that filly had her brat on the bench a month ago and old Phelton chewed his ears off about it, every time he hears the words 'woman in labour' he drives like he's going to a fire. He'll tip us over one of these fine nights, sure as hell."

"Medicine!" Duncan spat. "The healing art. Damned if I don't wish I'd taken up plumbing!"

"You did," Tom said. "Just what do you think surgery is? Where the blazes are we going, anyhow? All the way to Texas?"

"Down to the Irish Channel," Duncan said savagely. "Some Biddy is having a litle Mick. Lor' luv th' Irish! Dangblast it, Ned, I told you——"

"Might as well stop yelling at Ned, Dunc. He can't hear you," Tom Hendricks said.

They climbed down from the ambulance on Annunciation Street. The two big roans were covered with foam, their eyes rolling redly under the electric lights that had been installed as early as 1886, making New Orleans the first city in Louisiana to have them.

"Damn it, Ned," Duncan snapped, "if you kill those nags, or turn us over, we'll be in more trouble than just being late!"

"Sorry, Doc," Ned said, "but I'm plumb scared of ol' Doc Phelton."

"Hell, Doc, it was fun!" Fred Baynes said.

They heard the woman scream then, terribly.

"Come on, Doc!" Fred Baynes said.

"Don't let it get you, Fred," Duncan said. "Women just purely love to yell."

They went up those dark, rickety, foul-smelling stairs. The house was more than a hundred years old, and clearly on the point of collapse. And even though the streets had been wired for electricity seven full years ago now, it was still illuminated by gas, oil lamps, candles. The smell of greasy cooking assailed their nostrils. They heard the roars and shrieks of drunken, nuptial quarrels.

"Lor' luv the Irish!" Duncan said again, pityingly.

They knocked on the door of the flat. A fair-haired child opened it. She was dressed in rags. They couldn't tell what colour her dress had been for the dirt.

"Anybody at home but you, Sissy?" Tom said kindly.

She stared at him.

"Yessir," she got out. "Joey 'n Mike—an' Ma. Ma's gonna have me lil' sister. She promised me a sister, this time."

"We'll see that she keeps her word," Duncan said. "Where's your father?"

"He—ain't here. He got tired o' listenin' to Ma yell," the child said.

"Damn them!" Fred Baynes muttered. "They're my people, but damn them anyhow! The bloody drunken bastards, they——"

"The kid can hear you, Fred," Duncan said.

They found the woman lying on a bed as filthy as the rest of the flat. Filthier. She was very pale and thin, except for her abdomen, which was enormous.

"Twins," Tom said.

"Guess again, Tom," Duncan said. "That brat's in a transverse position. We'll have to use podalic version."

"Here?" Tom snorted.

"Hell, no! That would be asking for puerperal fever. We'll have to get her to the hospital."

"But you can't," the woman whispered. "There's no one here to keep the kids——"

Duncan stared at her. Her accent was definitely cultivated, her grammar correct. That was damned strange for the Channel.

"We'll send one of the Sisters of Charity," Tom said.

Duncan was staring at the two smaller children, fast asleep on pallets on the floor. The pallets were bundles of rags. They had been various colours once. Now they were all one colour, black. Greasy black.

He turned to the woman.

"How long have you been having your pains?" he said.

"Since day before yesterday," the woman murmured.

"Lord God!" Duncan said. "Tom, go get Ned! Bring the stretcher. We've got to get her to the hospital in one hell of a hurry!"

"But the kids?" Tom said.

"Knock on the first door you come to. Find anybody in this fire-trap that even looks sober, and send them here to watch. Tell them if they don't come, you'll put the law on 'em. Get going now!"

"It's too late," the woman whispered. "I'm going to die."

"Not on my life, you aren't!" Duncan snapped. "Buck up now, Mrs. O'Leary. You're in good hands."

"I know I am—Duncan," the woman said. "Just as I knew you'd get to be a doctor, in spite of everything."

Duncan stared at her. He came closer, bent over the bed.

His lips moved, shaping her name. But he didn't say it. Not with Fred Baynes there. Not with tomorrow's paper not yet printed and there being time enough for the reporter to write this up, too.

"How," he choked, rage and pity strangling him, "did you—you!—come to this?"

"I—I stopped trying, Duncan," she whispered. "Stopped aiming so high. I married a man who wasn't as high as the stars above me—like you were."

"Instead you got one a million miles below you," Duncan snarled. "Oh Jesus—God! No! This shouldn't happen! This shouldn't be allowed to happen; not to the finest and the sweetest and the best——"

"No, Duncan. He wasn't so bad at first. Let me tell you. I—I haven't got much time. I—I got a job in the five and ten. I worked hard. You see, then I still believed I could get to be somebody. Fat chance! I should have known I was only—a thing. A thing to be beaten and kicked, and left alone to die from having his kid. Die and leave my brood to grow up to be whores and thieves, because that's all there ever is for kids born in the Channel."

"I was born in the Channel, remember," Duncan said. He turned and saw that Fred Baynes had his notebook out and was making the little pot-hooks and spiral scrawls of shorthand.

"Goddamn you, Fred," he screamed. "Print this, and I'll kill you!" Then he paused. "Sorry," he said. "Take your notes, boy. Then print it! Twist their guts with it! Rub their noses in it. All this! All the hunger, filth, misery! I know how it feels, Fred! I was born here. Only—I escaped. Most of 'em never get a chance to."

"Then," Fred said very quietly, "they should be rescued. Doc, I'm going to start the goddamnedest campaign! I'm going to find out the names and addresses of the fat pigs who own these ratholes! Then I'm gonna list 'em, along with a full description of the conditions I found here."

"You'll get fired," the woman said wearily. "The same people who own these places own the newspapers—or their friends do. Forget it, mister."

"Look——" Duncan began, but she cut him off, her voice low, husky, tender—like the memory of love; like the dull ache of loss.

"You got out," she said, "because you were different. One like you, Duncan, is born maybe every thousand years. The only happiness I ever had was knowing you, loving you—that never stopped, Duncan. But I guess it's going to stop—tonight——"

"No!" Duncan got out. "I——" He was being very careful not to say her name. He didn't want Fred Baynes to scrawl that down in his pot-hooks, look it up in the old files.

She doubled her two hands across her middle, caught her lower lip between her teeth and bit it through. But she didn't make a sound. She was very pale. The blood showed starkly against her skin.

'Anæmia,' Duncan thought bitterly. 'That too. Malnutrition, mistreatment, neglect. And drunkenness. The four horsemen of the Irish Channel. Why are they like this? Name of God, why? Other people are poor, but——"

Tom and Ned came through the door. With them was a fat, blowsy woman with a kindly red face.

"Mrs. O'Higgins will stay with your children, ma'am," Tom said gently. "It was she who telephoned for us in the first place."

"Heard you up here a-weeping 'n a-wailing, dearie," Mrs. O'Higgins said. "So I ups and takes myself down to Harry's Bar and called the hospital. Knew that drunken pig of an Irishman you married would never think o' it. Sure an' you jist rest aisy now, dearie. You ain't got a thing to worry about, not a thing i' th' wurrrld. I'll take care o' your bairns jist as if they was me own."

"Thank you, Mrs. O'Higgins," the woman wept.

They took her down the stairs—all five flights of them. Duncan climbed into the ambulance beside her.

"Mind if I come, too, Doc?" Fred said. "This is just the kind of thing I need—the real human touch. The touch of tragedy, you might say."

"Tragedy?" she whispered. "Tragedy only happens to great people, mister. Like kings and queens. Read the books, mister. Never to God's cockroaches, like us. We only get stepped on, mashed flat. Let him come in, Duncan. I won't say anything that——"

"All right, Fred," Duncan said tiredly. "Come on."

Tom climbed up on the seat beside the driver. The ambulance moved off in a jingle of harness, an explosion of whip cracks, a shower of oaths.

"Tell us about it," Duncan said. "You said you had a job?"

"Yes——" she got out between set teeth, "in the five and ten. And I met Tim there—worst luck!"

"Tim?"

"My husband. He was something to see, Duncan! Dressed to kill: bowler hat, gold tiepin, silk shirt. Thought I'd die laughing the first time I saw him. He was everything that vulgar people think is fine. But he was nice. He came up to my counter to buy some trinket or another. After that, he came back almost every day. I started going out with him on Sunday, and very soon he proposed. He had a good job then: Mr. Timothy O'Leary, Assistant Superintendent at the Ice Plant. As I said, he was nice. For one thing, he wasn't—fresh. That was a relief. And I was lonely. And you were gone. Gone for ever. I wanted a home. Kids. I figured I could do worse. I was wrong. I couldn't have."

"But that flat, ma'am?" Fred Baynes said. "Seems to me the Ice Plant Superintendent wouldn't need——"

"Assistant Superintendent, mister. No. We had a very clean and pretty flat. We got down to that one by stages. Always moving, each flat worse than the last. Started when he lost his job."

"Why'd he lose it?" Duncan said.

"Drink. When the babies started coming, he started to worry. You see, Duncan, he made quite enough to take care of me and the kids. But not enough to do that and drink and gamble with the boys at the same time. He wasn't a skirt-chaser, though. I'll say that much for him. But it was one thing or the other; so he kept on cutting down on the house money to spend it on his fun."

"And you quarrelled with him?"

"Of course. What wife wouldn't have? That made him worse. He started getting ugly. Drinking more and more. Even slamming me around once in a while. Let his work slide, so they kicked him out. That really got him wild. Took all the money, and went off on a four-day drunk. Came back nastier than ever. Every two words

It was: 'Cheap little counter-jumper!' and, 'Tell me, baby, how many times did you do it for the boss?'"

'Let me be blasted from earth by lightnings,' Duncan thought bitterly; 'destroyed by earthquakes. Let me die in catastrophes, be cut down bloodily in combat with giants! Anything but this—this being nibbled to death by the rats of time. Anything except one of these pitifully banal annihilations, this slow grinding underfoot of cockroaches—God!'

"He left me more than once, after that. Then he'd come back brimful and overflowing with contrition and beg me to forgive him. But as soon as I did, it was right back to the bottle for my Tim! Cuffing and kicking me around. I don't suppose you noticed that my youngest boy is a cripple, did you? Tim did that—kicked me in the stomach while I was carrying little Mike. He—he's lost nine jobs in the last two years. Now—he doesn't even—try any more—Oh, Lord God, here it comes again!"

Duncan opened his bag, drew out the hypodermic. He sponged off an area in the crook of her arm, placed the needle on it, shoved it home. Then he pressed the plunger in, slowly. He sat there, watching her face. Her breathing slowed, quietened.

"Thanks, Doc," she said drowsily.

When they got her up to Maternity, they found everything in a turmoil. There wasn't even a nurse in the emergency delivery room. Tom raced downstairs to Surgery. In minutes he was back.

"One of us will have to act as anæsthetist, Dunc, then assist. No nurses available. There was a big fire at one of the cotton warehouses. They've got fifteen smoke-poisoning cases in there now, and more coming in every minute. They're all giving artificial respiration. Old Phelton says for us to carry on. He'll look in as soon as he can."

"A fire!" Fred Baynes roared. "Lemme out of here!" He whirled, already running.

They scrubbed in grim silence. A podalic version was nothing to be taken lightly. One of them would have to work his hand up into the uterus, catch the child by one or both of his feet, and turn him into a vertical position so that he could be extracted without too much damage to the mother.

"God, she's small!" Tom said.

"She's had three kids before, remember," Duncan said.

They had to do it all: bathe her, shave the *mons veneris*, give her additional anæsthesia so that the pain would not kill her.

"You take it, Dunc," Tom said.

"No. Put out your hand. The one who has the smallest paw is it."

Tom had slim, tapering fingers. Much smaller than Duncan's rawboned, large-knuckled, pianist's hands.

"I lose," he said quietly. "Where the hell are the gloves, Dunc?"

"Over there in the steriliser. But if you've really scrubbed, you don't need them. I hate the bloody things. You lose too much feel."

"I know. But you ever run a microscopic examination of nail-parings—after a ten-minute scrub?"

"Yes. Full of crap, even then. Colon bacillus, mostly. Strep. Every bloody damned infection-breeding microbe on the globe. You're right. The risks are too great. Use the gloves."

Tom bent over the patient. He was already sweating. The woman groaned fitfully.

"She's not out, is she, Dunc?"

"No. Can't put them all the way under. You need a little consciousness, or sometimes they don't contract. Got it, boy?"

"Not yet," Tom whispered. "There!"

He worked on in silence.

"Dunc," he said, his voice thick. "I—I can't! I don't know why; but I can't! The kid's deformed or something. I simply can't budge him!"

"Let me try," Duncan said.

He had much more difficulty, inserting his hand. He was, perhaps, a trifle stronger than Tom. But the results were the same. The baby, wedged crosswise in the womb, could not be moved.

He straightened up. Looked at Tom. Licked bone-dry lips.

"We'll have to do a Cæsarean," he whispered.

"She'll never make it," Tom said. "Safer to crush the head, go in there, and section it——"

"Tom, that child's alive!"

"I know it is. But you've got to choose between the child and the mother, Dunc. And this poor filly's got two more depending upon her . . . No, three. I forgot the little crippled one."

"Think she would survive that, either, Tom? A Cæsarean's quicker. And if it works, we save them, both."

"What for?" Tom said bitterly. "So she'll have another mouth to feed? Make herself one more filthy pallet in that unspeakable room? Have it grow up to be a hoodlum, if a boy, or a hustler, if a girl?"

"Those are not medical considerations, Doctor!"

They turned. Doctor Jarvis Phelton stood in the doorway. His eyes were bleak with weariness. He was, they both knew, one hell of a fine doctor. One of the best, among the older men. Perhaps even because he was as cold as ice.

"Glad you're here, Jarvis," Duncan said. "It's a hell of a thing to decide. The child's transverse and——"

"I have eyes, Doctor. Podalic version."

"Doesn't work," Tom said. "We've both tried. Dr. Childers thinks destroying the child, and extracting it in sections, would take too long."

"Besides which," Doctor Phelton said coldly, "it is murder."

Tom stared at him. He had forgotten momentarily that Dr. Phelton was a Roman Catholic. The rules, again. The rules which he, as a Protestant, wouldn't know. But which he stood accused, in Dr. Phelton's eyes, of rejecting, even before he knew them. *A priori* and *a posteriori*, he thought grimly.

"Will you examine the patient, Doctor?" he said, trying to keep the note of defiance out of his tone.

"Of course," Dr. Phelton said.

The examination took him thirty seconds.

"Cæsarean section," he said.

"It will kill her!" Tom said hotly.

Dr. Jarvis Phelton studied him. Even the distant sounds in the hospital came over to them crystal-clear in that long, long silence.

"That is your opinion, Doctor," Dr. Phelton said at last, quietly; "which has the saving grace of the possibility of error—since it is opinion. Whereas, the other——" He crossed to the door in two long strides. In it, he turned. "I'll send Nurse Regis to you as anæsthetist," he said; and was gone.

"The bastard!" Tom cried. "The icy cold bastard!"

"He's right, Tom," Duncan said.

"Yes! But for the wrong reasons! Damn it all, Duncan, you can't base medicine on theology! I tell you——"

"She would die without it," Duncan said quietly. "I'm just as sure she'd die if we took her baby piecemeal. There's one chance in a million of saving her—of saving them both. And that's a Cæsarean. As doctors, Tom, we've got to take that one chance."

"All right, Dunc," Tom said tersely. "You do it, then. I'll assist."

The operation was beautifully done. Perfectly done. Doctor Duncan Childers did all that human skill, and his own very great talents, could to save her. But the patient died on the operating table. And the pitiful, blue, undersized bundle of flesh they took out of her lived five minutes, despite such measures as their taking turns blowing into its tiny, opened mouth.

"I told you!" Tom said grimly. Then he saw Duncan's eyes.

176

"Lord God, boy," he whispered. "You—you're crying! Don't take it so hard. You were entitled to your judgment, and—who knows? —maybe you were even right. Probably nothing could have saved her."

"It's not that," Duncan mumbled. "I—I knew her, Tom. We were——"

He looked up to see Fred Baynes walking in at the door. Everyone was so tied up that nobody had stopped him from walking into Surgery in his street clothes.

"Damned fire was out when I got there," he growled, "so I came on back." Then he, too, saw Duncan's face. "Jesus, Doc!" he said, "what's wrong?"

"Our patient died," Tom said wearily. "It seems that Dr. Childers knew her in the past. It's upset him."

"I gathered that much on the way over," Fred said. "Tough luck, Doctor."

Tom stared at his friend. This kind of emotion disturbed him. It clawed too deep. He took refuge in anger.

"Are you a doctor or aren't you?" he shouted. "Damn it, Duncan, snap out of it! Who the hell was she, anyhow?"

Duncan didn't answer him. He stood there, his head bent.

Fred Baynes came over to him, put an arm around his shoulders. "You can't save 'em all, Doc," he said gently. "Come on, tell us, who was she?"

Duncan straightened up, his face tear-streaked, his eyes bloodshot, red.

"Just a girl called—Calico," he said. Then he strode out of there.

Tom Hendricks and Fred Baynes stood there, looking at each other.

"Calico? Now that's one hell of a funny name," the reporter said.

Chapter 13

RIDING HOME IN A HIRED CAB ON CHRISTMAS EVE, 1903, Duncan Childers, M.D., could feel the weariness in him down to the very marrow of his bones. He patted his breast pocket. The little case containing the necklace gave back a reassuring thud to his fingers. The necklace was his combined Christmas and Anniversary gift to his bride.

'Three years,' he thought. 'Of work, of married life. Funny how curiously mixed it's been. Too bright; too dark. Am I three years older only—or the fifty that I feel?

'Married to Hester. I never expected that. I suppose I always knew I'd marry some day. But I never thought it would be—Hes. Not really. Not even then. Even though I did fall head over heels in love with her at seventeen. That was nothing but puppy love, anyway. Got over it, outgrew it, forgot it. So did she, though she claims she didn't. Sentimental beasts, women. Rot. The two who met when I came back from Europe three years ago weren't those same kids at all. Two strangers thrown together, in part by an irrelevant memory of childhood, in part by her loneliness and my grief. A man and a woman seeking in each other surcease from the torment those damnable little glands pour into the bloodstream, from their still childish fears and hurts inflated by their too active egos into a *Weltschmerz*, a universe of pain.

'Love? That too, I guess. Though it's too simple an explanation, even too meaningless. Love: a catch-basket for a variety of emotions, most of them a hell of a lot less pretty than our naïve romantic bent will let us admit.'

He leaned back against the cushions, closing his eyes, his mind, groping wearily for definitions, for the magic formula that would clarify everything: love equals sex equals companionship, liking, mutual respect, belonging—"and ye twain shall be one flesh"—hogwash. 'We're a thousand miles further apart now than we were when we were kids kissing each other in the woods. We twain are still twain and becoming twainer—why? Name of God, why?

'Sex? That's all right. Better than all right. Very good. Not like —Calico; but, after all, boy, poor Callie had reasons for being expert. Thank God she's out of it now, and at peace. Hold it,

178

Doctor! Whatever it is that your blushing bride lacks, it is not expertness. Far from it. Which is a thing you never wanted to go into, did you? All right. Go into it now. You've eliminated all other gods but that one; yet you still bow down and worship—truth. She had two days of marriage with Gino Rossini. Two days that can cover a multitude of sins, since virginity cannot be lost but once. Two days. Time and to spare to acquire a skill that most women don't attain in a lifetime of nightly practice. Remember Marta, you fool? That was innocence. That's how purity behaves. The tears. The shame. The shocked awakening to what her own body was capable of. The pleas that could and did unman me. All right; accept that. Don't dig into it. Leave what Jarvis calls the saving grace of a little decent doubt. Say that she had unusually acute aptitudes. Forget Hans Volker's pained expression when you told him you were going to marry her. The old boy knows something, all right. Something he isn't telling. Why? Why else but that it's a thing it would be a violation of professional ethics to reveal? Again, all right. Say that Hes is extraordinarily talented in that department. Say—anything but what you know is so: that you weren't number two on little Hester's list, not even—oh, skip it! All right, Truth-worshipper, there's your truth. Like it? Pretty, isn't it? Like the little boy with the coaster wagon, you've got it now; but what the hell are you going to do with it? Live with it, boy; that's all—as most men learn to live with what they know, and are; not with what they dream and hope. Rationalise it. Justify it. Say that she made you no promises, that even if she had, they would have been meaningless because the distance between sixteen and twenty-nine is one of the longest and crookedest journeys that there is. Admit that she didn't belong to you then; even that she doesn't now; that no amount of desire or will can really make one human being belong to another. Acknowledge that jealousy is an atavistic emotion, and that the past doesn't matter anyhow. Not unless you take it as a signpost to the future, as it too damned often is. What was it that Oscar Wilde said? Oh yes: "The future is only the past again, entered by another gate."

'Leave it. Leave your eyeless, faceless, ugly truth. That aspect of it, anyhow. What remains is your fault. "He who hath sons hath given hostages to fortune." Sons—or a wife. You've grown up finally. You've found out what medicine is. Found out that you really are a doctor. Or that you could be. That you're capable of embracing that life of monkish dedication. Embracing and loving it. Only you hadn't quite got there until—until you butchered poor

179

Callie trying to save her; matched your skill, your judgment, against death, and had death win!

'Until that night you wanted the dedication, all right, but without the monkishness; to have your cake and eat it, too. Remember the evening you came home after four operations, two scheduled, and two emergencies that came in—ruptured appendix, one of them already showing acute peritonitis—and she wanted to go dancing? And what happened, Doctor? You went dancing. You drank champagne. You came home and made love. So the next day, in the middle of one of the two dozen or so œsophagus reconstructions that Phelton had scheduled since he found out you could do them, you had to ask Tom to take over, because in another minute you were going to kill the patient; speed gone, skill gone, sureness gone, light-headed from champagne, shaky from fatigue, hollow-boned from the aftermath of love. . . .

'Remember how she cried the first time you attempted to tell her you meant to go back to Caneville-Sainte Marie and really be a doctor? That you wanted to leave New Orleans, gay New Orleans, bright, frothy New Orleans, where all you do is skilled butchery instead of practising medicine? So you didn't go back. You signed on the staff of Phelton's Knife-Happy Hollow for another six months. Six months that end tonight.

'But add the other side, too. That she's been good to you. That, in her way and after her fashion, she loves you—truly. The touching way she gives you the little things she's bought you with her old man's infernal money. Things that you can buy yourself now, with your beautiful, beautiful damned lying fees obtained from rich hypochondriacs under false pretences! Things you'd rather do without than get that way. But you can't tell her that, can you? You haven't the heart. That lovely binocular microscope. The finest set of instruments any young doctor ever had. A calfskin bag to carry them in. Coming to you like a child, those young-old eyes so full of pride, as if to say: 'See—see what I have for you in my hands!''

'And when you suggested that she ought to learn something about medicine instead of sitting there moping in the flat—because you were afraid of what loneliness might force her into, knowing that she hates being alone worse than death or hell; she who married a member of the profession whose mates must necessarily lead lives lonelier than those of any other women, with the sole exception of seamen's wives—she signed on as a Nurse's Aide; emptied bedpans, scrubbed floors, worked so hard and learned so much that even that old combination buzzard and battle-axe, Regis, swears that she could make R. N. in six months! She, who didn't know the sun rose before eleven o'clock in the morning, who had never had breakfast out of bed in all her life! And she was good at it. Very good. Not because she likes it, or really wants to do it; but because it pleases me . . . God damn it, I——'

"This the address you told me, Doc?" tne cabby said.

But, as he went up the stairs, it was no longer Hester he was thinking of, but Calico. Calico, who hadn't got the world on its own terms. Or maybe she had. Didn't the world's terms include precisely that sort of lonely, pitiful dying?

'Bless her,' he thought. 'If there's a heaven, I know she's there. She had her hell on earth. Yes, bless her. For, by dying like that, she saved my own meaningless equivalent for whatever people mean when they say "immortal soul".

'She did that for me. Cracked the last of my already dented armour. Got to me. Hit me down deep where I live. I've got to go now. I've got to. If life is meaningless, then I must give it meaning, pour into this tiny interval between two everlasting darknesses all that I have of light.'

'Pretentious bastard, aren't you?' his mind mocked him. 'Go on, little glow-worm, let's see you glow!'

He grinned. 'I was being sententious, wasn't I? But damn it all, man doth not live by bread alone!'

'Nope,' his mind gibed; 'a glass of wine helps; not to mention a good piece of the common commodity from time to time. But the rest is hogwash. Makes you feel better? Fine! Go to it; but for Christ's sake stop piling eternities on top of it. You aren't that big, boy.'

He paused at the landing below his apartment and put his hand in his coat pocket to find the key. As he did so, his fingers touched the heavy, embossed envelope. Doug's and Grace's wedding invitation.

"Mr. Ernest Swithin Harvey requests the honour of your presence at the wedding of his daughter, Grace Elinor, to Mr. Douglass Putnam Henderson on New Year's Day, This Year of Our Lord, Nineteen hundred and four, at Christ Church Cathedral, at eight o'clock post meridian."

That had happened fast enough! As he had known it would. The workings of human emotions under those particular circumstances were as predictable as the course of—yellow fever, say. 'What can we buy them? They've both got everything.'

Even before he put the key in the lock of the apartment, that beautiful apartment that Nelson Vance had bought them, saying:

"Know you ain't had a chance to make yourself a pile yet, son, but, till you do, I don't want my baby living like no nigger scrub-woman", he heard the sound of music and voices and laughter.

"Oh, no!" he groaned. "Oh, God, no!" Then: 'All right, take it easy, boy. It's Christmas Eve, after all—and you don't have to get up in the morning. Not unless some damned woman starts to have a baby at four a.m., or some drunk falls out of a buggy and breaks his arm; or two liquored-up good friends decide to carve each other up instead of the turkey. Which will happen. It always does. If he were anywhere around, I'd round myself up a posse and go lynch Alexander Graham Bell for having invented his bloody telephone. Before that, they at least had to go to the trouble of coming and getting you."

He opened the door.

"Darling!" Hester cried, and hurled herself upon him, swinging by both arms from his neck, bending her knees so that he bore her entire weight, and kissing him endlessly—great moist kisses that tasted of champagne.

"Take it easy, baby," he laughed. "After all, there are people present."

"Not people," Tom gibed. "Doctors. Subspecies. Not entirely human."

"Oh, don't worry about them!" Hester said. "They don't even think you're going to get excited. They know better. When you come home, you're dead. In fact, I'm thinking of getting them a substitute doctor, so you can get some rest. Or, better still, me a substitute husband, so you can put on some weight, skinnybones!"

"Ma'am," Lester Ryan said with drunken gravity, "you have a volunteer!"

"I'll keep you in mind, Lester," Hester said.

"So will I," Duncan growled in mock wrath, "when I want to try out a surgical innovation. Without anæsthesia, of course."

"Keep him away from me!" Lester said. "He's mean!"

Millicent, Tom's wife, came up to Duncan with the tray.

"Have some champagne, Doctor," she said.

She was pregnant again, enough to show, and little Dan, their first, was only eleven months old.

"Aren't you kids rushing things a bit, Milly?" Duncan said.

"No. We want to have lots and lots of babies," Millicent said. "At least a dozen. Babies are nice. Instead of you and Hester being so lazy, you should——"

"It's not laziness, Milly!" Hester laughed. "At least not on my

182

part, dearest. I just think old Doc Skinnybones here needs a vacation. In the country, where I can feed him lots and lots of eggs!"

"That," Doctor Jarvis Phelton said, "is rubbish, Hester. Superstitious rubbish. Many couples are married ten or twelve years before they have a child. Sometimes it is a physical impossibility, impotence on the part of the husband——"

"Impotent he is not, Doctor!" Hester said merrily. "That I can assure you!"

"Hes," Duncan said. "All right, this is nearly 1904, these are modern times; but there are limits, baby——"

"We are speaking scientifically, Doctor," Phelton said. He, too, was a little drunk, Duncan saw. His voice was taking on the rotund tones of the lecture platform.

Duncan moved off. He had heard enough lectures.

"Come sit by me, Doctor," Miriam Phelton said to him. Dr. Phelton's wife was one of those impeccably groomed, middle-aged women who fancy themselves exceedingly skilled in diplomacy, or, for that matter, in any kind of intrigue. She was, of course, like all women, to any man with an I.Q. above the moronic, as transparent as window-glass.

Duncan crossed to the sofa where she sat, thinking as he went: 'Is it because we indulge them in it that they persist? Or are there actually men as stupid as women think we all are?'

Mrs. Phelton patted the cushion beside her, arch, maternal, graceful. "Sit down, my boy," she said.

Duncan sat down beside her, glancing over to where Hester and the three men were engaged in a deep, drunken discussion of the reasons why women did, or did not, have babies.

"It's most strange," Jarvis Phelton said, "but there were these couples, married, as I said, for years, and nothing happened. Yet the minute they——"

"Perhaps," Lester Ryan suggested brightly, "they didn't!"

"They didn't what, Lester?" Tom said.

"They didn't——" Lester said. He used the short, explicit, Anglo-Saxon word.

"Lester," Miriam Phelton said, "you want me to wash your mouth out with soap, you naughty boy?"

"Why don't you find Lester a wife, Miriam?" Duncan said pleasantly. "That way maybe he'd leave mine alone." 'Nice gambit,' he thought; 'my King's Bishop's pawn is out now, one space.'

"Jealous, Duncan?" Miriam said.

'Cleared her own Bishop now, or her Queen. Now all I've got

to do is to move any other pawn except my Queen's or King's, and she's got me. Fool's mate. Let's see: guess I'll move out my Rook's pawn. Really set it up; leave myself helpless.'

"Frankly, yes, Miriam—at least, a little."

"Is that why you haven't renewed your contract with Jarvis, Duncan?" Miriam said.

"Checkmate!" Duncan said aloud.

"What's that?" Miriam Phelton said. "What did you say, my boy?"

"Nothing. Just an expression of mine. Do you want me to stay on, Miriam?"

"Very much. Jarvis likes you, son. You and Tom——"

'You mean he likes the hard cash that our knowledge of a little modern surgery brings in,' Duncan thought. He said brightly, "Does he?"

"Of course, Duncan! Jarvis is so undemonstrative, that's the trouble. He says that you and Tom are exceedingly competent and——"

"And what, Miriam?" Duncan said.

"And he needs you, Duncan," Miriam said, laying her hand on his arm.

"Unhand my husband, you villain!" Hester cried. "Say, just what are you two chatting about so cosily?"

"I'm trying to persuade your husband to stay on with us," Miriam said. "You do agree, don't you, dear?"

"I'm with you all the way, Miriam!" Hester said. "I just love New Orleans."

"Then come over here and help me," Mrs. Phelton said. "I appear to be getting nowhere, very fast."

Hester got up, and came over to them. She sat down on the sofa beside them. Jarvis Phelton came over, too.

"Let me in on this," he said cheerfully.

'I'm outnumbered, three to one,' Duncan thought. 'But they can't win—not even with Hes helping them. Have to stand up for what I believe. Reached the point now where the retreat must rally, or become a rout. Can't call my soul my own now. My soul that I don't believe in. What the hell am I fighting for anyhow? My dignity as a man. The dignity of a cockroach. What difference does it make? The good or ill that one does in the world is equally meaningless. As meaningless as the actions of cockroaches. Damn Beth anyhow, for putting that notion in my head! Besides, she's wrong. It does make a difference to—me, who've got to live with myself. And even if a man's life is only a lightning flash in the

184

eternity of time, he owes it to himself to flash gloriously. Since this
little life is all we'll ever have, so much better to live it with internal
splendour, to stand erect, not crawl—like a cockroach.'

He threw back his head and laughed aloud. Hester stared at
him.

"What ails you, darling?" she said.

"Nothing!" Duncan said. "I'm well, now—entirely well at last."
He looked at them, smiling. "Here you are," he said, "all of you,
asking me to bow to your selfish interests, bow even to my own.
Hester loves New Orleans. She can't see being cooped up in that
miserable, backyard swamp town again. And I don't blame her.

"You, Jarvis, are aware that I have a certain value to you; and
Miriam knows that value extends even to herself, since it is
measured in the currency of the realm."

"Agreed," Jarvis Phelton said. "You are valuable, Doctor.
Damned valuable. If it is the question of salary that's troubling you,
I'll put you on a commission basis and you'll make a fortune."

"You already pay me more than I can hope to make in Caneville,
Jarvis," Duncan said. "It's not money. Beyond the bare necessities,
and a few simple luxuries that I can gain anywhere, it simply
doesn't matter. What does matter to me is that I do what I was
born to do—practise medicine."

"But you are practising medicine," Phelton said. "I don't
see——"

"You can't see, Jarvis. And I can't make you. Here in New
Orleans, for a year and a half, I've been resectioning œsophaguses,
expirating aortic aneurysms, even bobbing the too long noses of
women who have too much money and not enough brains to know
that beauty comes from inside, from the heart. Saving the lives of
people who nine times out of ten would benefit humanity if they
died and got the hell out of the way. Keeping alive rich old types
whose arterio-sclerosis comes from eating too much, whose bills at
Antoine's for one week would keep one of those starving families
down on the Channel alive for a year. I'm a surgeon, all right.
But I'm also a medical doctor. Hell, after a year and a half with
you, I've damned near forgotten the symptoms of the common
cold! Cut and sew, cut and sew—as if we could cut out what's
really eating humanity; as though we could sew up the wounds
that bleed them to death slowly: want, rejection, prejudice, loss
of self-respect, failure of hope. . . ."

"That's not our job," Jarvis said. "We're neither social workers
nor priests."

"I know. But up there in the Twin Towns they need me more

than I'm needed here. I'd like to give them what I can. I want to go where people need me. Where—don't smile, Lester, I know I'm being inconsistent and contradictory—I can do some good. I want to place whatever skill I have at the disposal of the sick. All the sick, not just those who can afford thousand-dollar operations."

"You're being unfair, Duncan," Phelton said. "We do take charity cases."

"Now you do. In the new wing I got you. Before that, almost none. And those few were chosen for the spectacular nature of their cases, so that they paid for themselves in free publicity for the Clinic. You and I have performed more heart operations in a year than a surgeon normally sees in ten. We've kept the mortality down under thirty per cent, which is good. All right. But I want to go back to my parish, where young mothers die of puerperal fever every day just as though Semmelweis had never existed. Where we've got doctors who don't believe in the existence of microbes. Where the incidence of yellow fever is the highest in the state, and the town council won't drain the swamps, won't pass a screening law, won't have cisterns and rain barrels covered, because they insist that mosquitoes have nothing to do with it, blaspheming over Jesse Lazear's grave! I want to fight pellagra, hookworm, do something about gonorrhœal ophthalmia——"

"Fine," Lester Ryan broke in, "but you know what's going to happen, boy? You're going to spend your life giving placebos to congenital inadequates, treating colds, grippes, flu's that we don't know how to cure; malaria, ditto, typhoid, ditto, yellow fever, triple ditto. Only surgery you'll ever get to do will be a hell of a lot of tonsillectomies, a few appendectomies that'll come in too late, ruptured, and stinking of peritonitis; and your quota of anal fistulas. Snatching babies, of course. Up all night every night in the wet and the cold, riding through muddy back roads to attend patients who've waited so damned long to call you in that they'll most likely be dead when you get there. For which noble and self-sacrificing life you'll be paid—on the rare occasions that you do get paid—in sacks of potatoes, chickens, and eggs. Every time I see chickens or eggs now, I go 'Ugh!' and run to throw up. That's what you want, boy? If so, you can have it!"

"Yes," Duncan said; "that's what I want, Lester. All of it I can get."

"But, Duncan," Hester wailed, "you're asking me to go back up there—to bury myself in that dull, horrible——"

"Yes. Precisely that, baby. I'm asking you whether that 'for better, for worse, for richer, for poorer, in sickness and in health, till death do us part,' meant anything. Or whether it was just words. I'm asking you whether I can stop selling myself, my knowledge, my skill, stop being a kind of medical whore."

"Duncan——" she whispered.

"New Orleans is fun. All right, baby. But I wasn't born to have fun. I was born to be my brother's keeper; to be a responsible practitioner in a pain-racked, dirty, hopeless, helpless world. Perhaps, knowing that, believing that, I shouldn't have married. I shouldn't have inflicted upon you the painful consequences of my personal dedication. I was wrong to do it, and I'm sorry."

"Oh, Duncan, love—I——"

"So I'm giving you your choice. For I haven't any choice, Hester. I have to go back. I have to do what I was made, born, created to do. But you can stay if you like. I'll give you a divorce, so you can marry some gay blade, opera buff, dance king, champagne-swilling type who has enough common sense to enjoy life. If that's what you want, I——"

But she was off the sofa by then, kneeling before him, holding both his hands in hers, staring at him, her eyes luminous with tears. Then she said it, speaking the words slowly, impressively, and with great dignity. They had, he realised afterwards, the rare and bitter beauty of the truth.

"No," she said. "I don't want that, Duncan. I want—you. I want you on my own terms; but, since I can't have you that way, I'll take you on your own. At least I'll try. What you're asking of me requires a kind of courage I haven't got. Maybe I can find it somewhere. Maybe you'll give it to me. But I will try. I wish I could promise you more. I wish I could be sure I won't fail. But I can't promise you I won't, because I know what I am. All right. You've got the floor, darling. You want it like that? You want to gamble I won't revert to type; that I won't even leave you, perhaps, because the little I'll have of you won't be enough, and the lot I'll have of Caneville will be a damned sight too much?"

It was quiet in the room. There was no goblet tinkle, rustle of breathing, sound of voices; nothing but the echoes of her words.

"Yes, Hes," Duncan said quietly. "I'll gamble on that. I'll bet on you."

Lester Ryan put down his glass.

"Let's get out of here," he muttered, thickly. "Leave them alone. Quit sticking our noses into what's not our business."

Miriam Phelton got up. She took Lester's arm, and her husband's.

"You're perfectly right, Lester," she said. "Come on."

Chapter 14

DUNCAN PUT THE RECEIVER of the telephone back on the hook. Then he turned to where Hester lay, supine and totally relaxed, in the big bed. That bed had been Minna's. It was strange to see Hester in it. He had the sudden conviction that his foster-grandmother would not have approved of Hester's being in her bed. Nor, for that matter, in the Bouvoir house at all.

"Who was it, darling?" Hester said sleepily.

"Abbie Fontaine," Duncan said.

Hester popped up in bed like a jack-in-the-box, all sleep gone from her eyes.

"Abbie Fontaine!" she said. "What the devil does she want?"

"It seems there's been an accident. Jeff fell out of his wheelchair. She says he's got a rather nasty cut."

"Probably a lie," Hester said flatly. "We've only been in Caneville two months, and she started trying to get her hooks into you the very day we arrived. She wants a perfect score. Every man in town."

"I don't think so, Hes," Duncan said. "Abbie's not that stupid. If that call were a fake, she'd have said she was sick. Illness can be feigned. A cut can't."

"Maybe she cut him. I wouldn't put it past her."

"Oh, come now, Hes, stop meowing. Besides, if you distrust her—and your ever faithful husband—that much, why don't you come along for the ride? In fact, I'd appreciate it. To be perfectly frank, I don't trust little Abigail, either."

"And lose my beauty sleep? Not on your life, darling. Call Jen. She's just as interested in keeping you out of Abbie's clutches as I am. And I don't have to worry about *her*."

'The one woman on earth you do have to worry about,' Duncan thought bitterly; 'but you can't see it. And they talk about feminine intuition!' He said: "Jen can't come. She's got the flu. All this rain——"

"Poor dear. I'm so fond of her. Duncan! She's not all alone in that house?"

"No. Hans put her in Tompson's Nursing Home. She needs attention. And since her father died there's nobody——"

"I know. Fat lot of attention she'll get at Tompson's. It's a pity your new hospital which you squeezed so nicely out of Dad won't be ready until next spring . . . Tompson's is a disgrace. Apart from Martha Tompson's being slovenly, the darned place is right across the street from Crazy Mike's. With all those roaring drunks going in and out of the saloon all night, she'll never get a wink of sleep. I'll bring her here. I can take care of her. You made me learn how."

He stared at her. Hester did have her good impulses.

"She wouldn't come," he said.

"I'll convince her. Tell her she'll be properly chaperoned. And that I've tamed my rampaging husband considerably. Besides, as I said, I don't have to worry. Jen's a one-woman Purity League."

"There've been times when I've wished she weren't," he teased. He bent and kissed Hester. " 'Bye now, baby," he said. "I'm off."

He found Abbie, to his vast relief, amazingly subdued. No. Subdued wasn't the word for it. Frightened. She was greenish. She looked as if she'd been sick. For the first time since he had met her, she didn't try any of her bright, girlish prattle on him.

"What the hell ails you, Abbie?" he said.

"Threw up. All that blood! Ugh! Nope. Can't blame it on the blood. I've thrown up three mornings in a row."

Duncan studied her. He looked for certain tell-tale signs. Found them. Kept his mouth shut. 'None of my business,' he thought. He said: "Where's the patient?"

"In there——" Abbie whispered.

He walked into the house. It smelled. Abbie was a damned poor housekeeper. But then, she did work. Secretary-typist for old Tobias Smithson, of the Mertontown Mills. Smithson was seventy-two. The wives of men just a little younger wouldn't let them hire Abbie. He'd heard she wasn't a bad secretary. And she did support poor Jeff. Chalk up one good mark for little Abbie!

He went into the bedroom. Jeff Fontaine wasn't there. Somebody had been there, though—or Abbie was the damned most restless sleeper in this world.

He walked on through it; came to a cubbyhole that had been the pantry of the house. Jeff was there, lying on his cot, his face toward the wall, his pitiful wasted legs bent into the sitting position he could no longer straighten them out of. And he was crying. Very softly, but endlessly. Staring at that wall. That blank wall he'd come to. And crying for the loss of hope, in him who had already lost so many things. Like manhood. Like pride.

"Jeff," Duncan said, "buck up, old-timer. You're going to be all right."

"All right?" Jeff muttered. "Me? Don't be a complete jackass, Doctor!"

"I fight the tendency," Duncan said cheerfully, "but sometimes it gets the better of me. Mostly on Saturday nights. During the week I usually manage not to bray. Come on, let me have a look at you."

"Look then, damn you!" Jeff said.

The cubbyhole was too small. It stank. Of sweat. Of bedclothes unchanged for weeks. Of urine. And, even on that bright March day, it was too dark for him to see Jeff's face.

He switched on the electric light. Fifteen watts. Less. It compounded confusion, making him see things he thought weren't there.

He shoved his arms under Jeff, lifted powerfully.

"What the devil are you doing?" Jeff snarled.

"Taking you out of here. Can't work by touch. I have to see."

Jeff weighed practically nothing. Duncan guessed he wasn't eating. Part of the pattern. What the hell did Jeff Fontaine have to live for, anyhow?

He walked, carrying the paralytic, into the bedroom. Laid him down on the bed.

He looked at Jeff Fontaine. And rage burst inside his viscera like shrapnel. He licked bone-dry lips. Shaped the word. Forced it out.

"Who?"

"What the hell is it to you?" Jeff Fontaine grated. "You're just like all the rest! Abbie's always saying——"

Duncan turned, lifted his head, called: "Abbie! Come in here, goddamn you!"

She came.

Duncan looked at her.

She tried to meet his gaze. She couldn't.

"Who was it, Abbie?" Duncan said. "Stan Bruder?"

Abbie's yellow eyes flamed. She lunged past Duncan, caught her husband by the shoulders, shook him furiously, screeching:

"You dirty cripple! I told you not to tell! Filthy little half a man!"

Duncan's hand closed on her arm, jerked. She came upright. He turned her, swung his hand, open-palmed, far back. Held it there. It ached with anticipation of the impact. He could almost feel it smash across her quivering, frightened mouth. But he couldn't. He just wasn't built that way.

Jeff looked at him. His cracked, swollen lips spread into a grin. "Go on, Doc!" he croaked. "Paste her one! Belt the living hell out of her!"

Duncan shook his head.

"No," he said. "I've dirtied my hands enough already."

He bent, picked up his bag, opened it.

"Now," he said, "let's see if we can't clean that face of yours up a mite, Jeff."

Abbie stood there watching. Her face was green with terror.

Duncan swabbed the bruised, torn, savagely beaten face with alcohol. The bruised, torn, savagely beaten face of—a cripple. The rage came back, made him shake. He could see the edges of the gash above the dirty bandage Abbie had wound around Jeff's head. It would require sutures. So he mustn't think about that. His hands mustn't shake.

He looked at Abbie. When he spoke, his voice was ice.

"Go heat me some water. Bring it here when it's ready."

She left the room at once.

He turned back to Jeff. "Where's your razor, old-timer?" he said gently. "I'm going to have to shave your head."

"Bathroom," Jeff said.

Duncan went and got it. He clipped the hair from around the gash. While he waited for the hot water, he picked the slivers of glass out of it.

"Whisky bottle?" he said.

"Yes," Jeff whispered.

"Tell me about it, boy. I've got to make a report, you know. Criminal assault."

"Doc—don't. Please don't. Please, Doc, please!"

"Why? He won't touch you again. I'm going to see to that."

"No. You don't understand. I'm not afraid of Stan. But it— it will all come out, if—I press charges."

"You don't have to. Assault with a deadly weapon—and a whisky bottle's damned well a deadly weapon—is a felony. The State'll press the charges."

"No, Doc! I don't even want him arrested. I want it kept quiet! Promise me you won't report it! For the love of God, Doc, promise!"

"Why?" Duncan said softly.

Jeff looked at him. The tears flooded his broken face. Flooded, not streaked.

Duncan looked at him. "He comes here, Jeff," he said very quietly, "at night. While you're still awake. He doesn't even have the decency to take her out into the fields. No. Here in the house. With you listening. Until you couldn't take it any more. Until, half paralysed or not, you played the man. He was drunk. First he battered you to a pulp with his fists. Then he saw, or touched, that whisky bottle. And being Stan Bruder, being a thing they'd have to write a whole new dictionary of filth and foulness to describe, he picked it up and—that was it, wasn't it, Jeff?"

Silently Jeff nodded.

Abbie came back into the room with the hot water. She stood there watching while Duncan shaved Jeff's head. Before it was done, she began to laugh hysterically.

Duncan looked at her. The laughter died. He turned back to his patient.

"This is going to hurt, old-timer," he said.

"I can take it, Doc," Jeff Fontaine said.

Duncan sutured the wound. Cauterised it. Jeff didn't make a sound. He lay there, and took it. He'd had a lot of practice at taking things, Duncan thought.

"That does it," Duncan said. "Now I'm going to take you into town so that Dr. Volker and I can go over you. Abbie, go get something to put around him."

She went and came. In her hands was a blanket. It was dirty too.

"Duncan——" she got out.

He looked at her.

"What the hell do you want?" he said.

"Step outside a minute? I—I got to talk to you!"

"Talk?" Duncan said; "I'd think you barked, Abbie."

"Oh!" she whispered. "Reckon I—I had that coming. You must think I'm pretty low."

"You, Abbie, would have to reach up to scratch the belly of a snake. Besides, I know what you want. The answer is: 'No, Abbie.' Before you even ask me."

"You—you mean you can tell? Already?"

"I'm a doctor, Abbie."

"And—you won't—help me?"

"Not even if you were dying," Duncan said.

He carried Jeff Fontaine into Hans Volker's office. Through the back way, so that people in the waiting-room wouldn't see his face.

Hans Volker looked at Jeff. At Duncan.

"Who in the name of the bleeding, martyred Christ——?" he roared.

"Give you one guess, Doctor," Duncan said, and crossed to the door. In it, he turned. He said: "Look him over, Doctor; there may be internal injuries as well."

"All right. Damn it, Jenny would have to be sick just now!"

"Want me to have a look at Jen?" Duncan said.

"Yes. Damn it, boy, you make me nervous! Come back in here! There're half a million patients——"

"No," Duncan said. "I've got a thing to do."

Hans Volker stared at him. Saw his eyes.

"Duncan!" he thundered.

"So long, Doc," Duncan said. "Come see me—in jail."

He went to Muller's General Store.

Jan Muller greeted him with evident pleasure.

"Vhy, Duncan," he began, "it's been a long time——"

Duncan cut him off.

"I want a whip," he said. "A mule-skinner's whip. Nine-foot lash. Leaded."

"Name of God, Duncan! Vhy do you vant——"

"To beat a mule with, naturally. No. Not a mule. A swine."

Jan Muller watched him leaving the store. He turned to Hilda.

"Poor boy!" he said. "He vorks too hardt. I better call Doktor Volker. I think his mind——"

Duncan went to Crazy Mike's. He left the whip in his buggy. He pushed open the swinging doors of the saloon.

"Stan," he said, "will you step outside with me?"

The other men stared. Stan blustered.

"Why the hell should I——?"

"I've just come from the Fontaines'," Duncan said. "Now are you going to come outside?"

Stan came. Fell into a crouch. Put up his fists.

Duncan stood beside the buggy, his hand inside.

"Don't mean to fight you, Stan," he said. "I don't put my hands into polecat's puke. You know what you did last night? You remember?"

"Yes," Stan said. His voice had a quaver to it. His eyes shifted from side to side. They fell on Jenny Greenway, standing by an upper window in the Nursing Home across the street. She was wrapped in a pink bath-robe. She was very pale and thin. The sight of her seemed to give Stan Bruder courage.

193

"What the hell business is it of yours?" he roared.

"I'm making it my business," Duncan said, and brought out the whip.

From her window across the street, Jenny saw it all. Duncan didn't see her. It wouldn't have made any difference to him if he had.

A mule-skinner's whip is a terrible weapon. With it you can kill a man. Duncan didn't kill Stan with it. Not quite. Stan's coat protected him somewhat. After Stan's first attempts to rush him and take away the whip had been beaten back with a few deadly stripes across the face, Duncan simply slashed him to the earth, left him clawing the ground and crying. He wasn't hurt badly; Duncan could have done nearly as much damage with his fists. But the crushing humiliation of being horsewhipped in public, before a rapidly gathering crowd, was the thing that counted most. None of the men dared enter that nine-foot circle around which the lash whined viciously, to crack pistol-shot-clear as it removed another inch from Stanton Bruder's hide. They stood there and watched Duncan finish, some of them—those with pretty wives or sweethearts—with great pleasure.

Duncan tossed the whip to the ground. Turned.

"You're under arrest, son," Sheriff Bruno Martin said.

"Wait," Duncan said pleasantly. "This is a private matter, Sheriff. And I don't believe Mr. Bruder wants to press charges. Do you, Stan?"

"Don't—want to press—charges?" Stan got out. "Why the living hell—do you think——"

"I don't think. I know. I've got a friend of yours in my office. Jeff Fontaine. You want me to step in there with Sheriff Martin, and bring him out here to show the crowd?"

Stan hung there on his hands and knees. Like a dog. Like a whipped dog. He opened his mouth.

"No, Sheriff, reckon I won't press charges after all," he said.

Duncan crossed to the Nursing Home. Mrs. Tompson's eyes were blobs of terror in her fat face. Her throat quivered.

"Good morning, ma'am," Duncan said. "May I freshen up a bit before I go upstairs to see Jen?"

"Y-yes, Doctor," Mrs. Tompson said.

He washed his face and hands, and combed his hair. Then he went upstairs.

Jen was in bed, propped up on the pillows. Her face was deathly pale. She was shaking. When he came over to her, she lay there, looking at him in perfect silence.

He put out his hand to feel her pulse.

She shrank away from him, cringing.

"Don't touch me!" she said, her voice hoarse with horror. "You unspeakable beast, don't you dare!"

Hester's reaction was a trifle different.

"I knew dear Abigail had her charms," she drawled, "her dainty, unwashed charms. But I had no idea they were so potent. Tell me, love—before I pack—just what it is that Abbie has that made you nearly kill a man?"

"Don't be a fool, Hes," Duncan said drily. "Abbie had nothing to do with it. Or very little. You're asking the wrong questions. Ask me why Stan Bruder didn't dare press charges. Or, better still, ask him. He might tell you. I won't."

"You mean that I'm to accept these cryptic remarks as sufficient reason not to leave you?"

"If you don't, you're crazy," Duncan said.

She whirled. Fled up the stairs.

The telephone rang. Duncan picked up the receiver.

"Duncan!" Hans Volker's voice came over the wire. "It's all over the place! Never saw a scandal spread so fast! It's even got to Mertontown. Carter phoned. Wants an emergency meeting of the Parish Medical Association to press charges against you before the State Board. I told him to call it and be damned!"

The line wasn't clear. He had a hard time hearing what Hans said.

"What charges?" he said.

"Conduct unbecoming to a member of the profession. Carter's screaming to have you expelled. You know how those Mertontowners are. They hate our guts. Say we're uppity. They're right. We are. I'm going to show 'em Jeff Fontaine's face. Prove to 'em, the way Stan Bruder beat him, the provocation was gross."

"They'll say I should have left it to the law."

"Damn it, you should have! But I know why you didn't. Jeff asked you not to, didn't he? Didn't want that much dirty linen aired to the public gaze?"

"Right. And we can't air it. Professional confidence. Let them expel me."

"The hell I will! I made Jeff no promises. You don't have to say anything. And, boy——"

"Yes, Doctor?"

"Speaking not as a doctor, but as a man, you should have killed that dirty swine!"

Duncan put the phone back on the hook. Turned.

Hester was coming back down the stairs. Her eyes were very wide. Tears traced liquid sunlight down her face.

"Duncan," she whispered, "I—I listened in. On the extension upstairs."

"So?"

"Will you forgive me, please, love?" she said.

He didn't get expelled. He received a unanimous vote of censure from the Parish Association. Even Hans Volker signed it. Because it was just. His conduct had been outrageous. He made his apology in person to the Association. And he didn't lose his wife. Not then.

But what happened was just as bad. Perhaps worse.

Jenny Greenway started going out with Forsythe Bevers. Which was the next thing to going out with Stanton Bruder, Duncan thought. Only Jenny didn't know that. Forsythe spent all but a month out of the year in New Orleans, gambling, wenching, amusing himself mightily, instead of attending to his job as Vice-President of the Bevers' Knitting Mills in Mertontown. Duncan suspected that his father, old Winthrop Bevers, was just as happy to keep Forsythe out of sight and sound as Martin Bruder had been in the case of Stan. Why did rich men's sons turn out so badly? And why in the name of everything unholy couldn't Jenny realise that for Forsythe to be Stan's number-one crony they had to be much the same sort?

Jenny despised Stanton. But she hadn't known anything about his friend. Even though Mertontown and Caneville-Sainte Marie were only ten miles apart, the bitter enmity between them had always made any sort of social intercourse between the younger people impossible. Jenny, then, was taking Forsythe upon face value. Why the hell hadn't he stayed in New Orleans?

Now, damn him to blue blazes, he was always underfoot. Playing the gentleman; playing the lovesick swain. 'And,' Duncan admitted bitterly, 'playing them damned well. Why not? He's got the equipment. He's a fine-looking cuss. He's considerably less of a swine than Stan. And he's rich. No way for Jen to find out what degree of a swine he is. Less than Stan, all right; but far too much to suit Jen, if I know anything about her. No way, unless I tell her. Hold it, Doctor! That weapon's dirty, even though its steel be true. Dirty—and two-edged. Cuts the wielder worse than the intended victim.

'So—no. Jen all but hates me anyway, now. Had to almost beg her to take the job as Head Nurse of our hospital once it was finished. And when she did accept finally, she reminded me at least three times it was for purely professional reasons! Oh God, I——'

That summer the whole town was divided into two warring camps over the controversial young Doctor Duncan Childers. The Antis far exceeded the Pros. On his side were only Hester; Nelson Vance, whom Hester had told the truth; Doug and Grace Henderson, out of pure gratitude to him; Hans Volker; the doctors of the Parish Medical Association who had seen Jeff's face; the Mullers; and Professor Bergdorf.

Even Jenny Greenway seemed to have joined the Antis. She whirled by his door in Forsythe Bevers' racing sulky, smiling at Bevers, her arm through his.

And that hurt. It hurt almost beyond his capacity to bear.

Chapter 15

ON THE NIGHT OF SEPTEMBER FIRST, 1904, Doctor Duncan Childers received a telephone call.

"You'd better come at once," the voice said. Its tone was strangely muffled. It sounded like someone talking through cloth. "There's a woman out at the old McPherson place, bleeding to death!"

"At the McPherson place?" Duncan muttered sleepily. "But nobody lives there."

"An accident, Doctor. She was taken into the house."

"Say! Who the devil are you?" Duncan said.

There was a click. The line went dead.

Duncan turned, started dressing, all his nerves sounding signals of alarm.

But he went just the same. He had to. His vocation was Medicine.

A little while later, the phone rang in Sheriff Bruno Martin's home. A very little while. Just the right interval. Calculated to a hair.

"Sheriff Martin?"

"Yes." The Sheriff yawned copiously. "Who's calling?"

"A friend. If you'll get dressed right now and rush out to the old McPherson place, you'll catch Dr. Duncan Childers doing something he damned well oughtn't!"

"Say, who are you?" Sheriff Martin roared.

"I told you. A friend."

The sound, quick and sharp, of a receiver being put back on its hook.

Then silence.

Sheriff Martin was undecided. He liked young Doctor Childers. But still——

But still he saw his duty clear. He was the Sheriff of the Parish. He got dressed. Went.

And found Duncan Childers bending over Abigail Fontaine's lifeless form. She lay on the kitchen table. The six-months' foetus that had been taken from her by an operation illegal in every state in the union was in a tin pail, under the table. It was fully formed.

A boy. The kitchen was a shambles. There was blood all over the place.

Sheriff Martin saw his duty crystal-clear.

He arrested Doctor Duncan Childers.

Hans Volker was the first to reach the jail. He stood there looking through the bars at his young colleague. His old face was drawn. A knot of muscle above his jaw jerked.

"Son," he rumbled, "tell me one thing. I hate to ask, but I've got to. Son—did you?"

Duncan stared at him. His brown eyes were bleak as death. When he spoke, his voice was low but harsh. He said:

"You've seen the cadaver, Doctor?"

"No, son, I——"

"You've seen me operate. Many times. So go look at Abbie, Doctor. Go look at that poor, pitiful hunk of butchered meat. Then come back here and ask me that, if you dare!"

"Son, I'm sorry. I didn't think——"

"It doesn't matter. I fell into the neatest trap in history. Forgive my tone. Naturally, I feel like hell right now."

"You should, son. Don't worry; you'll be out of here in no time. I'm going to convene the Parish Association."

"Lord God, Doctor, why?"

"First you tell me something, Duncan. In your considered opinion, could that job have been done by a surgeon?"

"It was done by a butcher. An apprentice butcher. And he was drunk."

"Then, after I've had a look, I'm going to convene the Association. On the unanimous opinion of all the physicians that the operation could not have been performed by a practising surgeon, the hearing magistrate will be forced to find there's no valid charge. With that evidence before him, he can't possibly remand."

"Damn, but you sound like a lawyer!" Duncan said.

"Some of that legal jargon rubbed off on me. I've had to testify in court God knows how many times—usually in bastardy cases. Has your bail been set?"

"You're forgetting your law, Doctor. It can't be, until they have a preliminary hearing before the magistrate. This isn't a minor felony. I'm charged with—homicide."

"All right. Duncan, one more thing."

"Yes, Doctor?"

"You think Stanton Bruder did this. So do I. But, after I get you out of this hellish mess, you're not to lift a finger against him.

You can't take the law into your hands again. He'll make a slip, one day. He's not that smart. Promise me, boy?"

Duncan looked at him. His brown eyes flamed, cooled down very slowly. Became ice.

"Yes, Doctor, I promise," he said.

Next, Hester came with her father.

"Oh, darling!" she wept. "We're doing everything we can! Dr. Hans came and told us. I was so worried when you didn't come home this morning! Why didn't you phone?"

"Yep, why didn't you, son?" Nelson rumbled.

"Didn't feel up to it," Duncan said. "Besides—I wasn't sure what you'd believe, Hes."

"Duncan, you hurt me! Don't you think I know you better than that? Besides, it's stupid. The only people who get mixed up in the abortion business are old quacks, too shaky and whisky-soaked to maintain a practice. Why the devil should you?"

"Out of consideration for Abbie, maybe," Duncan said, "or even for poor Jeff."

"Then you'd have done it successfully. You'd have brought her into your nice clean operating-room, written out a diagnosis that her continued pregnancy was dangerous to her health for this or that reason, and snatched that brat as clean as a whistle! You would not, Doctor, have operated on a filthy kitchen table in an unoccupied house without anæsthesia, apparently with a blunt butcher's knife and a pair of pliers. The description's Dr. Hans's. Naturally, I haven't seen her."

"Hes," Duncan said, "did I ever tell you, you're a great girl? Now give me a kiss and get going. You and Father Nels do what you can to get me out of here."

"I'm phoning the Governor at noon," Nelson roared. "Damn 'em, they can't do this to me!"

That night, Jenny came. She was fighting mad. The tears had misted her glasses so much she had to take them off. So Duncan could see her eyes. Every time Jen had her spectacles off, he became convinced all over again that she was one of the loveliest girls in the world. But when she put them back on again, his vagrant attention wandered.

He didn't say anything. He waited for her to speak. He wanted to see at whom that fury was directed. After all, their last conversation had been somewhat less than cordial.

"Oh!" she gasped, "I'm so mad I could spit! The fool! The blithering idiot! The unmitigated ass! With hairy ears at that!"

"And who, may I ask, Nurse Greenway," Duncan said, "is the object of your excessively complimentary remarks? Me?"

"Oh no, Duncan! I was talking about Henry Carter. Do you know what the fool said?"

"Of course," Duncan drawled. "He said I did it."

She stopped short.

"Well, not exactly. At least not so baldly. He had to get up his nerve. He hemmed and hawed and 'wal now-ed' for twenty minutes. Then he came out with it: yes, a young, unskilful surgeon could have done such a botched-up job in his august opinion!"

"Unskilful? Why, the old bastard! I've forgotten more surgery than he'll ever——"

"I know. Dr. Hans slapped him down. He roared just like a lion: 'You're calling the doctor who performed the first successful operation on the human heart that anybody hereabouts ever heard of, unskilful?'"

"What'd he say to that?"

"Can't you imagine? 'Successful, Doctor? *My* successful cases are walking around!'"

"And he's filled three cemeteries singlehanded with his failures. Go on, Jen."

"I thought Dr. Hans was going to kill him. But he controlled himself beautifully. Spelled it out for Carter: several successful heart operations in New Orleans. Mortality under thirty per cent. Plastic reconstructions of the œsophagus; that thyroid transplant—the works. I thought Dr. Hans had him then; but I was wrong. He just sat there smiling like an evil old coot. Then he said: 'I have no doubt that your young man is exceedingly skilful, Doctor. But have you considered the factor of emotional strain? The best hand can slip when that's involved, which is why most surgeons won't operate on their own wives and loved ones. I can imagine that a young man might have been under considerable strain, performing that operation upon the body of a woman with whom he is reputedly in love, and extracting the fœtus of what, conceivably, may have been his own child!'"

"Jesus!" Duncan cried. It was a cry of pure agony.

"And," Jenny whispered, "that's already all over town. It's the favourite theory. You were upset. Knowing she was married to a man who couldn't possibly have fathered the child, you tried to mend matters. Being shaky, you botched it."

Duncan looked at her.

"Is it," he said, "also—your theory, Jenny?"

"No," she said icily. "I demonstrated my theory about you—my very mistaken theory, it seems to me now—the day Dick Willis tried to kill you. I'm sorry! That was rotten of me. Forget I said that, Duncan."

"No. So now you regret having saved me? You agree with the considerable number of our citizenry who want to make me guest of honour at a nice, sociable little hanging?"

"Don't be a fool, Duncan! I haven't regretted it. And I most certainly don't want you hanged. I have been disappointed in you, yes. Terribly disappointed. Because of so many things: your—New Orleans tart they talked about so much at Dick Willis's trial. Your utter, bestial savagery, seen with my own eyes. Forsythe told me about the other time: how you kicked Stan when he was down, ground your heels into his face. That was true, too, wasn't it, Duncan?"

"Yes," he said miserably.

"True, and my punishment for misplaced faith. I'd put you so high, Duncan. So far above all other men. But feet of clay are a common enough condition, aren't they? Don't know why it shocks me so to find *you* have them."

Anger tore him.

"So to my feet of clay," he snarled, "you prefer a whole mud image? What you've put in my place is not flattering, Jen!"

"Nor what you've put in mine," she said tartly. "Forsythe is really quite decent, once you get to know him. And he loves me. Which does have its appeal. But only one man on earth could tower from your special hill."

"And he is?" Duncan grated.

"You," she said very quietly. "The day you get to be what I dreamed you already were."

Then she turned upon her heel and left him there, walking very softly, and with no special haste.

The magistrate, confronted with Dr. Carter's flat belief that Duncan Childers not only could be, but probably was, guilty as charged, and Doctor Harris's hesitations over the point of whether or not the butchery of Abigail Fontaine could have been done by a surgeon's hand, handed down a true bill and bound the prisoner over until the court should sit some six weeks from that day. Duncan's bail was set at twenty-five thousand dollars, the largest in the history of the Parish.

Nelson Vance posted it for him. Duncan hadn't that much money any more. Hester had run through much of his bank account with her extravagances. And Duncan had poured a small fortune back into the Irish Channel, into a settlement house project started after Fred Baynes's articles on conditions there had created such a furore.

Hans Volker came to see him. Stood there looking at him with troubled eyes.

"Dr. Hans," Duncan said, "what is it now?"

"You stay here, boy! Don't stir from the house. Keep away from the windows. I've had Bruno Martin station some men——"

"So now they're going to lynch me?" Duncan said.

"Stan Bruder's stirring them up. Goddamn him, he——"

"You mean that many people care what happened to Abbie? Care that much?"

"No. But Bruder knows mobs. Got the same mentality himself, I reckon. He's playing on their sympathy for poor, betrayed, crippled Jeff. Whom he probably put the horns on to, himself."

"Probably!" Duncan snorted.

"I know. Surely. Only he's got a point. What the hell will become of Jeff now?"

Duncan sat there. A fly buzzed across the room. The noise of its wings was thunderous.

"We put him in the hospital. In a private room, Dr. Hans," Duncan said quietly. "And I pay the expenses for his care."

"Good idea. Only you don't. I do. Don't you see they'd take it as an admission of guilt?"

"You're right," Duncan sighed. "Can I get you a drink, Dr. Hans?"

"Yep. Need it. No. Haven't time. Got to get back and keep tabs on that bastard, Bruder!"

"Stay," Duncan said. "What difference does it make?"

"A hell of a lot—to me. I've never had a son. You've damned near made up—the lack."

Duncan looked at him. He had had many things, good and bad, said to him in his life. But nothing had ever moved him like that. Nothing so much. He choked the rough-edged boulder in his throat back down. He said: "Thank you, Doctor Hans—for that."

"Don't mention it. We've just got to hold 'em down until *The Clarion* comes out. Jeff was kind enough to sign a statement stating his belief that you didn't do it. I didn't even have to ask him. He suggested the idea. You've got a friend, there, boy."

"Bless him," Duncan said.

"Amen. The paper'll be out in two hours. An extra. That should end all the shouting. But even after that, I don't want you to budge. Stay home and play the piano. I'm going to clear you. I know how."

"Even with Henry Carter testifying as an expert for the prosecution?"

"Even with that. If you stay the hell out of my way and let me work it. All right?"

"All right," Duncan said tiredly. He didn't particularly care one way or the other. Not after all the things that had happened to him. Not after that last interview with Jenny. Especially not after that.

Hans Volker turned detective. Unlike the sleuths of fiction he knew who the culprit was. What he had to do was to obtain proof his culprit had committed the crime Duncan was accused of. And that was hell.

He made the rounds of the doctors, midwives, Cajun *sages-femmes*, of the Parish. Of them all he asked one question: "Do you know of any girl of respectable family who is unmarried but who is going to have a child?"

It was not until two weeks before the trial that he found one. One, in all the Parish. Which spoke well for the morals of the Parish. It had been a lovely, flowering spring. Her name was Berta Schultz. Good, solid Lutheran family. She was dying of terror that her father might find out.

He talked to the girl. Suggested a name, his heart sick at this violation of all he believed in, even though he had no intention of letting her go through with it. He offered to pay, saying that she could pay him back later. Poor stupid, desperate Berta rose to the bait, took the marked bills he gave her, departed into Smoketown to seek out——

Charity Mance.

As Berta had promised, she told him: time, date, place.

At the name of the place, he stared. Then it came to him: Why not? Duncan Childers stood convicted in the minds of almost the whole community of having used McPherson's farm for his crime. Now he was out of the way, it would not be watched. It was almost the safest place Charity could have chosen for the occasion.

He waited, Sheriff Bruno Martin at his side, the two of them hidden in the underbrush near the house, the ten minutes they'd decided it would take Charity to strip the girl and put her on the table. Then they entered the house, he by the front door, the Sheriff by the back. They were in time. Charity was just picking up the long steel knitting-needle she used to pierce the walls of the uterus, let in the life-destroying air.

She turned, faced them. And on that face grown old in sin was, incredibly enough, a smile.

"Come to 'rest me, gentlemens?" she cackled. "All right, I'se yore prisoner—for now!"

"For now?" Hans spat. "What the devil do you mean by that, Charity? Put the cuffs on her, Bruno!"

The Sheriff's stride awakened Berta from her frozen horror. She scampered, fat and naked, from the room, seizing her clothes from the chair as she went.

"No need o' that, Sheriff," Charity grinned. "I won't run. Don't have to. You gentlemens gonna turn me loose."

"You outa your mind, ol' nigger woman?" the Sheriff said.

"Nosuh. 'Pears to me, y'all is tryint' to 'rest Charity. Y'all thinks I'se dumb—like whitefolks?"

Bruno Martin drew back his hand, slapped her to the floor.

"You ol' black bitch!" he roared, "I'll——"

"That's enough, Sheriff!" Hans Volker said. "Abuse of a prisoner during arrest is a felony, and actionable as such. Pick her up."

The Sheriff picked her up, his face red with fury.

"What makes you think we'll turn you loose, Charity?" Hans Volker said.

"Don't think. I knows. You see this?"

She put her hands in the voluminous pocket and came out with two copies of a printed paper.

Hans took them, read:

I, ————————————, hereby release, discharge, and free Madame Charity Mance from any responsibility for accident, injury, or my death, occurring during her treatment of my condition. Signed, ————————————, this ——— of ———, 19———.

Berta had signed them both.

Hans threw back his head and laughed aloud.

"Who the hell ever told you a quit claim would do you any good against a felony charge?" he said.

"Nobody, Doc. My lawyer friend down in Nawleens ain't that dumb. He coloured, too. We's learning to be just as crooked as you whitefolks. When we done learned all yore tricks, we gonna take over, us."

The Sheriff took a step forward.

"No, Bruno," Hans said. "Tell me something, Charity. Did you do that job on Mrs. Fontaine?"

"Shore did, Doc. Pore gal, she were a bleeder. Some of 'em's like that. Cain't nobody save 'em."

"Got that, Bruno? You're a witness. You heard what she said, Berta?" he called, raising his voice.

"Yessir!" Berta whimpered from the next room.

"Y'all don' need no witnesses, Doc. 'Cause ain't gonna be no trial. Y'all's gonna turn me loose."

"What the living hell makes you think we'll let you go?" Bruno Martin snarled.

"Them papers. I'm smart, me. Notice I got two of 'em?"

"So?" Hans Volker said.

"I saves 'em. In two different strong-boxes. One in the vault of th' Caneville Bank. The other in th' Mertontown one. That one's the best. That one's got five different keys to it. Had 'em made special, so nobody could stop 'em all." She grinned at them wickedly.

" 'N five coloured folks y'all don't even know by sight, let alone by name, got them keys. You mought find one. Maybe two. But five? Nosuh. I'm plumb smart, me."

"Go on, Charity," Hans Volker said.

"Day I'se 'rested or hurt or kilt, editor o' *The Mertontown Courier* gonna get five keys. Five letters tellin' him to go to the bank 'n open that box——"

"Lord God!" Bruno Martin got out: "Lord Jesus, Doc!"

"And in it he's a-gonna find Lord knows how many o' these heah fancy printed papers. With the names, writ by theyselves, of all them pretty, sweet, highfalutin lil' Caneville whitegals, who walks so dainty 'n so uppity; like they don' sweat 'n pant 'n cry same as a blackgal do with her lovin' man in th' dark!"

Hans hung there. He knew some names on that list. He had had to go in more than once to repair the damage Charity had done: debriding gangrenous tissue, scraping the uterine wall, stanching hæmorrhages. He knew one name on that list. One name in particular. He had saved Duncan Childers. For what?

Sweet martyred Christ, for what?

"An' if y'all don't think young Mister Tim Evans won't print them names 'n how 'n why, right on the front page so ever'body kin read 'em, bustin' half th' good families in Caneville all to hell, 'n a-startin' a mighty heap o' white menfolks to shootin' n' killin' each other, 'n beatin' they ever-lovin' wives, why then, gentlemens, y'all don't know newspaperfolks; an' y'all sho Lawd don' know Mertontown!"

"Doc!" Bruno Martin groaned. "She's got us. You know how much hell's gonna pop loose when Tim Evans prints that tale?"

He didn't say 'if'. He said, 'when'. It was as sure as that.

Hans Volker thought: the life of one man. The career of a boy who is going to be a great surgeon. A good boy. Who's worked hard, seen hell to get there. Measured over against the happiness of God knows how many families. Against that boy's own happiness.

His face hardened. Anger rose in him. Towered.

Against the happiness of a pack of cheap little perfumed sneaks, who couldn't keep their skirts down and their pants up! To hell with them! They'd made their beds with sighing and delight. Let them lie there now, in their bitter beds of shame. The tune being danced to, the piper must be paid. And Duncan Childers was worth more than all of them!

"Arrest her, Sheriff," he said; "afterwards, we'll see."

Duncan was playing the piano when Hans came into the house. Snatches from Rimsky-Korsakov: 'Antar', 'Coq d'or', the enchanting 'Scheherazade'; a passage from the 'Capriccio Espagnol'.

Hans hated to interrupt him. But he had to. His music—and his life. But he didn't say anything to Duncan. It was to Hester that he spoke. He said: "Hes, want to come for a little drive with me?"

"Oh no, Doctor!" Hester said. "Not while Duncan's playing. He hasn't played for me in so long."

Then she met his eyes.

"Hester," he said slowly, "you'd better come with me, child."

"Say, Doc, what's this all about?" Duncan said.

"Go on playing, boy. You'll know soon enough," Hans Volker said.

"No!" Hester wept. "I can't, Doctor Hans! I can't! You've got to turn that old witch loose! All right, he can't practise medicine any more; but Father'll take him into the business! We'll be all right! We'll be—all—right——"

"When?" Hans said grimly. "Twenty-one years from now, when he gets out of jail? Homicide carries that penalty, Hester. Twenty-one years out of his life. You think you're worth that, Hester? And the boy completely innocent?"

She clung to him, sobbing.

"Besides, it's too late. By tomorrow Tim Evans will have those keys. I'm going over there and beg him not to print that story. But he won't listen. What Mertontowner would? A chance like this to get back at us for forty years of insults? Not on your life, child. So you'd better tell him. Before he reads it in the newspaper. Ask his forgiveness. He's a good boy; he'll——"

Blindly Hester shook her head.

"No," she choked. "He won't! Not that. Not considering *who* it was. You—you won't turn Charity loose, Doctor Hans?"

He looked at her. His eyes were very stern.

"Charity Mance is guilty of murder, Hester," he said. "And you, and others like you, are partners in crime. I'm an old-fashioned man. I believe the preservation of virtue is important. But, quite frankly, I don't give much of a damn for maintaining a reputation after virtue's gone—especially not by such rotten means. And one thing I know: a child, once conceived, has a right to the life it didn't ask for. To me life is sacred. Far too sacred to be snatched away for the dirty reason of preventing people from calling you the cheap little bitch you are!"

"No!" she stormed. "You don't understand, Doctor Hans! Not for me! For—him! He'll be so hurt—so—hurt——"

"Which, being a man, he can take. Take and grow upon. But less hurt, more inclined to forgive, hearing it from you than reading it in Tim Evans's dirty scandal sheet. For he will read it there. Even if we were to let Charity go now, it would be too late. The minute we brought her in, it already was——"

"Then why did you bring her in?" Hester sobbed. "For God's love, tell me that!"

"Because I had to," Hans said tiredly. "She's committed a crime, and I know the law. What's going to happen to those also involved, the fate of a pack of rutting females in perpetual heat, is immaterial and irrelevant. Are you going to tell him, child?"

Hester lifted her tear-scarred face, met his stern old eyes.

"Yes," she said, not without pride. "I'll go tell him now."

He listened very quietly. His expression did not change.

Only, behind his eyes, quite visibly, something died.

"Who was it, Hester?" he said. His voice was soft, gentle. Patient with a curiously terrible patience.

"A man," she sobbed. "What does it matter? You want to shoot or horsewhip him? What good would that do, Duncan? Tell me: what good?"

"No," he said. "Neither, Hester. You didn't belong to me then. I don't intend to do anything. It's none of my business, really. I'd just like to know. It was Stan Bruder, wasn't it?"

She lifted her tortured eyes.

He held them pitilessly.

"Yes," she said.

"Stan—always Stan," he said, his voice flat, lacking tone. Then: "Why didn't he marry you?"

"I didn't want him! I was sick of him! I preferred to risk——"

But he would not leave her even that. Coldly he stripped away her last shred of pride.

"Hester——" he said, the word long-drawn-out, deep.

"All right! All right!" she screamed. "You've tortured me enough! I'll tell you! He wouldn't have me! I begged him on my knees! On my knees, Duncan Childers! Not that I wanted his love. I *was* sick of him, by then. But that he'd be man enough, kind enough, even, to spare me the disgrace. He wouldn't. Said the woman he finally took to wife wouldn't have callouses on her back from going over on it for anybody—like me! And he was right! You hear me, Duncan Childers, he was right!"

He sat there, unmoving.

"See what you've got now! Stan Bruder's leavings! The cheap little tramp even he didn't want! I hope you're proud, Duncan Childers! 'I—hope—you're—very—proud!'"

She threw herself upon the sofa, sobbing.

He got up. Pushed open the door. Went out.

Her sacrifice was useless. There is a sombre thread of mockery woven through the very warp of life. For, the next day, Hans Volker sat in the office of *The Mertontown Courier*, pleading his foredoomed cause.

Tim Evans shuffled the quit claims through his fingers like cards.

"The hell you say, Doc!" he laughed. "Give up the greatest story of my career to spare your fancy Caneville fillies a black eye or two? Not on your life! Go back a long ways, don't they? Here's one dated 1898. I was in Cuba then, covering the War——"

He stopped. Held the quit claim dated 1898 between his two hands to steady it. He couldn't steady it. It shook.

He raised his eyes. Met Hans Volker's gaze.

"I've changed my mind," he grated. "There'll be no story! Here, damn you; take them and get out! No, not this one! This one I'll keep."

Hans Volker picked them up. Stuffed them into his coat-pocket. Said: "Thank you, Tim." Went out of there.

Tim Evans sat there alone, holding that one quit claim he had kept. Stared at the name written in the blank space. Bent his head very slowly, looked at the picture on his desk. It was inscribed: "To my darling husband, with eternal love, Frances Ann."

He leaned his head upon the desk, cradling it upon his arms. He wept. Not for the past, but for the future. For all the bitter years he had left to live, knowing what he knew.

Chapter 16

"I CAME HERE TO PRACTISE MEDICINE," Duncan said, "but it looks like all I've been practising is open warfare."

"You could do with a mite more discretion, son," Hans Volker said. "What with horsewhipping people, being jailed for abortions you didn't perform, damned near getting lynched—it's been rough, hasn't it? Still, since you came back home—let's see, it was just after New Year's Day, wasn't it? That makes——"

"A year and a little more," Duncan said. "From January, 1904, until February, 1905. Thirteen months, during which I appear to have gotten exactly nowhere."

"Nowhere?" Hans Volker snorted. "I'd like to see what you call somewhere, then! You got us this hospital——"

"The James Buchanan Vance Memorial Hospital," Duncan said wryly. "Contributed largely by my esteemed father-in-law, in memory of one of the worst damned scoundrels who ever drew breath. I could do with a sight less of life's little ironies, Hans. I got Twin Towns this modern, up-to-date hospital, not intentionally, but because I'd lost a battle with Father Nels. Tried to get him to let me blow up that old dam that keeps the Bayou Flèche full of water, and our swamps nice and wet, and teeming with *Culex fasciatus*, or, according to Theobald's classification, which even Walter Reed has accepted now, *Stegomyia fasciata*."

"Just call 'em mosquitoes, and let it go at that," Hans said. "They kill you just as dead under either name."

"All right," Duncan said. "Incidentally, Hans, it *is* a dam. That old landslide story is pure rot. And five will get you ten that my father-in-law, years ago, seeing the Bayou and the marshes drying up on him, and with them his fur profits, invented that landslide to cover his own intervention into the workings of nature."

"Wouldn't doubt it. But what has that got to do with your getting the money to build the hospital out of him?"

"Didn't get it out of him. He offered it. Kind of a bribe, I reckon, to shut my big mouth about swamps and mosquitoes. And I took it. Dishonourable as old hell, but I saw in it a way to salvage some good out of the all-pervading evil. I knew I couldn't win on the swamp drainage question. About matters affecting their self-interest Nelson Vance and the Town Council think as one man."

"What did you do," Hans gibed, "to get our fine maternity ward and that beautiful X Ray machine out of Mrs. Douglass Henderson? I never figured that your tactic of turning evil into good extended to a little quiet adultery."

"If it weren't for your grey hairs," Duncan said, "or, more accurately, your flowing, snow-white mane, I'd——"

"Come on, son, how did you prise it out of her?"

"By a method a dirty-minded old coot like you will never believe. I just asked her—and in her husband's presence. Doug made no objections. In fact, he encouraged her to do it. Tell you another thing, Doc: that has been a good marriage. Never saw a happier-looking critter than Doug. It appears that Jenny did him a good turn when she wouldn't marry him. And I put my two-bits' worth in by introducing him to Grace Harvey. Worked out just fine, didn't it?"

"Doug's a fine boy," Hans Volker said. "And with that lovely kid they've got—nothing like children to cement a marriage, son."

"Hinting, Doc?" Duncan said softly.

"Frankly, yes. I've heard rumours that things could be happier between you and Hester than they are. And it's my fault, damn it! Interfering old fool that I am!"

Duncan's eyes were bleak suddenly.

"The circumstances being what they were, you did what you had to," he said. "Anyhow, it's not your fault. Put the blame on God. He made us the way we are. Deuced dull subject. Let's drop it, shall we, Hans?"

'So it's true,' Hans mused sadly. 'I thought they'd patch it up by now.'

"By the way, Hans," Duncan said, "you sent for me. What was it you wanted to see me about?"

Hans Volker's face became even more serious.

"Tell me, son," he said soberly: "is it true that you infected Will Thompson with malaria to prove to him that there actually are germs, and that mosquitoes carry them?"

"Heck, no! He did it himself. You know that series of slides I was preparing to illustrate the life cycle of the malarial parasite in *Anopheles claviger*? Well, I'd just finished the series when he came in, and I showed them to him. So he just snorted: 'Them damn lil' bits and pieces cause malaria? Who're you tryin' to kid, boy? Anybody with any gumption knows you get it from miasmic airs from the swamps.' Well, I had a gauze cage filled with infected

Anopheles, buzzing around like mad. So I said to him: 'You don't believe it, Doctor? Well, just stick your hand in there!'"

"And he did it? Why, the poor ignorant old fool!"

"He did it, all right. You ought to go and see him. He's lying up there, with books piled up all over the bed, reading every living word I could find him on microbes! Every time I go in there, he croaks, between shivers: "Got any more litrachew on these damn lil' bugs? Gawdamnit, Doctor, this is great stuff!'"

"Hell of a conversation," Hans chuckled. "But we'd better pull him through. Be a valuable ally. He's always been the one old Vance and the Town Council relied on to refute our new-fangled ideas."

"Well, he's just like Saul after that journey to Damascus now. You go in and talk to him, Hans. Be gentle, though. Don't rub his nose into it."

"I won't. Glad it was that way, though. Because otherwise I was going to have to act like the Head Doctor of this establishment and read you one hell of a lecture. Now you go get yourself some rest. We've got an appendectomy and an exploratory scheduled for tomorrow morning."

"Exploratory? What's up, Doctor?"

"Miller, who runs the feed store. Sounds a hell of a lot like an aortic aneurysm to me."

"The cat-house king," Duncan mused. "Storeyville's pride. We don't need to do an exploratory, Hans. If it sounds like an aneurysm —it is. You know that nine times out of ten when you get one in the aorta, the cause is—syph. And Miller's been supporting every whorehouse from Basin Street to Storeyville ever since I was a kid. Wages of sin, Doctor."

"Well," Hans Volker said, "we have to go in there, anyhow. You know how to patch those things up. And even if you are Vardigan Childers's nephew, you aren't going to let a man die of something you can fix. Besides, there are mitigating circumstances. Madge Miller hasn't thawed out since the blizzard of eighty-eight."

"'Neither do I condemn thee,'" Duncan said quietly. "All right, Doc, be seeing you."

When he got downstairs to the street entrance, Mrs. Morris, the receptionist, stopped him. That was the kind of establishment he and Hans Volker were running now. With a receptionist. Not for swank, but because they needed one. And a telephone switchboard which Mrs. Morris handled. They had five young graduate nurses, hand-picked by Jenny Greenway. They were all good, competent girls, every living one of them as homely as home-made sin. Duncan wondered whether Jen had done that on purpose. She was a marvellous Head Nurse, whatever her reasons for accepting the post were. And she was becoming more friendly now.

"Doctor," Mrs. Morris said, "there's a nigger man waiting to see you. I made him wait outside. Nerve of him, coming in here, asking for you! And the way he talks, Lord God, you'd think——"

"What would you think, Nellie?" Duncan said.

"That it was a white man talking, if you don't look at him. Gingercake-coloured nigger. Always did say them mulattoes is the worst! And dressed! Got a suit on good as yours, Doctor. Shirt and tie. Silk shirt, or I miss my guess. First time I ever did see a nigger out of overalls, except a preacher."

Duncan stood there, staring at her.

"Mose!" he exploded. "Lord God, it's Mose!"

Nellie Morris got up from behind the desk and went to the door. What she saw shocked her so that afterwards she had to send an orderly to the dispensary for smelling-salts. Duncan Childers had gripped the young negro in a huge bear-hug, and was pounding him enthusiastically on the back.

"Better let go of me, Dunc," Mose grinned shyly, "or you're going to lose every damn patient you've got. This is still Louisiana, boy. South Louisiana."

"Why, damn me for a sinner!" Duncan laughed. "Don't reckon I've been so glad to see a body in ninety years! Just got back, boy?"

"Well, not exactly," Mose said. "Been home long enough to put on double harness."

"Renée?" Duncan said.

"Yep. She waited. Thought she wasn't going to; but she did."

"Happy, boy?" Duncan said.

"If," Mose said fervently, "heaven's any better, I don't want to go there. Couldn't stand the strain. Heard you married Miss Hester. Reckon you're happy too, Dunc."

Duncan's smile wavered.

"Yes," he said. "Very."

Mose looked at him gravely.

"You always were the world's lousiest liar, Dunc," he said quietly. "Want to tell me what's wrong? Good to talk it out, sometimes. And it's not like talking to one of your white friends. It'll go no further than here. I won't even tell Renée."

Duncan stared at him. The need to tell someone was very strong. And this was Mose. Good old Mose.

"She—oh, hell, Mose, it's nothing much. She doesn't like it here

214

any more. Had a taste of New Orleans while I had a residency there. Big city. Lights. Gaiety."

"She wants you to give up your practice here," Mose said slowly. His words were affirmative, not interrogative. "Your brand-new hospital that you squeezed out of her Pa. Go back down there and be a fashionable doctor with a nice bedside manner. That's it, isn't it, Dunc?"

"Yes," Duncan said miserably. "That's it."

He didn't add the rest. He couldn't. Not even to Mose. You didn't tell any man, negro or white, that your wife had adopted a tactic that went straight back to Aristophanes: that she slept in a separate bedroom behind locked doors now, and had done so for five months, waiting, as she put it, for him to come to his senses. 'As if,' he thought bitterly, 'there were anything in our case that could be arranged by sense. The damage is done. We've both been wounded unto death. Our marriage is gone. She says we need that hectic life again. That this place has too many bitter memories. As if we'd leave them behind if we went. As if they weren't in us like a sickness. As if evil did not for ever vanquish good. A hell of a note! She's been true to me. A good wife after her fashion. And I've been a pretty fair husband. And yet—I'm glad of that locked door! Because to touch her now would be an abomination. Stan Bruder's leavings! What difference does that make? Who am I, anyhow, God?'

"Too bad, Doctor," Mose said. "Got to practise calling you that, Dunc. Be a hell of a thing if people around here were to hear a nigger calling you by your first name."

"Oh, to hell with them!" Duncan said savagely.

"No, Dunc, not to hell with them. That's not the answer. Don't really know what the answer is myself. Reckon the closest to it that any man can come is, 'Father forgive them, for they know not what they do.'"

"Rot," Duncan snorted. "Christian resignation will get you exactly nowhere, Mose."

"It'll keep me alive long enough," Mose said gently, "to do something for my people."

Duncan looked at him soberly.

"You're right," he said. "That's the principal thing, isn't it?"

"I told Renée," Mose said, "that I was going to bring you home for supper tonight—if I could. She didn't exactly believe me. You see, Dunc, she never met a white man like you. And I want her to. Part of her education. Stop her from over-simplifying things."

"White is black, and black is white in her book, eh, Mose?"

"Something like that. Will you come, Dunc?"

"I'd be delighted. And not just to educate Renée, but because it'll be a real pleasure for me."

"That's settled, then," Mose said. "Say, Duncan, I meant to tell you how sorry I was to hear about your grandmother. Didn't have your address to write you a sympathy note back then when it happened; and Ma had written me that you were away."

Duncan's face tightened. That hurt still.

"Yes," he whispered. "Coronary thrombosis. Of course I wasn't a doctor then; but I should have thought to have her examined before I left for Harvard. She—she looked so well——"

"Those things, Dunc, just happen. She was a great lady, your grandmother. The best."

'And the wisest,' Duncan thought. 'She saw through Hester, even when Hes was a child. Only I didn't. Maybe I still don't. Hes lives in this world, and is of it. She knows how useless dedication and self-sacrifice are. All right, they're useless. All human actions are, finally. But I'm made like that. I can't help it. And she knows it. Just as,' he added bitterly, 'she can't help it—and I know it. It's not me she's rejecting. She still loves me—I think. She wants me in her ambiance, her own milieu, apart from which she is a fish out of water, just as I am—out of mine. Life is such a simple thing: you're born; you pass a few days under the sun; you die. But, God in heaven, how we complicate it! I am sick unto death of wounds dealt me before I dreamed of wedding Hes. I flee happiness for reasons that exist not in my head but in my viscera. I should forget. Be practical. Enjoy life. Hester is right. I think I'm performing the high and holy mission of saving lives. But nobody can save lives. The best we can do is to prolong them. So, what am I shouting about? "Stern Duty, immortal daughter of the Voice of God——" Hogwash! I ought to give in. Go down to New Orleans, develop my bedside manner. Only, I can't. I can't——'

He was aware then that Mose's eyes were on him, pityingly.

'Am I that transparent?' he thought. "Look, Mose," he said, "I've a couple of calls to make. Want to come along with me for the ride?"

"No," Mose said gravely. "That was all right when we were kids. But now you can't afford it. You're a big man around town. It's a fool trick to buck the world, boy. Ride with the punches, and save yourself to get done what you've got to do. Be seeing you, Doctor Childers. This heah po' chile is plumb honoured——"

"Stop it!" Duncan snapped.

"Take it easy, boy," Mose said. "You don't want to end up there at Pineville like that poor Mrs. Rosemary Vance, do you? If you want something good for the nerves, I can prescribe——"

"All right, all right," Duncan smiled wearily. "What time shall I come tonight, Mose?"

"About eight, Dunc," Mose said.

As he moved towards the Cajun section, Duncan looked at the splendid dappled grey he drove. The horse was a gift from Hester, as was the smart and saucy little buggy. He had never particularly resented his wife's wealth. It simply hadn't mattered one way or another. But it did now. 'Trying to buy me,' he thought savagely; 'can't she see I'm not for sale?'

He could see Jean Baptiste La Veau's cabin before him now, perched on its stilts above the Bayou. He had come out there to look at Brigitte, Jean's wife. She was pregnant again—as usual. So he needed someone to pole him out to the cabin in one of the dug-out boats that the Cajuns called *pirogues*. But of all Jean's twelve children—with the thirteenth on its way—only one was in the garden on the bank before the house. Thirteen, he thought, and they couldn't really feed or clothe two. 'If that's the will of God, like Father Gaulois says, then God is sure as hell overdoing things.'

He got down from the buggy and approached the child. She was so busy hoeing weeds that she hadn't noticed him.

"*Bonjour, ma petite,*" he began. "Are your folks at home? I've come to have a look at your mama."

The child whirled, her eyes wide with terror. Then she turned and ran, as though seven devils were pursuing her, down to the Bayou's edge, flung herself into the *pirogue*, and paddled furiously towards the house. And it was then that Duncan realised that he had never seen this particular child before. Pity held him rooted to the spot. The child's face had been a horror: cross-eyes and the widest, most hideous hare-lip he had ever seen in all his practice.

His mind raced into techniques: a strabotomy, of course. Not even a difficult operation. Been done hundreds of times since Stromeyer first cut the eye muscles of a cadaver back in 1838 and returned the eyes to their normal position. Dieffenbach had done a successful one on a living patient the very next year. And with George Critchett's improved method. 'But that hare-lip! Lord God, that hare-lip! I could see four teeth through it! No question of scarifying the edges and ligating it. Plastic, no less. Let's see. I could lift a flap of the inner surface of the forearm, and make a graft, binding the arm over the upper lip until it takes. Then a second operation to separate the arm and the mouth, and to shape her a new lip. Colour? It wouldn't have any. Be as white as the rest of her skin.' He stood there frozen, light washing over his mind in blinding waves. 'Tattoo! Of course! Get one of those filthy beggars up from New Orleans who stencil naked women on sailors' chests! Make him sterilise his instruments, or sterilise them myself. Pick out the right shade—Get on with it, boy; time's a-wasting!'

"Jean!" he called out. "Jean! For God's sake come and get me! I want to talk to you about that child!"

When he left, an hour later, it was all settled. Jean would bring little Marie Louise into the hospital the following afternoon. Fee? None. Expenses? He would pay them out of his own pocket, for the simple joy of restoring this child, who for years now had been running and hiding every time she heard a stranger's step, to life. He could see in that small face even the beginnings of beauty. It made a warmth in him, just thinking about it.

As a result, his examination of the pregnant woman had been somewhat perfunctory. He realised that, but he didn't worry about it. Brigitte La Veau was as healthy as a horse. Nor did he reckon the consequences of another thing he had done. He gave Jean a year's supply of contraceptives, and growled at him: "Use them, man! You've got too damned many brats now!"

His mood of exultation held him until he reached Smoketown, where the negroes lived. He had not visited it for years, largely because he didn't even want to remember what it was like: the narrow, crooked alleys, with filthy water standing stagnant in the middle of them, the tumble-down shanties that stank of greasy pellagra-breeding cooking, and the stench of unwashed humanity. The children in their filthy rags playing upon the heaps of refuse that nobody ever bothered to collect. The number of cases of conjunctivitis he could count in less than half a block. The cripples, out of all proportion to what they should have been, considering the negroes' percentage in the population. The razor scars on the faces of men and women alike, scars which he realised were the visible marks of the endless, daily, hourly frustrations and psychic hurts, exploded into physical violence—and against the available, unprotected neighbour, instead of the alien master race that inspired them. The grim silence, no laughter and no song, none of that happy-go-lucky spirit that white Southerners told the world and each other about so much they had become to believe it true. Up in Caneville the blacks, knowing what was expected of them, might turn their matchless mimicry to a counterfeit of the gaiety the

218

white man said they had; but here they stared at Doctor Duncan Childers with eyes that glittered with undisguised hostility.

And then, in the midst of the misery, hopelessness, and filth, an island, an oasis: the homes of Smoketown's upper class. The Baptist preacher's imposing two-storey mansion. The undertaker's neat brick bungalow. The steamboat gothic house of the semi-gangster who owned every barrel-house, bar, dwelling of ill fame in town. Last of all, Big Mack Johnson's neat, white-washed shotgun cabin, become Doctor Moses Johnson's residence now, with his gold-lettered shingle swinging in the breeze before the door.

Mose came out and greeted him. They shook hands solemnly. Duncan could see the two women on the porch. He recognised Mose's mother. Luvinia hadn't changed much, except that now her Indian straight hair was snowy white. Looking at her now, he put into explicit thought what he had often felt before: in another time, another place, this striking woman would have been a princess —or a queen.

"Howdy, Doctor," she greeted him with massive calm. "Meet my daughter-in-law. Renée, this here is Doctor Childers."

Duncan stared at Mose's bride in frank and open admiration.

"Lord God, she's pretty, Mose!" he said.

Renée blushed. Duncan was a little surprised to note he could see that blush. Her skin was *café au lait*. When she blushed, it turned dusky rose. Her features had been softened and rounded a little from the Caucasian's rigid aquilinity by her African forebears, but only a little; and her figure, under a gown quite as much *à la mode* as anything that Hester or Jenny wore, was a joy for ever.

"Thank you, Doctor," she said. "You're very kind."

"Sit down, son," Luvinia said. "Been a long time since we seen your face around here."

"Too long," Duncan said, and sank into the rocking-chair that Mose pushed forward.

It was hard to get a conversation started. They accepted him, he knew. Mose had told them that he was kind and good. But he was —white. And in Smoketown, in the house of a man who had died in dignity and in grief because of a white man's doings, the colour of his skin was like a leprosy, a brand of ugly memories and old pains.

Then the girl came out on the porch. A lovely girl, some sixteen years old. A white child, having no trace of negro in her at all.

"Come here, baby, an' meet th' Doctor," Luvinia crooned.

The girl hung back. Duncan sat there and stared. Luvinia was too old. Mose had been away from home for years. But surely that undimmed, unalloyed tenderness with which he gazed upon Renée could not have survived——

"She's not my baby, Doctor," Renée said drily. "She's Mose's sister's child. We adopted her."

'And Jim Vance's,' Duncan thought grimly. 'Hester's niece. My niece-in-law. Lord God, is there no end to the evil that bloody bastard spewed out upon the world?'

He found himself talking, saying without caution or previous thought: "Moses, you can't! You ought to send her away where she——"

"Can be white?" Mose said gently. "I've thought of that. But she's too young yet, Dunc; and she needs us."

"I'm sorry," Duncan said quickly. "I spoke without thinking. You all know I didn't mean any harm."

"Course not," Luvinia said. "Poor baby, she's a-gonna catch it —from white folks and niggers both. Whitemen gonna want to make a fancygal outa her, and niggers already picking on her cause she's so light. But my Mose'll fix that. See that she gets a good education; train her to be secretary, or a nurse, send her North——

North to freedom, Duncan thought. The warmth with which negroes pronounced that word always shamed him a little.

"Come here, missy," he said. "I'm your uncle. At least I'm your uncle-in-law."

Luvinia threw back her head and laughed aloud.

"Why, that's a fact, ain't it? That's a pure-Lord, nachel fact!"

Going away in the darkness, Duncan had the good feeling that he had won them at last. Around the table, over the inevitable fried chicken, beaten biscuits and collard greens, the talk had been slow and warm. Even Renée was clearly convinced that here was one white man with neither hate, prejudice, nor condescension in his heart. When he had started to talk medicine with Mose, he had been surprised and delighted to find out how much his old friend knew. He left them, finally, with the idea of starting a clinic for the negroes moving through his mind.

But, as he jogged up to the Bouvoir house, he was thinking, oddly, not of his idea for the new clinic, but of children: Doug's and Grace's infant, and Jim Vance's two daughters, separated by the unbridgeable chasm of race. 'Maybe if Hes and I were to have a kid,' he thought, 'things would be different. But she doesn't pay much attention to little Ruth. Never even offered to take her off the old man's hands. Not that he'd let her go. Lord, how old Nelson loves that child! Just as he loved Hes herself—and Jim. That's his good side, I reckon. He's a fool over kids.'

He saw, suddenly, that the lights were on downstairs. And, stranger still, a carriage stood before his door.

"Now, who the devil?" he muttered, and climbed wearily down from the buggy. He went up on the porch, unlocked the door, went into the living-room.

Hester sat there, alone. She was dressed for travelling. There were valises piled up all around her. Her valises—and his.

"I'm leaving," she said flatly. "And I do hope you'll come with me, Duncan. You've done your part here, Duncan. You've got the town a hospital, improved the sanitation in this burg a hundred per cent, reduced infant mortality and childbed fever cases down to a third what they were. And I—I'd like to have my husband again. If that's possible. If he can stop brooding over a past that doesn't concern him. Forget, finally, that the girl he married played the fool, perhaps because he wasn't here to keep her from playing it— to save her. I want you with me, darling, living like a civilised human being. Working with Dr. Phelton, coming home to me at least some nights. Will you come, Duncan?"

"Hes," he said, moving towards her, "Lord God, Hes——"

"Don't touch me, Duncan! Let's not be emotional, please!"

"Hes, you know I can't go to New Orleans—leave my work——"

"It's your work or me, Duncan. Choose."

The question was false. The choice had long since been made. He stood there, looking at her.

"Hes, if you walk out of that door——"

"It'll be the end. I know. So be it. Oh, driver!"

The man's footsteps sounded in the passage. He came shuffling through the door.

"Take the valises out to the carriage, will you? No, not those— only these."

He stood there watching her make this absurd little drama of their physical parting. As if it mattered. They had parted months before.

She put out her hand to him.

She smiled.

"Good-bye, Doctor Duncan Childers," she said.

Then she went through the door, closing it so gently it made no sound at all.

Chapter 17

JENNY PASSED HIM THE SCISSORS with the tip of one blade flattened horizontally like a miniature spatula, so that when heavy bandages were cut away it could not pierce the skin. On the other side of the room Marvin Roberts, the local photographer, waited with his heavy camera ready on its tripod, holding the pan of flash powder up in his left hand, gripping the rubber bulb of the shutter mechanism in his right. Dr. Volker and Dr. Carter stood by the bed; across the room, Dr. Thompson sat wrapped in a heavy dressing-gown and shivering.

"Oh, Duncan," Jenny said. "My teeth are chattering!"

"Why?" Duncan said. "It's going to be all right. Just like her eyes."

"Beautiful job, Doctor," Carter said. He was being excessively nice now, out of his sense of guilt over his rôle in the Fontaine case. "First strabotomy ever done in this parish. Glad you thought of taking those photographs before you operated. Nobody would believe it's the same child."

"Damned if she didn't look like her right eye was trying to peek behind the bridge of her nose," Will Thompson said. "Got yourself one hell of a fine boy, Hans. Always did have faith in him, didn't you?"

"I've operated for hare-lip," Henry Carter said, "but in a case like this I wouldn't even have attempted it. Of course skin-grafting is almost as old as surgery, but——"

"It was a hell of a thing to do," Hans said. "Poor little tyke lying there day after day, with her arm stitched to her upper lip, and never a murmur out of her. Damn it, boy, this better be good, or I'll have your hide!"

Duncan straightened up. He smiled at them.

'When he smiles now,' Jenny thought, 'only his mouth moves. His eyes don't change. They stay—dead. Oh, damn her! Damn her evil soul to hell and begone! This shouldn't be done to him. Not to him. He deserves everything good the world has to offer. It shouldn't be done to any man, but especially not to—Duncan. Nor to me. Dear Lord, how long can I stand seeing him like this? How long can I, without stretching out my hands to him and——"

"Gentlemen," Duncan said, "I am not a miracle worker. Marie Louis is not going to have a normal mouth. She will have two scars at the outer junctures of the graft. I'm hoping those scars will be very nearly invisible. Also, the reconstructed section of the lip will remain white. However, in about two weeks, we're having it tattooed to match the rest of the lip. From then on, the child should look not a bit worse than any kid who has had a slight accident—fallen off a bicycle, say."

"All right, get on with it, son," Hans Volker said.

Duncan began snipping through the bandage. He peeled it off, and stood back.

"Glory be!" Will Thompson said.

It was—rebirth. The pitiful little monstrosity, with her right eye turned inward so that it stared straight at the bridge of her nose, and the great gap in her upper lip through which teeth and gums showed hideously, was gone. In her place lay an almost normal child. A decidedly pretty child. It wasn't perfect. Two thin red lines, that looked as though they had been neatly traced with a ruler, outlined the place where the gap had been. Between them the lip was white. It looked rather like a birthmark—nothing worse.

"Well?" Duncan said.

"Oh, Duncan!" Jenny got out. She was crying quite frankly.

Marie Louise stared at her. The straight, fine, intelligent eyes were troubled suddenly.

"*Est-ce que je suis si laide?*" she whimpered.

"Oh no, darling!" Jenny cried. "You're not ugly! You—you're beautiful! I'm crying because I'm so happy!"

"Will *Mademoiselle l'Infirmière* be so kind as to permit me a mirror?" Marie Louise said.

Jenny looked at Duncan.

"Give it to her," he said gravely.

The child took the mirror. She sat there staring at her new face. She did not move or speak for a long, long time.

"I find myself very pretty," she announced primly; "but there is something rare. My lip, it has not the colour that it should. Will it remain *comme ça, docteur?*"

"No, baby," Duncan said. "In a few more days, we're going to colour it to match the rest. It will hurt, I'm afraid. But you have the courage, is it not so?"

"Yes, *docteur*," Marie Louise said firmly. "To be pretty like other girls I can support very much pain. My eyes are nice. Nicer than my mouth. But we will see, *n'est-ce pas, docteur?*"

"Yes, baby," Duncan laughed. "We'll see. Now we are going

223

to do a thing. That m'sieur there is going to take a picture of you, as you are now. To do so, he will ignite the powder he has in that pan. It will make a very bright light, but also a big noise. You will not have fear, will you, *ma petite*?"

"No, *docteur*, I will not have fear."

"All right, Marvin," Duncan said. "It's all yours."

The magnesium flash powder went off with a roar. Smoke drifted thinly against the ceiling. Marie Louise blinked once or twice; that was all.

"Reckon that does it," Duncan said tiredly. "Now if you will excuse me——"

"Where are you going, Duncan?" Jenny said sharply.

"Promised to stand by while Mose snatches an appendix," Duncan said. "Why?"

"Because you shouldn't!" Jenny said wrathfully. "I'll bet you haven't had two hours' sleep any one night this week!"

Duncan stared at her.

"Keeping tabs on me, Jen?" he said.

"Yes. Somebody has to. You're a walking skeleton. You always were lean—but you never were a bag of bones, before. I tell you——"

"Leave him be, Jen," Hans Volker said quietly. "There is something to be said for hospital discipline, after all. You don't want me to start enforcing it, do you, Nurse? We've been pretty slack around here. Never made you get up when a doctor came in. Didn't insist upon the use of the title. He's a doctor, child. A real one. They're rare. When he's older, he'll learn that he has to sleep sometime—for the proper protection of his patients even. In the meantime, leave him be. We surrender to practicality mighty slowly when our heart's in this thing."

"I'll never surrender," Duncan said.

"Your body will. It'll just quit on you one of these fine nights. But having a strong-minded female pestering you won't do, either. Hank, you want to take a look at Miller? Got a blooming aortic aneurysm, the poor fellow."

After they had gone, Jenny made her rounds, holding hard against even the tendency to think. She went through the ward, where they had an unusually large quota of yellow-fever patients for so early in the spring, segregated, each of them lying under a canopy of mosquito-netting to prevent the ravenous *Stegomyia* from getting at them and spreading the disease. The hospital was itself screened; but Duncan had insisted upon this additional precaution against any stray mosquito that might get in when somebody

opened a door. They were very careful about the doors. Jenny hated
to enter that ward. It was so very nearly hopeless. Of course, if the
disease were diagnosed early enough, if you kept them absolutely
quiet, gave them nothing at all to eat, not even milk, during the
febrile stage; gave them divided doses of calomel, followed by
magnesium sulphate upon admission, mostly you saved them. Since
Duncan had convinced the town's doctors of the necessity of hos-
pitalising every patient even suspected of having yellow fever, and
beginning treatment at the appearance of the premonitory symptoms,
some twenty-four to forty-eight hours before a positive diagnosis of
yellow fever could be made, the mortality had been held to a low
fifteen per cent. In other parishes it hovered around forty. In bad
years it went up to eighty-five. The awful thing was that you didn't
know. Duncan said that it was caused by a filterable virus. That
was all anybody could say. Nobody had ever seen the yellow-fever
microbe, not even with the highest-power microscope in the world.

Not knowing was bad. You couldn't even swear it was the treatment that saved them. Back Bayou people got it, and some of them
got well without any treatment at all. But in the bad years, in spite
of everything you could do, they died. You got used to death in a
hospital, but the way people with yellow fever died you never got
used to. They came in with a chill, headaches, pains in the arms
and legs, in the back, vomiting, constipation and inability to urinate.
Then they calmed down, got better. Some of them, thank God,
kept on getting better until you could send them home. But when
the third stage set in, nine times out of ten, you could give them up.
They burned up with fever, turned yellow, started to vomit black
mucus. Their gums bled. Their kidneys. In not too rare cases they
hæmorrhaged into the skin. They befouled their beds with urine,
with fæces, with black vomit, with the peculiarly vile stench of
their sweat. When they died finally, the excess of pity you had
suffered from made you almost—glad.

But tonight they were doing fine, all of them. She was happy
over that. For one thing, it meant she could go home on time—at
midnight. She could go home and lie in her bed, wide-eyed all the
night through, thinking of him, and dying on the inside, very, very
slowly. Which was too much. Far too much.

Or, forcing him from her mind, she could occupy herself with
the problem of whether or not to marry Forsythe Bevers. Bevers was
considered a catch. He was very rich, and quite good-looking, even
if his eyes did have something in them—that was disturbing.
Another thing that bothered her was the number of people who
genuinely didn't like Forsythe. She was beginning to hear things—

a snatch here, a phrase there, that troubled her. Only, there didn't seem to be anything concrete about that dislike; nobody ever said exactly why they didn't like him. That was because he wasn't from Caneville and nobody really knew him, she guessed. Except Stan Bruder. Well, she had weaned him away from Stan completely. But, apparently, Duncan also knew Forsythe in New Orleans. And the contempt in his eyes was unmasked when Forsythe's name was mentioned. Only, he wouldn't say anything, either. He was too much a man to belittle—a rival. If that were the word. If there were a word for the relationship between Duncan and herself. But what if the expression she saw in Duncan's eyes when he looked at her new suitor was more than—jealousy? What if the things she didn't know about Forsythe were more important than she thought?

And, basically, was it right to marry a man you knew very well you didn't love, whom you merely liked, instead of waiting to see if the one you did love would ever win free? It was hopeless. Hester would never, never let Duncan go.

Well, she was going down to New Orleans herself in June, to attend the annual seminar for head nurses they held at Tulane. Sort of a refresher course. There was a thing or two she could find out in New Orleans about Forsythe Bevers. And about—Duncan.

She went back to her office and busied herself with her charts, reports, lists of needed supplies. But tonight even this routine paperwork took her a long time. Duncan's face kept getting in between her and the pages on which she was trying to write. She made mistakes; had to do the same reports over two and three times before she got them right. When she was in the act of signing her name to the very last of them, she heard, astonishingly, the sound of footsteps in the corridor. Nurse Griffiths, surely, coming to relieve her. Looking at the clock, she saw it was ten minutes after twelve.

She greeted Nurse Griffiths tiredly, gave her instructions. Then she slung her cape about her shoulders and went downstairs. When she came out of the door, she saw Duncan sitting in his buggy, waiting for her.

"I was passing by on my way home," he said. "Happened to look at my watch and saw it was five to twelve. So I waited. Thought maybe you could use a ride home."

She looked at him, and her fingertips ached to touch his face.

"I could," she said quietly, "but not home, Duncan. Let's just ride a while and you talk to me. I need some air. Besides, you won't sleep when you get home anyhow, like you should. All you'll do is to sit there and pound the piano the rest of the night."

Duncan stared at her.

"How did you know that, Jen?" he said.

"Because I've heard you. Don't ask me when, or even how I happened to hear you. A woman has some right to her little secrets, Duncan. But I don't think I've heard that piece you were playing, before. It's lovely. So—sad. What is it, Duncan?"

"A little thing of my own. Been trying my hand at composing. It's called 'A Fugue for Damned Souls'."

"Oh, Duncan!" Jenny said.

"Sorry," he said brusquely. "Melodramatic title, isn't it? Where do you want to go, Jen?"

"Oh—anywhere. Down by the Bayou, I reckon. It's warm enough for that. Strange to think that the century's already five years old. Come on, the ride will do you good, after your labour of love on little Marie Louise."

"Brave as hell, wasn't she?" Duncan said. "Some of it was painful. And she lay there and let me whittle away and hem-stitch——"

"Duncan," Jenny said softly, "when you decided to do that, were you thinking of—your hill?"

"My hill? I'm afraid I don't follow you, Jen."

"Then you weren't. I'm glad. I'm very glad. You do have that side, too. I guess I always knew you had."

"What side are you talking about? You cook up more damn riddles, Jen. . . ."

"No, Duncan, I'm very clear. Almost transparent. You know nearly everything about me."

"Except why you keep going around with Forsythe Bevers," Duncan said drily.

"I'll tell you that. I like him—and he needs me. Besides, Duncan, I'm not a girl any longer. You know my age, though, being a woman, I wish you didn't. I don't want to stay single all my life. Tell me—who else is there?"

"Not me," he said bitterly, "until I get the gumption or the guts to——"

"Let's not go into that, Duncan," Jenny said.

"All right," he muttered, and turned away, staring out over the Bayou. "No fit subject for discussion anyhow, is it?"

Jenny didn't answer him. She was too busy studying his profile. The moonlight over the Bayou exaggerated its bony contours. 'A moon,' she thought furiously, 'painting the waters silver. The reeds standing up like spears, piercing the night. Indian Summer, so soft and warm. So lovely, so romantic. And we sit here—with her evil between us like a presence, separating us like an invisible wall.'

"Jen," he said, "what did you mean by my hill?"

227

She smiled.

"Strange that you forgot, Duncan. It's very simple. The one I used to put you up on as being different from other men. Better, finer—even kinder. I thought maybe you were trying to get back up there, by means of Marie Louise. Vain of me. I should have known better."

"And have I got back?"

"Not quite. Let's say you've shown me I wasn't entirely wrong," she said.

"And if I ever do get back up there?" he whispered.

"You'll still be guarded by—your dragon. Your beautiful, absentee dragon. But guarded very well, for all that."

"Oh, damn!" Duncan said feelingly.

She looked away from him, out over the silver waters.

"We've talked enough for tonight, I think," she said, "and I am very tired. Will you take me home now, Duncan, please?"

"All right, Jen, we'll go," he said.

Duncan drew the grey up before Jenny's door, jumped from the buggy, and helped her down. It was, curiously, the moment she had been dreading. What was worse, seeing Duncan's face under the new electric street lamp, she realised that he knew she had been dreading it. There was pure mocking deviltry in his eyes.

"Well, Jen," he said, "aren't you going to invite me in? Offer me a nightcap? Or—even kiss me goodnight?"

She looked at him. Her brown eyes were very dark behind those ugly glasses.

"No, Duncan," she said. "None of the three."

"Why not, Jen?"

"Because—that's a dead-end street, Duncan. It has no exit. I am no longer a child."

"No," he said gravely. "You're a woman now. A rarely lovely woman, Jen."

"Thank you, Duncan," she said, just as gravely.

"Let's cut out the play-acting, shall we, Jen? I know you're fond of me."

"No," she said, "not just fond. I'm in love with you, Duncan. I always have been. I always will be. And with that kind of feeling one doesn't play games."

He stood there, looking at her.

"And Bevers?" he grated.

"Will have to be content with what crumbs of affection I have left to offer him. If I can bring myself to be that selfish, that unfair.

228

I think, perhaps, I can. I've been taught a few lessons, Duncan, since you came home. Bitter lessons."

"Lord God, Jenny, I——"

"Goodnight, Duncan," she said. Then, very quietly, she turned and left him there, standing in the darkness that was, and was not, of the night.

Chapter 18

DUNCAN SAT ON THE VERANDA of the Bouvoir house, looking at his watch. One minute to eleven. In exactly one more minute they——

The crisp hoofbeats of Forsythe Bevers's black trotter cut through his thoughts. He looked up, seeing them coming up the road. Jenny was dressed precisely as he had known she would be: in a big, white picture hat that did wonders for her dark hair and eyes. The saucy white lace parasol trailed with studied negligence over her shoulder. Wearing those new glasses of hers that detracted less from a woman's looks than any specs he had ever seen.

'Right on schedule. Every Sunday morning at eleven o'clock sharp. Making damned sure that I——'

He stopped short, staring at the oncoming sulky. The critical, analytical side of his mind, that somehow stopped him always just short of folly, held him now. 'You've spent your life underestimating Jen,' he told himself. 'Damned well time you quit it now. So she goes riding every Sunday with Forsythe. Why shouldn't she?'

They were abreast of him now, in front of the house. He lifted his arm and waved to them. They waved back, sped on.

'Why shouldn't she? Forsythe's single and unattached. He's got all that money. And what have I really against him? That he's Stan's best friend. That birds of a feather flock together. That I know how he spends his time in New Orleans. The saloons, the race track, Basin Street. A whoremonger, a gambler, a drunkard. Hell! Whom am I trying to fool? I'd object to him if he had a halo, wings, and a harp. I'd object to any man who looked at Jen. Dog in the manger. I, who haven't even got what it takes to win free of Hes, even knowing that a desertion charge——'

Hes. He straightened up, sat back, staring blindly at the road. He didn't want to think about that. That hurt. In some ways, it hurt worst of all.

He had gone down to New Orleans the day after his ride with Jen. He had gone to ask Hester to free him, so that he could do something about Jen. Only it hadn't turned out the way he expected.

She had opened the door to the flat. She had been clad in a dressing-gown, her blond hair loose.

And the surge of remembered passion, of wanting her, that exploded through his veins had left him speechless, white-faced, weak; the motives that had brought him drowned by the thunder in his blood.

"Come in," she said. "I'm glad to see you, Duncan."

She made coffee for him. She seemed really glad to see him. But those ancient eyes measured him with the precision of a micrometer. She saw his faded shirt with the frayed collar; his ill-pressed blue serge suit, shiny in the knee and seat. He could almost see the words forming behind her eyes in cool and pitiless contempt: 'Country doctor. Horse-and-buggy practitioner. Hayseed Medic, gone back to the grass roots from which you sprang.'

"Hes," he got out at last, "I've come to ask you——"

"To come back to you?" she said. "No, Duncan. I'm sorry, but —no."

He sat there, staring at her. The sickness of desire was in him, belly-deep, shredding the remnants of his pride, his will.

"And if I agreed to—to give up my practice and come here?" he said, already knowing what her answer would be; but driven by an almost masochistic desire to have her say it, hear her speak the words.

"I'm sorry, Duncan," Hester said.

"Not even——"

"Not even that. You see, Duncan, I don't want you. What I see before me now, I simply don't want. What you were before—yes. But that's gone, isn't it?"

"Hes——"

"Gone for ever. You've remade your life. Like that line from the *Rubáiyát*, you've reshaped it nearer to your heart's desire. And it shows. Don't blame me, Duncan. I married a brilliant young surgeon. You destroyed him. Reduced him to a Back Bayou pill-pusher. So you've got to accept the consequences of your own actions. They're very simple, Doctor. The amputation was success-ful. You no longer have a wife."

He stood up then, looking at her with sick-hurt eyes.

"Then you'll give me a divorce?" he said.

"Of course, darling. One of these years. When I have a likely replacement in view. But now—no. Dear little Jen will wait. She's waited until now."

"Why not—now, Hester?" he said.

"My pride, darling. My tender feminine pride. Don't want people

231

pointing their fingers at me as the abandoned wife whom you got rid of to clear your way to legalise the little affair you're prob'bly having with your Head Nurse. Rather put the boot on the other leg. Your strong, masculine shoulders can carry the load. Mind you, I'm not refusing. I will co-operate very fully—when it suits my convenience."

He stood there a long time, looking at her. Then he came away without another word. He knew there was nothing to be said.

He got up, leaned against one of the columns of the porch. 'Back Bayou pill-pusher. She may even be right. I've lost three cases in the last five months that I shouldn't have lost. Wrong diagnosis in one. The second I gave a prescription to that nine times out of ten cures the disease. Quinine for malaria. Name of God, whoever heard of a person's dying from taking quinine? But Josiah Martin did. It poisoned him. Why? Dear God, why? And that Renfrew boy. Brought in by his folks for a tonsillectomy. An operation that any quack can do blindfolded and with one hand tied behind his back. He bled to death. Damn them to hell, they knew there was a history of hæmophilia in the family! And they didn't open their mouths because that kid had miraculously reached eight years old without ever having cut himself, so they thought he didn't have it. But I should have investigated, asked questions—admitted that I'm not infallible. I'm just a doctor. The undertaker's best friend. I think sometimes that the practice of medicine should be banned for a year in a controlled experiment to see if the world wouldn't be a hell of a lot better off.

'Leave it. Stop torturing yourself. Give way to that sort of thing, and you'll murder your next ten patients in a row. Think about something else. Think about—Jen.

'Why was it you could never see her, before? Once in a while, at long intervals, you'd open your eyes and admit to yourself that she is pretty. Only it's not that any more. She's pretty. All right. She's softly, darkly lovely. Again all right. It doesn't matter a damn.

'What does matter is that she's changed. Grown up, matured into something I was not perceptive enough to see was there all the time. She's changed all right, but I've changed more. When I saw Hes, I wanted to climb into bed with her. That was all. That was, perhaps, enough. But seeing Jen, I want something else. Something I've always needed, without recognising it: a wife. Not just legally sanctioned sex.

'Funny, but I've a notion now that that will be all right, too. She's beautifully controlled. But not cold. Not ever cold. . . .

'Which doesn't matter either, because I've lost her, too, now. Nothing to offer her, nothing. While Bevers—goddamn Bevers to deep blue hell!'

He saw the surrey pull up before the door. A negro was driving in. In the back seat sat Nelson Vance and little Ruth. Duncan went down the walk to greet them.

Little Ruth was pretty. After all, her late, unlamented father, Jim Vance, had been a handsome man. And poor Rosemary, while plain, had never been ugly. But Ruthie was one of those children who improve upon their parents. And now, in his lonely old age, she was Nelson Vance's whole heart.

"You sit right here with ol' Uncle Jasper, honey,' Nelson rumbled. "Me'n Uncle Doc got to have ourselves a talk. Grownfolks' talk."

"Hi, Uncle Doc!" Ruthie said.

Duncan leaned into the surrey and kissed her. She wound her arms around his neck, tight. Her little mouth was sticky from peppermint candy. She smelled fresh and fragrant, as always. Nelson saw that the negroes took very good care of her.

"Shall we sit on the veranda, Father Nels?" Duncan said, "or would you rather go inside and have——"

"Heck no, son," Nelson said. "I'm off the stuff for now. Sit right here on the veranda where I can keep an eye on my baby. Come on, now. Won't take much of your time. Howcome you're home?"

"Sunday morning. No office hours, no calls. Dr. Volker's orders. Swears I'm killing myself. I was laid up a while last winter. Touch of pneumonia. Now he says that if I don't get some rest, I'll go into a decline."

"He's right. You look like pure—deep hell. Sick doctor won't do his patients no good."

He sank tiredly into the rocker, looked at Duncan.

"Tell me, boy," he said, "you heard from Hes?"

"No," Duncan said.

"That's funny," Nelson said. "That's damn funny. I was sure she'd give in, by now."

"Why should she?" Duncan said. "If she hasn't changed her mind in all this time, I don't see——"

"When you told me she'd left," Nelson said, "I cut her off. Figgered that when her money run out, extravagant like she is——"

Duncan stared at him.

"Father Nels," he said quietly, "that was almost three months ago."

"I know," Nelson said. "Maybe she got herself a job."

"Maybe," Duncan said.

He was hearing, inside his mind, Nellie Morris's words. Yesterday at the hospital. Not a week ago, not a month. Yesterday. "Ran into your wife down in N'Awleens, couple o' days ago, Doctor. Sure was looking fine! Dressed to kill! I was on Canal Street shopping and——"

Yesterday, plus Nellie Morris's a couple of days ago, added up to three days, not three months. He knew what it cost to maintain that flat. To dress the way Hester did. To frequent the opera, the theatres, the finest parties, soirées, balls. Hester who never had had a dime left out of the money he had given her for the week's expenses two days after he had given it to her. Three months without funds. Three months without a peep out of her—Lord God!

The question was simple. Very simple. Who? No. That's not the question. It doesn't matter. He repeated the thought, hearing exultantly its ring of absolute verity. 'It doesn't matter. It doesn't matter at all. Let her. I don't give a damn to whom she's selling herself for the kind of life she craves. The point is, she's finally opened a door for me. I can get out now. I'll go down there with —Doug, say, and——'

"Reckon I'll be running along," Nelson said sadly. "You're a fine boy, son. I was hoping my trick would work. But nothing ever did work with Hes. She's the most mule-stubborn lil' filly in the whole blamed world."

But after his father-in-law had gone he examined the matter more carefully. And the door of escape from his marriage that was no marriage at all closed very quietly in his face. Adultery was grounds for divorce. All he had to do to be free, to have a chance to put Forsythe Bevers out of the running, was to do—something he was completely incapable of. Gather witnesses. Hire private detectives. Stage a raid. Expose her shame to the eyes of the world. Hers—and his own. It was just too dirty. Whatever Hes was doing, he couldn't do it. He simply wasn't made that way.

There still remained the means he had thought of constantly from the very night that Hester left. Under the stern Napoleonic Code that was the basis of much of Louisiana's law, desertion was also valid grounds. That was still an ugliness, but less. Even on that basis, a certain amount of dirty linen must be aired in public. Well, he'd damned well air it, now!

'I wouldn't do anything,' he thought; 'but—Forsythe Bevers!

234

That smug, fatuous son of a bitch! I'll see Attorney Byron Willis first break in the rush tomorrow.'

But he didn't. First there were his office patients, and, as their numbers slackened off toward eleven o'clock, Father Gaulois stalked in, his face the picture of righteous wrath.

"Is it true," he snapped, "that you have been teaching birth control to my parishioners, Doctor?"

Duncan looked at him with a wry grin.

"Guilty as charged, Father," he said.

"Then may I ask you," Father Georges said icily, "to cease leading my people astray. You should consider their immortal souls, Duncan!"

"I consider their pitiful bodies," Duncan said. "That's my job, Father. You take care of their souls. That's a little out of my line."

"Yet you interfere——"

"Look, Father," Duncan said, "I'm not up to a long, metaphysical argument. That's way beyond me. You're dedicated to faith, and I to rationality. Don't you see there's no ground on which we can possibly meet?"

"Oh yes, there is, Duncan," Jenny said. "The one where you two always meet. On the ground of human compassion. I think I can prove to you, Father, that he does meet you there. Just a minute, while I find something."

She opened the drawer and drew out the two pictures of Marie Louise. As she held them up for the priest to see, the solitary diamond on her third finger, left hand, caught the light and glittered. Every ray of it went through Duncan like a blade.

"Jen," he whispered, "that ring. Is it——?"

"Yes, Duncan," Jenny said. "Any objections?"

"No," Duncan said; "no, Jen. I—I wish you every happiness."

"Thank you, Duncan," Jenny said gravely.

And it was then, at that moment, that the telephone rang.

"James Vance Memorial Hospital," Jenny said crisply into the mouthpiece. "Doctor Childers's office. Yes? What's that? Oh, my God! Yes, I'll tell him! I'll tell him right away!"

"What the devil's wrong now?" Duncan said.

"They—they're going to lynch Mose!" Jenny said.

In a shade under five minutes the three of them reached the street corner where Sheriff Bruno Martin stood, pistol in hand, trying to hold off the mob. That mob was led by Forsythe Bevers, stupidly acting as lieutenant for the man who had already learned the effectiveness of throwing a stone and hiding his hand. Forsythe was a fool! For all his glibness, he had not Stan Bruder's warped cunning. Or else, Duncan thought grimly, he would see that acting in a coward's stead is the world's most bootless business.

Behind the Sheriff, Mose stood. He was afraid. He was terribly afraid; but he contained his fear, bore it with dignity.

Duncan was down from the buggy at once. Father Gaulois was a second behind him. Then Jenny. She found, oddly, that she had Duncan's bag in her hands. It was pure reflex, born of long habit. She hadn't realised that she had picked it up as they left the hospital.

"What the hell is going on here?" Duncan said.

"This damn nigger cut a white child's throat!" Forsythe Bevers cried. He was not quite reeling, but he was obviously drunk. "Different place from where you cut, Doc! They say you're good. Let's see you save her!"

"My good people!——" Father Gaulois began.

"Shut your trap, Padre!" Forsythe cried. "We're none of your candle-lighting bead-counters! Get out of the way, Martin, and let us string the black bastard up!"

Duncan stared at him. Then at Jenny. He didn't say anything. He had no need to. He saw, exultantly, what was in her eyes now.

"Wait a minute!" he called out. "Let's get to the bottom of this! Moses Johnson is a medical doctor, and a damned good one. Why should he cut a child's throat?"

"Why does a nigger do anything?" Forsythe jeered.

"Mose?" Duncan said quietly.

"Diphtheria," Mose said. "She was choking to death. Her ma came out and asked me to get a doctor. There was no time. So I went in and did what was indicated: breathing-hole at the base of the throat. Only the child's father came home just as I was inserting the tube——"

"Don't let 'em get away with it!" Harry Turner cried. "Him'n Dunc's great friends! Look, boys, we gonna stand here and let a nigger-loving son of a bitch——"

"You're going to do just that, Harry," Duncan spat. "You and all the rest. Any man who touches Mose will have to answer to me! And if you think that's easy, ask the yellow-livered coward who sent you out, with his loud-mouthed friend to lead you. Ask Stan Bruder what happens to those who cross me! You'll answer, damn you! You, Harry, who have a wife now, because I got there in time. You, Bob, whose baby can see, because I took those cataracts off her eyes. You, Murphy, whose intestine I patched. Damned near all of you! You miserable, ungrateful pack of rats! Two hundred of you against one man, and that man a doctor! You don't know what a

236

doctor is, do you? You think the colour of his hide makes any difference? A doctor saves lives. He does not kill!"

They stood there, silent now.

"If that child dies, it'll be because you interfered with a doctor at work. She had diphtheria, you damned fools! The operation Dr. Moses Johnson performed on her was the correct one—the only known means to keep these cases from choking to death!"

"Look, Doc——" Harry whined.

"Shut up! I'm going in there and try to save that child. I'm taking Mose with me to assist. I want four of you as witnesses. You, Murphy. You, Harry. You, Bob—and you, Mister Forsythe Bevers!"

"Count me out," Forsythe drawled. "I've never stayed in the same room with a nigger in my life, 'less he was waiting on me. Besides, this isn't over yet! Boys, you gonna listen to this cheap, woman-butchering quack? Even if he did get it put off on that old nigger woman, I still say it was him who——"

Jenny crossed to him in three long strides. Slapped him, hard across the mouth.

He staggered back, staring at her.

"You shut up, Forsythe!" she almost whispered. "Shut up, or I'll slap you again! To think I was letting myself get fond of you! A thing like you!"

Her hand moved, clawing at her finger. The diamond glittered briefly. She did not give it to him. She opened her hand and let it fall to the ground.

"If you want it, pick it up," she said. "Get down and pick it up—out of the dirt where you belong!"

Then she turned.

"Come on, Duncan," she said. "We've got work to do."

Duncan stood there.

"The rest of you go home," he said.

They hung there a moment longer, muttering. Then, one by one, they began to slink away.

The child was choking, blue. Her father stood by the bed, the bloody tube Mose had placed in the incision still in his hand.

Duncan looked at him.

"You get out," he spat, "before I throw you out, you blundering would-be murderer! You heard me, get!"

'Like he is now," Jenny thought triumphantly, 'there's not a man alive who can face him. I'm going to make an exit to that dead-end street now—even if I have to blast!'

Then she looked at the child.

"Duncan!" she breathed. "She—she's gone!"

"The hell she is, Nurse," Duncan said. "Hypodermic. Adrenalin. Hurry now."

His voice, speaking, was very calm.

Jenny prepared the needle, thanking God for the impulse and the trained reactions that had made her bring that bag.

Duncan sponged off a spot on the child's chest, just above her heart. He took the needle, pushed it in without any hesitation at all. His hand closed over the plunger, forcing the liquid in, slowly. He drew out the needle. Stood back.

The child's heart began to beat again. Wildly, erratically. Then it slowed, steadied.

"Lord God!" Mose breathed. "What is that stuff, Doc?"

"It's new," Duncan said. "J. J. Abel isolated it in 1898. Adrenalin —extracts of the adrenal gland. Most powerful heart stimulant known. Let's get busy, Mose."

In minutes they had the blood and phlegm mopped from the incision. The child's breath came whistling through. Jenny was in the kitchen, boiling a section of tubing on the gas stove.

"Henry," Duncan said, "phone the hospital to send the ambulance. And next time, damn you, don't interfere!"

It was mid-afternoon by the time they had the child safely in bed. Duncan and Jenny watched beside her, keeping that tube clear. She was winning the fight; that was certain now.

Jenny got up and went to the window. She turned away from it, her face white.

"Duncan!" she whispered. "That mob—they're running through the streets again!"

"Good Lord! I told Mose to stay down in the kitchen until I could take him home myself! Jen, go see if he's still there. If he's not——"

But Jenny was already gone.

She was back in minutes.

"Mose is still there," she said happily. "Thank God for that!"

"Amen," Duncan said. "But I wonder what the devil——?"

In a little while they knew. Forsythe Bevers had whipped up the mob again, aided and abetted by Stanton Bruder. Duncan's remarks had been repeated to Stan, verbatim. He couldn't take that. He found courage—with two hundred men to back him up. He took the stump after Forsythe had finished, lashed the mob to wild fury. Set them searching for Mose Johnson. And any white man willing to protect him. Such as Duncan Childers. But he held them back from attacking the hospital. His coward's cunning told him they couldn't get away with that. Instead he sent them sweeping down upon Smoketown. They burned it, starting with Mose Johnson's house. Mose's family weren't there. They were in the Catholic Church with Father Gaulois. Sensing the mob's temper, after Duncan and Jenny had gone back to the hospital with Mose and the child he had gone directly to Smoketown and bullied Luvinia into accepting sanctuary.

Cheated of their prey, the mob sought others. They shot, stabbed, and beat five negroes to death. Wounded twenty others.

Then, tiring of their sport, they went home again.

Duncan sat there staring at Jenny, as she told him the message that had come over the phone. His eyes were bleak.

But Jenny's were invisible behind a wall of tears.

"Forsythe was the leader," she whispered. "I—I was going to marry him. I was that lonely—that desperate. Oh, Duncan, I——"

Duncan stood up then. Took her in his arms.

"Don't worry," he said gently. "You'll never be lonely again. I promise you that."

Her hands came up, resting palms outward against his chest.

"No, Duncan," she said.

"Why not?" he growled.

"Because nothing has changed between us," Jenny said.

Chapter 19

NOR HAD IT. Nothing had changed at all. There was, of course, no more Forsythe Bevers. Even though Southern *mores* had dictated his and his band's acquittal, he was out of Jenny's life. He had gone down to New Orleans to let things cool off before returning to his father's mill in Mertontown. But there was still Hester, and the cool inflexibility of Jenny Greenway's will.

Duncan was defeated now. July's warmth entered into him. That bright July day in 1905 that Jenny came back from her nurses' seminar in New Orleans. Came almost back to him.

He drove toward the station at the breakneck speed of seventeen miles an hour. He wasn't late. Jenny's train wouldn't arrive for half an hour yet. The truth was, he simply enjoyed going fast.

'Compensation for these last three weeks Jen has been down there in New Orleans attending that nurses' seminar. What the hell could they teach her? She knows more than any of them. Only went down there in the first place to get away from what's threatening between us now.'

He swung the tiller bar in his curved-dash Olds hard over, and brought the car to a stop beside the kerb. He had ordered the gas-buggy the day Jenny left. It had been delivered a week ago. He sat there waiting. His check cap, gauntlets, goggles, and linen duster were thickly covered with dirt. 'Ought to do something about these miserable roads,' he thought. 'Cobblestones, or paving blocks, maybe. Glad I thought to bring a duster along for Jen.'

He heard the whistle of the train with relief. He called a boy he knew, gave him a quarter and asked him to stand guard over his new, gasoline-burning buggy. That was absolutely necessary. The Olds was the only automobile in town, and if it were not guarded every minute, some fool would fiddle with it. And then, likely as not, it wouldn't start when he came back with Jen. Likely as not, it wouldn't start anyhow. The automobiles of 1905 were temperamental beasts.

He waited on the platform. He saw her immediately; but he was aware that she had not seen, or perhaps had simply not recognised, him. She didn't have her glasses on, which meant he was a vague blur to her. He employed the circumstances to study her. She was dressed in the very latest mode: a dark red linen bolero and skirt with inverted box-pleats, the sleeves slightly puffed at the shoulders, but much less than the discarded, ugly, leg-of-mutton style. The skirt was very high at the waist, showing off her lithe slimness. Under the bolero jacket she wore a tailored shirtwaist with a tall, standing collar like a man's, ornamented with a tiny black velvet bow tie. A flat saucer-shaped hat of deep rose straw, decorated with black egret plumes, perched on the high-piled masses of her dark hair. She looked stunning. He fairly ached to kiss her.

'Damn it all, I'm going to!' he thought, and, marching up to her, took her in his arms.

She stiffened in pure astonishment, blinked at him, groped in her handbag, where her glasses were.

"Later, Jen," he growled, and found her mouth. He kissed her slowly, lingeringly, taking all the time about it in the world.

"Why, Duncan!" she laughed tremulously. "I—I must say I didn't recognise you in that get-up. Wait a minute; let me see." She found her glasses, fitted them. "What on earth is this masquerade for?" she said.

"Come outside and you'll see," he grinned. He turned to the negro porter. "Bring those bags outside, George," he said.

She tripped along on her high heels, the tips of her toes peeping out from under that skirt. It was an inch or two off the ground. Daring as all hell, Duncan thought, disapprovingly. The crowd was so thick around the Olds, she couldn't see it.

"Please folks, clear the way!" the negro porter said.

"Duncan!" Jenny breathed, clasping her hands together like a child. "A motor-car! You've bought a motor-car! Oh, but it's just darling! It even matches my dress!"

"Had it painted that colour on purpose," Duncan said. "I knew how you like red . . . Put the luggage up behind, George. That's it." He flipped the porter a half-dollar. "All right, Jen, get in," he said.

He helped her up into the seat.

"Please don't drive fast," she said. "I'm frightened to death, now!"

"It's not as fast as the train you were on," Duncan said. "About eighteen miles an hour is all it'll do."

"That's much too fast for anything not on tracks," Jenny said. "You will be careful, won't you, deares——" She stopped, her face flaming redder than her dress. She had been afraid that the word, 'dearest', she always called him in her mind was going to slip out one day. And now it had, before she had been back five whole minutes. She felt like crying, from pure chagrin.

Duncan pretended not to have noticed it. "Here," he said. "Slip this on over your dress, Jen."

"What on earth for, Duncan?" Jenny said.

"Keep the dust from ruining your clothes. It's called a duster, and, believe me, in a gas-buggy you need it!"

He spun the crank. Docilely, as if not to embarrass him, the one-cylinder motor caught. He ran round, jumped in, released the brake, put the Olds in gear, and they were off. He held the car down to an easy ten miles an hour. Jenny laughed delightedly.

"I think it's positively marvellous!" she said.

"I'll take you for a spin tonight. That is, if you'll come," he added darkly.

"Of course I'll come," Jenny said. "Why shouldn't I?"

Duncan stared at her in astonishment. Things were definitely looking up—at last.

"Nine be all right?" he said.

"But, Duncan, it'll be starting to get dark by then. You don't mean you drive this thing at night?"

"Why not? It's got perfectly good acetylene headlamps. Brightest things you ever did see. I'll make it earlier, if you like, though."

"No, nine is quite all right," Jenny said.

．　　　．　　　．　　　．　　　．

"Now I think it's more wonderful than ever," she said, watching the headlamps bore holes in the darkness. "They're as bright as a train's headlight. The world is certainly going fast, these days. Saw in the paper in New Orleans that a couple of bicycle manufacturers out in Dayton, Ohio, have built a successful airship. I cut the clipping out to show you, but I lost it."

"People have been flying in airships for years, Jen," Duncan said.

"No. I got it wrong. Not an airship—a flying machine, Duncan. A heavier-than-air flying machine. With a motor just like this car's. Do you believe that? The paper didn't seem to—not really."

Duncan considered the question.

"Yes, Jen," he said, "I do. I think there's no limit to what applied science is capable of. Dayton, eh? Reckon I'll run up there one of these days, and have a look."

"No, you don't, Duncan! You'd end up buying that fool contraption for sure; then you *will* break your neck!"

He looked at her. It was too dark for him to see her eyes.

"Would you care, Jen?" he said.

242

She didn't answer him for a long time. They had to shout to be heard above the motor, anyhow, which was hardly conducive to romance.

"Yes," she said at last. "I'd care, Duncan. In fact, I think I'd die."

Instantly he brought the gas-buggy to a halt. He put his arms around her.

"Jen—Jen, darling——" he whispered.

She didn't resist. She kissed him back, tenderly. They kept it up a long time. Too long.

"Let's go for a walk, Duncan," Jenny said. "I—I'm tired of riding." Her voice sounded odd. Its lower tones were a trifle—harsh.

They walked with their arms about one another, down by the Bayou's edge. There were willows trailing their sorrowing branches in the water.

"Let's sit here," Duncan said.

"All right, Duncan," Jenny murmured. Then: "Duncan, I—I want to tell you something. I met Fred Baynes in New Orleans. No, that's not true. I looked him up, because you told me about his interviewing you that time. To tell the truth, I was being nosy. I wanted to find out about your life down there. Well, he told me. About your work. How you spent nearly all the money you made on the poor. I visited the settlement house that you were the main one in starting. Oh, Duncan—Duncan, dearest, will you forgive me, please? I was disappointed in you! When even those rages of yours were good rages—hatred of injustice, of cruelty. I asked Jeff Fontaine right out, the day I left, what happened that time you whipped Stan. And he told me how Stan had beaten him—a cripple! And about Stan and Abbie, and——"

"Hush, Jen," he said gently. "Those things are dead now, and best forgotten."

"No they're not! I'll never forget them. Oh, my dearest, that hill is occupied again! I've kept it vacant far too long!"

Then, for the first time in all the years he had known her, she kissed him. Freely, tenderly, even—with passion.

They lay in the sweet-smelling grass, kissing each other endlessly. She no longer pushed away his searching hands.

"No, Duncan," she said, "we mustn't! This is wrong. You know it's wrong, dearest——" Then, clasping her hands behind his head, she drew his face down to hers, silencing her own protests against his mouth.

"Oh, Duncan, no!" she wept. "No, no, no——"

The no's trailed down a diminuendo into defeat.

"Oh, Duncan, I——" she whispered—"I want you so!"

It was then, of course, at that exact, maddeningly frustrating moment, that they heard the voice. It was coming from their left, higher up among the trees. It kept coming clearer all the time, as the speaker approached them. Jenny sat up, frantically brushing the leaves and twigs out of her hair.

The voice was close enough now for them to hear what it was saying.

"I can see them now!" it boomed, "all the fornicators, all the adulterers, twisting and shrieking in the fires of hell!"

"Uncle Vard!" Duncan groaned. "My sainted Uncle Vard!"

"What's he doing, Duncan?" Jenny whispered. "Why is he shouting like that?"

"Practising next Sunday's sermon," Duncan told her. "He often does that—goes out in the woods and bellows at the trees."

Jenny started to get up, but Duncan caught her wrists.

"Lie down!" he hissed. "If he sees us, he'll include us in the sermon. Not by name, but so clearly that the whole blamed town will know. Oh, why in the name of his favourite hell and damnation did he have to show up now!"

Jenny lay there, trembling. The Reverend Vardigan Childers was much closer now.

"So I say unto you," he roared, "all of you lately risen from your filthy beds of sin——"

"He knows we're here!" Jenny wept. "He knows, Duncan! Else why would he have picked that particular subject?"

"Didn't pick it out," Duncan whispered. "It's his favourite. He's preached it at least ten thousand times. For the love of God, Jen, keep still!"

Vardigan Childers passed on, not five yards from where they lay half-hidden in the grass. He was too intent upon his sermon to notice them. He boomed out his rolling phrases, itemising with singular relish the various types of fleshly sins. They lay there, scarcely daring to breathe until his voice grew dim in the distance.

With profound relief, Duncan heard it die out into silence. He turned back to Jenny.

"Jen——" he said.

"No, Duncan," Jenny said. Her tone was decisive, crisp.

"Why not, Jen?" he groaned.

"Because it's wrong. I was about to do something—to let you do something—we'd both regret."

"Speak for yourself, Jen. I wouldn't regret it, one damned bit!"

"Well, I would. I'm grateful to your uncle. There was the hand of Providence in his passing by just when he did, Duncan."

"Then I wish Providence would mind its own ruddy business, just like it usually does," Duncan said.

She looked at him bleakly.

"Take me home now, Duncan, please," she said.

And that, it proved, was most decidedly that. No night rides in the Olds. No day rides, either. In Hester's pet phrase, the mixture as before. Only worse now. Infinitely harder to bear.

To compound his misery, Caneville was enjoying a period of unusually good health. He did not have enough calls to provide him with the blessed opiate of fatigue. He had too much time for thinking, and his thoughts made for ever the same refrain: 'Jen, Lord, Jen. If there were only some way——'

There was. Grace Henderson came riding up to the Bouvoir house, the very next Sunday morning. She sat there in her buggy looking at him.

"Duncan," she said, "I want you to come with me down to New Orleans. Now—today. I've been told that the reason Doug's been making trips down there for three months now is your—Hester."

"So," Duncan said tiredly, "why don't you just let them?"

"No. It's got to stop. He's bankrupting the business, spending money on her. If it is she. It may be somebody else, for all I know. It started because he was jealous of our baby. He said I had no time for him any more since that dratted kid showed up. He's right, I guess I did neglect the poor boy . . . But I won't let this go on. I've got to stop it."

"Hes does have her charms," Duncan said drily. "But tell me one thing, Grace: once you've gone down there, what then? Just what do you mean to do about it?"

"I don't know. That depends upon so many things. But I do need your help. Will you come?"

"Lord, Grace, I——"

"I'll get someone else if you don't," she said; "and, after all, you're involved. In fact, you're responsible. You made it possible for me to marry him, by giving me my looks back."

"Are you sure your father's dying and leaving you all that money hadn't anything to do with it, Grace?" Duncan said cruelly.

"Perhaps. I don't care. However I got him, he's mine. And I mean to keep him. Will you come, Duncan?"

245

He stood there, looking at her. 'Seize time by the forelock,' he thought; 'for behind he is bald.'

"Yes, Grace, I'll come with you," he said.

They reached New Orleans early in the morning. Duncan had brought his key to the flat with him. He had kept it, not intentionally, but from the normal oversight that makes people forget to dispose of things they no longer need.

They went to the flat. He opened the door. They walked quietly into the bedroom. But Grace was wrong. Dead wrong.

Hester lay there sleeping the sleep of the just—absolutely alone. He heard suddenly, startlingly, the intake of Grace's breath.

"Oh, Duncan," she said. "I'm so sorry!"

Hester opened her eyes. In her there was no slow transition between sleep and wakefulness. She woke up all at once. Totally. She sat up in bed, looking from one to the other of them.

Then she began to laugh; peal after peal of silvery, bell-toned laughter.

"Dear Grace," she whispered, "and my darling husband! Staging a raid—how wonderfully, wonderfully funny!"

Duncan smiled ruefully.

"My apologies, Hester," he said, "not for this implied insult to your morals, if any; but for my lack of respect for your intelligence. Stupid of me to think you'd let yourself get caught."

"Of course not, darling. First, I never receive gentlemen guests at home. Second, I never go to their diggings, either. There are too many discreet little hostelries in this town, as you probably know. And one can change them, frequently. Every night, if necessary. So where does that leave you, Duncan?"

"I'll bite," Duncan said. "Where does it leave me, Hes?"

"Nowhere, darling. Adultery is out. That leaves—desertion. In this state, you have to file that plea. Then I have to be notified, asked to come back to you, before the court would lift a hand. And do you know what I'd do in such an event?"

"What would you do, Hester?"

"Come back to you, darling," Hester said. He stared at her. "Which is the last thing on earth you want. Foul up all your plans for Jen—or is it Grace, here? Incidentally, Grace, dear, you're wrong about Doug. When he comes down here, all he does is to sit in some saloon and drink. No women, though that's what he's trying to make you think. He loves you terribly, Gracie dear. . . ."

"Thank you for that, Hester," Grace said.

"Don't mention it. Where was I, Duncan?"

"You were saying," Duncan said, "that you'd come back to me."

"Oh yes, darling! Just long enough to make sure all your shining plans go smash. Then I'd leave you again. Meantime, it would be the mixture as before. Our silent meals together. That locked door——"

"Duncan," Grace said bitterly, "why don't you beat her?"

"How quaint!" Hester laughed.

"Wouldn't solve anything," Duncan drawled, "and she's hardly worth the expenditure of energy. Come, Grace, let's go."

" 'Bye-'bye, angel-lambs," Hester called. "If you two feel amorously inclined, I can suggest a few addresses——"

"Oh, hell!" Duncan said, and walked out of there.

He put Grace on a train, sent her home. But he stayed in New Orleans himself.

He didn't know why he stayed. Certainly not to do anything more about Hester. Perhaps because going back to Caneville-Sainte Marie now took more courage than he had.

So he remained. He went to the theatre, the opera, the horse races. Even to church. And found it strangely comforting, non-believer that he was.

He stayed away from Tom Hendricks's as long as he decently could. Seeing all that happiness hurt too much. But when he did go at last, it was not happiness that he found.

Tom opened the door himself. His face was grey.

"Lord God, Dunc!" he cried. "Where the devil have you been? I've been looking all over town for you for three days!"

Duncan stared at him.

"How'd you even know I was in town?" he growled.

"Dr. Hans phoned me long-distance. After having called damned near every decent hotel in the city. It's—it's yellow fever, Dunc. Dr. Hans swears he's never seen it like this before. The whole town is hard hit. Looks like a major epidemic, boy."

Duncan licked his lips.

"Is—Jen—all right?" he said.

"Didn't you tell me she had it as a child? The theory is you only have it once. After that, you're immune—or supposed to be."

"I hope so," Duncan said. "When's the next train?"

"Midnight, same as usual. I told Dr. Hans I'd come too, just as soon as I found you. My aunt's here. I insisted that she come. Uncle Matt—refused. Said that, as a druggist, his duty was to the community."

"Bless him," Duncan said.

"Amen. Uncle Matt is something mighty fine. Dunc—do you think there's any point to ringing Phelton or Ryan?"

"No. But ring them just the same. They just might find us some-one else to ease their squeamish consciences. Come on, boy, let's get on that phone."

Dr. Phelton, of course, refused. The pressure of affairs did not permit. He was sure that Dr. Childers was unaware of a small but significant increase in the number of cases in New Orleans itself. Wouldn't it be rather awkward if he rushed off to save a neigh-bouring parish and left his own clients—that was the word he used: clients, not patients—in the lurch?

But, to Duncan's and Tom's vast astonishment, Lester Ryan rose nobly to the occasion. "Of course I'll come," he said. "Meet you at the station tonight at a quarter to twelve."

They got off the train in the morning to find themselves in what appeared to be a ghost town. No one at all was in the streets. They had to walk to the hospital. On the way, a huge wagon passed them, with a melancholy-looking negro driving it. On the wagon was piled up what seemed to be a mountain of packing-cases. Long, narrow packing-cases. They had gone on several yards when it hit them, all three of them simultaneously, what those packing-cases were. They turned, staring at the retreating wagon. It was drawn by a six-horse team. There must have been more than fifty of those cases on it.

"Good God!" Lester Ryan breathed.

"Have mercy upon their souls," Tom added softly.

"Amen," Duncan said.

The hospital was full. The cases overflowed into every ward, every corridor. They had them on army cots, even on pallets on the floor. The whole place smelled of them.

Hans Volker's face was grim. He didn't waste a word in recriminations over their tardy arrival.

"We're not accepting any more in the hospital," he barked. "Can't. No room. Carter, Thompson and I will hold the fort here. You young fellows take the house calls. There're hundreds of them—all bad. Mortality inside the hospital's up to thirty per cent. Outside, it's seventy-five—and rising. That's it. Get going now!"

"Wait!" Duncan said sharply. "Doctor, you know any way of curing yellow fever?"

"No. You know damned well there's no—say, what are you getting at now, boy? Got another one of those damned near miracu-lous hunches of yours? If so, let's have it!"

"To hell with the patients, Doctor Hans. What we'll have to

248

be concerned with are the people who haven't caught it yet. Do you remember that article about the Laredo, Texas, outbreak in the *Journal* of the American Medical Association, last year?"

"Yes," Hans Volker said slowly. "I put that issue aside. Meant to study it. Never got around to it, as usual. Struck me at the time as being the right procedure, the only procedure. Goddamn it, boy, you're right! Forget the patient, except to make him as comfortable as you can; and go after the bloody damned mosquitoes! It saved Laredo."

"And it'll save us," Duncan said. "Where is that issue, Doctor? The time we spend in reading it again is time gained, not lost."

Hans Volker began to look for the *Journal*. All three of them helped him. But in the end they had to send for Jenny to find it for them. She did so almost at once, not without giving the four of them a piece of her mind for calling her away from the desperately sick.

The article they sought was in the issue of 9th July 1904. It was written by Dr. G. M. Guiteras, and entitled: "The Yellow Fever Epidemic of 1903, at Laredo, Texas". There, beautifully detailed, was set down for them what became their battle plan.

"Now what to do?" Lester Ryan said, looking at Duncan with uneasy eyes. "This is a tough proposition. We need the city authorities solidly behind us to even have a chance to make it work."

"We'll go see the Mayor," Duncan said. "Right now."

"No, you don't," Hans Volker said. "I'll phone the old fool to come here. I'll be telling him, not asking. He'll come. He's scared enough now. Tom, you and Dr. Ryan stay here and help me pound some sense into his head. He'll listen to you big city bedside slickers quicker than he would me. Duncan, you've got the hardest job. Though maybe it won't be so hard after all now—seeing that poor little Ruth hasn't got a hope nor a prayer. You go see your pa-in-law. Unless we have Nelson Vance behind us, Mayor Matthews won't dare make a move. Make it a professional call. Jim's kid is—dying."

"Lord God!" Duncan breathed.

"Nelson has been over here a hundred times, asking for you. Phones every half an hour or so to see if you're back. Touching faith he's got in you, boy. Seems to think you can perform miracles. Anyhow, go. I think he's in the mood to listen to reason, now."

Hans Volker was right. Little Ruth was dying. She was already vomiting black mucus. When that set in, death inevitably followed, especially in a child.

And Nelson Vance, big, roaring, blustering Nelson Vance, sat there holding her fever-wasted little hands and crying.

"Not you, too!" he choked. "You ain't a-going to tell me there's no hope, like the rest of them quacks, are you, son?"

Duncan had a hard time mastering his pity. He was close to tears himself. But he knew what he had to do. He looked at the walls. Just as he expected, there were three or four *Stegomyia fasciata* posed on them in their characteristic position. He moved quickly, pinched one of the blood-gorged insects gently between his thumb and forefinger, taking care not to crush it.

"You out of your mind, boy?" Nelson roared. " 'Stead of doing something for my poor baby, you're catching bugs!"

"Not just bugs," Duncan said icily. "A mosquito. A mosquito filled to the gullet with Ruthie's blood. You've always shouted me down when I told you these nasty little murderers carried yellow fever. Well, I'm going to prove it to you. Stick out your hand, Father Nels!"

Nelson Vance stared at him, his round face white. Only his bald head remained pink now.

"What you aiming to do, son?" he growled.

"I'm going to put this mosquito on your hand. Let it bite you, leaving a few millions of the virus that causes the disease in your blood. In forty-eight hours you'll have your first chill. In four days you'll burn with fever, turn yellow, start puking black. In five you'll be a stinking hulk of carrion that not even the buzzards will touch! Come on, Father Nels, stick out your hand! There's nothing I can do for this poor baby. She's going to die. But by heaven and hell I can execute her murderer! You, Nelson Vance, who condemned damn near a whole town to death to safeguard your filthy profits on your stinking musk-rat skins. You hear me, Father Nels: put out your hand!"

Nelson Vance sat there, staring at him. Then slowly, quietly, he stretched out his hand.

Duncan took a backward step.

"All right, boy," Nelson said. "Get on with it. I don't care, now."

Duncan squeezed his thumb and forefinger together. A drop of black blood popped out, staining his flesh.

"No," he said. "I'm not God. But there is something you can do to make up for it. You get on the phone and call the hospital. Mayor Matthews is there now. You tell him you're behind our clean-up programme, two hundred per cent. Tell him, if he so much as hesitates, you'll have his hide. Now hop to it. I'll see what I can do for Ruthie."

Which was—nothing. He knew that very well.

By nightfall they had it all: three squads of eight men each, one of the eight always a carpenter. Three mule-drawn carts, each containing sulphur and pyrethrum powder, twenty-five pots, twenty-five pans, five-gallon cans of wood alcohol, rolls of paper, shears, knives, buckets of paste, brushes, brooms, wall-brushes, mosquito-netting, lath, nails, hatchets, saws, and five-gallon cans of kerosene oil.

They moved out like an army composed of three divisions. Lester, Tom and Duncan each commanded one of the divisions. But, as they moved to the attack, a thing that none of them had dreamed of happened. There was a deep, slow-rolling boom, and a wall of earth and smoke rose beyond the trees at the far end of the Bayou.

"What the devil!" Tom said.

"Father Nels," Duncan said. "Ruthie died this afternoon—after I'd accused the old man of murdering her, because he wouldn't let us drain the Bayou and the swamps. So he's gone and done it himself. Tell me, Tom," he added softly, "you ever know a really wicked man—all wicked, I mean?"

"No. Not now. Old Nelson was the last one on my list—and he's just scratched his name off. I'm glad."

"I've got one left," Duncan said drily. "Stan Bruder. Hans says he's out at the plantation now. Well, boys, we're in for it. I'll see you when I can."

.   .   .   .

They moved out, taking three different directions. House by house, they covered Caneville-Sainte Marie. In every house where the disease was found they made the sickroom mosquito-proof. They screened the windows. Hung a screen door between that room and the rest of the house. Draped a mosquito-net over the bed. Then they nailed up laths or pasted paper strips over every crack in that house, blocked the chimney, closed every window, carried the sick and herded them well outside, and fumigated with sulphur and pyrethrum not only that house, but every house in a block where yellow fever was found. In the water pans, placed on the floor to lessen the danger from fire, they always counted, just as Dr. Guiteras' article said they would, anywhere from a dozen to over a hundred dead mosquitoes. It was man-killing, back-breaking work. There was no end to it. They poured oil into rain barrels, down wells, instructing the people to let buckets drawn from wells stand until the oil rose to the top, then skim it off, or siphon the water from below it. The water would taste horrible, they admitted, but that was a small sacrifice that must be made to keep the town alive.

As the volunteer workers insisted upon at least eight hours' sleep a night, Tom and Lester philosophically made the best of it, and slept in their turn. But Duncan was driven, haunted by the spectre of what is one of the ugliest ways that a human being can die. He very nearly didn't sleep at all. He scarcely ate. His eyes sank into skeletal hollows in his face. His mouth was lined and drawn. Nightly he made his rounds, driving his old buggy, for the simple reason that the horse would bring him home even if he fell asleep, while the Olds would probably kill him; plus the fact that no automobile was yet sufficiently reliable for him to gamble on its not breaking down before he reached a desperately ill patient. He visited the cabins of the trappers, perched over the muddy sink that had been the Bayou, the swamp people, the outlying farms, trying to cure a disease for which, fifty years later, a cure still would not have been found; staring death in the face hourly, occasionally even winning, by pure luck, but mostly sitting there, giving what comfort he had to give to the families of men, women, children, condemned to die.

The disinfectant squads, murdering mosquitoes by the thousands, were slowly winning their fight now. Daily the number of new cases reported dropped. It made no difference to Duncan Childers. He went on driving himself beyond his own, or indeed any man's, strength. Jenny, seeing him like that, was goaded into making a hysterical scene, weeping and storming at him, telling him he was sure to kill himself, that way.

"So," he croaked, "what difference does it make to you, Jen?" Then he stalked out into the night.

When he came back to the hospital, somewhat refreshed by the catnaps he had caught while his grey plodded from house to house not needing his guiding hand, it was mid-morning, and the sun was hot and bright. He stumbled wearily up to his office on the second floor; put out his hand to open the door; and stopped, staring owlishly at his own trembling fingers poised in mid-air, curved already to seize the brass knob, but arrested there in a curiously ludicrous suspension of motion by that husky voice he knew so well: no longer purring now, but rising to a feline snarl, saying:

"Of course I came after you, Lester! I'm unaccustomed to sleeping alone. But don't be unnecessarily flattered. I could replace you, you know."

"Hes——" Lester Ryan croaked.

"Only"—Hester's voice sank back into its normal, mocking tone; into something else, a sort of bleak clarity, Duncan thought—"I don't seem to want to. Which is not a tribute to your boyish charms, Lester; but to my weariness. This incessant changing of men has gotten to be damned tiresome. So—I seem to be stuck with you. All right. You're nothing much, Lester, darling; but you're all I've got now. And that's awful. While you, my beamish boy, are also stuck with me, which must be awful, too. Our mutual punishment for being what we are, instead of being—what Duncan is, say."

"And what is he?" Lester said.

"A man. Perhaps even a—great man. I don't know. Anyhow, I've come to take you back. Let Duncan play the dedicated, sacrificing Medic, heroically giving his life for his people. He's cut out for it. You're not."

"I know," Lester said. "Only—it rubs off on a fellow, some of that dedication you're talking about, Hes. He does that to me. Makes me remember when I wanted to be a doctor instead of a fee-grabbing quack. And I've seen a sight too many people die lately, Hester. Which reminds me I've got to, one day. So I want to be able to face it. Go to my Maker with a few good marks. Be able to say: 'All right, I've been an adulterous swine; but I did save a few lives—and I risked my own doing it.' They say He's merciful, so maybe——"

Duncan heard the silvery lift and soar of Hester's laughter.

"My poor penitent!" she mocked. "The next thing I know, you'll be scourging yourself. Come off it, Lester! I have no patience with——"

"Hester!" Ryan's voice was edged with sudden alarm. "What are those welts on your neck?"

"Mosquito bites, darling. Probably the fever-bearing kind. I had to wait at the station nearly two hours for a hack. Which never came. The damned place was swarming with them. Nearly ate me alive."

"Lord God!" Lester breathed. Silently, outside the door, Duncan echoed him. "Hes," Lester quavered, "you've got to go to bed! I'll give you divided doses of calomel and——"

"Rot," Hester said succinctly. "Does no good and you know it. If I've got it, I've got it. Funny thing—this morning I didn't even

253

slap them off. Don't think I really care. What am I living for anyhow? What good did I ever do? I've fouled up the works for every single man I've known: Gino, Stan, Duncan, you——"

"Hester, for God's love!"

"Oh, stop it! If I've been infected, what the hell could you do, Lester? I'm almost a nurse, remember. I'll go over to Father's and lie down. Take your damned calomel. Even light a candle before the image of the Virgin, if that pleases you. One form of mumbo-jumbo works as well as another, Lester. If I have it, I'll die. Which might be a good thing. Free you to marry some sweet little Irish biddy who's had sense enough to wait for a special dispensation from the Pope before she takes off her——"

"Hester, please!" Lester said.

"All right. I'll wait for you at Father's until day after tomorrow. Mostly because I'm too tired to go back to New Orleans right away. But if you don't come with me then, find yourself another playmate, boy!"

Duncan heard the click of her heels as she turned. He did not move. She opened the door. Stopped. Stared at him. Her full, sensual mouth curved into a smile.

"Eavesdropping, Doctor?" she said.

"Yes," Duncan said evenly. "Lester's right, Hes. You'd better take care——"

"Duncan," Lester said painfully, "you don't know how sorry I——"

"Forget it," Duncan said. "I don't think Hester's even worth our quarrelling over. What's more, she knows it. But, the situation being as it is, Hes, don't you think it's time you gave me that divorce and made an honest man of Lester?"

"No," Hester said. "You're forgetting something, Doctor. Dear Lester is numbered among the members of the True Faith. He's got a special book. It says: 'Till death do ye part'. Death, not the divorce courts. So—no soap, no dice, no nothing. I'm not altruistic. But when I find a worthwhile replacement, I'll do it. For you—and Jen. So you can come in from the woods and make love in a proper bed, with the framed certificate hanging over the headboard to prove it's all nice and legal and proper, and take all the fun out of it."

"You know, Hester," Lester Ryan said suddenly, "I've found the word for you. You're—vile. I never realised before how vile you are!"

She smiled at him.

"Thanks, Lester," she said. "I think you're darling, too."

254

She turned back to Duncan.

"You look positively awful, Doctor," she said. "Why don't you go lie down somewhere?"

"Can't," Duncan said wearily. "I've got a few more calls to make."

Chapter 20

JUST A FEW MORE CALLS.

He had started out, when he saw he wasn't going to make it. He recognised he had reached the stage where the simplest action had to be forced, had to be conscious, or his body would refuse to respond to his mind's command. His thoughts were vague, not entirely rational: 'If I lift my arm, put it against that crossbar, I'll be uncomfortable enough not to fall asleep—Go on, arm, lift! Damnit, I said lift! Thaaat's it . . . How weary, flat, stale and unprofitable seem to me all the uses of this world. Oh God, I could be bounded in a nutshell and count myself master of infinite space were it not that I had bad dreams. . . .

'Hes. Ruth. Poor baby. Poor, poor baby never had a chance, never a chance, for *elle était du monde où les plus belles choses ont le pire destin, et rose, elle a vécu comme vivent les roses l'espace d'un matin* —who said that? Mal—Mal—Malherbe! *Consolation à M. Pierre sur la Mort de sa Fille.* True. Beautiful things do have the worst fates and the best of them live like a rosebud the space of a morning. True. But don't we all don't we all don't we all?

'Ah! The house dwelling residence of my sainted Uncle who hath full many a sinner sent down to dance in hell. Old Fire'n Brimstone himself predestination's favourite child—the elect are saved before they're born the damned are damned before they're born and we should all resist wicked impulses but not because they're wicked only because giving way to wicked impulses is a sign of being non-elect and you never know. Have I got it right Uncle Vard? The doctrine of predestination that only the elect are saved and only Presbyterians and damned few of them are among the elect maybe there's nobody among the elect but you Uncle Vard sitting on the right hand of God the Father from whence you shall judge the quick and the dead the dead the dead——'

He climbed down from the buggy wearily. He went into the house. He went into his uncle's bedroom. Vardigan Childers was dying, too. He was dying just like the rest in the same bad, ugly way. What was worse, he was not dying a serene Christian death, secure in the arms of the Saviour. He was dying very badly, his eyes wild blobs of fright in his ugly, yellowed face, a dribble of black vomit streaking his chin. Duncan stared at him. The sight of the Reverend Vardigan Childers, as he was now, cleared his mind briefly of fatigue.

"Duncan, boy," Vardigan Childers croaked, "so glad you got here—afraid I was going to—to pass on before you got here to—to give me the time I need . . . Can't die—now, you understand, Duncan, I can't—I've done things unworthy of the cloth—I've had lustful thoughts—I've even——"

"No, Uncle Vard," Duncan said, "don't tell me about it. I'm just a doctor, not a minister of God. And as for saving you, I can't. Nobody could now. You'd better pray. You've always claimed it helps."

"Pray?" Vardigan Childers muttered. "No good, boy. Those who're saved, are saved; those who aren't, aren't. Praying doesn't change anything. Only I'm afraid—afraid—if I'm among the saved why do I have thoughts like I do? Why am I even afraid?"

Duncan stood up, swaying a little from weariness.

"I don't know," he whispered. "I'm not a theologian. But tell me, Uncle Vard, don't the elect have any impulses toward charity? Toward forgiveness?"

Vardigan Childers stared at him.

"Yes," he croaked. "Why?"

"Just remembering how hard you worked to get Dick Willis rail-roaded off to prison. Even to getting my testimony in his behalf disallowed on the grounds that as a non-believer my oath didn't mean anything. Yet, non-believer that I am, I have those impulses; in me they're strong. I can forgive you now, even for the hell you made me see as a child. Far as I know, you never forgave anybody anything. But you'd better start now. Beginning with yourself. You've got a few hours left; maybe even a day or so. You might even recover. I've seen it happen, even in people further along than you are now. But don't bet on it. Occupy yourself with a slightly different turn of thought, Uncle Vard. Spend the next few hours seeing if you can figure out what Jesus meant when He said: 'Neither do I accuse thee: go and sin no more.' "

Then he turned and marched out of there, a quotation from Nietzsche running through his head: "Distrust all those in whom the impulse to punish is strong."

He drove wearily away. Toward the Bruder Plantation, Schwartz-wald. Where Otto Bruder, Stan's uncle, lay dying.

Schwartzwald. The black forest. What forests weren't black, these days?

He was still half asleep when he pulled the horse up before the house. But the screams coming from it awakened him. He got down, aching from fatigue. The door wasn't locked. He went in.

Uncle Otto lay on his bed. One glance showed Duncan he was past all pain. It wasn't he who had screamed. He had been dead a long time.

Stan came into the room. He was holding an oil lamp in his hands. Black vomit dribbled down his chin.

"I'm on my way to hell!" he shrieked. "To hell, Duncan Childers, to hell!"

"Shut up, Stan," Duncan said. "Let me have a look at you."

"No!" Stan bellowed. "No! Abbie won't let you! She won't let you save me! Look at her, Duncan! See her eyes! Just like when that old witch nigger cut her! She's dead and in hell, and she's come to drag me down with her! She's dead and Callie's dead and Jeff is dead and them niggers that I fried!"

Duncan looked at him. He hadn't believed he could feel pity for Stanton Bruder. But he did. Pity, not hate. No longer hate.

"I burnt 'em! I burnt 'em and I tried to get you hanged and I did it with that whore you married and nothing I could do would touch you! But I got you now, Duncan Childers! I got you, you rat-bastard Irish Channel son of a bitch who ruined my life! I got you! There!"

He hurled the oil lamp to the floor. There was a blinding whoosh of flame. It climbed up Stanton Bruder's body. His clothes caught; his hair. He came forward gibbering and laughing; seized Duncan in fire-wrapped arms. He was terribly, maniacally strong. And Duncan was tired unto death. He fought with all his ebbing strength. He could smell the stench of Stan's flesh burning.

Stan's mouth came open. He howled. It was an animal sound— a choking, gasping cry of purest agony. He turned Duncan loose. Fell over backwards, screaming.

Duncan beat the fire out of his own clothing. Backed out of there. Stood in the yard, watching Schwartzwald burn, until Stanton Bruder's screams penetrated that part of his mind that ultimately controlled him. The part that couldn't let a human being die like that. Not even Stanton Bruder.

He went back into that flaming house. Dragged Stan out of there. Wrapped him in a rug he found in the as yet unburned hall. Rolled him until the flames were out. Started to lift him into the buggy.

Saw that he was dead.

Duncan eased Stan down gently upon the grass. Out of some deep, obscure impulse, the words came to him:

258

"All right, boy—we're quits. Slate's clean. You're—forgiven. If I have any right to assume the power of pardon. Now you just go, and make your peace—with God."

He did not even add, as usual, "If there is a God."

He climbed into the buggy. He turned the horse back towards the hospital. The night sky, like a blanket, dropped quietly over his head.

When Jenny came off duty, she found him there, sitting outside the hospital in the buggy, fast asleep. She got up beside him, took the reins and drove him home. When they got there, she searched in his pockets for the key, found it, got down and opened the door, came back to the buggy, and dragged him down. She shook him until he was half awake, got him to walk, half-carrying him, guiding him so that he would not stumble or blunder into the furniture; forced him up the stairs and into his bedroom. He collapsed on to the bed, with a muttered, "Thanks, Jen . . ." asleep instantly, profoundly asleep.

She took off his shoes, his coat, his tie, his belt, leaving his clothes loose and comfortable. She switched on the lamp beside his bed, and left him there, while she went to look for the negro couple who took care of the house.

They were gone, deserting him because of fear, or, more charitably, even more likely, he had sent them away—out of the parish, perhaps, to avoid contagion. Yes, surely out of the parish. It would do no good to look for them in Smoketown, for the negro section was the hardest hit of all, forcing Mose Johnson to perform daily miracles.

She climbed wearily back up the stairs and looked at him. He was sleeping peacefully. He'd be all right, she decided. She'd look in on him at intervals—after breakfast, at lunch time, at supper, to see if he'd awakened. She doubted that he would wake up before noon tomorrow. He'd need at least twelve hours' sleep, she guessed. She looked at her watch. It was long after midnight. She turned and scampered down the stairs. She got into the buggy and drove home. Once or twice the horse stumbled. 'Poor old fellow,' she thought, 'you need rest, too. Have to leave you at Jenkins's stable in the morning so you can be watered, brushed, and fed.'

But the next noon, when she rushed over to tell him the joyous news that no new case of yellow fever had appeared since yesterday, he was still asleep. She went back to the hospital with a troubled mind. The work was lighter now. They were beginning to discharge patients to convalesce at home. Hans Volker had time to confer with Nelson Vance, the Mayor and the City Council over the swamp drainage and mosquito control project to be financed jointly by the town and the parish; to help them draft the new screening law, making it obligatory, under threat of fine, for a householder to protect his family against the mosquitoes by leaving no window in his dwelling unscreened against them; to listen to the dreadful reports coming in from all over the state. For Caneville-Sainte Marie, it now appeared, despite the appalling number of deaths, because of the quick adoption of the measures worked out by Dr. Guiteras of Texas, was to be one of the most fortunate of the fever-ridden towns. By the time they had won their fight, in the rest of those parishes where yellow jack appeared each summer the epidemic was just beginning. All over the state other towns were dying. Between Mississippi and Louisiana existed a state of undeclared war. With no yellow fever so far, the Mississippians set up a shotgun quarantine; patrols of armed men guarded the state line, threatening to shoot to kill any man who dared cross from Louisiana. Which threat, of course, had no effect whatsoever on the buzzing little murderers of the night.

As Jenny was leaving the hospital, she ran into Hester. She gave one look at her and snapped: "You go to bed, Hester. You're done —and you look like you're coming down with it. Report to Dr. Carter. Tell him to give you——"

"I know," Hester said. "Thanks, Jen, I will. Going to see—my husband?"

"Yes," Jenny said. "At least I'm going to look in on him. He's been asleep for twenty-two hours now. I'm worried. If he's still asleep when I get there, I'll have to wake him up."

"Oh, let him sleep," Hester said with tired mockery. "Even if you do wake him up, he won't be up to any hanky-panky tonight. Voice of experience, Jen."

Jen stood there looking at her.

"You know, Hes," she said at last, "you're vile. You're positively vile."

He was still asleep. Because she was afraid not to, she awakened him as gently as she could. He sat up at once, his brown eyes bright and clear.

"Lord, Jen!" he said. "How long have I been sleeping?"

"Twenty-four hours, just about," she said tenderly.

"Good God! Let me out of here! The hospital—my clean-up squad—the——"

She put her hand against his chest and pushed him down again.

"You stay right there, Duncan," she said. "Go back to sleep.

There hasn't been a new case in a shade over thirty-six hours now. Everybody who isn't already dead seems to be recovering. Your services can be dispensed with quite nicely, Doctor."

He sat up again, grinning at her.

"Duncan, you lie down!"

"No, Jen," he said. "No more sleep. A bath's in order. Don't think I've had one in two weeks. I smell like a goat!"

She leaned forward towards him.

"Not like a goat," she said flatly; "like fever, like sweat. All right, take your bath. Lots and lots of hot water. It'll do you good."

"Jen, darling," he said lazily, "you know where the kitchen is? There's a thing in it that you light."

"I know. I have the same system at home. Go ahead, Duncan. After you figure I've had time enough to light the heater, open the tap."

"All right, baby-doll," Duncan said.

When she came back upstairs, he was stretched out on the bed again. She could hear the hot water gushing into his grandmother's enormous tub. She went into the bathroom and saw that the tub was nearly full. She searched in the wall-cabinet, found some bath salts, poured them in. Then she came back to where he lay and, bending over him, caught both his hands.

"Get up, lazybones," she said. "Your bath is nearly ready. By the time you undress, the tub will be full."

Groaning, Duncan got to his feet.

"Thanks, Jen," he said. Then he went into the bathroom, closing the door behind him. He looked at his face in the mirror, seeing the fiery red beard that had sprouted while he was asleep. His mouth tasted foul. He shaved and brushed his teeth. He got out of his soiled, sweaty clothes, letting them fall in a heap on the tiled floor. Gratefully, he slid into the huge tub. The steaming vapour rose about his head. It smelled perfumed from the bath salts Jenny had put into the water. It was wonderfully soothing. He dozed off again.

"Duncan!" Jenny's voice was edged with alarm. "Are you all right?"

He noticed that the water had cooled considerably. He must have dozed for quite a while.

"Just fine, honey child," he called back. "I'll be out in a minute."

He dried himself with the big towels, rubbing briskly; wrapped himself in his dressing-gown. He felt fine now. He felt wonderful. His mind was singularly at peace.

Then he came out of the door. Saw her eyes.

He stood there, looking at her.

A long time. A very long time.

To her, it seemed for ever.

"Jen," he said gently, "you can go home right now. I won't stop you. Or you can stay. It's up to you. But if you stay——"

She leaned back against the doorframe of the bedroom, staring at him. Her eyes were very big. Luminous. No, illuminated. From within.

He could almost see the thoughts forming behind them; see the exact instant they ceased to be thoughts at all, igniting abruptly into purest feeling; then her mind taking hold again; but no longer trying to man the breached walls of denial or rejection; so that, ignoring very nearly the clamour of her heart, she contemplated the inescapable recognition of her need's validity, with a strangely calm acceptance far nobler than mere passion, with an honest, fine, curiously proud acceptance of defeat.

It was not a thing to be put in words. It required an exercise of courage; an act of grace.

"I'll stay, Duncan," she said in an odd, grave, little girl's tone of voice. Then she came to him. Her arms sought his. Her mouth bloomed under his deep and searching kiss. He caught her to him, lifted her as though she were weightless, bore her into the room.

"Oh, Duncan, I'm so ashamed!" she wailed; but he bent and stopped her speaking mouth.

After time was again, she lay there trembling in his arms. When he bent to kiss her, he saw that she was crying.

"Lord, Jen!" he said contritely. "I'm sorry! Look, angel, I didn't mean to—— "

"You didn't!" she sobbed. "You didn't! I'm not crying over this. I'm crying for all the time I've wasted—all the nights I could have been with you before, if I hadn't been a stubborn, stupid fool!"

"We'll make up for them, Jen," he said tenderly.

"Yes," she said darkly. "Duncan, there's a phone up here, too, isn't there? Or is there just the one downstairs?"

"Right over there on the wall, honey," he said. "I couldn't go on stumbling downstairs to take night calls."

"Oh," she said. "You know how blind I am without my glasses, dearest."

He rose up on one elbow, watching in pure delight the way she crossed that room.

It took her a long time to get Central to answer. When she spoke at last, her voice was cool and crisp: "Get me four oh four Central, please. That's right, Memorial Hospital. Ask them to ring extension three five, please."

She waited, turned sideways, so that he could see that matchless lift and thrust of breast that never, even when she had become old, would need any form of support, that in-curving, deep-hollowed abdominal line, hips almost boyishly slim, only there wasn't a boy on earth built quite like that; and the long, long flow of thigh and calf that no woman he had known, not Calico, not Hester, had ever really approached, not to mention equalled.

'And I,' he thought ruefully, 'was looking at her freckles, and her specs!'

"Nurse Griffiths? Head Nurse Greenway speaking. Tell me, have any new cases come in? No? That's good. What's that? Doctor Volker has ordered five more to be discharged? Wonderful. In which case, I'm sure the girls can manage without me tomorrow. No, I won't be in. Probably not the day after, either. You just tell Dr. Volker I'm taking the rest he says I need. 'Bye now, Griffiths, 'bye."

She hung up the phone and turned back to him.

"By the way," she said, "what was that you said about making up for lost time?"

"Your kisses aren't always the same," he said lazily. "Sometimes they're warm and slack with sleepiness. In the mornings they taste of mint-flavoured toothpaste. Later on, they're coffee-flavoured. Reckon I like the coffee-flavoured ones best."

"Is that a hint, dearest?" she said.

"No, wench, an order! Get out of here and go make me some breakfast. I'm famished!"

"Me, too, Duncan. You suppose they're worried about us at the hospital?"

"Let 'em worry. I don't give a damn. Do you?"

"No—even less than a damn. Where's your dressing-gown, dearest?" She was very careful never to call him darling, because she had heard Hester call him that.

"Hanging behind the door. You put it on when you get out in the hall, Jen. Then take it off before you come back in. I want to see you with clothes on as rarely as possible."

"Don't worry about that, love," she laughed. "As far as I'm concerned, I wish I never had to get dressed again!"

While she was gone, he thought the whole matter over. They had talked about it, of course. They had had a great deal of time

263

for talking during those three days. He found that surprising. He had believed there wouldn't be any, fondly overestimating both resistance to fatigue and desire.

Only they hadn't reached any definite conclusions. Perhaps because the means for reaching them lay in other hands than theirs.

Persuasion having failed, force was in order. 'But what force have I?' Duncan thought; 'what threat that means a damned thing, after all?'

She was gone a long time. When she came back, she had steaming mugs of coffee, mountains of flapjacks and sausages on a tray; butter, cane syrup, everything.

They destroyed the breakfast rather than ate it. Jenny took the tray off his lap and put it on the floor. Then she started to kiss him.

He chanted: "Coffee-flavoured. Flapjack-flavoured. Cane syrup-flavoured. . . ."

"And this one?" she whispered. Then she clung her mouth to his and would not let him go.

"That, baby," he said huskily, "wasn't flavouring. That was provocation!"

"What did you think I meant it for, dearest?' she said.

When that time, too, the wonderful, sinewy strength of her relaxed once more into languid beauty; those wide-spaced, tensed firepoints drew in again, night blossoms closing; when all that was left of desire lay on the bruised red petals of her mouth; when the smoke-cloud darkness of her hair was stirred only by the slowing spasms of his breathing; and her supine body lay bedewed with love, moist-warm and glistening, he felt an aching, primordial need to have something to pray to, an atavistic hunger for a God to thank.

Lacking that, he worshipped her with his eyes, dreamed of the future, become good now, become warm, safe, and sure. A way would be found for this to go on for ever. A way would be found, because it must.

The phone rang shrilly. She sprang from the bed.

"Better let me answer it, Jen," he said. "You don't want folks to think."

She unhooked the telephone before she spoke.

"To think?" she said flatly. "I want them to know!"

He stared at her.

"Jenny Greenway speaking. Yes, he's here. What's that? Oh——"

264

Then, very, very quietly: "Yes, I'll tell him. He'll be there right away."

She hung up the phone, turned back to him.

"What the devil is it?" he said.

"It's—Hester; they—think she's dying," Jenny said.

Chapter 21

OH, NO! Jenny's mind reiterated its shocked protest. Oh, no! No!

This was too much; this should not be asked of them. Her hands flew, trying to make some order out of the sweat-tangled mass of her hair. This brown autumnal glory, Duncan called it—that nobody in the Twin Towns had ever seen deranged by so much as a single strand since she was a small child. But more than her hair was deranged now: her life was deranged. And in the classic sense of demented rather than disordered. The pitiless clarity of her resumed glasses showed her mouth was bruised and swollen; that loss of virtue (whatever virtue was) lay written large and clear upon her face for all the world to see.

She had put back on the soiled and wrinkled uniform of three days—three centuries?—before; she, who sometimes changed her stiffly starched whites twice a day. She could not find her hairpins, scattered as they were on the tiled floor of the bathroom, hidden in the rug of the bedroom, lost, irretrievably, like——

"Ready?" Duncan's voice, harsh, peremptory, came up to her.

Ready? To face the world? No. To speed upon this errand of merciless irony, embark upon this necessary, unavoidable compounding of confusion, she was not ready; nor would she ever be.

"Just a minute, deares——" She could not say the word. What right had she? What right? What right had her freely rendered body given her? What right their shared ecstasy; their mutually slaked need?

"Hurry up!" Duncan said.

She gave it up, with one last desperate pat of the brown autumnal glory that was a wild and sticky mess. She gave it up and turned away from the mirror, the white armour of her calling tarnished, uncrisp; and she, whose personal cleanliness was almost obsessional behaviour, the spinsterish finickiness of an ageing maiden, was conscious that she needed a bath. She, who had always walked in a cool aroma of good soap, fresh linen and the faintest, most delicate aura of perfume, was going to enter the hospital, mouth bruised, hair wild, in soiled and wrinkled whites and—say it, add the last, unacceptable, bitter detail—smelling faintly of the sweats of love.

So be it. The sin, if it be sin, must carry its own punishment.

266

Having counted the world well lost, she must now reckon up, face the actual losing, with all the equanimity possible, with all the dignity and pride she had.

Coming out of the house, she heard Duncan's voice rising in pure strangled rage, spitting out a string of Anglo-Saxon expletives that not only he but even a dock worker shouldn't have known. These failing him, he shifted into German; the guttural harshness of that tongue adding great force and weight to his description of the balky Olds as a bedamned pig-dog of a fire-wagon, whose mother had been unchaste with a water pump.

Jenny stood beside him, covering her ears as he cranked and cranked in vain.

"Why don't you hitch up the horse?" she said. "It shouldn't take long——" Then she remembered: she herself had taken the horse to Jenkins's Livery Stable to be cared for until Duncan could call for him.

"The horse?" he spat. "Don't know where the damned nag is. The servants probably took him when they——"

"No," she whispered. "I—I've just remembered that I left him at Jenkins's myself."

"Doesn't matter," he growled, glaring at the Olds. "It was the right thing to do. Poor beast was blown. Come on, then; we'll just have to walk."

"All right, Duncan," Jenny said. To walk—all the way through town—like this. To shred her reputation with every step. She could see, in her mind's eye, Caneville's matrons racing for their telephones, hear their voices: "Honey, you oughta see her! A fright! A perfect fright—looks like an unmade bed. The one she's probably just got out of——"

Her head came up proudly. Her slender nostrils flared.

"Come on," she said. "We'd better hurry."

Yes—hurry. To compound confusion. To aid and abet life's drunken over-indulgence in irony. To slam the door of hope resoundingly in both their faces. That is—if they could. If they could! Panic seized her, clutching legs that three days of love had left boneless, hollow, anyhow; slowing her at last to a stricken halt. A yellow-fever patient recovered—or he died. What the doctor did, or didn't do, had no demonstrable relation with that fact. Different doctors did different things; but with the same results: the patient lived, or he died. And in about the same proportions, no matter what the treatment used.

"Come on!" Duncan snapped. "What the devil ails you, Jen?"

"Duncan—we can't!" she breathed. "Oh, dearest, we can't! Not you—not I!"

He stared at her. Then, misinterpreting her meaning, his voice came out, thick with shock: "So we're to let her die, Jen? To legalise our adultery, we're to fold our hands? Add to the felony— the rather pardonable felony—of illicit love the crime of murder? For it would be murder, Jen, murder by neglect! Look, baby, I don't think I could stop loving you. I think you're so branded on my blood and nerves that nothing but death can take you off. But if there's a way to do it, you've found it! I could betray Hester, because she didn't matter any more; but what you're asking me now is to betray us—to betray what we are!"

"No!" she wept. "No, Duncan, you don't understand! You can't! I can't! We have to get another doctor, another nurse. You don't imagine I could spend three days in your house without the whole town knowing, do you? And it's yellow fever, dearest! They said she was dying. Suppose she dies anyhow, in spite of all you can do? You know what they'll say then? Don't you know, Duncan?"

He looked at her, his eyes, grave and still.

"Yes," he said flatly. "I know. They'll say I murdered her in order to marry you. That I took advantage of the circumstances. You're right. I apologise for what I was thinking. You're perfectly right. They're quite capable of saying that; even of believing it. Only, Jen—darling, it doesn't make any difference——"

"Doesn't make any difference! Oh, Duncan, if she dies, they'll call for an investigation and——"

"Which will come to nothing. No doctor worth a tinker's damn will dare to testify to a thing he knows is not, cannot be, so: that I or any physician alive could save a yellow-fever patient once the third stage set in. The only thing that would be censurable, the only act for which I could be expelled from practice, would be my refusal to attend. So come on!"

"They won't have to expel you! They'll just go on whispering you to death! Talk, talk, talk, till no decent family, no family of means, would dare call you in on a case. You'd be left with the Cajuns and the coloured people as patients—left to starve, Duncan! Don't you see?"

"I see you're a woman," he said quietly, "with a woman's chilling practicality. If you want to talk to me, Jen, damn it, walk and talk at the same time!"

"But, Duncan, I don't want to see you starve! I don't want——"

"What you want, baby, doesn't matter. What any one person

wants never does in this world. I didn't take up medicine to make money. I undertook to heal, to the best of my poor ability, the sick. Goddamnit, Jen, come on!"

"I'm coming. Duncan—there's still one other thing——"

"What's that, Jen?"

"If there's an investigation, everything will be brought out—including that I spent three days with you. Does your dedication to duty include—ruining whatever reputation I have left?"

He looked at her again. His eyes were very bleak.

"Yes, Jen—I'm afraid it does," he said.

She caught his arms, came up, surged on, sought and found his mouth, there on the main street of Caneville-Sainte Marie. At least a dozen people saw it.

"I don't care!" she laughed gaily. "I'm all right now, dearest—come on!"

They rushed up the stairs of the hospital together. Nellie Morris was at the desk. She took in Jenny's altered appearance in one long sweeping glance of pure triumphant malice.

"Why, Nurse Greenway," she cackled, "what on earth's happened to you? You look like you got caught in a threshing machine!"

Jenny looked at her coolly, serenely.

"As if you didn't know, Nellie," she said.

They raced for the woman's ward. Nurse Griffiths was there, her eyes frightened.

Griffiths was quite right: Hester was dying. But she was managing it with a serenity worthy of a better soul. She was not delirious. Her gaze was cool and sane. Even when the terrible, racking spasms of nausea hit her, she held on to that serenity. It was a dreadful thing to watch. Jenny found her eyes scalding out of clarity as she bent to wipe the black mucus from her face.

The spasm stopped. Hester smiled. Her smile was very weak; but filled with sardonic glee as she swept Jenny with her eyes. Gathered the available evidence. Added it up. Tabulated it. Reached certainty.

"Welcome to the world's oldest sisterhood, Jen," she said.

"Hester, for God's love!" Duncan said.

"Not for God's love——" Hester got out. "For yours, Duncan —wasn't it? Tell me, how was she? No damn' fun I'll bet——"

"Hes——" Duncan whispered, "you mustn't. Don't you realise——"

"That I'm dying? Yes, Duncan, very well. So I mustn't
269

bitch it up, must I? It isn't done. Why not? Why can't I die the way I've lived? Tell me, was she more fun?"

They stared at her. Then Jenny said it. Spoke the words out of an infinitude of compassion.

"No, Hes, I wasn't any fun at all," she said.

Hester struggled upright, her eyes dimming out of life, even as they held Jenny's own. Her breath escaped in a rattle, a gurgle. But when she finally got what she wanted to say out, she was laughing. Or crying. Or both.

"Liar!" she whispered, "but—anyhow—bless you—for that, Jen. Dear Jen. Dear, dear Jen. Duncan!"

"Yes, Hester?" he croaked.

"Put your arms around me! It's getting dark. And I am cold, so cold——"

Duncan eased her back down again. Then, very quietly, she died.

Jenny whirled, clung to him. Her sobs tore her, racked her body like invisible giant hands.

"Not like this, Duncan!" she stormed. "I didn't want it like this!"

"Nor I," he said, "but there it is, Jen." Then: "Bless her, she did it well!"

It was more than a month later before Jenny would let him say what needed to be said.

"Look, Jen, pious sentiments be damned!" he growled. "Life must go on. So, before I forget: Nurse Greenway, Doctor Childers wishes to know if you will do him the honour of becoming his wife?"

She grinned at him impishly.

"Nurse Greenway," she said, "begs to inform Doctor Childers that she will take the matter under advisement."

"For how long?" he said.

"For—about three seconds, dearest! The answer is yes. Yes, yes, and again yes! Oh, Duncan, love!"

"When?" he said, after he had kissed her. "We will have to wait a decent interval, of course. Hes deserved it. How would Christmas suit you?"

She didn't answer him. But he could see the hurt in her eyes.

"I'm sorry," he said. "Guess I'll never learn. That was the time I married—her. That's it, isn't it, Jen?"

"That's it," she said. "But it doesn't matter. I forgive you, Duncan. You're a man. And the hows, whens, whys and wherefores matter very little to a man. Forget it. Tell me, Doctor; did you ever marry anyone on New Year's Day? Think hard, now. Search your memory."

He considered that.

"Come to think of it," he said gravely, "I don't believe I ever did."

"Then it's time you do one thing you've never done before. The possibilities are limited, I'm sure. You've had a crowded life, Duncan."

"Crowded? No, Jen. It was the world's most dreary wasteland until you came," he said.